MANOR BLACK™

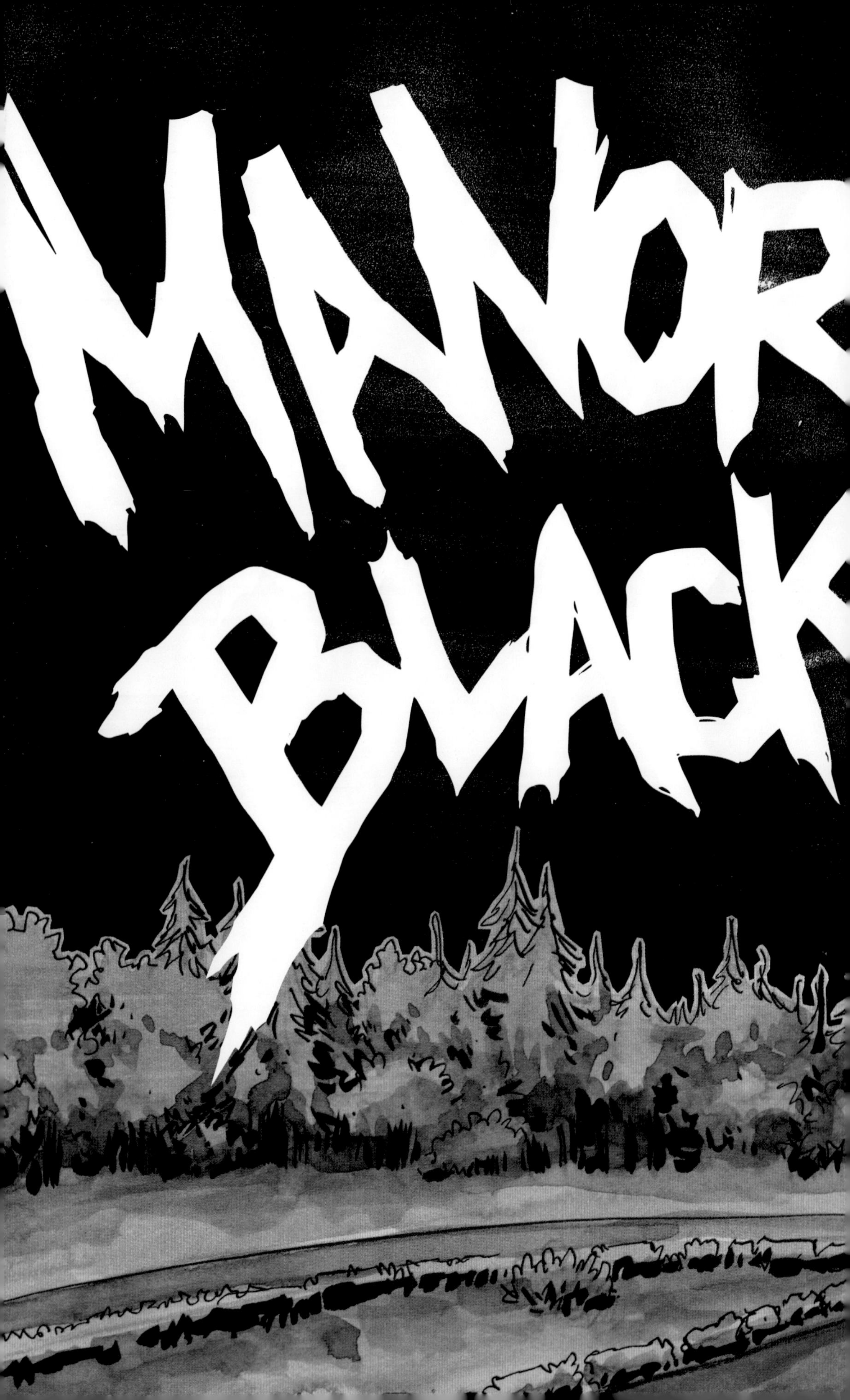
MANOR
BLACK

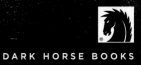

DARK HORSE BOOKS

VOLUME ONE

WRITTEN BY
CULLEN BUNN AND BRIAN HURTT

ART AND LETTERING BY
TYLER CROOK

COVER AND CHAPTER BREAKS BY
TYLER CROOK

MANOR BLACK CREATED BY
CULLEN BUNN, BRIAN HURTT, & TYLER CROOK

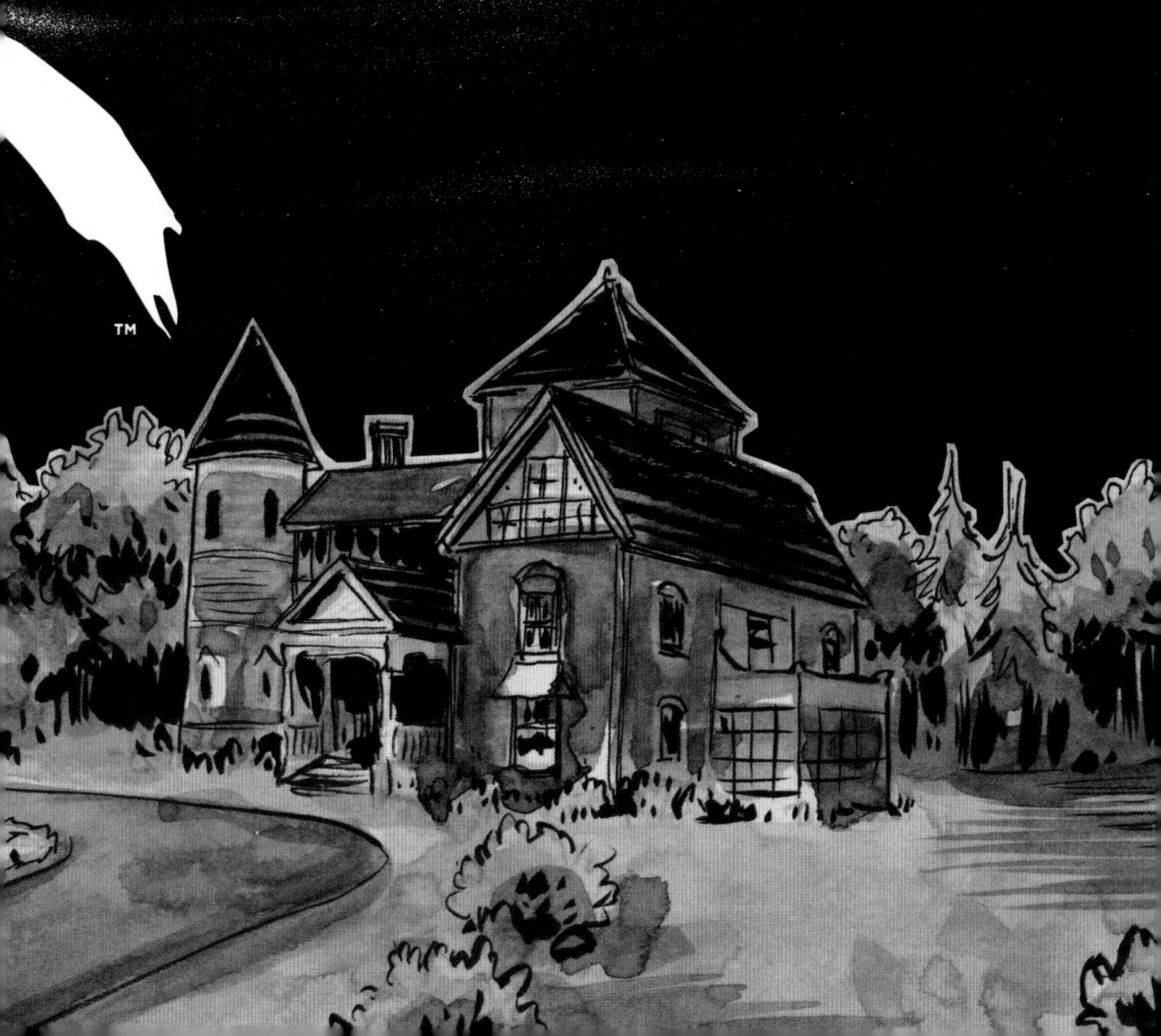

TM

Names: Bunn, Cullen, writer. | Hurtt, Brian, writer. | Crook, Tyler, artist, letterer.
Title: Manor Black / written by Cullen Bunn and Brian Hurtt ; art and lettering by Tyler Crook.
Description: First edition. | Milwaukie, OR : Dark Horse Books, 2020- | v. 1: "Collects issues #1-#4 of the Dark Horse Comics series Manor Black"
Identifiers: LCCN 2019039148 (print) | LCCN 2019039149 (ebook) | ISBN 9781506712017 (v. 1 ; trade paperback) | ISBN 9781506712802 (v. 1 ; ebook)
Subjects: LCSH: Comic books, strips, etc.
Classification: LCC PN6728.M359226 B86 2020 (print) | LCC PN6728.M359226 (ebook) | DDC 741.5/973--dc23
LC record available at https://lccn.loc.gov/2019039148
LC ebook record available at https://lccn.loc.gov/2019039149

Published by Dark Horse Books / A division of Dark Horse Comics LLC / 10956 SE Main Street / Milwaukie, OR 97222

DarkHorse.com

To find a comics shop in your area, visit comicshoplocator.com

First edition: February 2020
978-1-50671-201-7

10 9 8 7 6 5 4 3 2 1
Printed in China

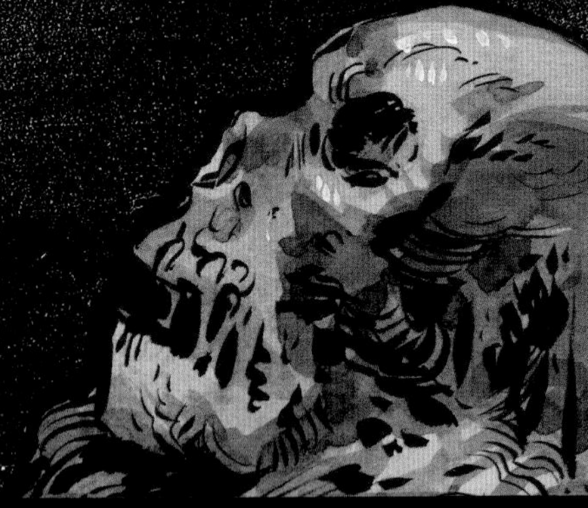

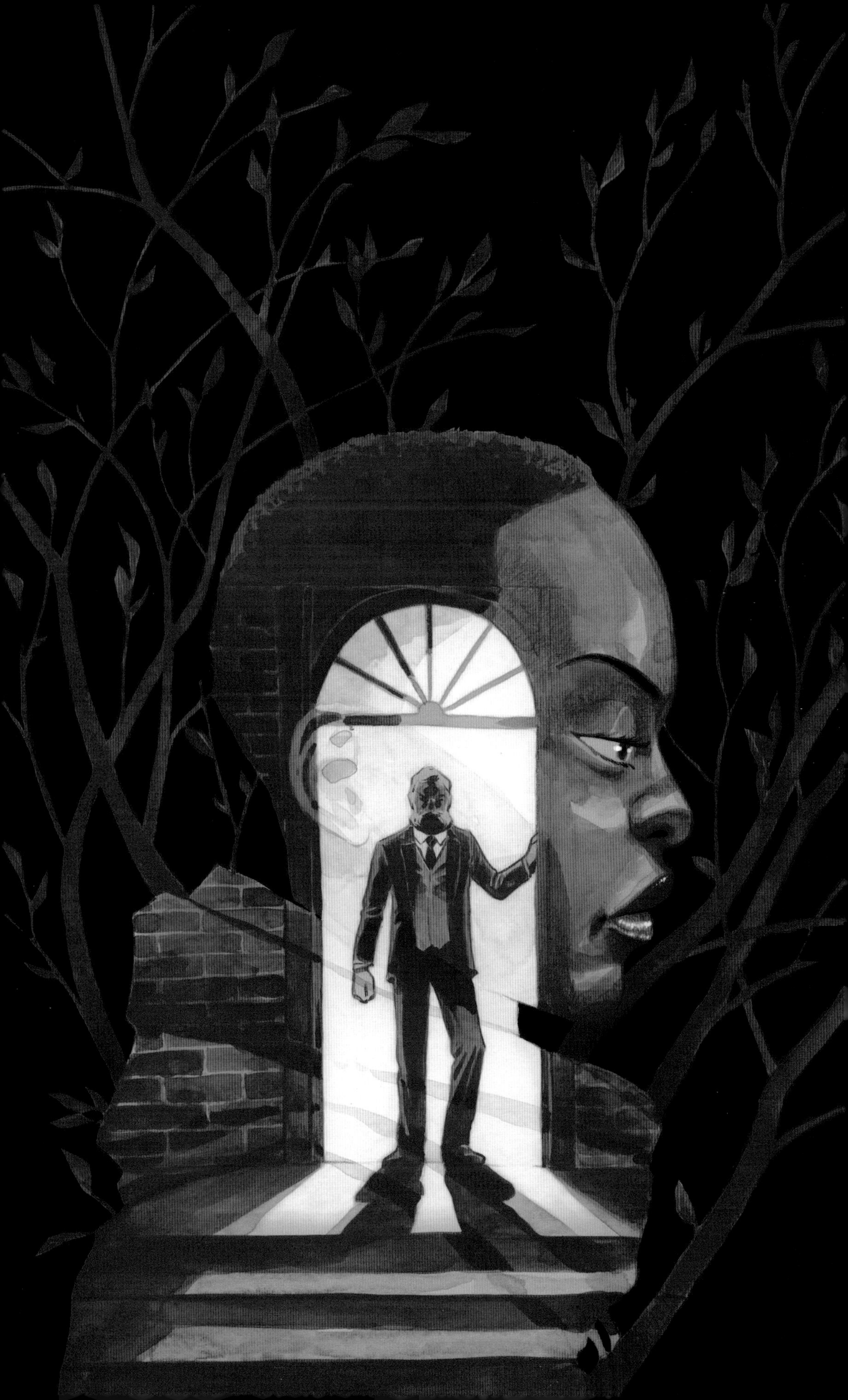

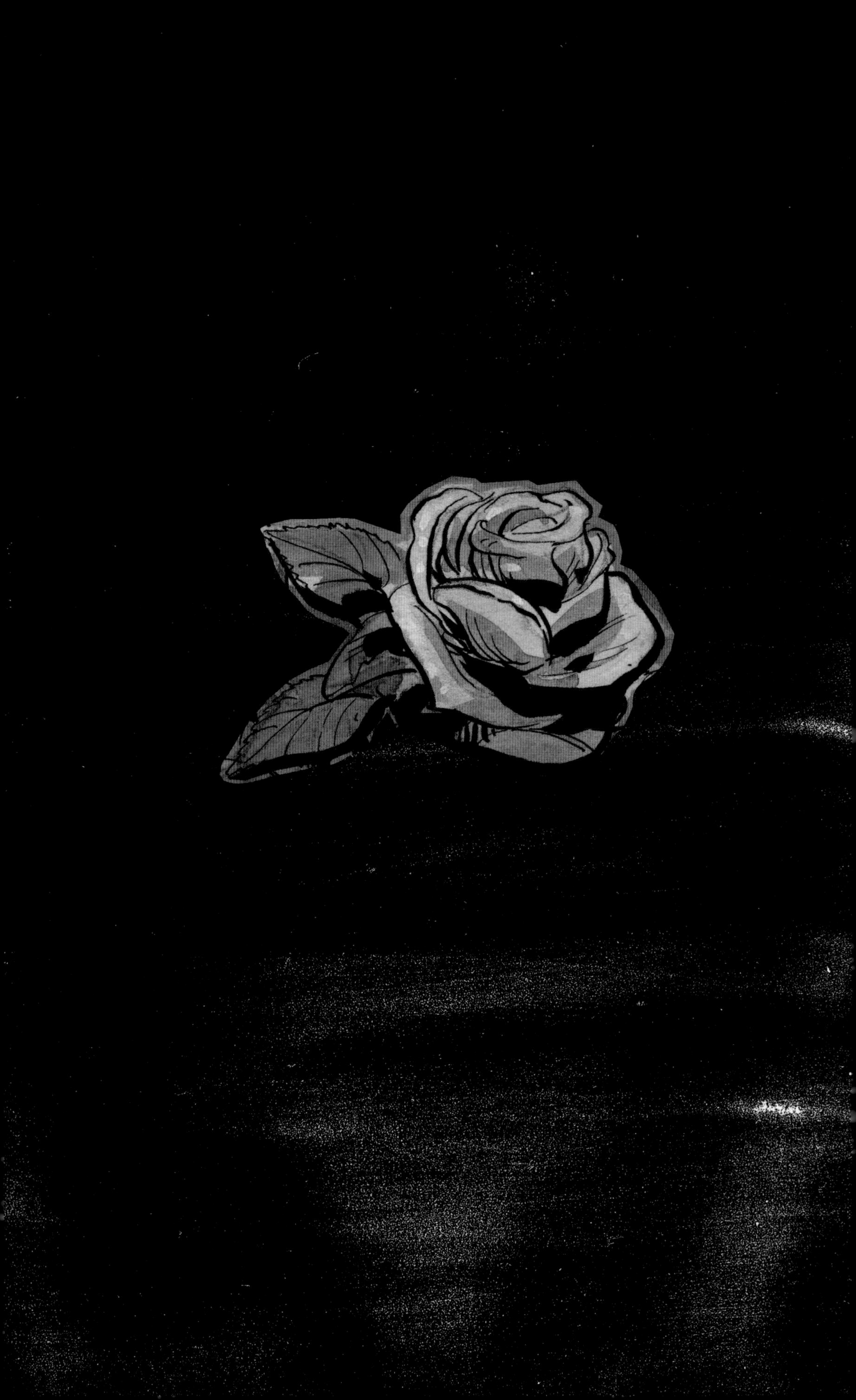

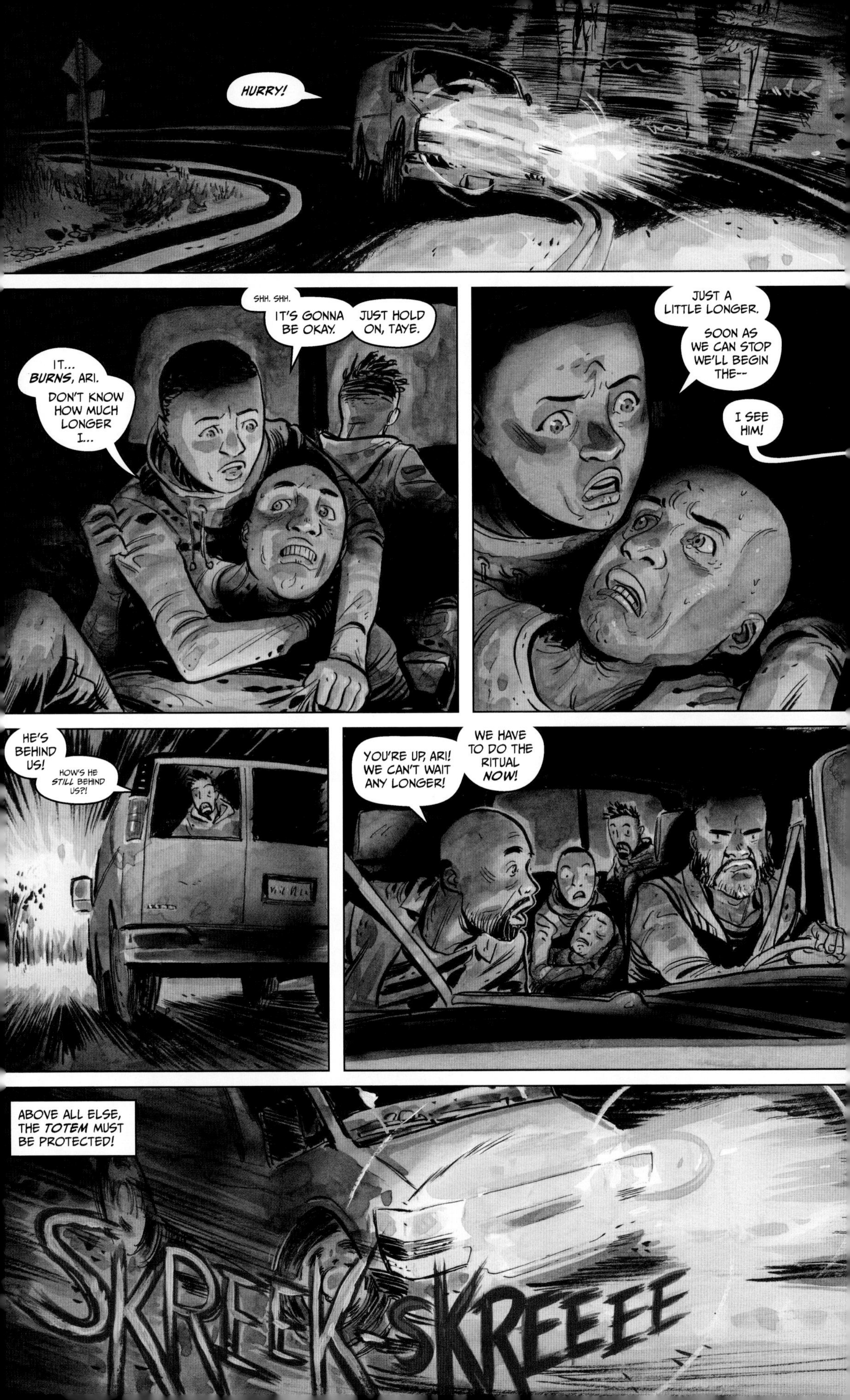
HURRY!
IT... BURNS, ARI.
DON'T KNOW HOW MUCH LONGER I...
SHH. SHH.
IT'S GONNA BE OKAY.
JUST HOLD ON, TAYE.
JUST A LITTLE LONGER.
SOON AS WE CAN STOP WE'LL BEGIN THE--
I SEE HIM!
HE'S BEHIND US!
HOW'S HE STILL BEHIND US?!
YOU'RE UP, ARI! WE CAN'T WAIT ANY LONGER!
WE HAVE TO DO THE RITUAL NOW!
ABOVE ALL ELSE, THE TOTEM MUST BE PROTECTED!
SKREEK-SKREEEE

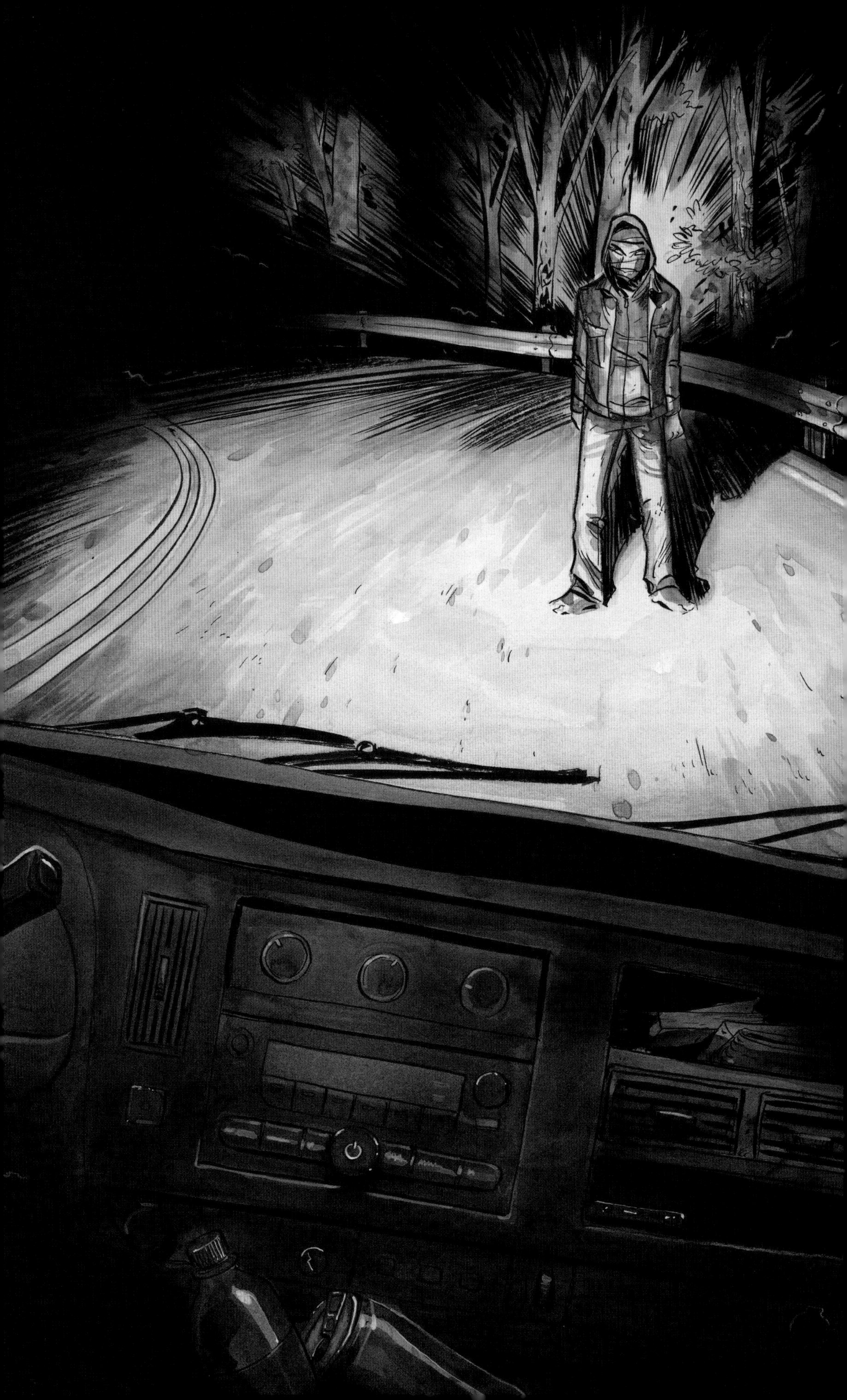

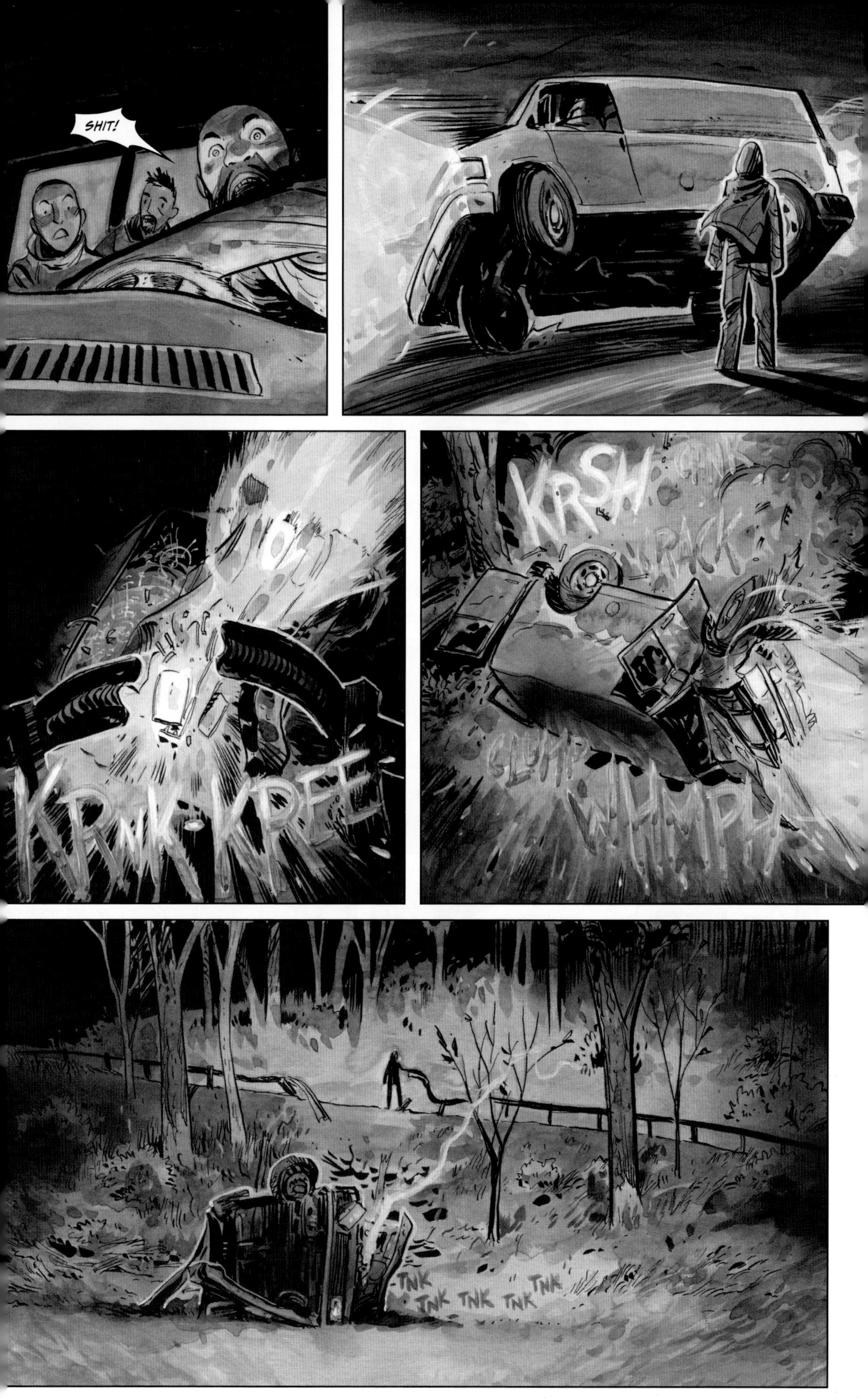
SHIT!
KRNK-KREE
KRSH
CHNK
KRACK
CLUMP
WHMPH
TNK
TNK TNK TNK TNK

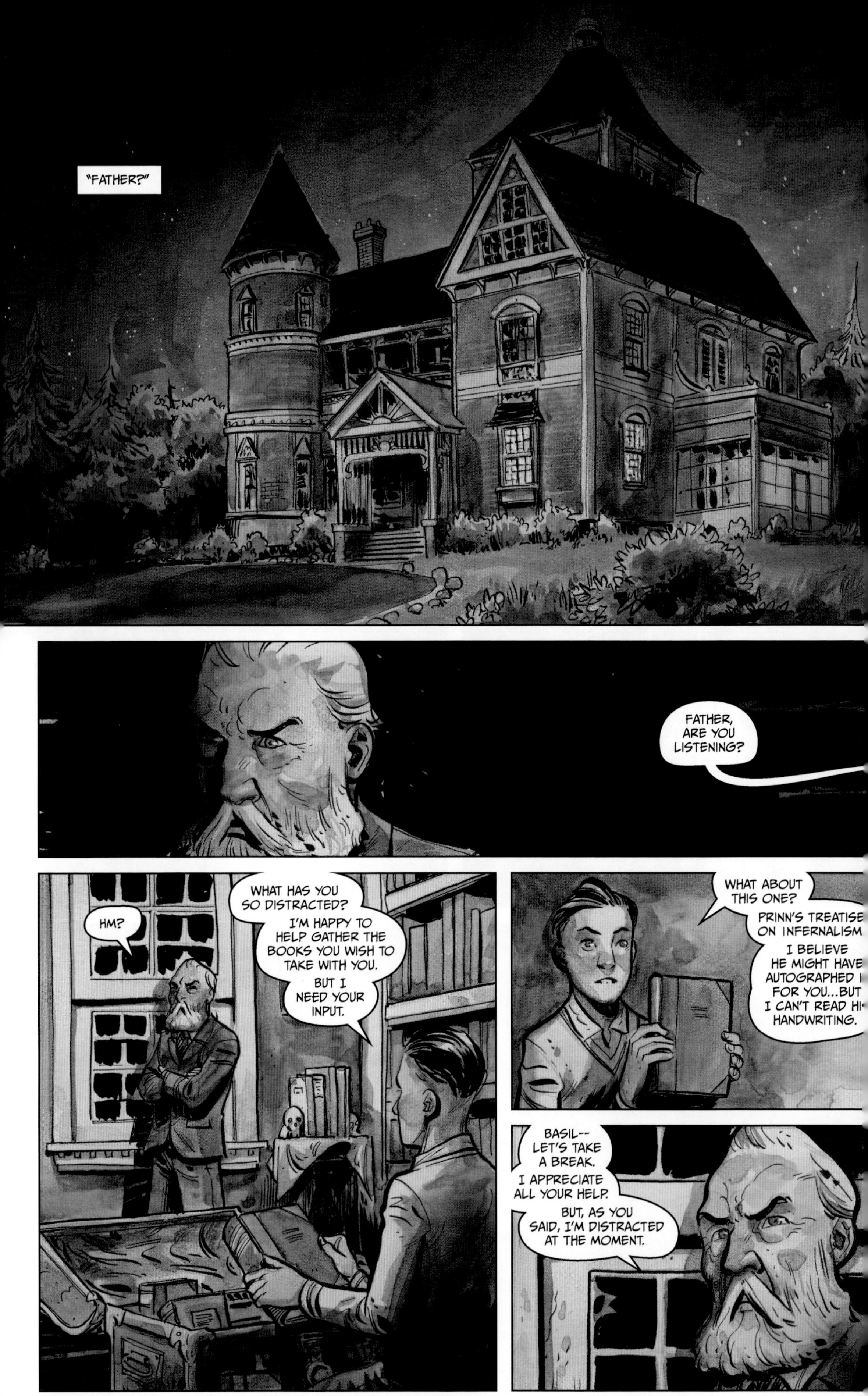
"FATHER?"
FATHER, ARE YOU LISTENING?
HM?
WHAT HAS YOU SO DISTRACTED?
I'M HAPPY TO HELP GATHER THE BOOKS YOU WISH TO TAKE WITH YOU.
BUT I NEED YOUR INPUT.
WHAT ABOUT THIS ONE?
PRINN'S TREATISE ON INFERNALISM
I BELIEVE HE MIGHT HAVE AUTOGRAPHED I FOR YOU...BUT I CAN'T READ HI HANDWRITING.
BASIL-- LET'S TAKE A BREAK.
I APPRECIATE ALL YOUR HELP.
BUT, AS YOU SAID, I'M DISTRACTED AT THE MOMENT.

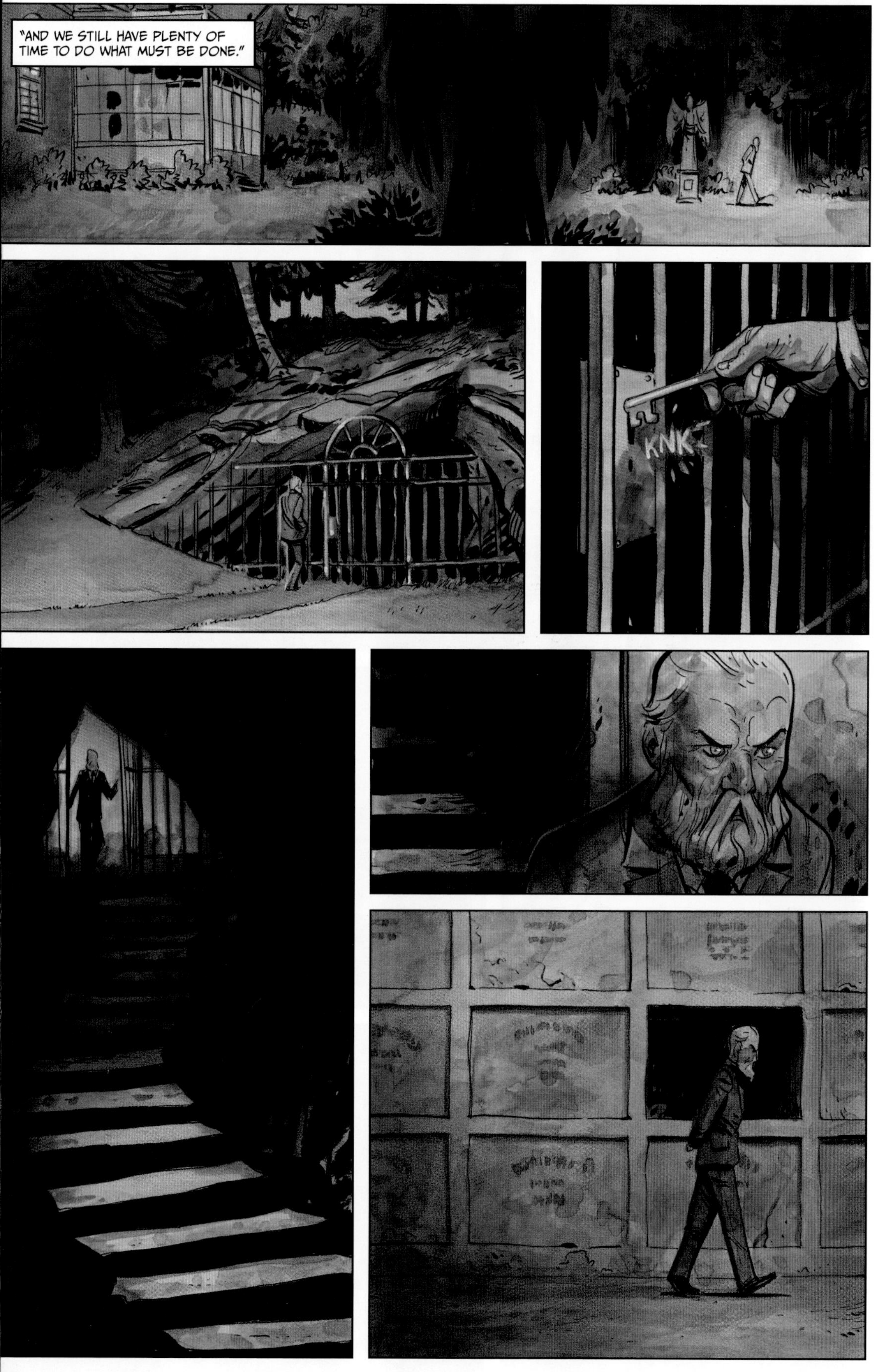
"AND WE STILL HAVE PLENTY OF TIME TO DO WHAT MUST BE DONE."
KNK

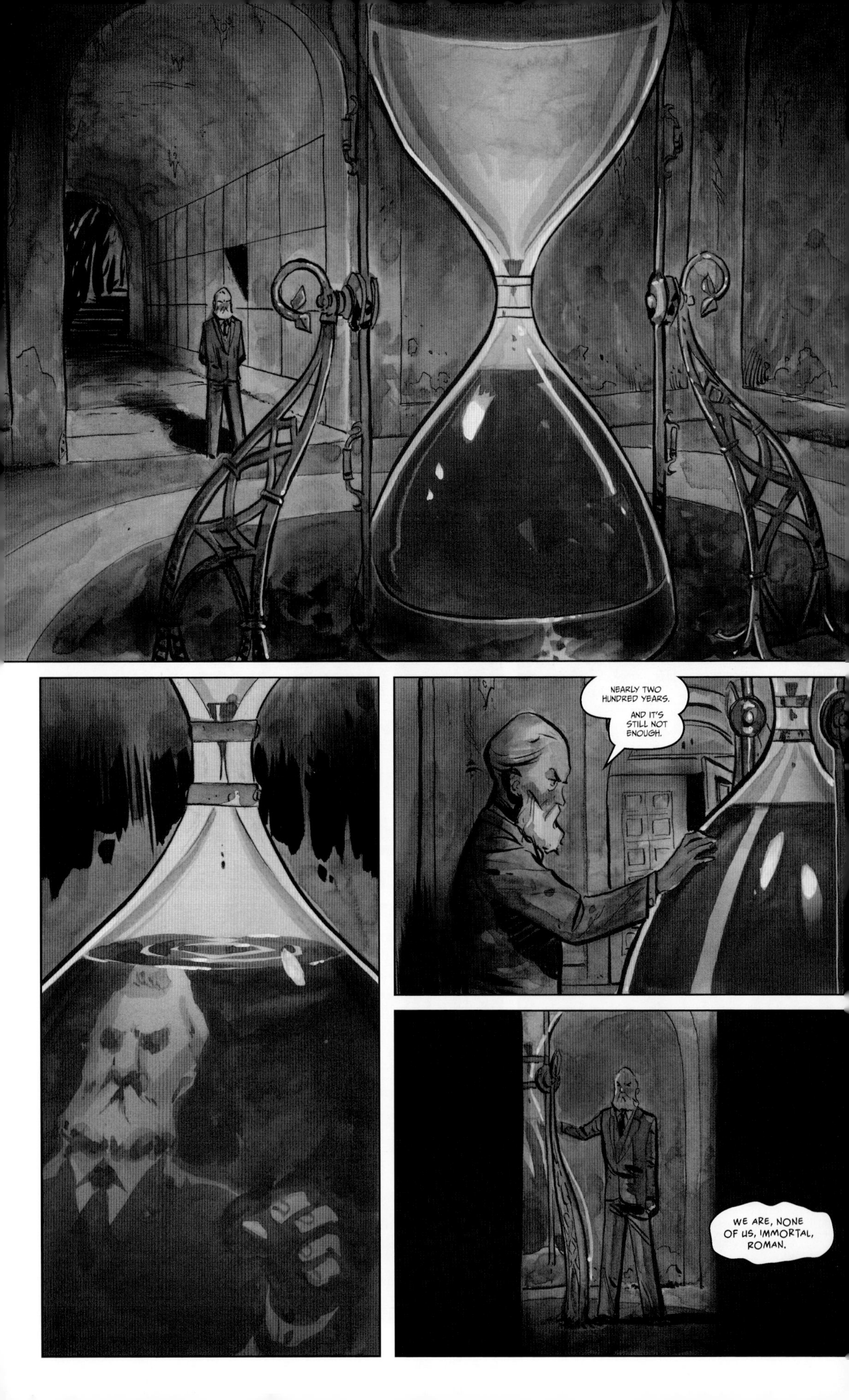
NEARLY TWO HUNDRED YEARS.
AND IT'S STILL NOT ENOUGH.
WE ARE, NONE OF US, IMMORTAL, ROMAN.

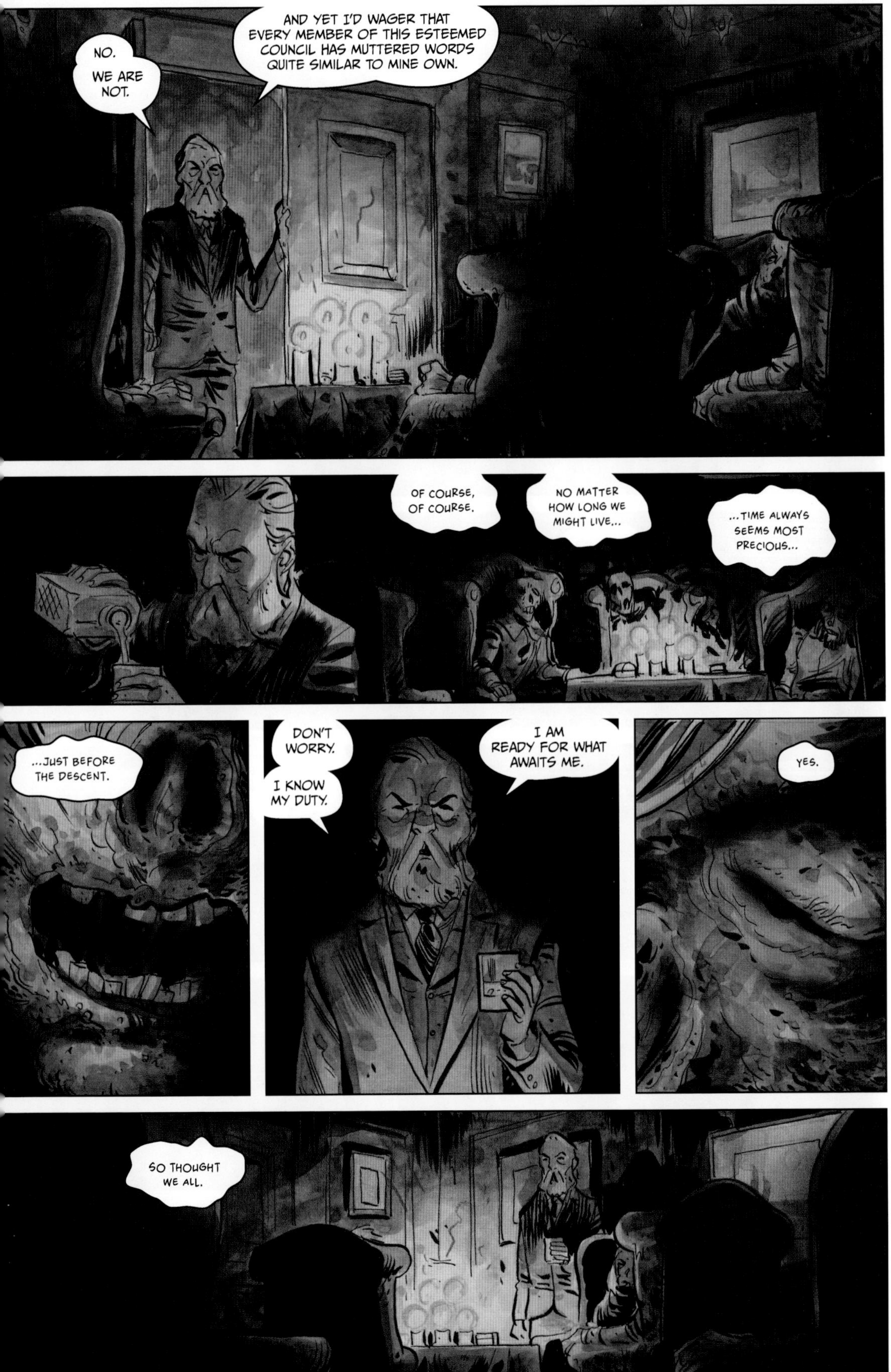
NO.
WE ARE NOT.
AND YET I'D WAGER THAT EVERY MEMBER OF THIS ESTEEMED COUNCIL HAS MUTTERED WORDS QUITE SIMILAR TO MINE OWN.
OF COURSE, OF COURSE.
NO MATTER HOW LONG WE MIGHT LIVE...
...TIME ALWAYS SEEMS MOST PRECIOUS...
...JUST BEFORE THE DESCENT.
DON'T WORRY.
I KNOW MY DUTY.
I AM READY FOR WHAT AWAITS ME.
YES.
SO THOUGHT WE ALL.

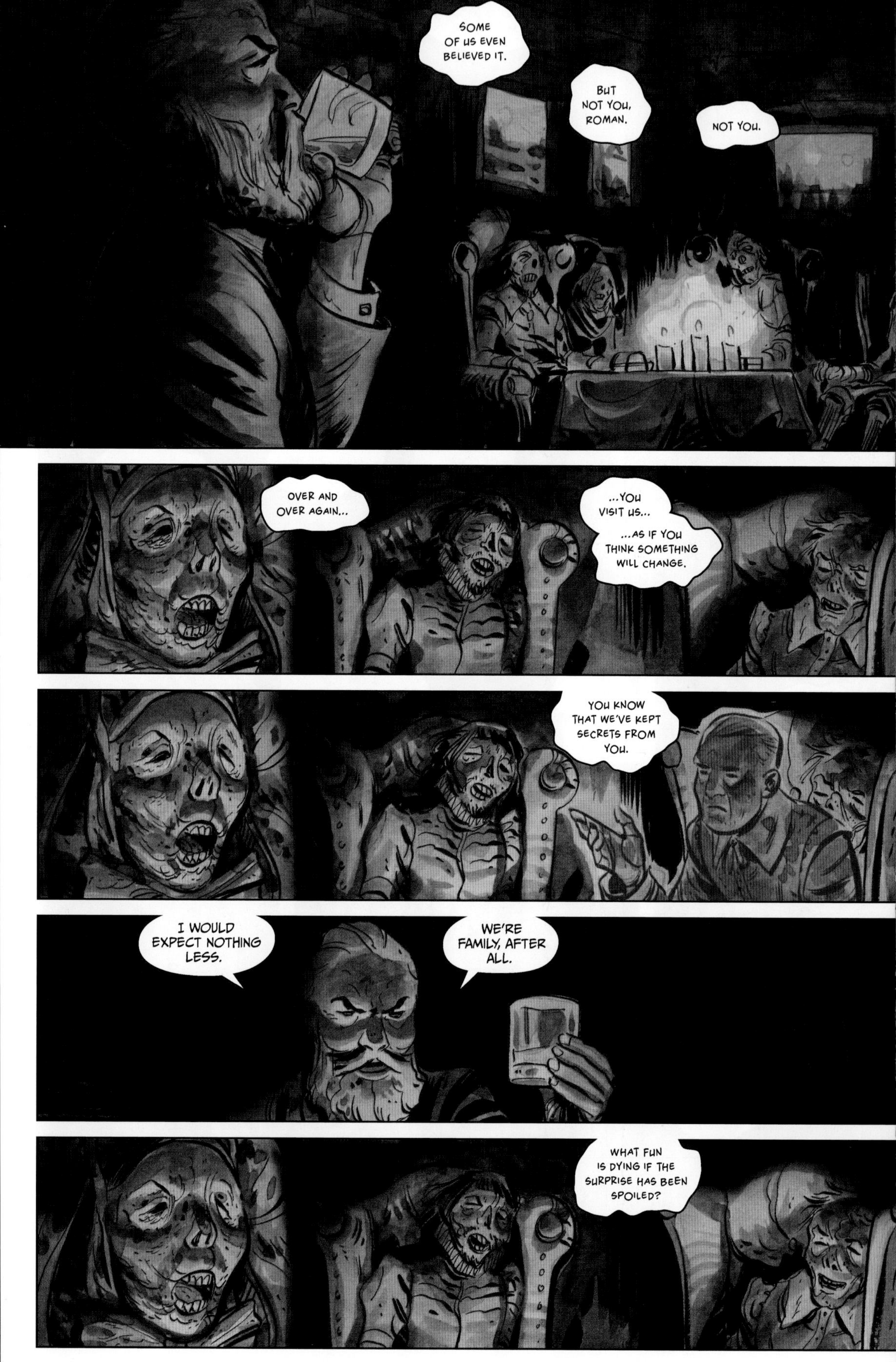
SOME OF US EVEN BELIEVED IT.
BUT NOT YOU, ROMAN.
NOT YOU.
OVER AND OVER AGAIN...
...YOU VISIT US...
...AS IF YOU THINK SOMETHING WILL CHANGE.
YOU KNOW THAT WE'VE KEPT SECRETS FROM YOU.
I WOULD EXPECT NOTHING LESS.
WE'RE FAMILY, AFTER ALL.
WHAT FUN IS DYING IF THE SURPRISE HAS BEEN SPOILED?

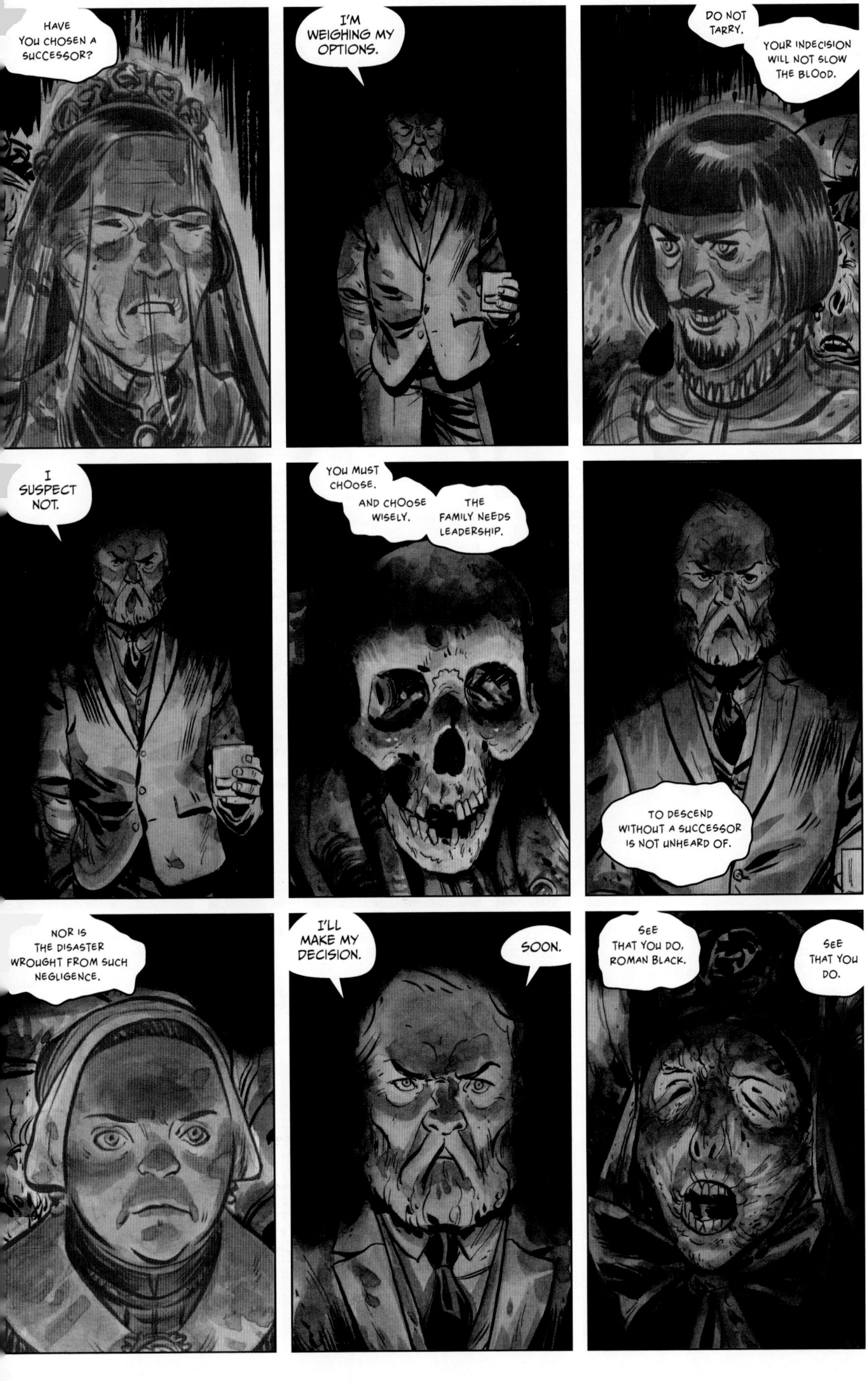
HAVE YOU CHOSEN A SUCCESSOR?
I'M WEIGHING MY OPTIONS.
DO NOT TARRY.
YOUR INDECISION WILL NOT SLOW THE BLOOD.
I SUSPECT NOT.
YOU MUST CHOOSE.
AND CHOOSE WISELY.
THE FAMILY NEEDS LEADERSHIP.
TO DESCEND WITHOUT A SUCCESSOR IS NOT UNHEARD OF.
NOR IS THE DISASTER WROUGHT FROM SUCH NEGLIGENCE.
I'LL MAKE MY DECISION.
SOON.
SEE THAT YOU DO, ROMAN BLACK.
SEE THAT YOU DO.

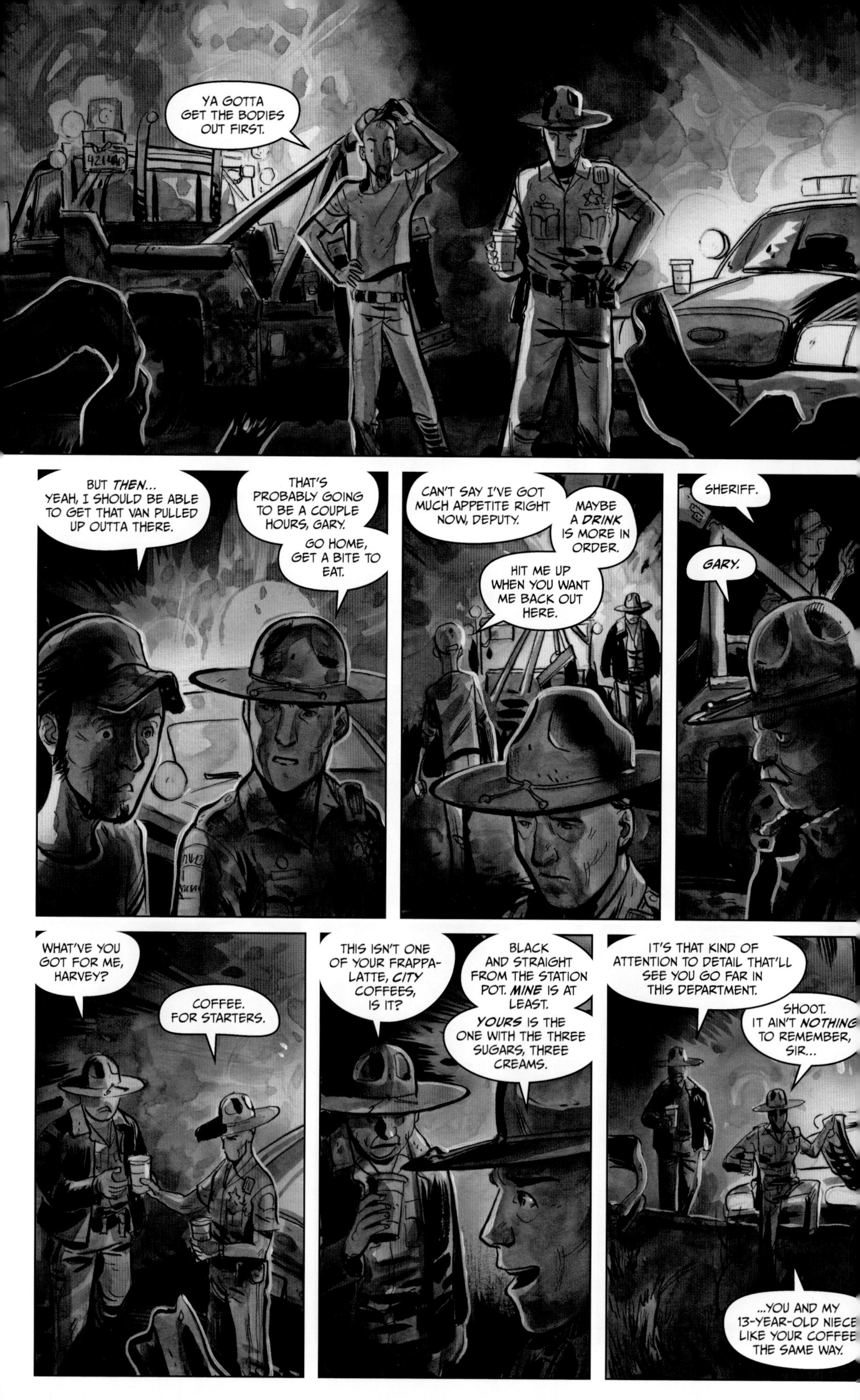
YA GOTTA GET THE BODIES OUT FIRST.
BUT THEN... YEAH, I SHOULD BE ABLE TO GET THAT VAN PULLED UP OUTTA THERE.
THAT'S PROBABLY GOING TO BE A COUPLE HOURS, GARY.
GO HOME, GET A BITE TO EAT.
CAN'T SAY I'VE GOT MUCH APPETITE RIGHT NOW, DEPUTY.
MAYBE A DRINK IS MORE IN ORDER.
HIT ME UP WHEN YOU WANT ME BACK OUT HERE.
SHERIFF.
GARY.
WHAT'VE YOU GOT FOR ME, HARVEY?
COFFEE. FOR STARTERS.
THIS ISN'T ONE OF YOUR FRAPPA-LATTE, CITY COFFEES, IS IT?
BLACK AND STRAIGHT FROM THE STATION POT. MINE IS AT LEAST.
YOURS IS THE ONE WITH THE THREE SUGARS, THREE CREAMS.
IT'S THAT KIND OF ATTENTION TO DETAIL THAT'LL SEE YOU GO FAR IN THIS DEPARTMENT.
SHOOT. IT AIN'T NOTHING TO REMEMBER, SIR...
...YOU AND MY 13-YEAR-OLD NIECE LIKE YOUR COFFEE THE SAME WAY.

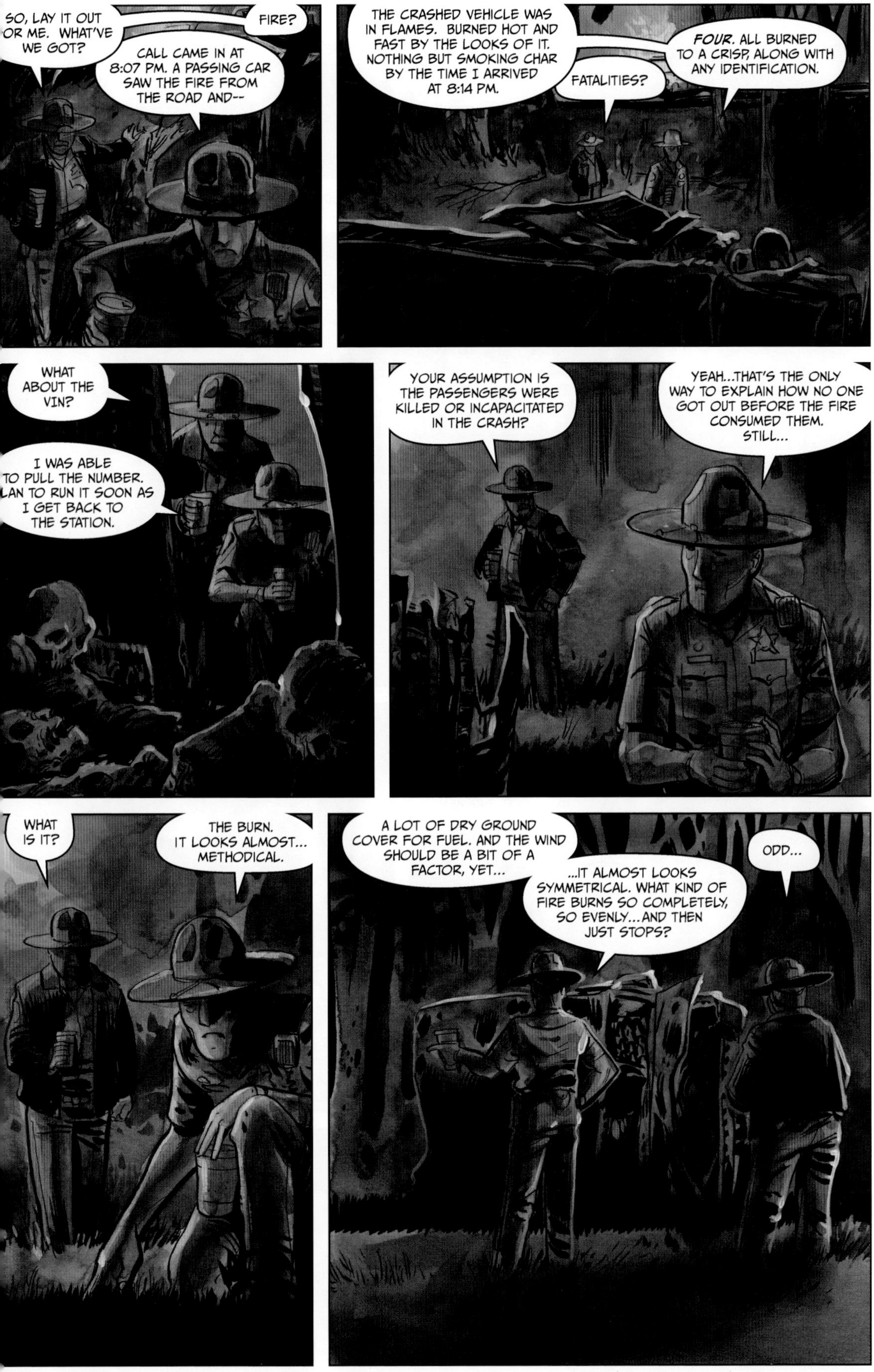

SO, LAY IT OUT OR ME. WHAT'VE WE GOT?
CALL CAME IN AT 8:07 PM. A PASSING CAR SAW THE FIRE FROM THE ROAD AND--
FIRE?
THE CRASHED VEHICLE WAS IN FLAMES. BURNED HOT AND FAST BY THE LOOKS OF IT. NOTHING BUT SMOKING CHAR BY THE TIME I ARRIVED AT 8:14 PM.
FATALITIES?
FOUR. ALL BURNED TO A CRISP, ALONG WITH ANY IDENTIFICATION.
WHAT ABOUT THE VIN?
I WAS ABLE TO PULL THE NUMBER. LAN TO RUN IT SOON AS I GET BACK TO THE STATION.
YOUR ASSUMPTION IS THE PASSENGERS WERE KILLED OR INCAPACITATED IN THE CRASH?
YEAH...THAT'S THE ONLY WAY TO EXPLAIN HOW NO ONE GOT OUT BEFORE THE FIRE CONSUMED THEM. STILL...
WHAT IS IT?
THE BURN. IT LOOKS ALMOST... METHODICAL.
A LOT OF DRY GROUND COVER FOR FUEL. AND THE WIND SHOULD BE A BIT OF A FACTOR, YET...
...IT ALMOST LOOKS SYMMETRICAL. WHAT KIND OF FIRE BURNS SO COMPLETELY, SO EVENLY...AND THEN JUST STOPS?
ODD...

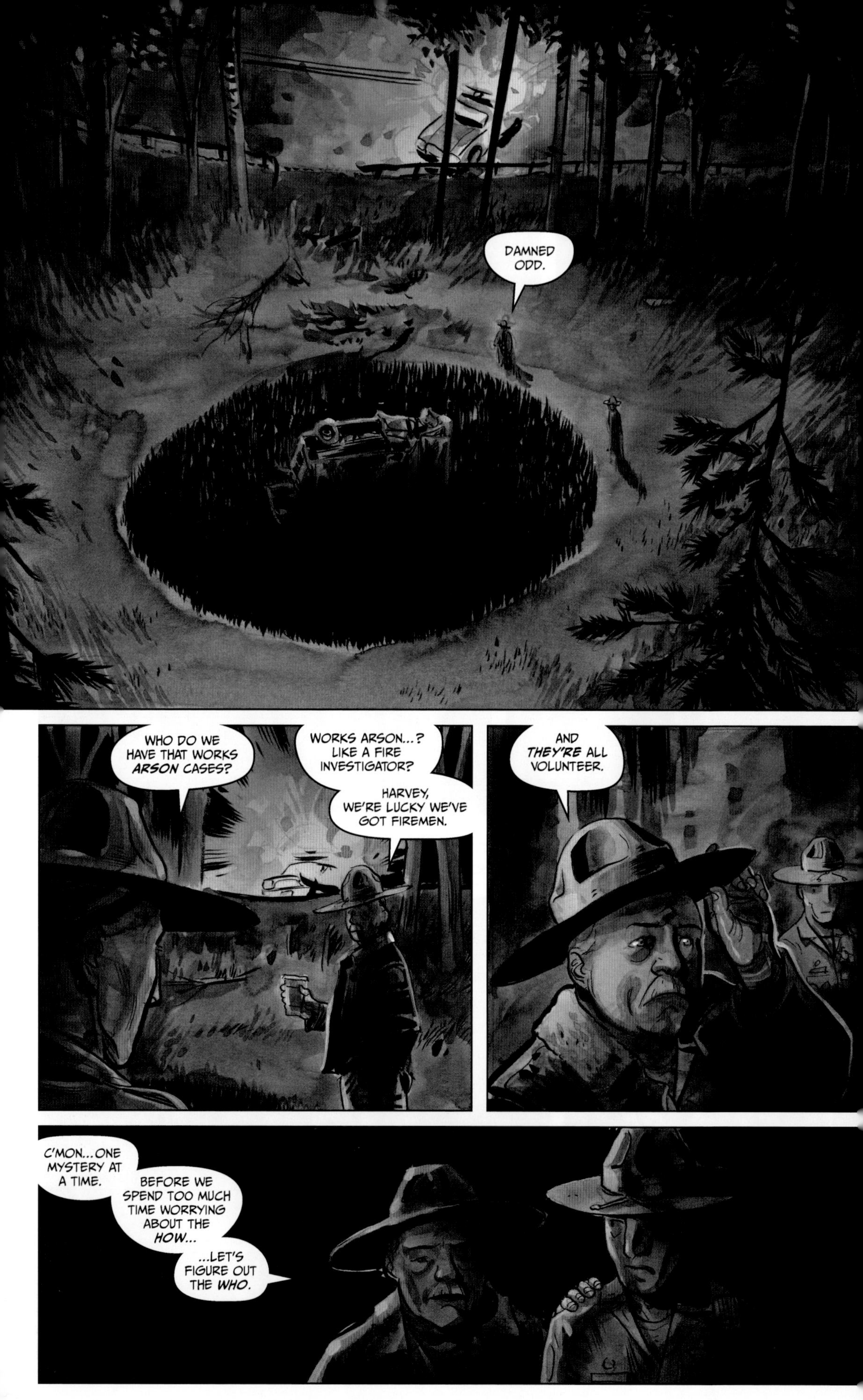
DAMNED ODD.
WHO DO WE HAVE THAT WORKS ARSON CASES?
WORKS ARSON...? LIKE A FIRE INVESTIGATOR?
HARVEY, WE'RE LUCKY WE'VE GOT FIREMEN.
AND THEY'RE ALL VOLUNTEER.
C'MON...ONE MYSTERY AT A TIME.
BEFORE WE SPEND TOO MUCH TIME WORRYING ABOUT THE HOW...
...LET'S FIGURE OUT THE WHO.

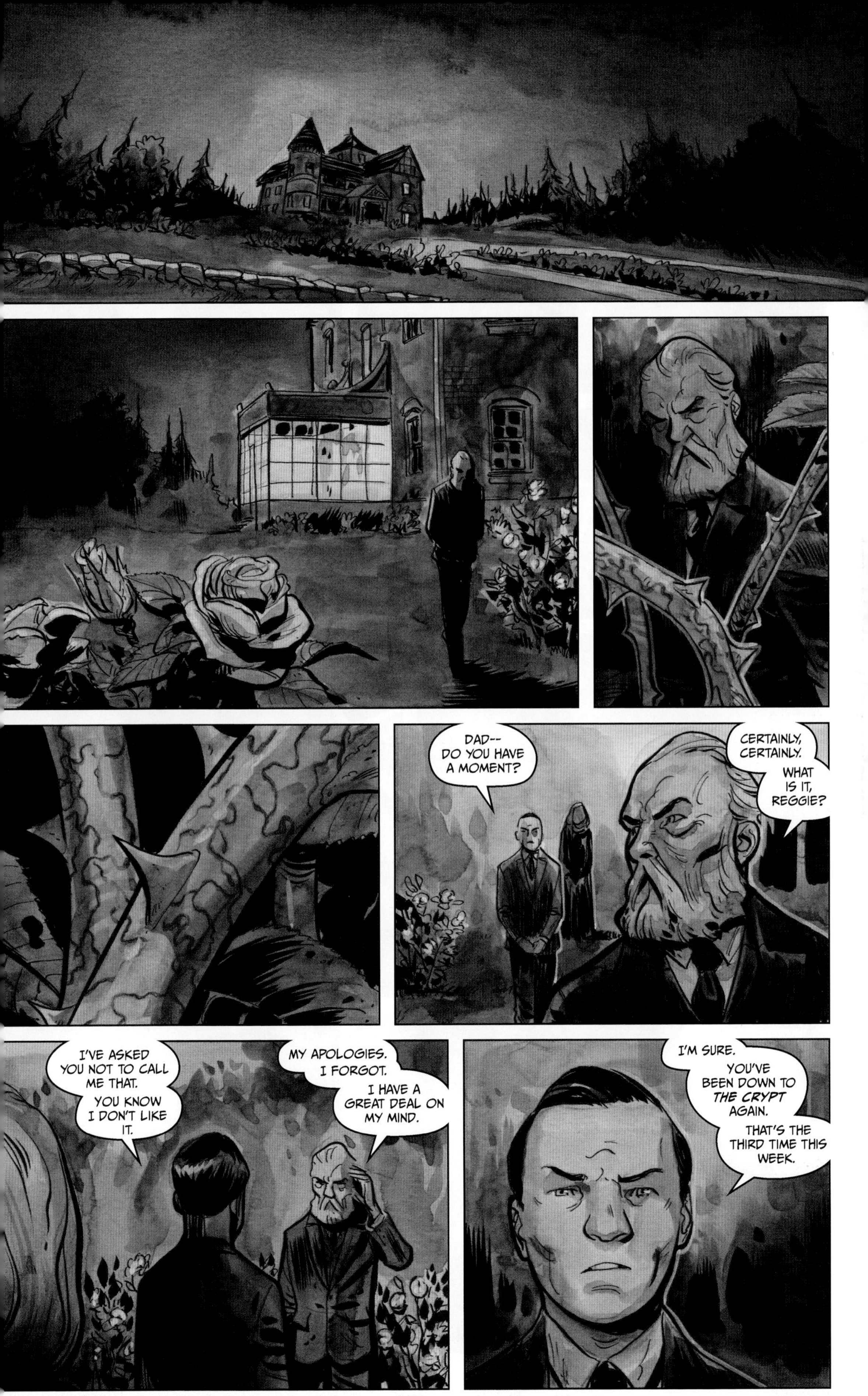
DAD-- DO YOU HAVE A MOMENT?
CERTAINLY, CERTAINLY.
WHAT IS IT, REGGIE?
I'VE ASKED YOU NOT TO CALL ME THAT.
YOU KNOW I DON'T LIKE IT.
MY APOLOGIES. I FORGOT.
I HAVE A GREAT DEAL ON MY MIND.
I'M SURE.
YOU'VE BEEN DOWN TO *THE CRYPT* AGAIN.
THAT'S THE THIRD TIME THIS WEEK.

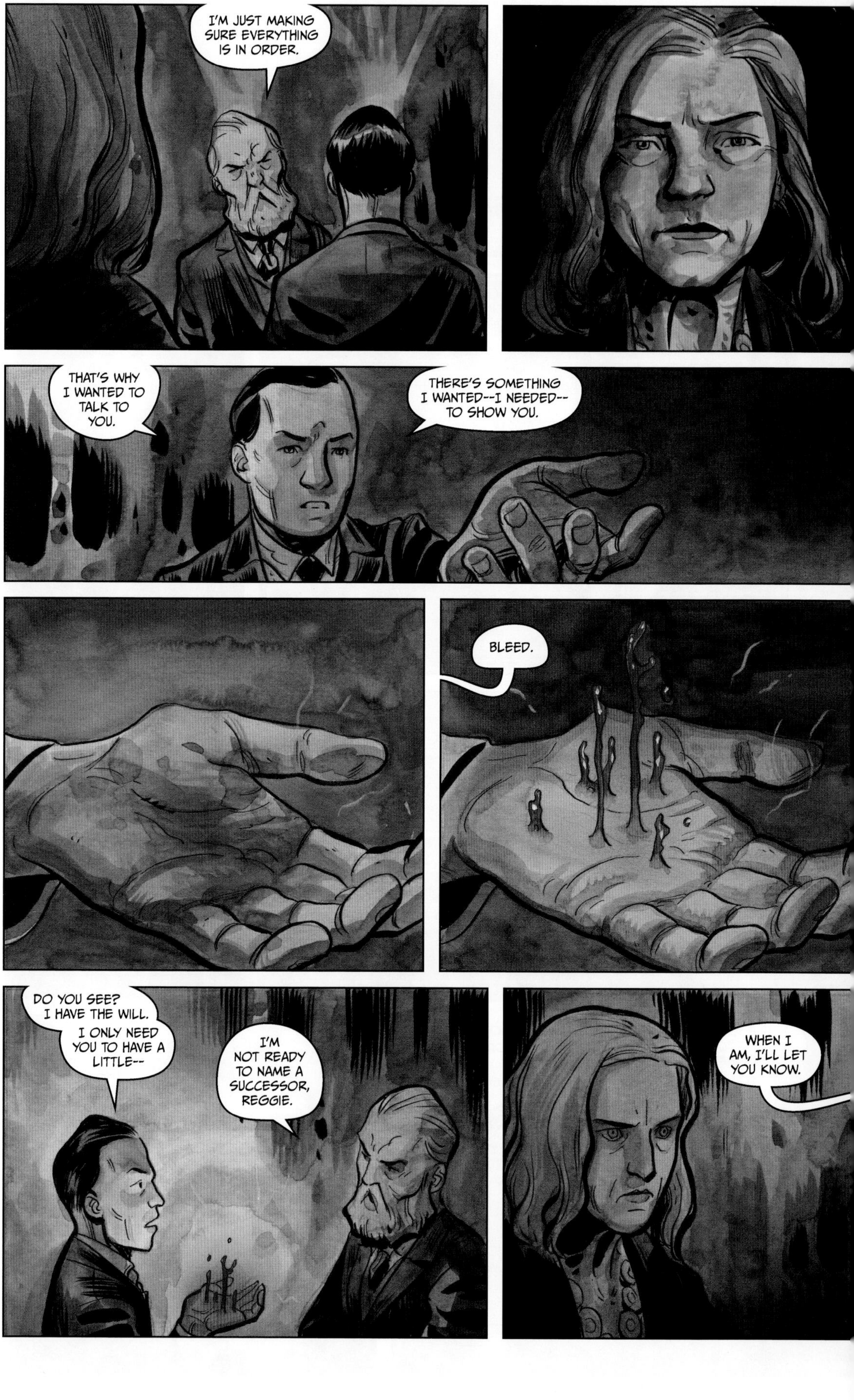
I'M JUST MAKING SURE EVERYTHING IS IN ORDER.
THAT'S WHY I WANTED TO TALK TO YOU.
THERE'S SOMETHING I WANTED--I NEEDED--TO SHOW YOU.
BLEED.
DO YOU SEE? I HAVE THE WILL.
I ONLY NEED YOU TO HAVE A LITTLE--
I'M NOT READY TO NAME A SUCCESSOR, REGGIE.
WHEN I AM, I'LL LET YOU KNOW.

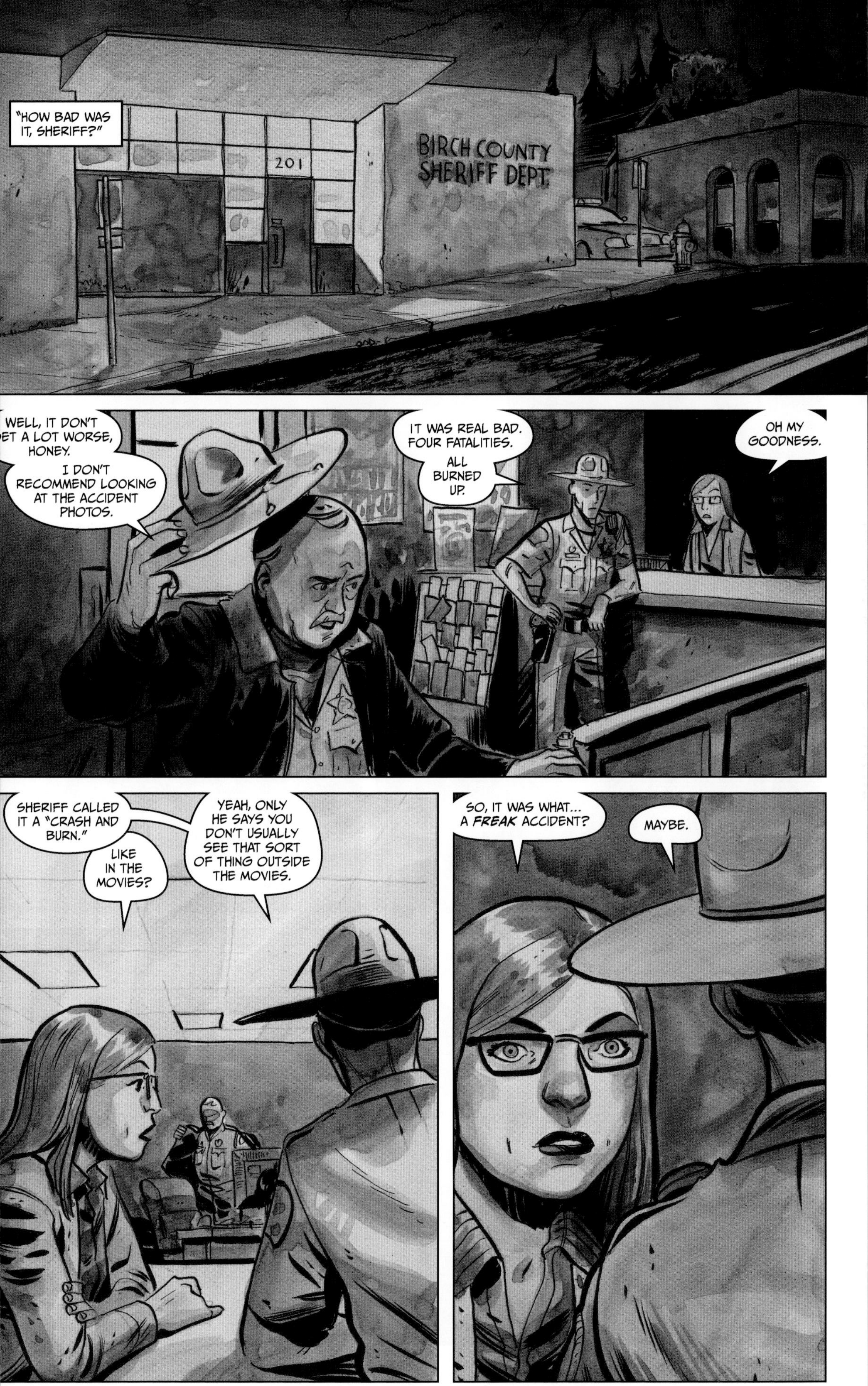
"HOW BAD WAS IT, SHERIFF?"
BIRCH COUNTY SHERIFF DEPT.
201
WELL, IT DON'T GET A LOT WORSE, HONEY.
I DON'T RECOMMEND LOOKING AT THE ACCIDENT PHOTOS.
IT WAS REAL BAD. FOUR FATALITIES.
ALL BURNED UP.
OH MY GOODNESS.
SHERIFF CALLED IT A "CRASH AND BURN."
LIKE IN THE MOVIES?
YEAH, ONLY HE SAYS YOU DON'T USUALLY SEE THAT SORT OF THING OUTSIDE THE MOVIES.
SO, IT WAS WHAT... A *FREAK* ACCIDENT?
MAYBE.

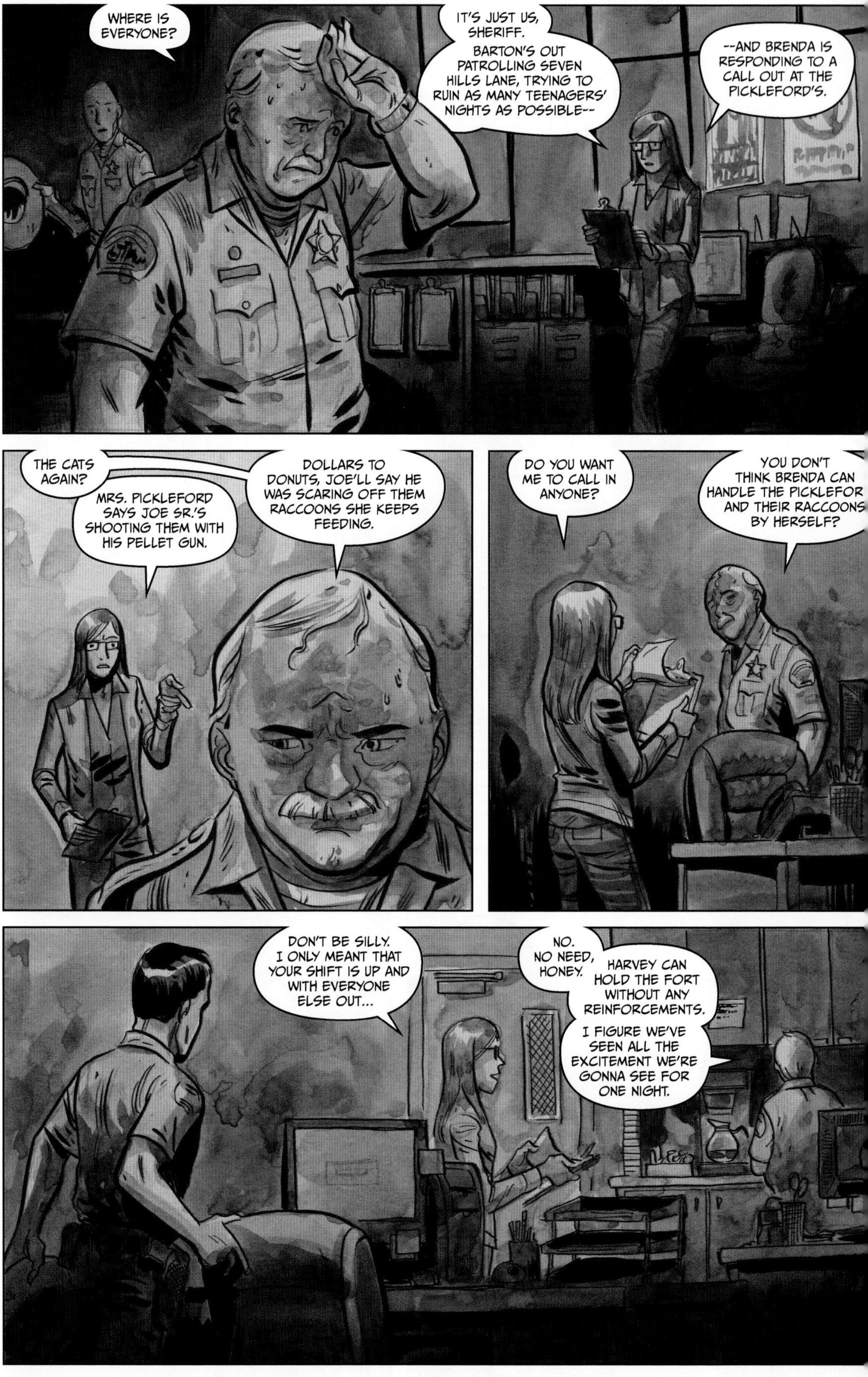

WHERE IS EVERYONE?
IT'S JUST US, SHERIFF.
BARTON'S OUT PATROLLING SEVEN HILLS LANE, TRYING TO RUIN AS MANY TEENAGERS' NIGHTS AS POSSIBLE--
--AND BRENDA IS RESPONDING TO A CALL OUT AT THE PICKLEFORD'S.
THE CATS AGAIN?
MRS. PICKLEFORD SAYS JOE SR.'S SHOOTING THEM WITH HIS PELLET GUN.
DOLLARS TO DONUTS, JOE'LL SAY HE WAS SCARING OFF THEM RACCOONS SHE KEEPS FEEDING.
DO YOU WANT ME TO CALL IN ANYONE?
YOU DON'T THINK BRENDA CAN HANDLE THE PICKLEFOR AND THEIR RACCOONS BY HERSELF?
DON'T BE SILLY. I ONLY MEANT THAT YOUR SHIFT IS UP AND WITH EVERYONE ELSE OUT...
NO. NO NEED, HONEY.
HARVEY CAN HOLD THE FORT WITHOUT ANY REINFORCEMENTS.
I FIGURE WE'VE SEEN ALL THE EXCITEMENT WE'RE GONNA SEE FOR ONE NIGHT.

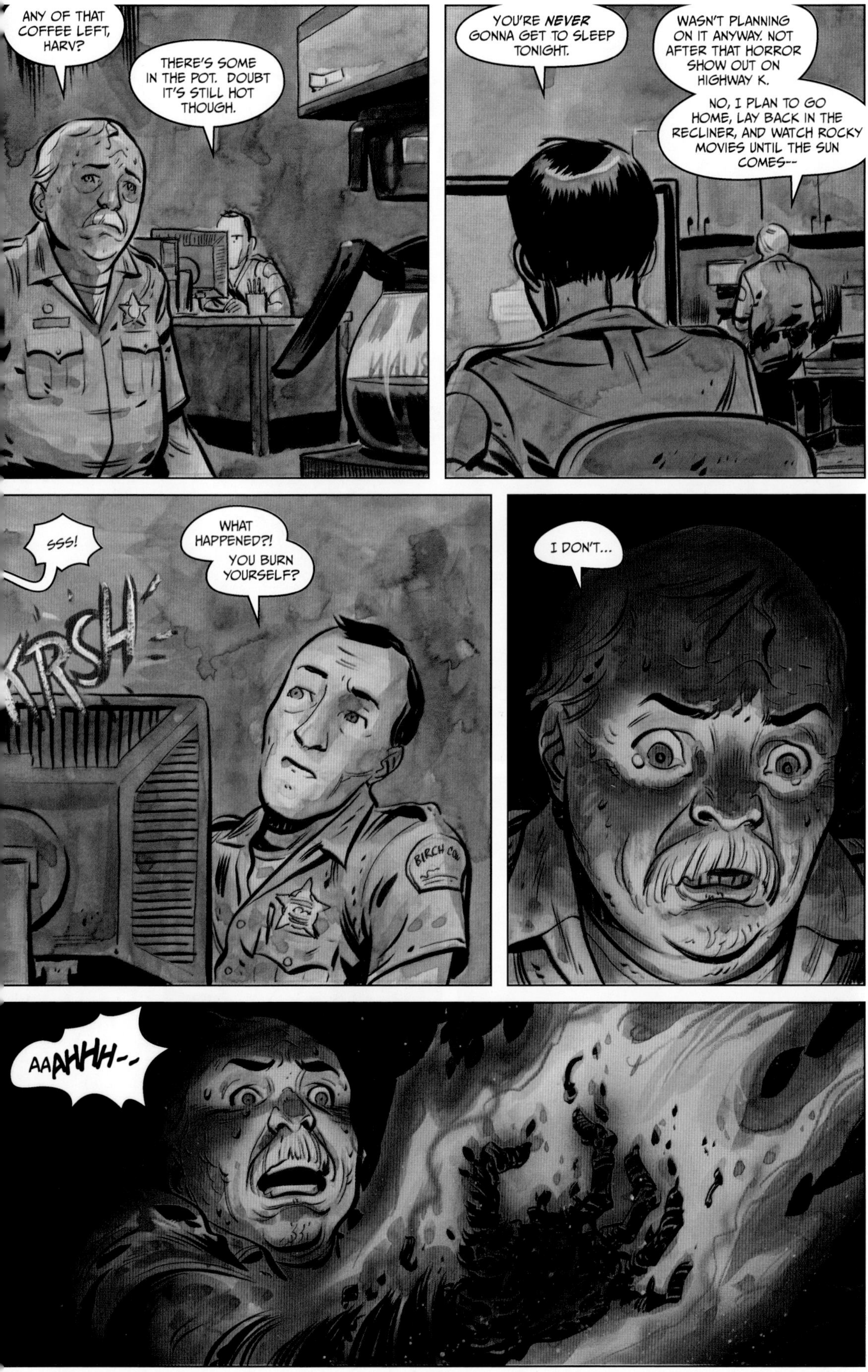
ANY OF THAT COFFEE LEFT, HARV?
THERE'S SOME IN THE POT. DOUBT IT'S STILL HOT THOUGH.
YOU'RE NEVER GONNA GET TO SLEEP TONIGHT.
WASN'T PLANNING ON IT ANYWAY. NOT AFTER THAT HORROR SHOW OUT ON HIGHWAY K.
NO, I PLAN TO GO HOME, LAY BACK IN THE RECLINER, AND WATCH ROCKY MOVIES UNTIL THE SUN COMES--
SSS!
KRSH
WHAT HAPPENED?!
YOU BURN YOURSELF?
BIRCH CO.
I DON'T...
AAAHHH--

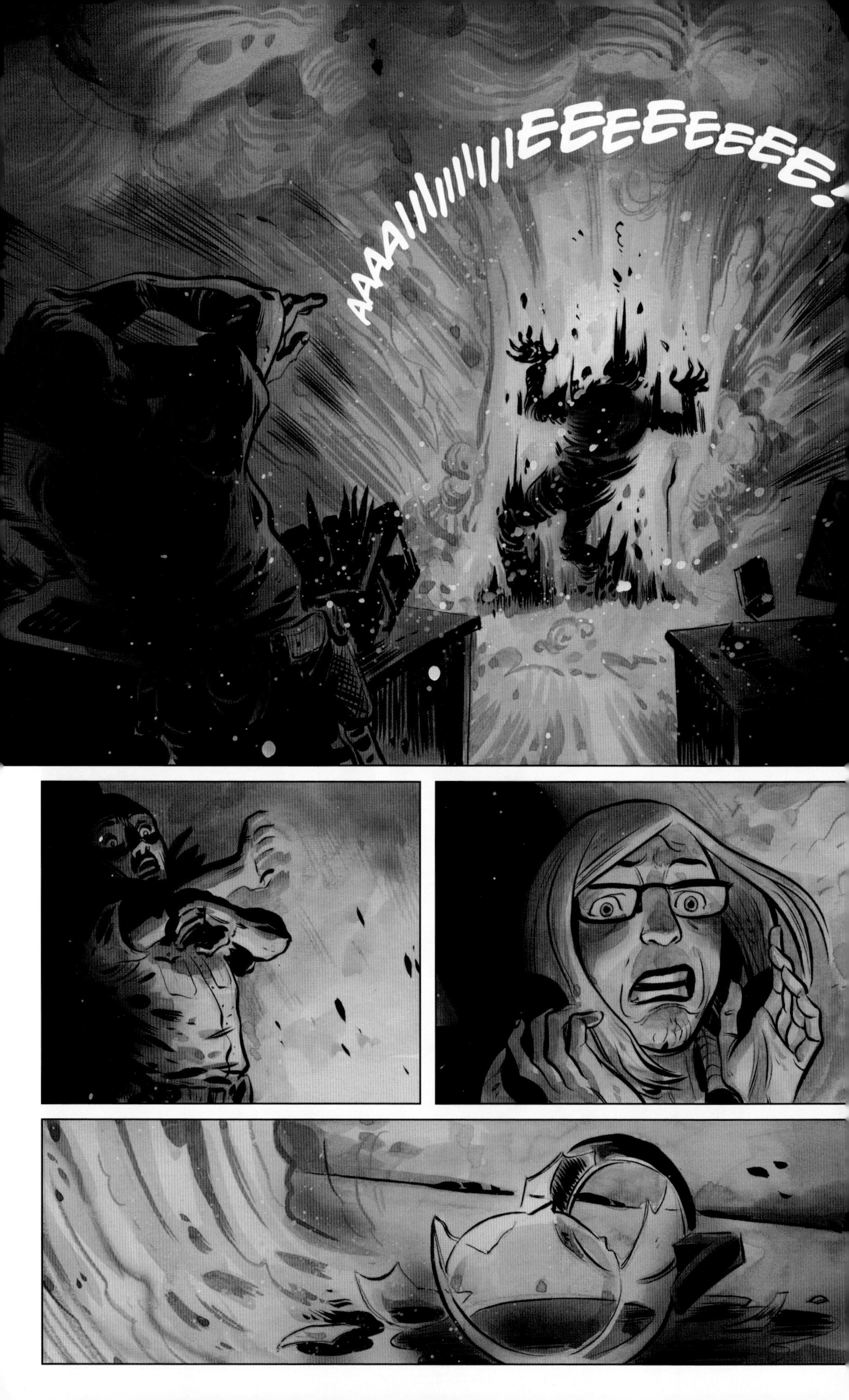
AAAAIIIIIIIIIIIEEEEEEEEEE!

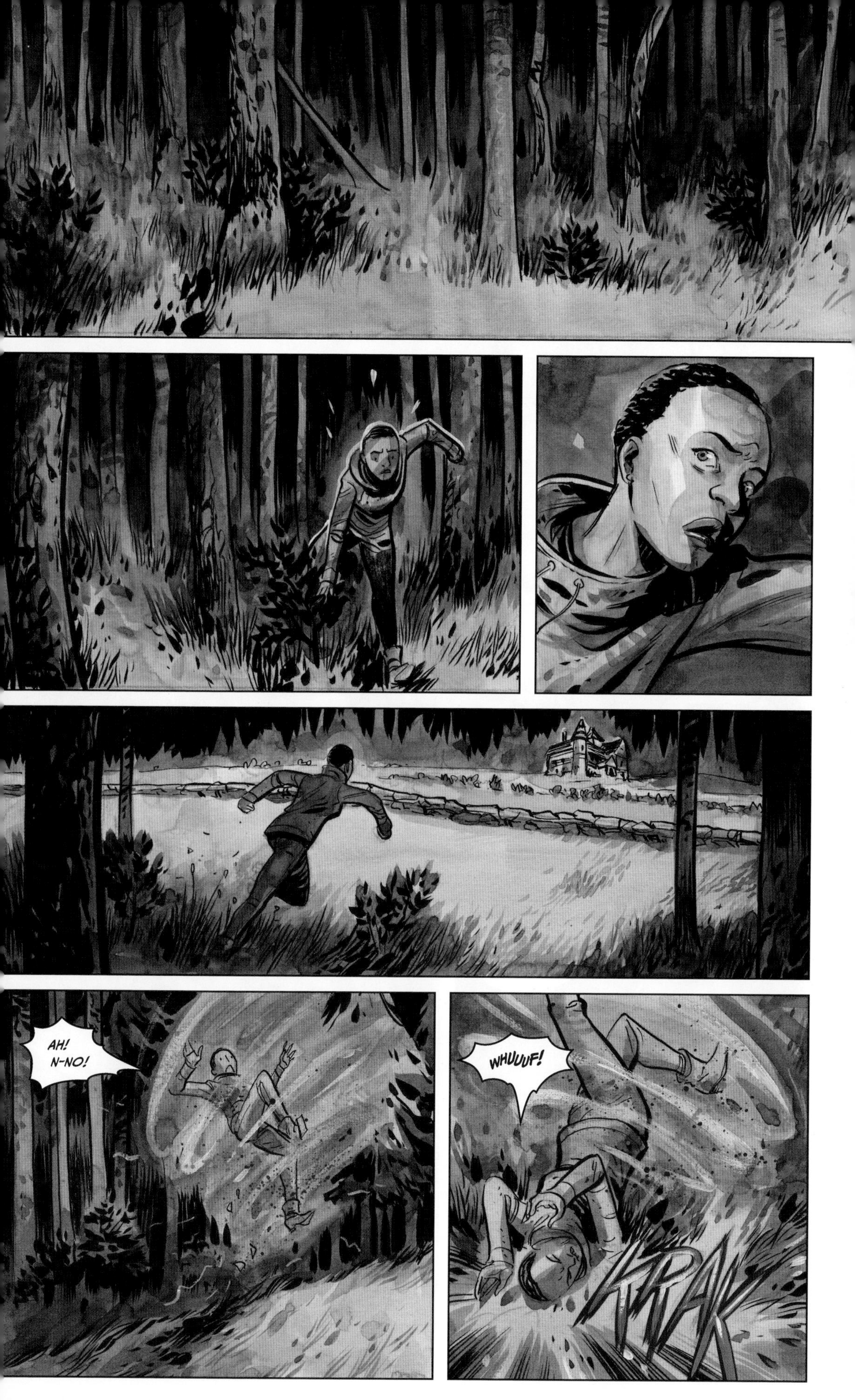
AH!
N-NO!
WHUUUF!
KRAK

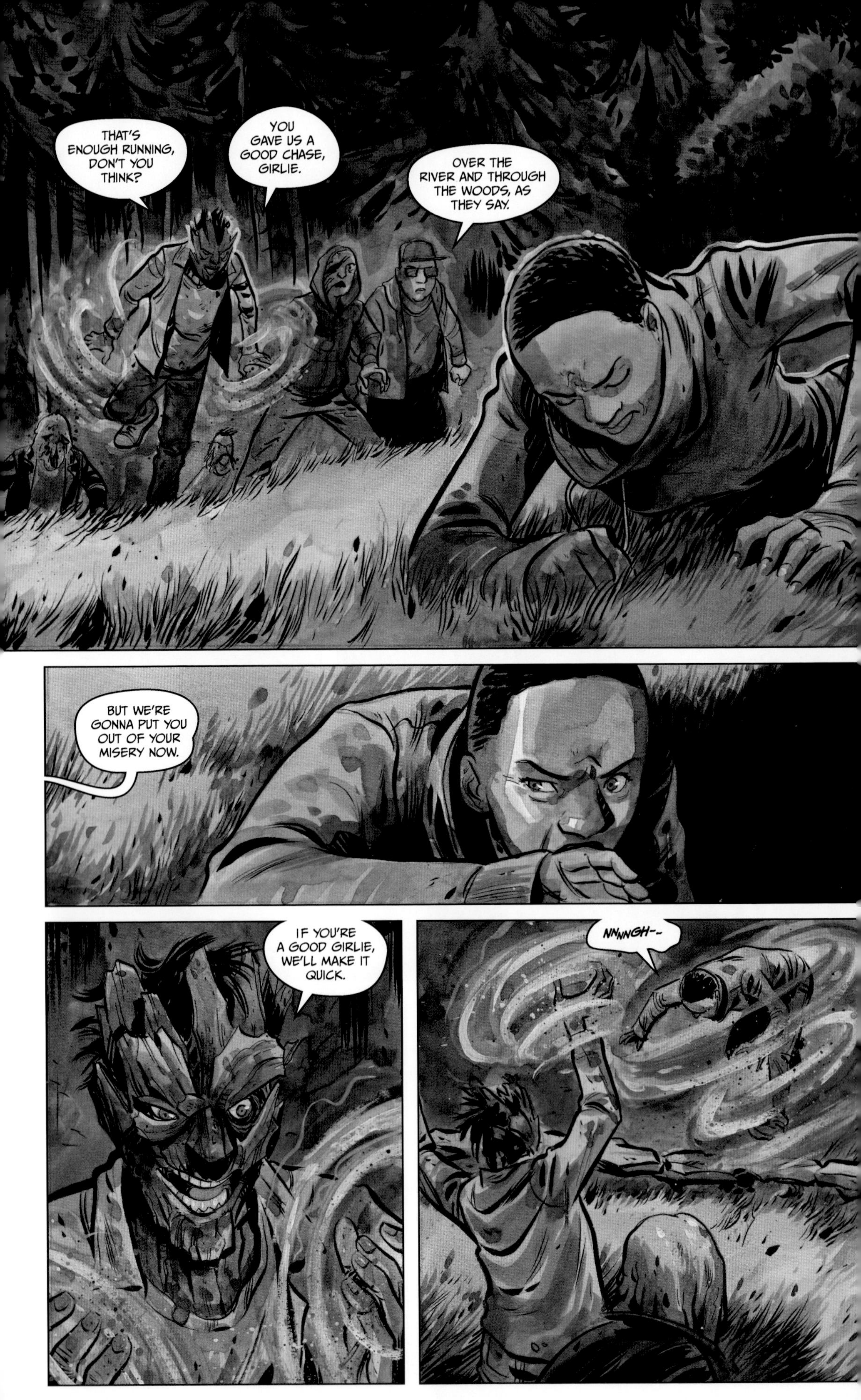
THAT'S ENOUGH RUNNING, DON'T YOU THINK?
YOU GAVE US A GOOD CHASE, GIRLIE.
OVER THE RIVER AND THROUGH THE WOODS, AS THEY SAY.
BUT WE'RE GONNA PUT YOU OUT OF YOUR MISERY NOW.
IF YOU'RE A GOOD GIRLIE, WE'LL MAKE IT QUICK.
NNNNGH--

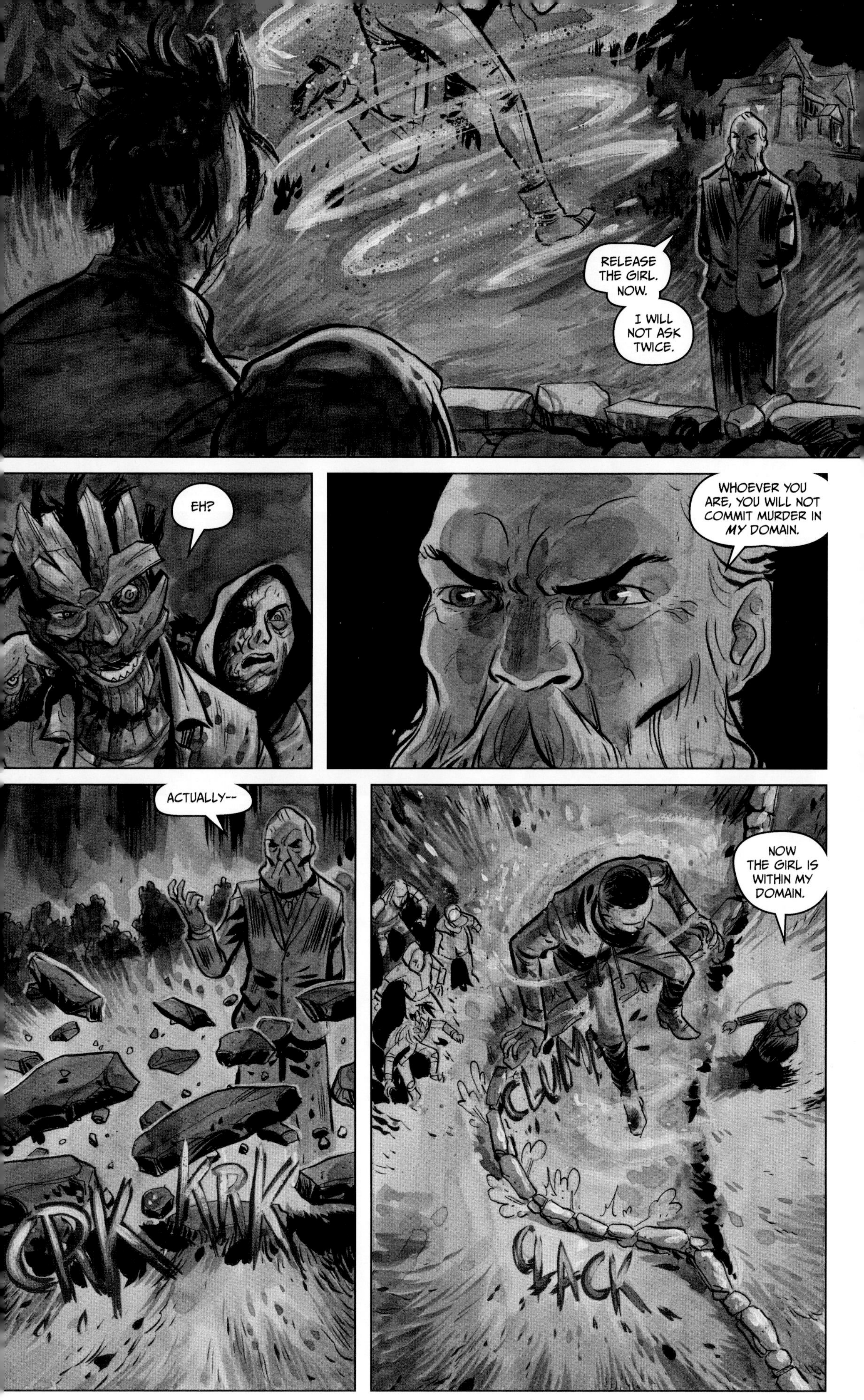
RELEASE THE GIRL. NOW.
I WILL NOT ASK TWICE.
EH?
WHOEVER YOU ARE, YOU WILL NOT COMMIT MURDER IN MY DOMAIN.
ACTUALLY--
CRK KRK
NOW THE GIRL IS WITHIN MY DOMAIN.
CLUMP
CLACK

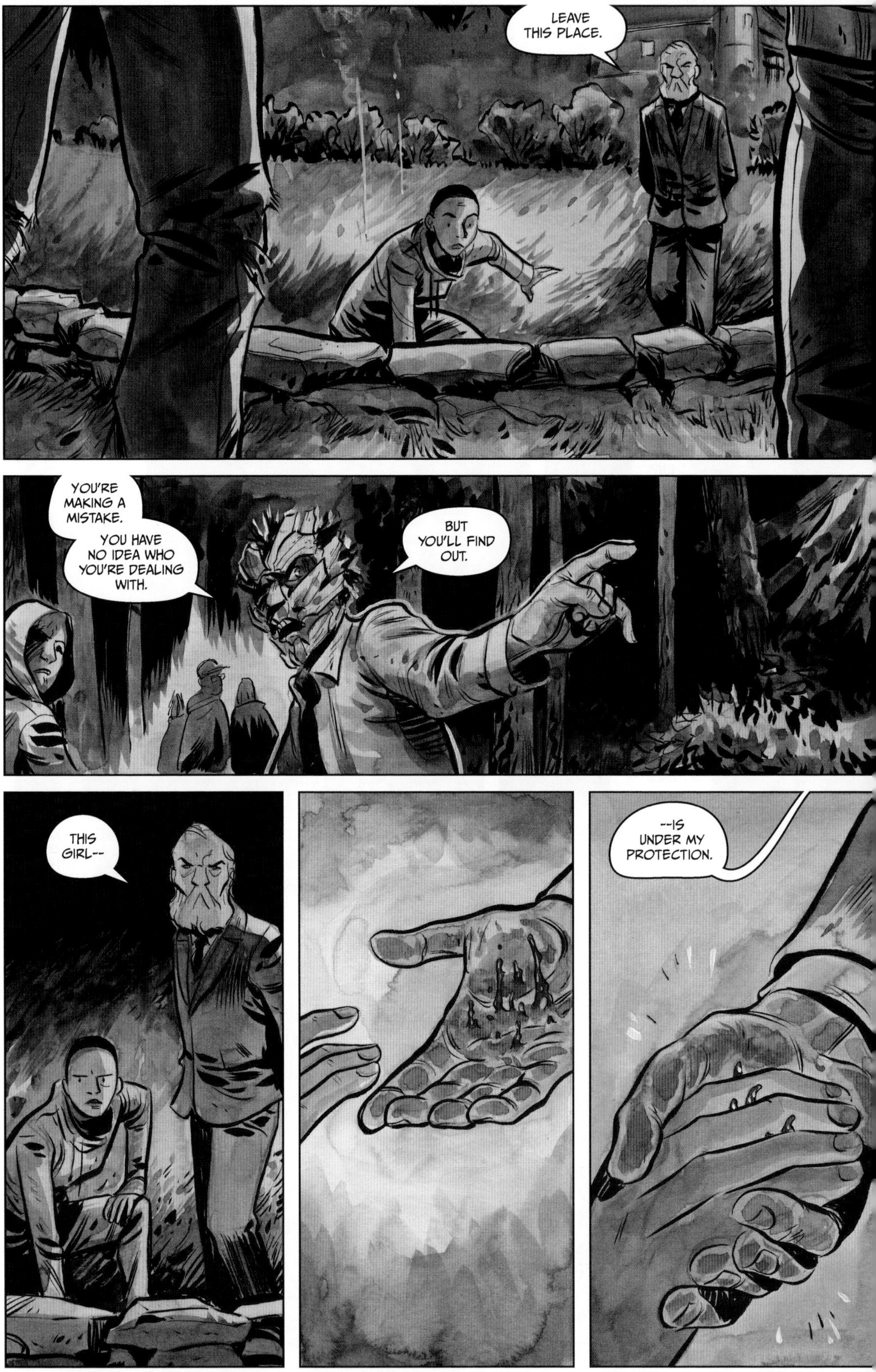
LEAVE THIS PLACE.
YOU'RE MAKING A MISTAKE.
YOU HAVE NO IDEA WHO YOU'RE DEALING WITH.
BUT YOU'LL FIND OUT.
THIS GIRL--
--IS UNDER MY PROTECTION.

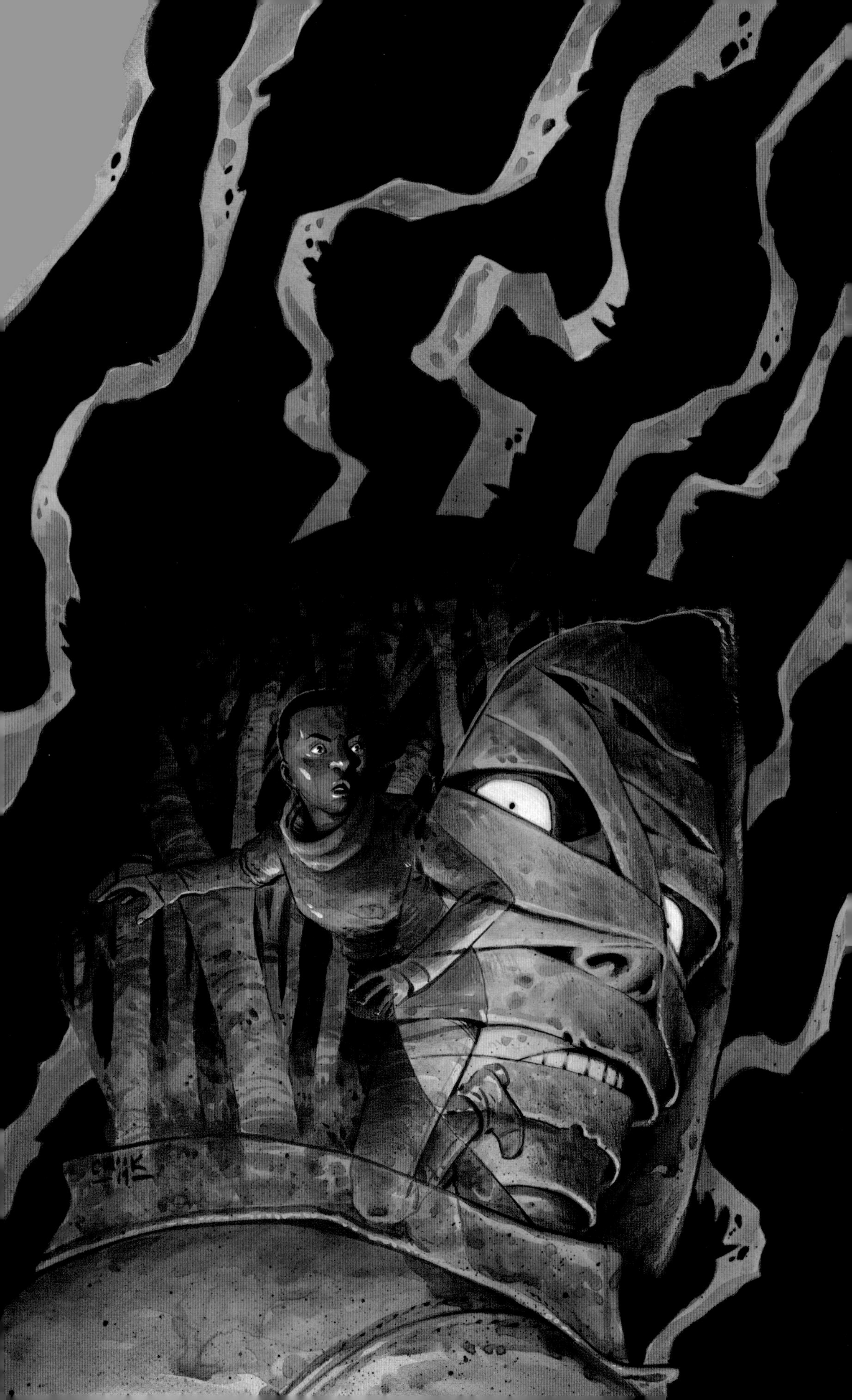

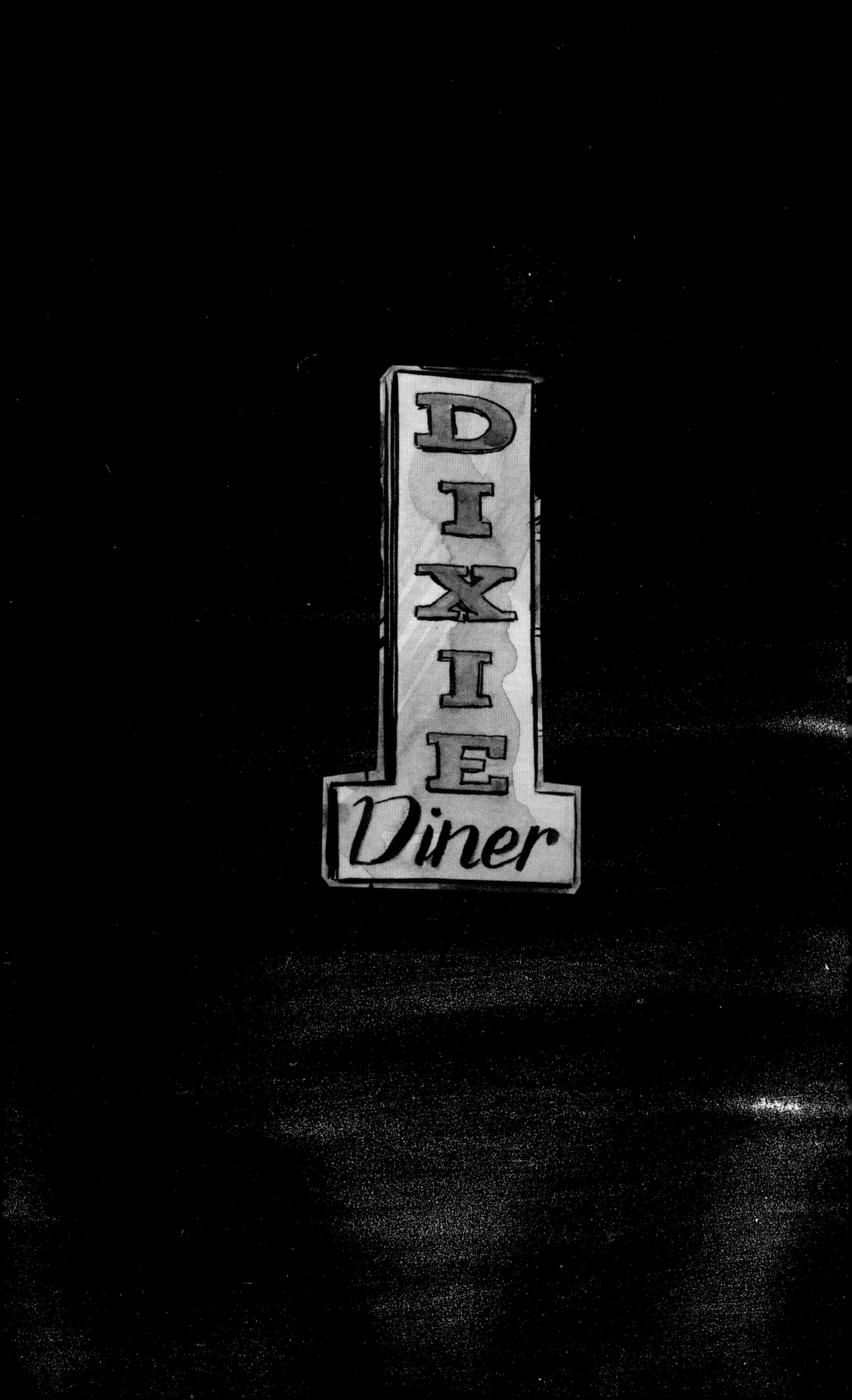
DIXIE
Diner

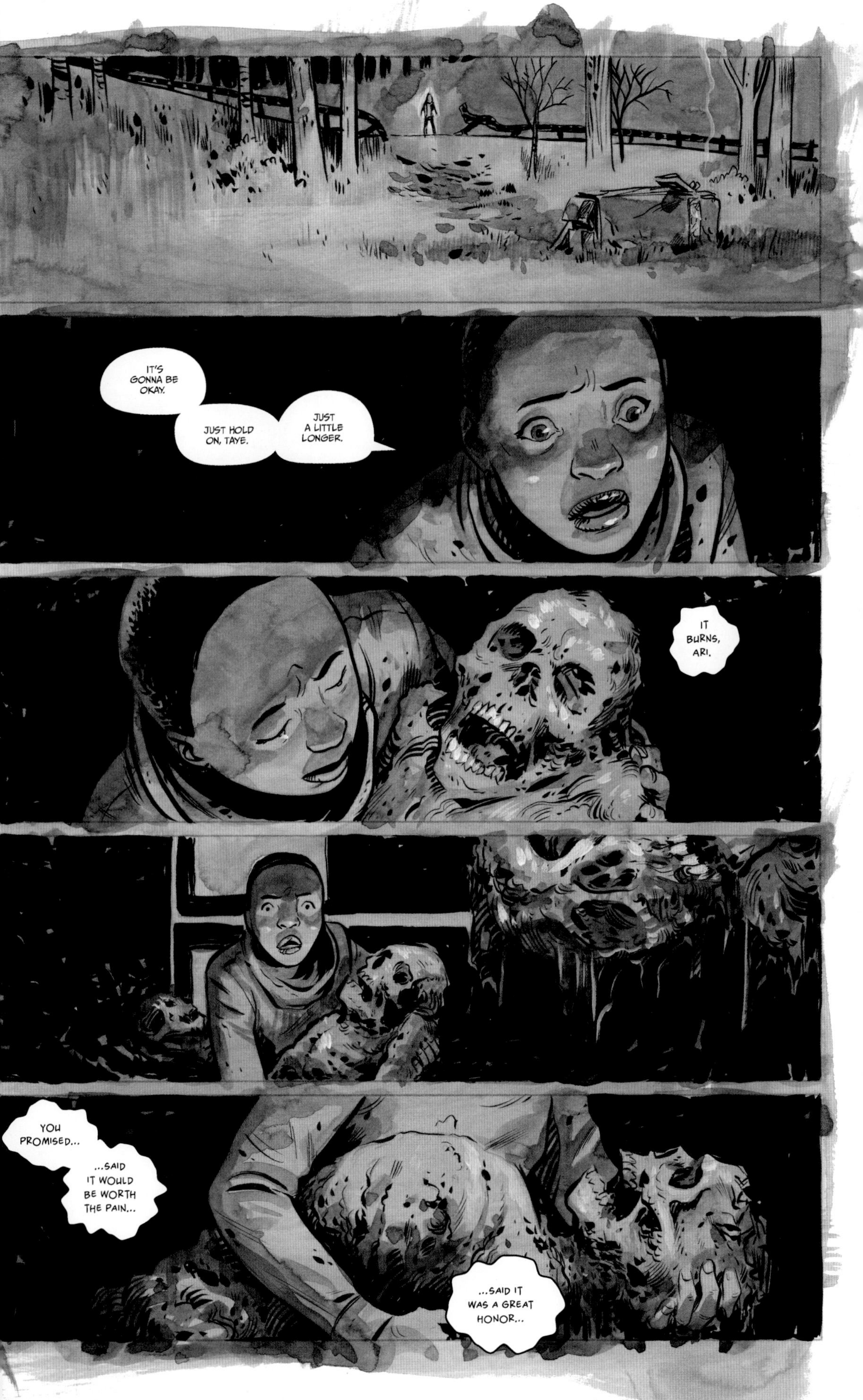
IT'S GONNA BE OKAY.
JUST HOLD ON, TAYE.
JUST A LITTLE LONGER.
IT BURNS, ARI.
YOU PROMISED...
...SAID IT WOULD BE WORTH THE PAIN...
...SAID IT WAS A GREAT HONOR...

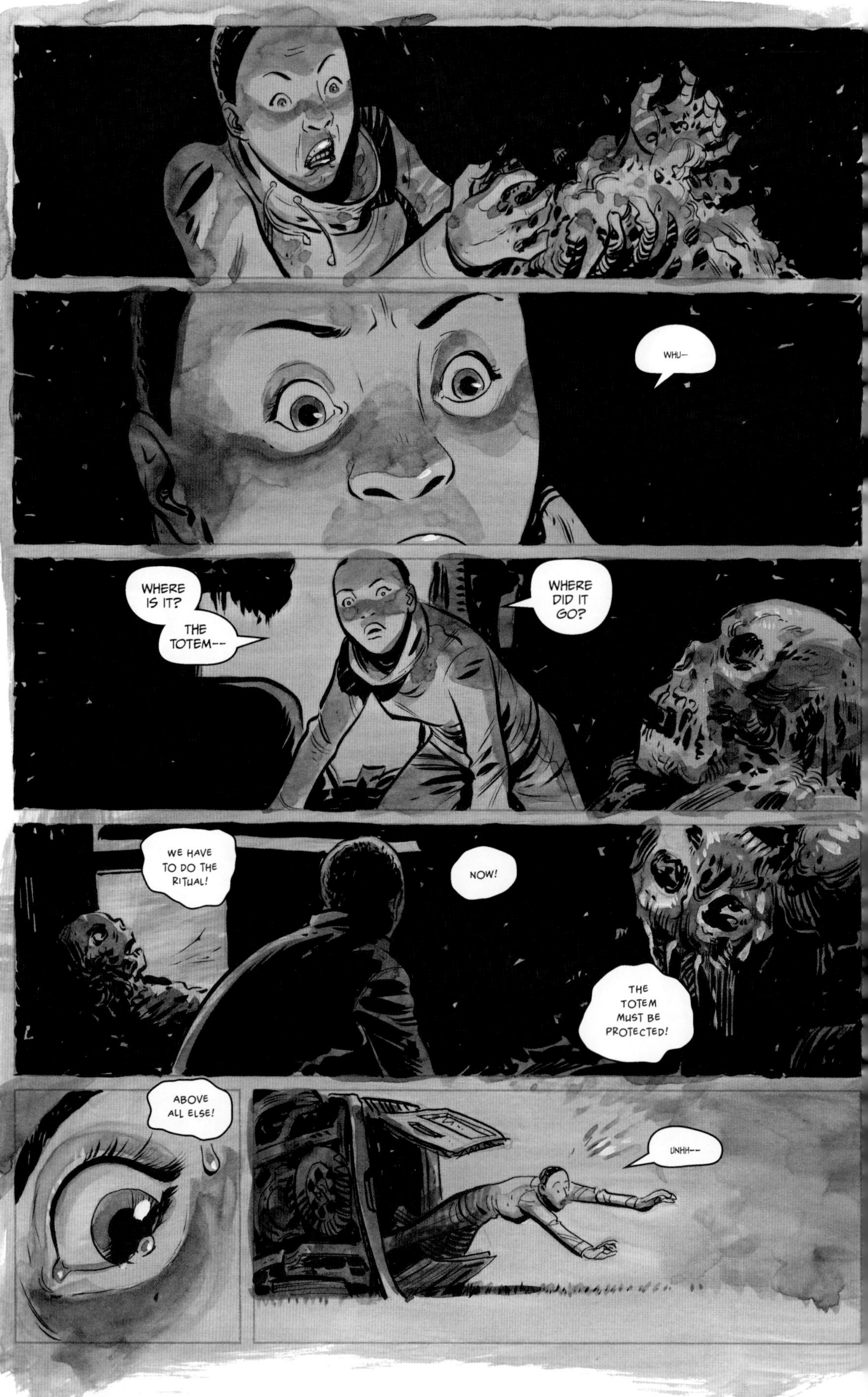
WHU–
WHERE IS IT?
THE TOTEM--
WHERE DID IT GO?
WE HAVE TO DO THE RITUAL!
NOW!
THE TOTEM MUST BE PROTECTED!
ABOVE ALL ELSE!
UNHH--

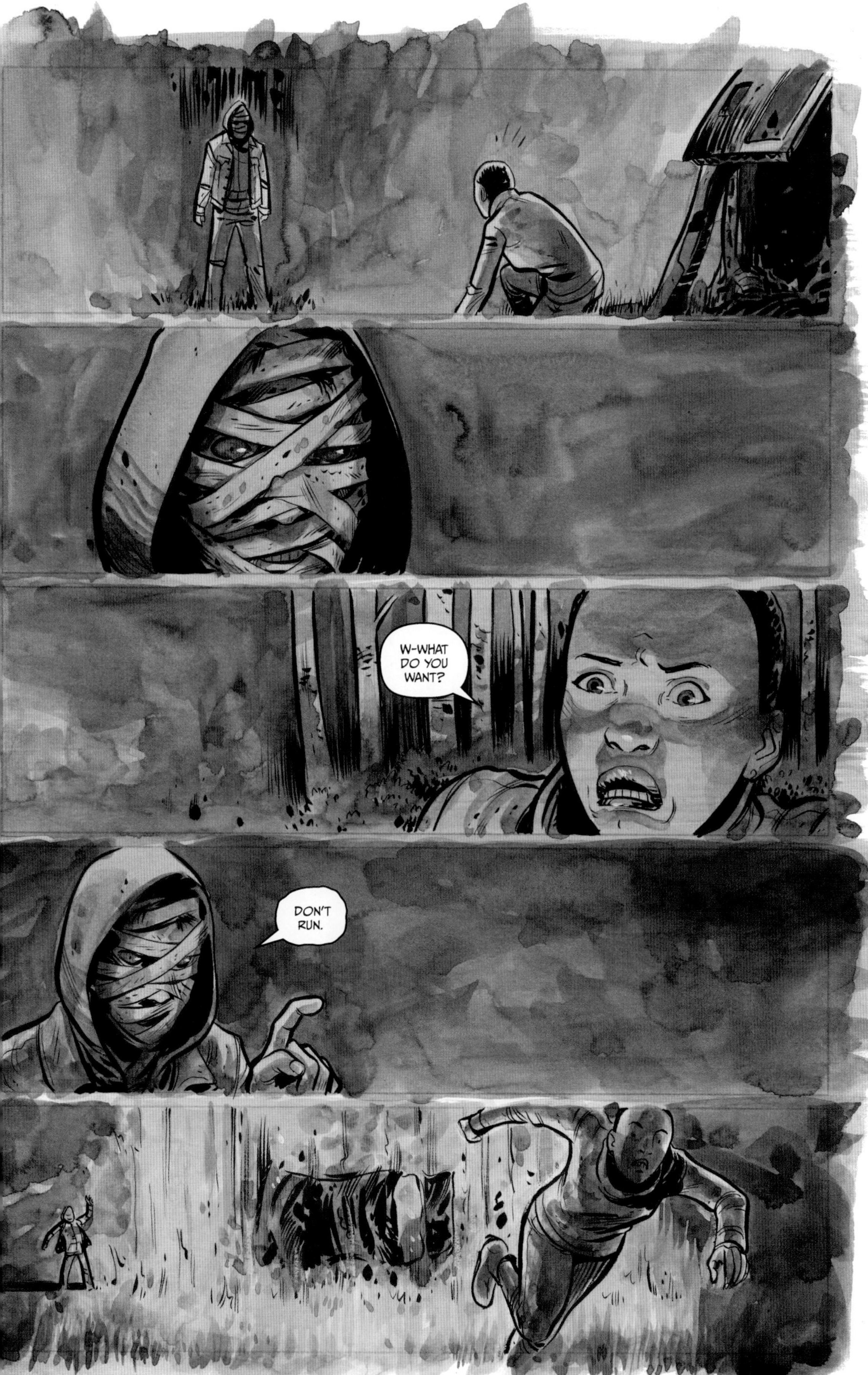
W-WHAT DO YOU WANT?
DON'T RUN.

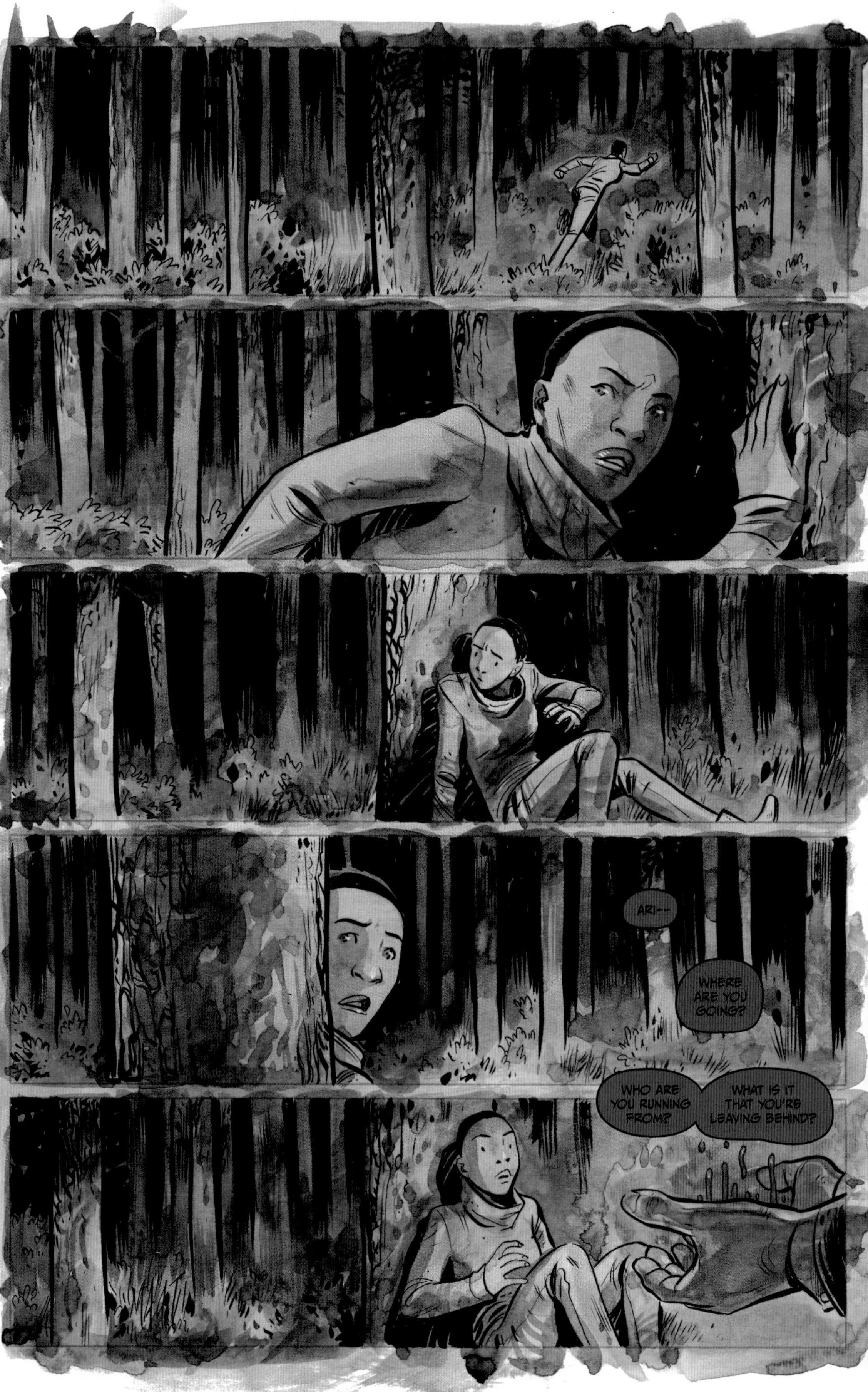
ARI--
WHERE ARE YOU GOING?
WHO ARE YOU RUNNING FROM?
WHAT IS IT THAT YOU'RE LEAVING BEHIND?

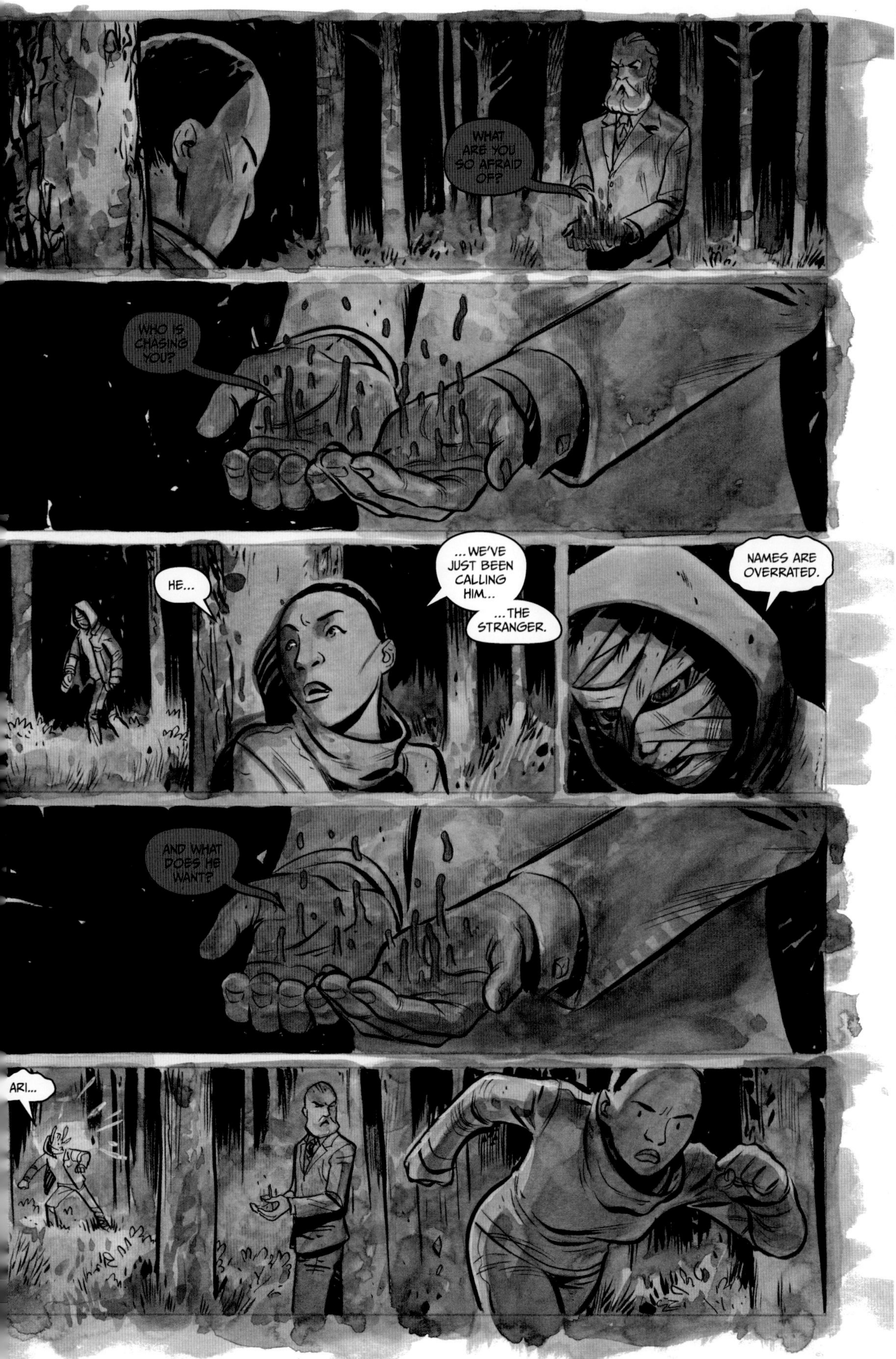
WHAT ARE YOU SO AFRAID OF?
WHO IS CHASING YOU?
HE...
...WE'VE JUST BEEN CALLING HIM...
...THE STRANGER.
NAMES ARE OVERRATED.
AND WHAT DOES HE WANT?
ARI...

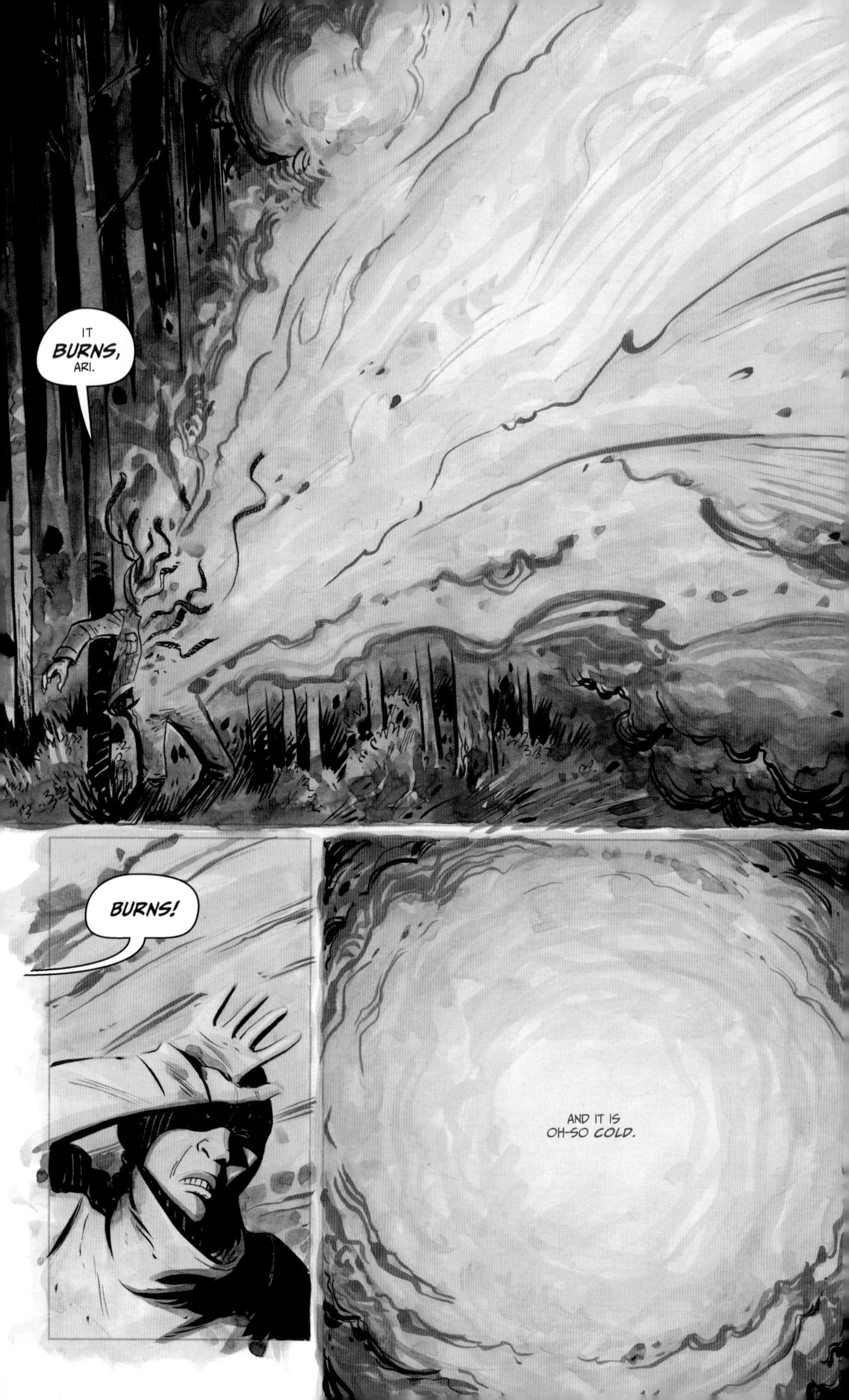
IT BURNS, ARI.
BURNS!
AND IT IS OH-SO COLD.

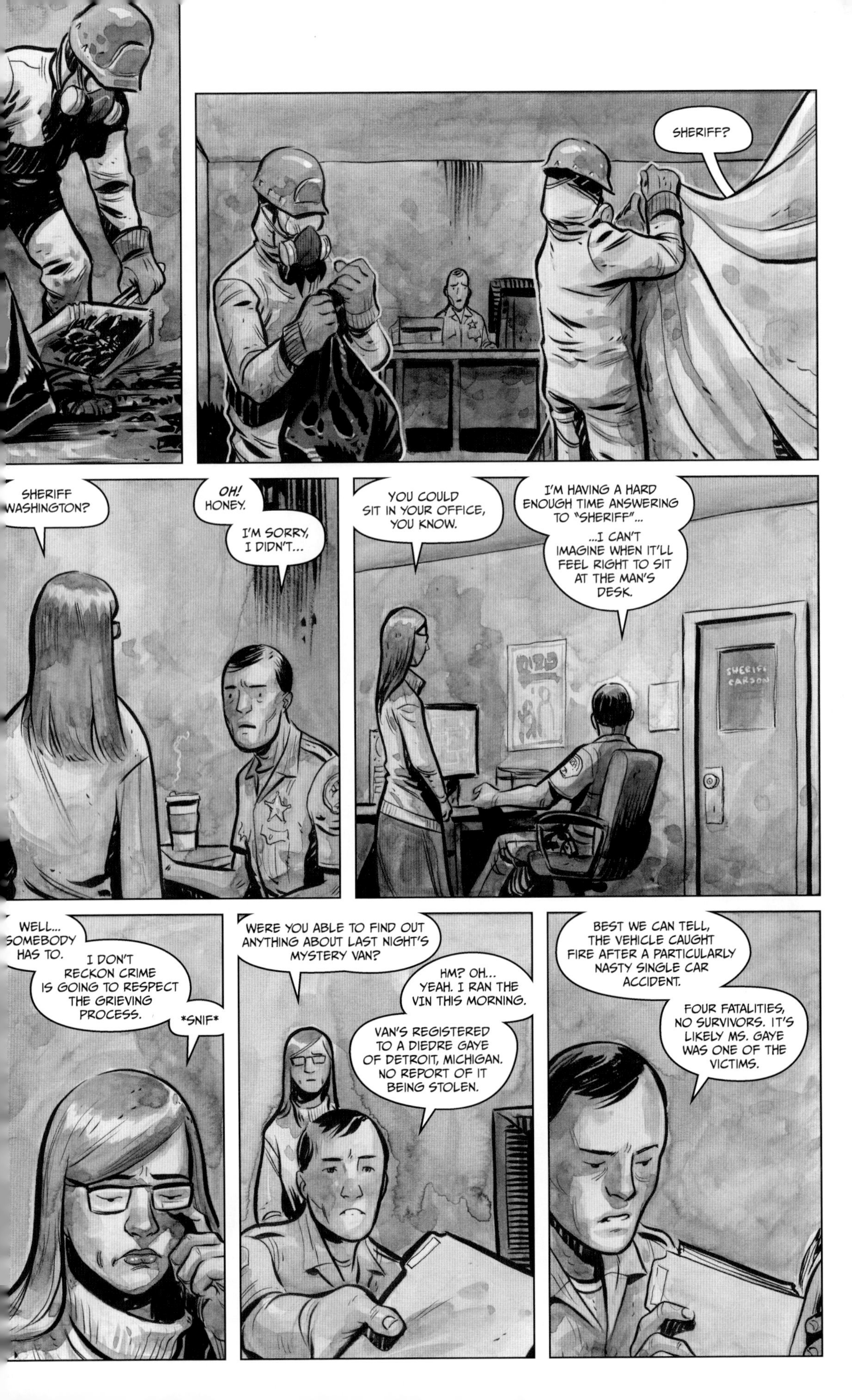
SHERIFF?
SHERIFF WASHINGTON?
OH! HONEY.
I'M SORRY, I DIDN'T...
YOU COULD SIT IN YOUR OFFICE, YOU KNOW.
I'M HAVING A HARD ENOUGH TIME ANSWERING TO "SHERIFF"...
...I CAN'T IMAGINE WHEN IT'LL FEEL RIGHT TO SIT AT THE MAN'S DESK.
SHERIFF CARSON
WELL... SOMEBODY HAS TO.
I DON'T RECKON CRIME IS GOING TO RESPECT THE GRIEVING PROCESS.
SNIF
WERE YOU ABLE TO FIND OUT ANYTHING ABOUT LAST NIGHT'S MYSTERY VAN?
HM? OH... YEAH. I RAN THE VIN THIS MORNING.
VAN'S REGISTERED TO A DIEDRE GAYE OF DETROIT, MICHIGAN. NO REPORT OF IT BEING STOLEN.
BEST WE CAN TELL, THE VEHICLE CAUGHT FIRE AFTER A PARTICULARLY NASTY SINGLE CAR ACCIDENT.
FOUR FATALITIES, NO SURVIVORS. IT'S LIKELY MS. GAYE WAS ONE OF THE VICTIMS.

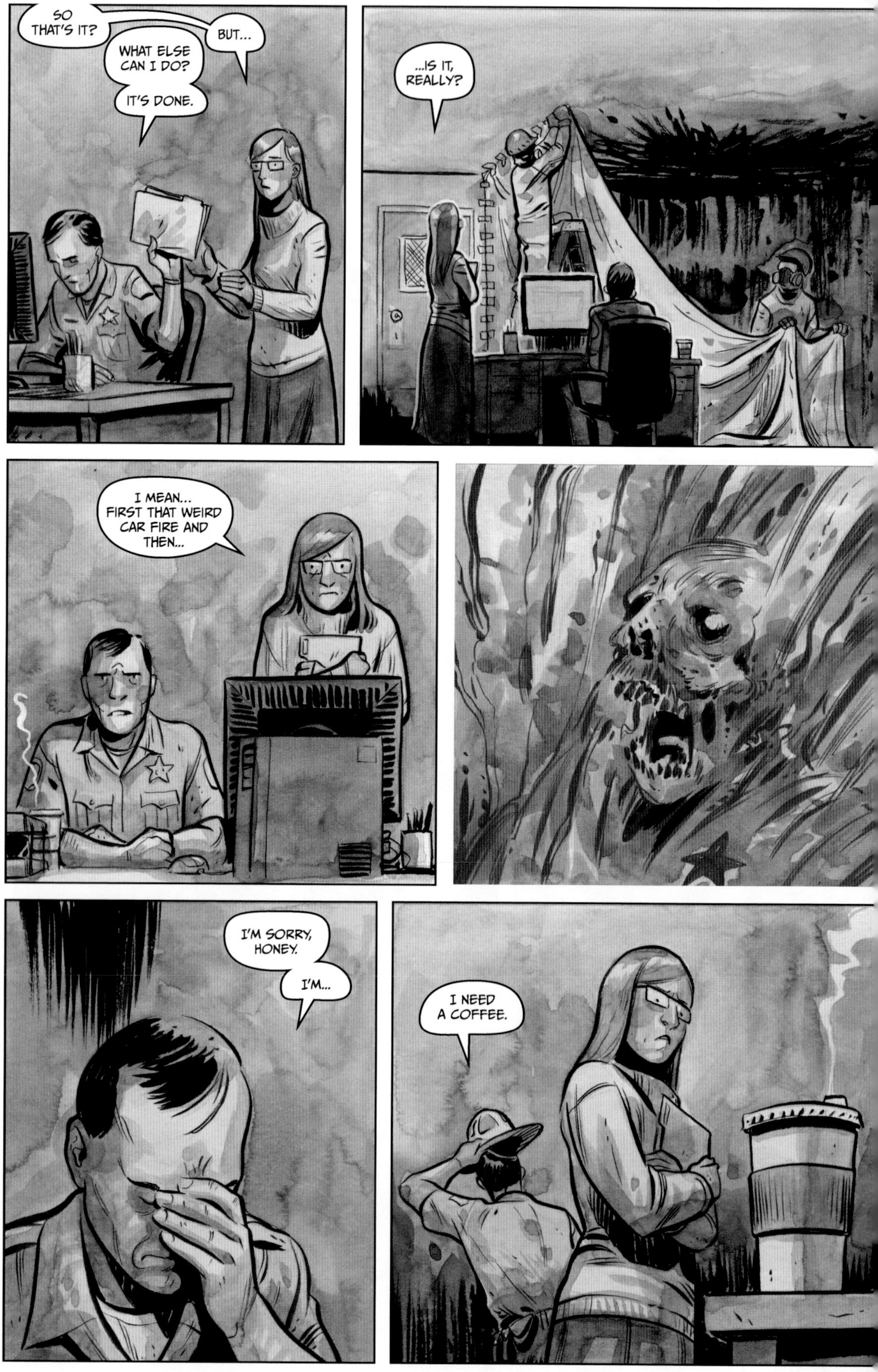
SO THAT'S IT?
BUT...
WHAT ELSE CAN I DO?
IT'S DONE.
...IS IT, REALLY?
I MEAN... FIRST THAT WEIRD CAR FIRE AND THEN...
I'M SORRY, HONEY.
I'M...
I NEED A COFFEE.

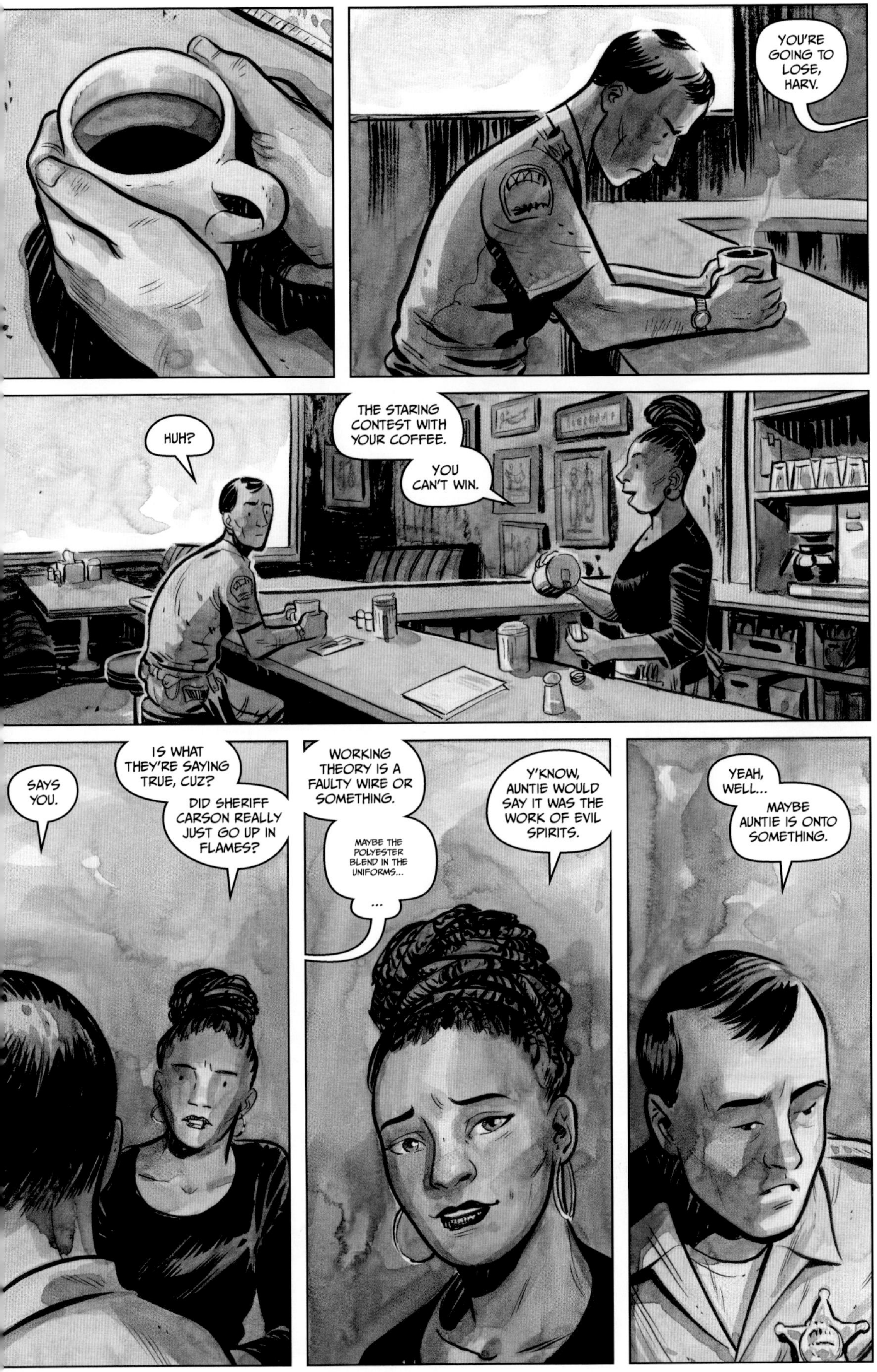
YOU'RE GOING TO LOSE, HARV.
HUH?
THE STARING CONTEST WITH YOUR COFFEE.
YOU CAN'T WIN.
SAYS YOU.
IS WHAT THEY'RE SAYING TRUE, CUZ?
DID SHERIFF CARSON REALLY JUST GO UP IN FLAMES?
WORKING THEORY IS A FAULTY WIRE OR SOMETHING.
MAYBE THE POLYESTER BLEND IN THE UNIFORMS...
...
Y'KNOW, AUNTIE WOULD SAY IT WAS THE WORK OF EVIL SPIRITS.
YEAH, WELL...
MAYBE AUNTIE IS ONTO SOMETHING.

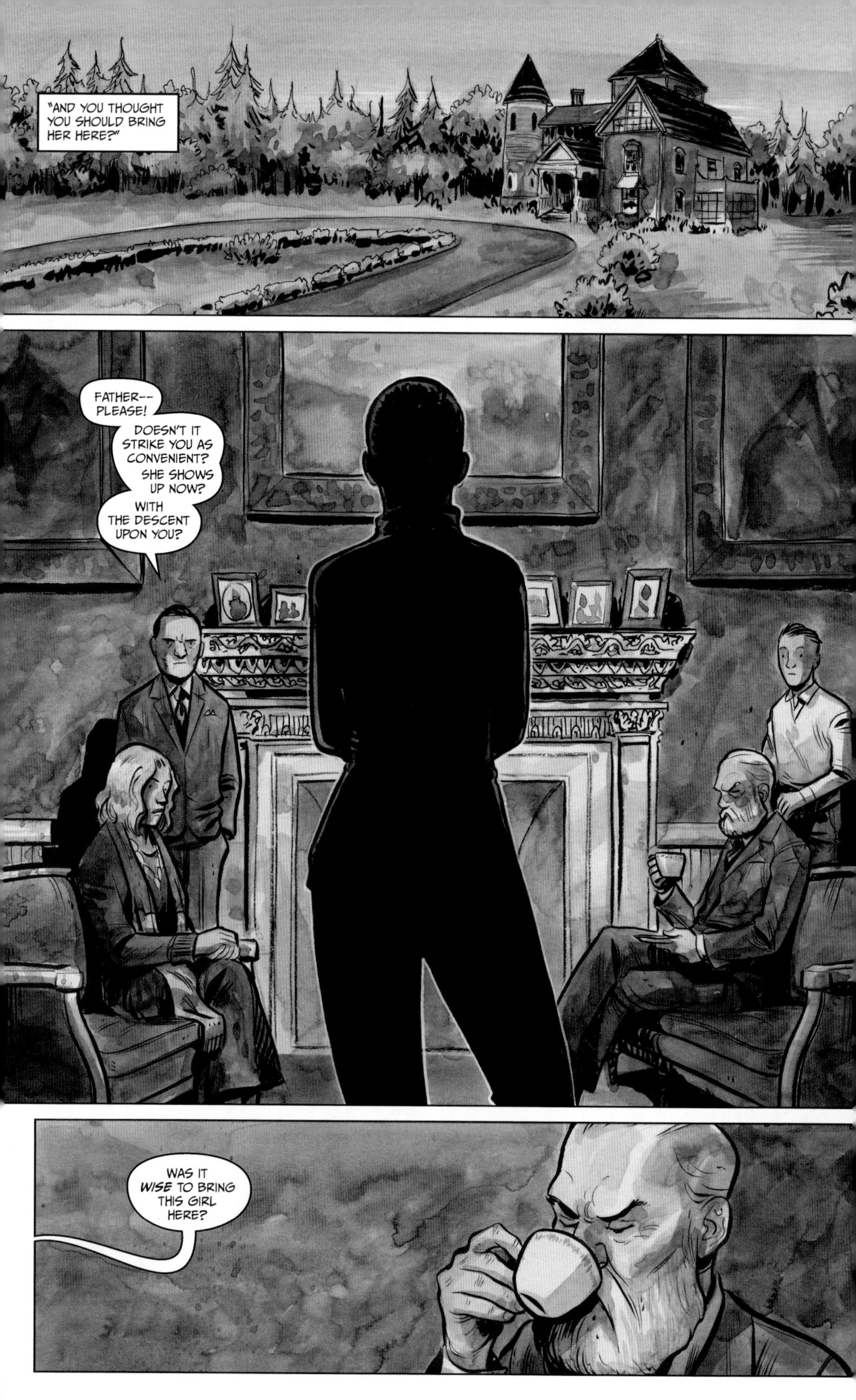
"AND YOU THOUGHT YOU SHOULD BRING HER HERE?"
FATHER-- PLEASE!
DOESN'T IT STRIKE YOU AS CONVENIENT?
SHE SHOWS UP NOW?
WITH THE DESCENT UPON YOU?
WAS IT *WISE* TO BRING THIS GIRL HERE?

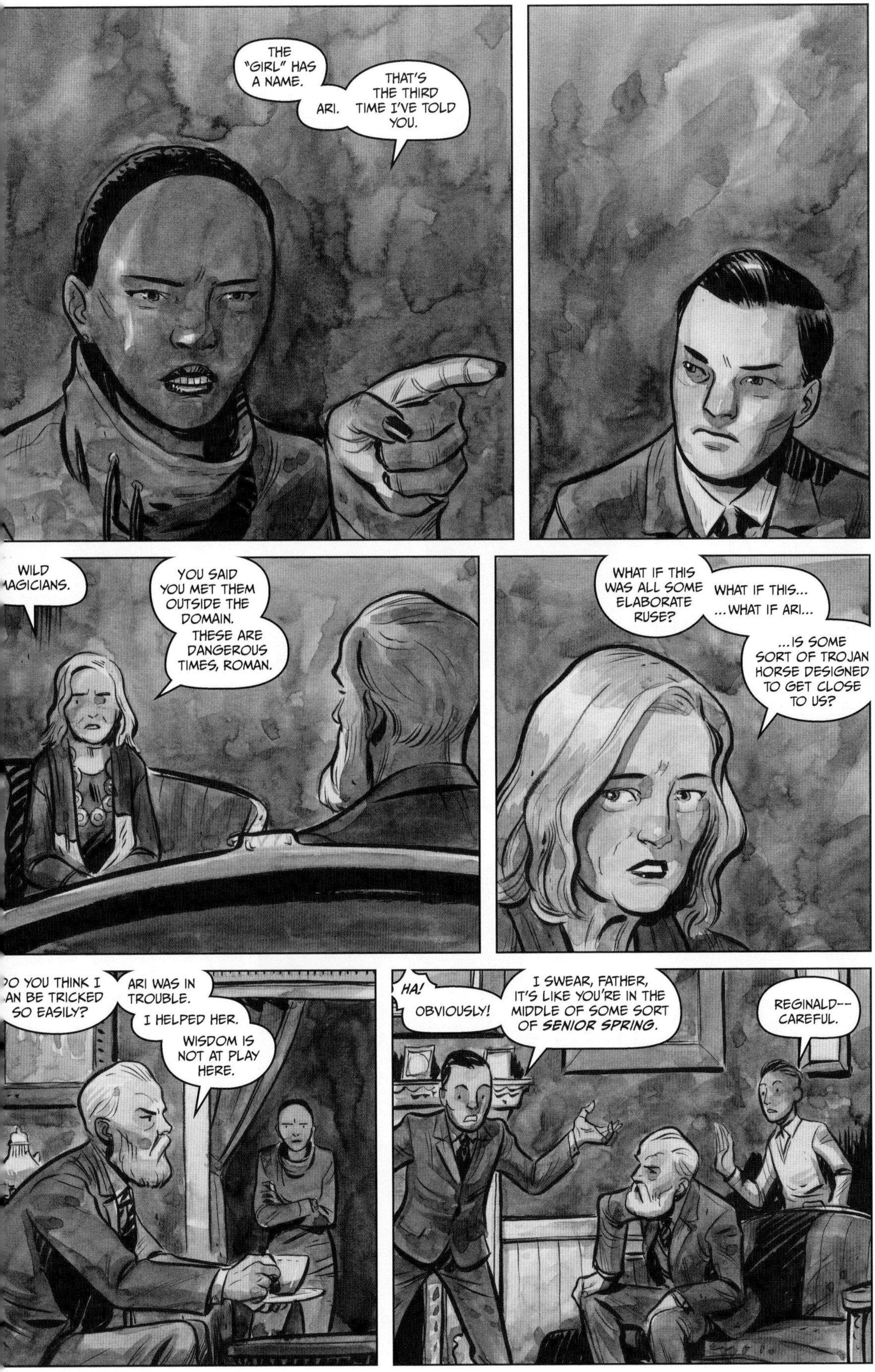
THE "GIRL" HAS A NAME.
ARI.
THAT'S THE THIRD TIME I'VE TOLD YOU.
WILD AGICIANS.
YOU SAID YOU MET THEM OUTSIDE THE DOMAIN.
THESE ARE DANGEROUS TIMES, ROMAN.
WHAT IF THIS WAS ALL SOME ELABORATE RUSE?
WHAT IF THIS...
...WHAT IF ARI...
...IS SOME SORT OF TROJAN HORSE DESIGNED TO GET CLOSE TO US?
O YOU THINK I AN BE TRICKED SO EASILY?
ARI WAS IN TROUBLE.
I HELPED HER.
WISDOM IS NOT AT PLAY HERE.
HA!
OBVIOUSLY!
I SWEAR, FATHER, IT'S LIKE YOU'RE IN THE MIDDLE OF SOME SORT OF SENIOR SPRING.
REGINALD-- CAREFUL.

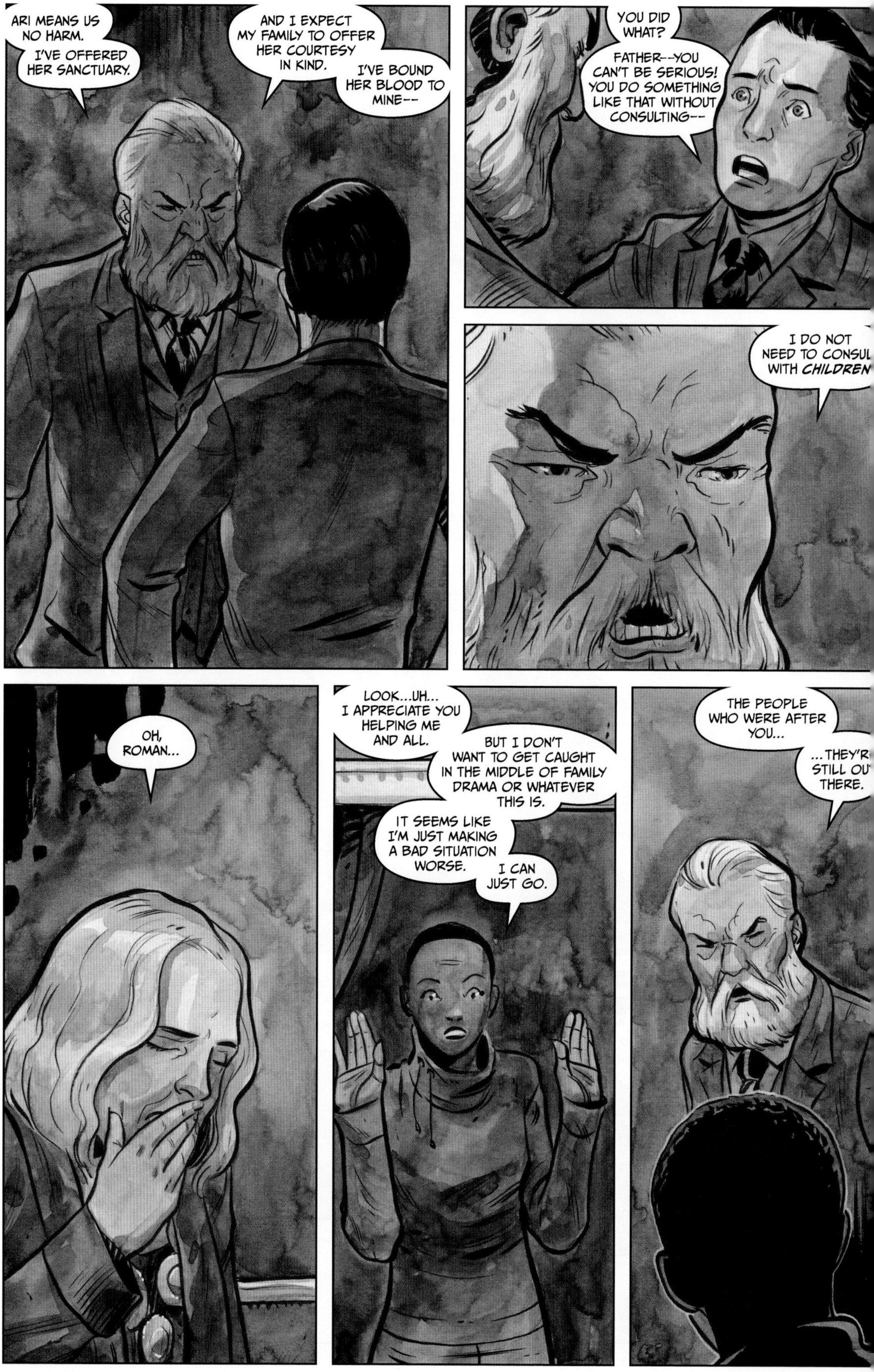

ARI MEANS US NO HARM.
I'VE OFFERED HER SANCTUARY.
AND I EXPECT MY FAMILY TO OFFER HER COURTESY IN KIND.
I'VE BOUND HER BLOOD TO MINE--
YOU DID WHAT?
FATHER--YOU CAN'T BE SERIOUS! YOU DO SOMETHING LIKE THAT WITHOUT CONSULTING--
I DO NOT NEED TO CONSUL WITH CHILDREN
OH, ROMAN...
LOOK...UH... I APPRECIATE YOU HELPING ME AND ALL.
BUT I DON'T WANT TO GET CAUGHT IN THE MIDDLE OF FAMILY DRAMA OR WHATEVER THIS IS.
IT SEEMS LIKE I'M JUST MAKING A BAD SITUATION WORSE.
I CAN JUST GO.
THE PEOPLE WHO WERE AFTER YOU...
...THEY'R STILL OU THERE.

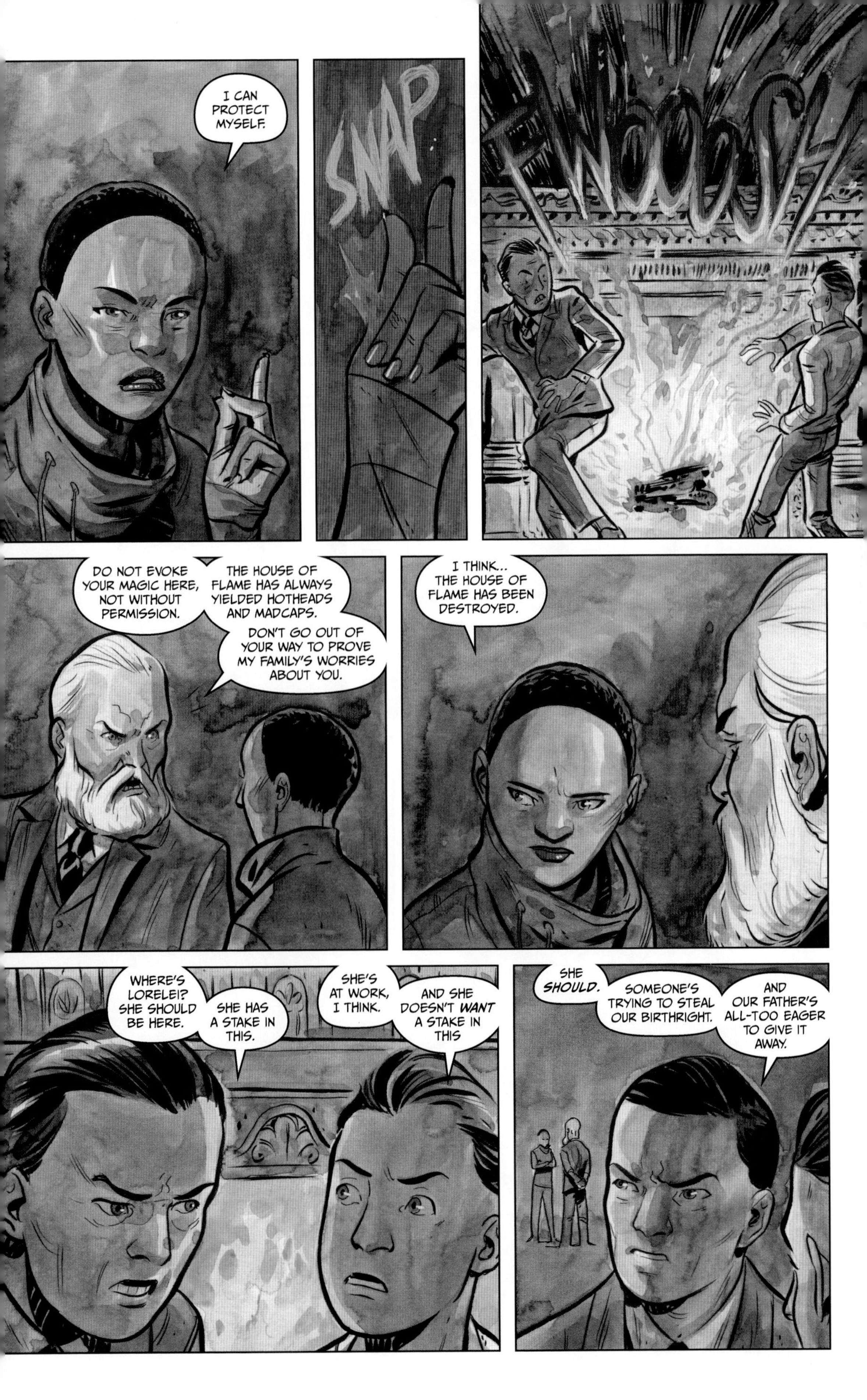
I CAN PROTECT MYSELF.
SNAP
FWOOOSH
DO NOT EVOKE YOUR MAGIC HERE, NOT WITHOUT PERMISSION.
THE HOUSE OF FLAME HAS ALWAYS YIELDED HOTHEADS AND MADCAPS.
DON'T GO OUT OF YOUR WAY TO PROVE MY FAMILY'S WORRIES ABOUT YOU.
I THINK... THE HOUSE OF FLAME HAS BEEN DESTROYED.
WHERE'S LORELEI? SHE SHOULD BE HERE.
SHE HAS A STAKE IN THIS.
SHE'S AT WORK, I THINK.
AND SHE DOESN'T *WANT* A STAKE IN THIS
SHE ***SHOULD.***
SOMEONE'S TRYING TO STEAL OUR BIRTHRIGHT.
AND OUR FATHER'S ALL-TOO EAGER TO GIVE IT AWAY.

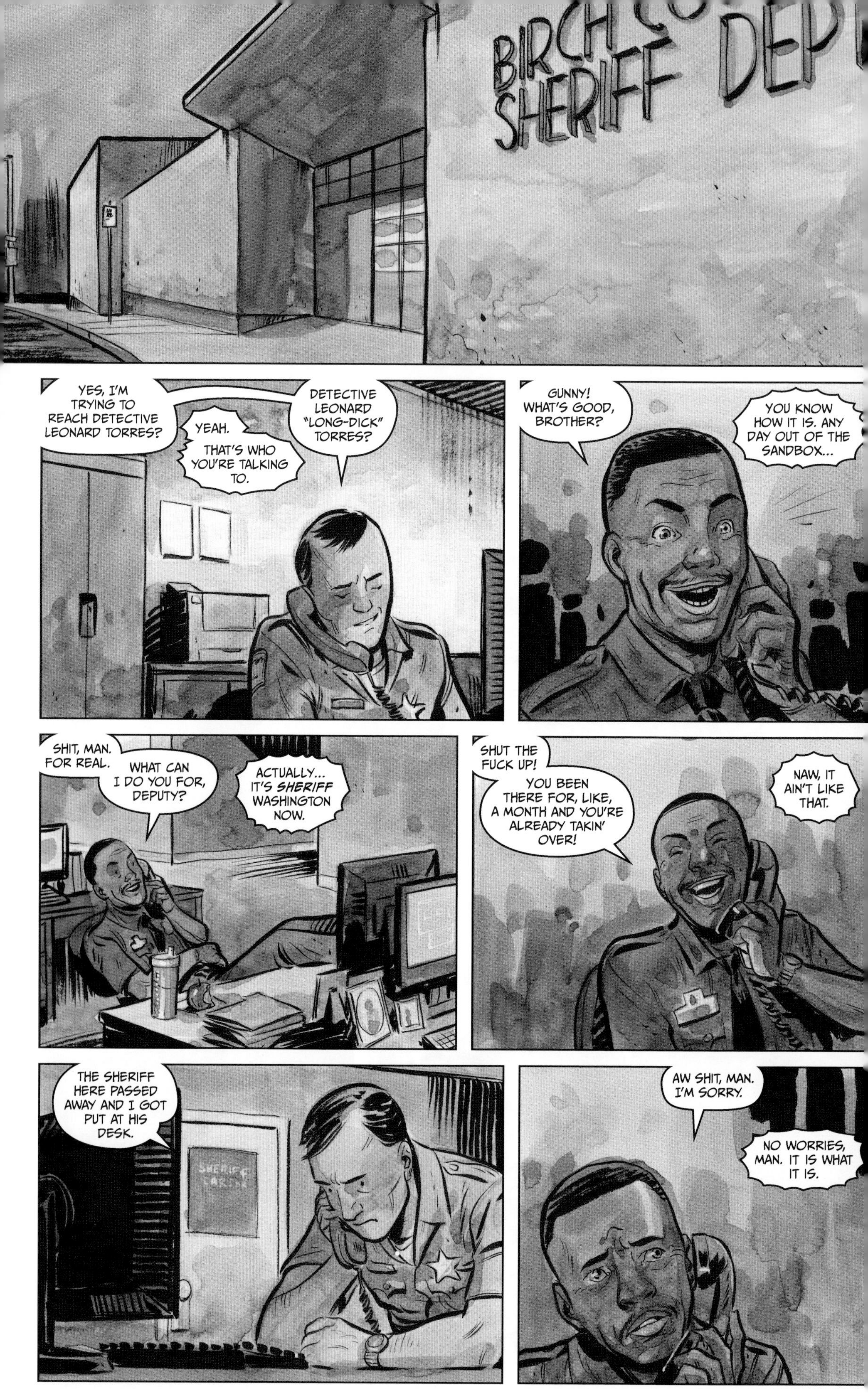
BIRCH CO
SHERIFF DEP
YES, I'M TRYING TO REACH DETECTIVE LEONARD TORRES?
DETECTIVE LEONARD "LONG-DICK" TORRES?
YEAH.
THAT'S WHO YOU'RE TALKING TO.
GUNNY! WHAT'S GOOD, BROTHER?
YOU KNOW HOW IT IS. ANY DAY OUT OF THE SANDBOX...
SHIT, MAN. FOR REAL.
WHAT CAN I DO YOU FOR, DEPUTY?
ACTUALLY... IT'S SHERIFF WASHINGTON NOW.
SHUT THE FUCK UP!
YOU BEEN THERE FOR, LIKE, A MONTH AND YOU'RE ALREADY TAKIN' OVER!
NAW, IT AIN'T LIKE THAT.
THE SHERIFF HERE PASSED AWAY AND I GOT PUT AT HIS DESK.
SHERIFF CARSON
AW SHIT, MAN. I'M SORRY.
NO WORRIES, MAN. IT IS WHAT IT IS.

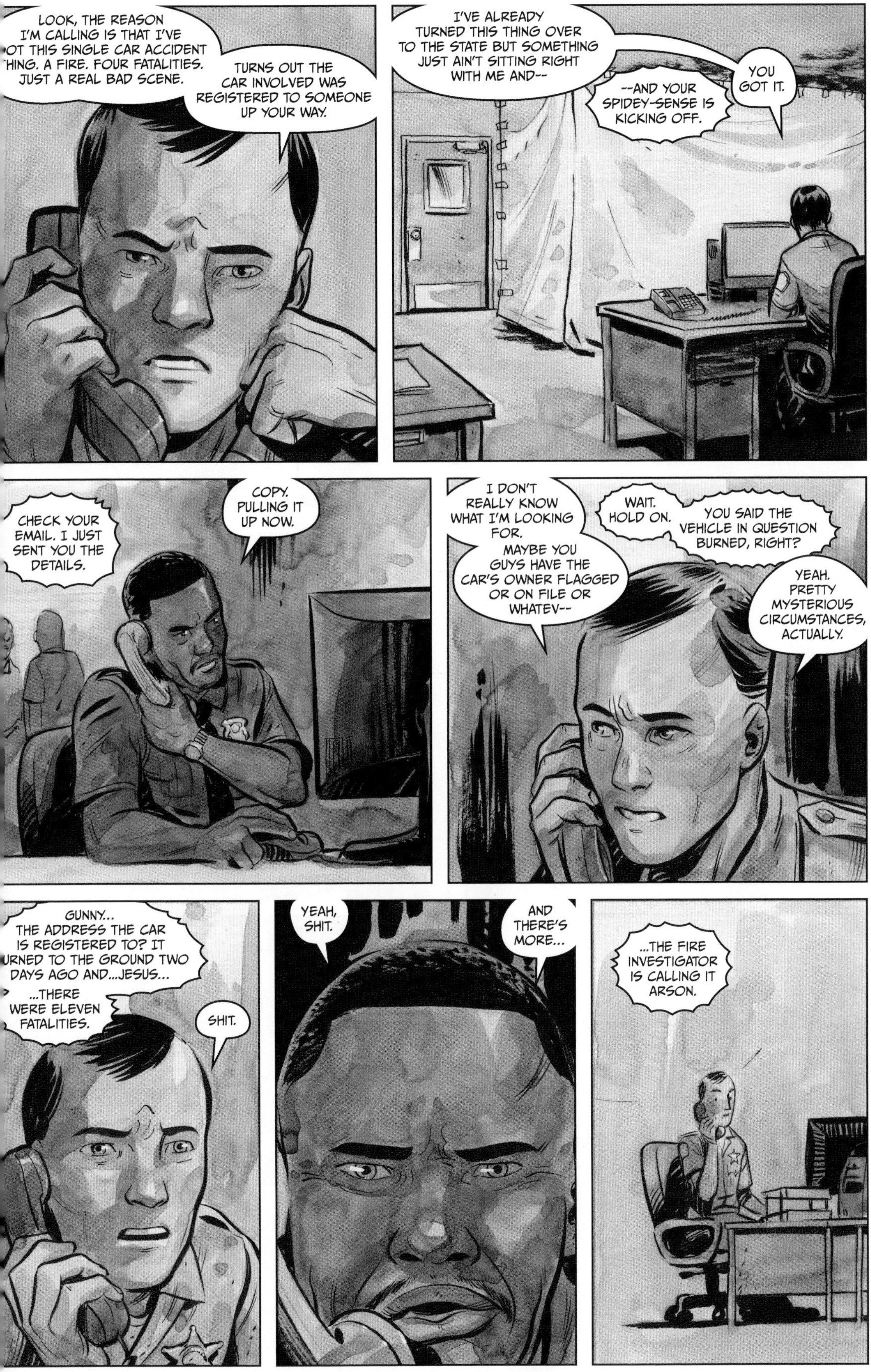
LOOK, THE REASON I'M CALLING IS THAT I'VE OT THIS SINGLE CAR ACCIDENT THING. A FIRE. FOUR FATALITIES. JUST A REAL BAD SCENE.
TURNS OUT THE CAR INVOLVED WAS REGISTERED TO SOMEONE UP YOUR WAY.
I'VE ALREADY TURNED THIS THING OVER TO THE STATE BUT SOMETHING JUST AIN'T SITTING RIGHT WITH ME AND--
--AND YOUR SPIDEY-SENSE IS KICKING OFF.
YOU GOT IT.
CHECK YOUR EMAIL. I JUST SENT YOU THE DETAILS.
COPY. PULLING IT UP NOW.
I DON'T REALLY KNOW WHAT I'M LOOKING FOR.
MAYBE YOU GUYS HAVE THE CAR'S OWNER FLAGGED OR ON FILE OR WHATEV--
WAIT. HOLD ON.
YOU SAID THE VEHICLE IN QUESTION BURNED, RIGHT?
YEAH. PRETTY MYSTERIOUS CIRCUMSTANCES, ACTUALLY.
GUNNY... THE ADDRESS THE CAR IS REGISTERED TO? IT URNED TO THE GROUND TWO DAYS AGO AND...JESUS...
...THERE WERE ELEVEN FATALITIES.
SHIT.
YEAH, SHIT.
AND THERE'S MORE...
...THE FIRE INVESTIGATOR IS CALLING IT ARSON.

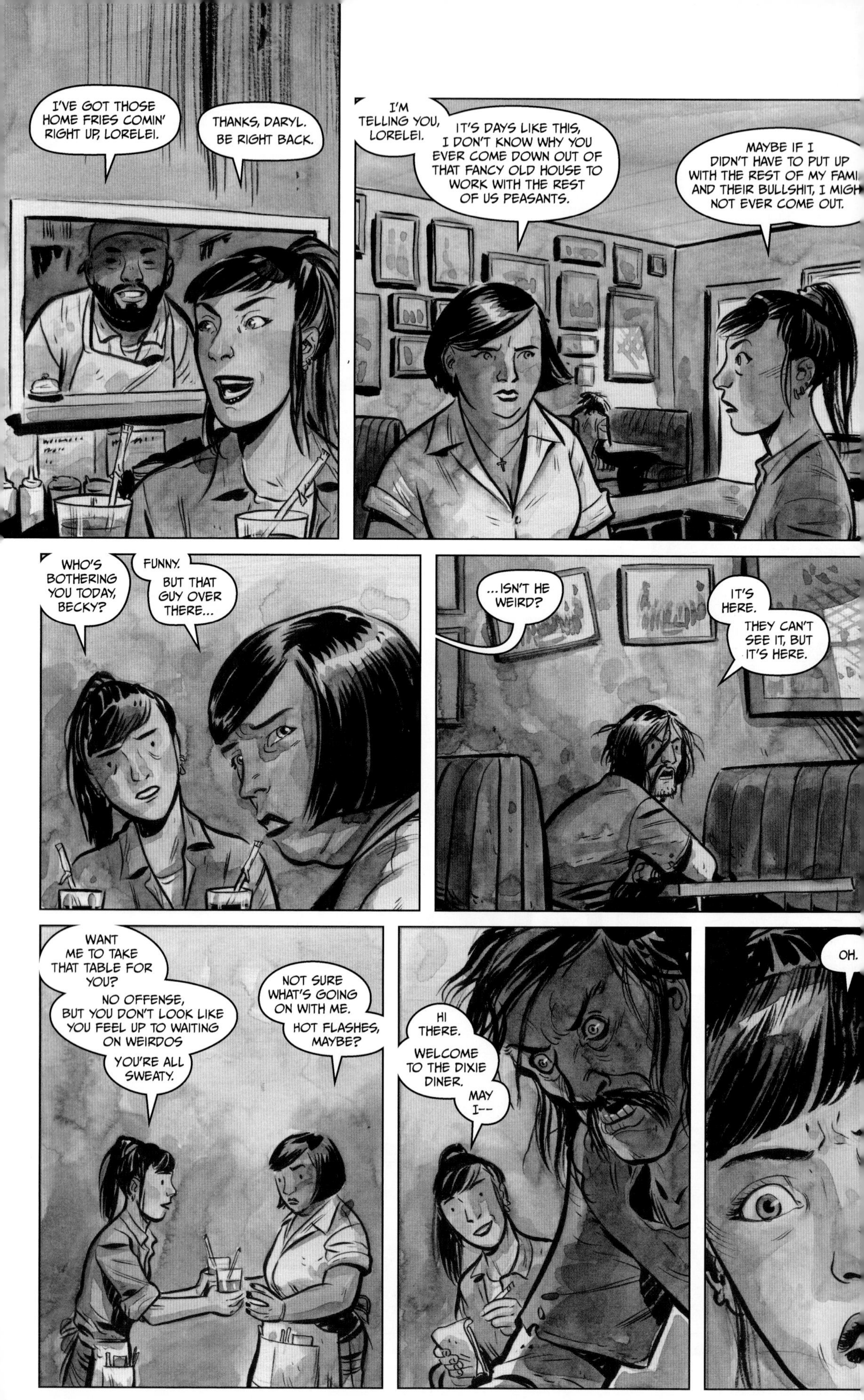
I'VE GOT THOSE HOME FRIES COMIN' RIGHT UP, LORELEI.
THANKS, DARYL. BE RIGHT BACK.
I'M TELLING YOU, LORELEI.
IT'S DAYS LIKE THIS, I DON'T KNOW WHY YOU EVER COME DOWN OUT OF THAT FANCY OLD HOUSE TO WORK WITH THE REST OF US PEASANTS.
MAYBE IF I DIDN'T HAVE TO PUT UP WITH THE REST OF MY FAMI AND THEIR BULLSHIT, I MIGH NOT EVER COME OUT.
WHO'S BOTHERING YOU TODAY, BECKY?
FUNNY.
BUT THAT GUY OVER THERE...
...ISN'T HE WEIRD?
IT'S HERE.
THEY CAN'T SEE IT, BUT IT'S HERE.
WANT ME TO TAKE THAT TABLE FOR YOU?
NO OFFENSE, BUT YOU DON'T LOOK LIKE YOU FEEL UP TO WAITING ON WEIRDOS
YOU'RE ALL SWEATY.
NOT SURE WHAT'S GOING ON WITH ME.
HOT FLASHES, MAYBE?
HI THERE.
WELCOME TO THE DIXIE DINER.
MAY I--
OH.

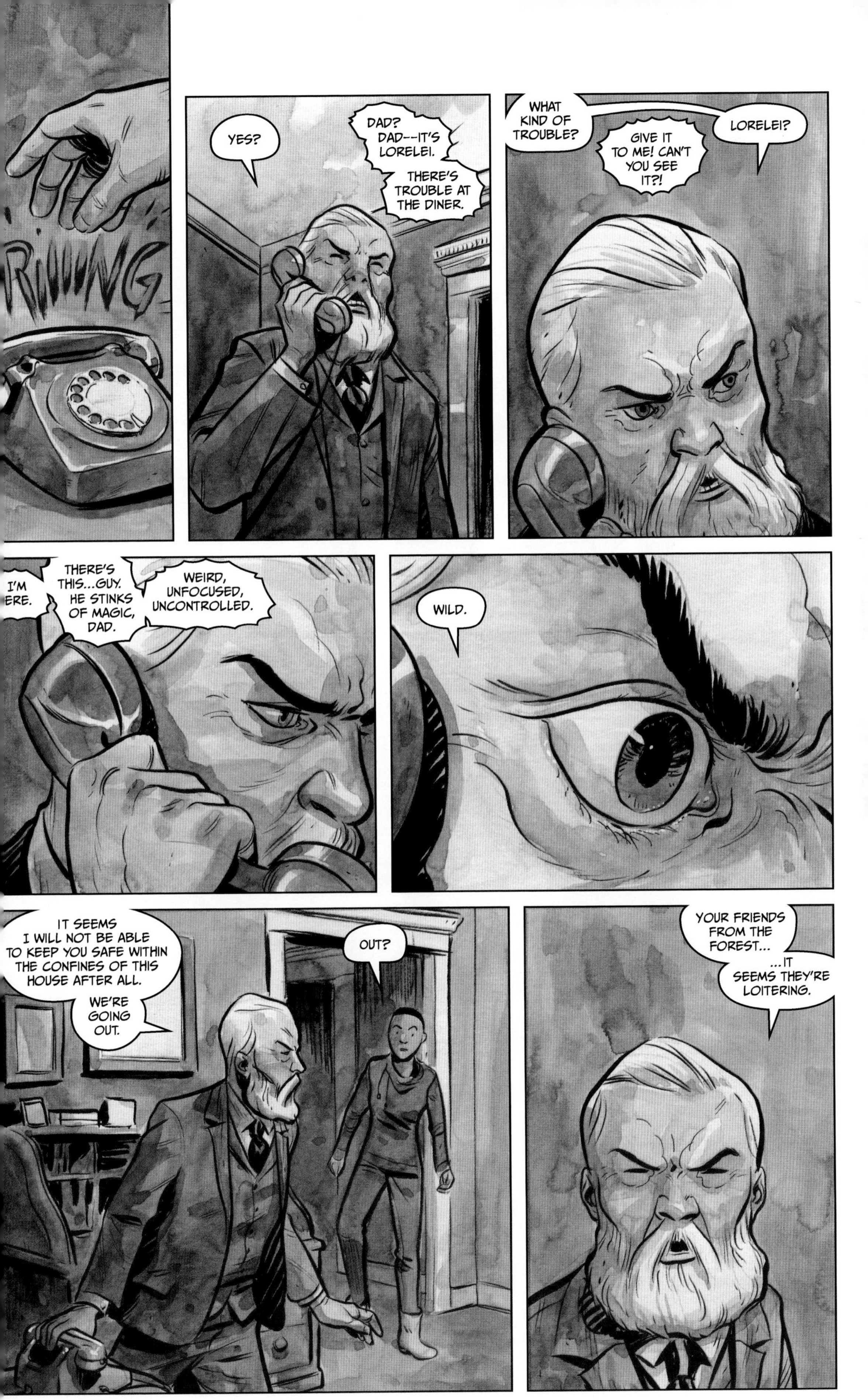
RIIING
YES?
DAD? DAD--IT'S LORELEI.
THERE'S TROUBLE AT THE DINER.
WHAT KIND OF TROUBLE?
GIVE IT TO ME! CAN'T YOU SEE IT?!
LORELEI?
I'M ERE.
THERE'S THIS...GUY. HE STINKS OF MAGIC, DAD.
WEIRD, UNFOCUSED, UNCONTROLLED.
WILD.
IT SEEMS I WILL NOT BE ABLE TO KEEP YOU SAFE WITHIN THE CONFINES OF THIS HOUSE AFTER ALL.
WE'RE GOING OUT.
OUT?
YOUR FRIENDS FROM THE FOREST...
...IT SEEMS THEY'RE LOITERING.

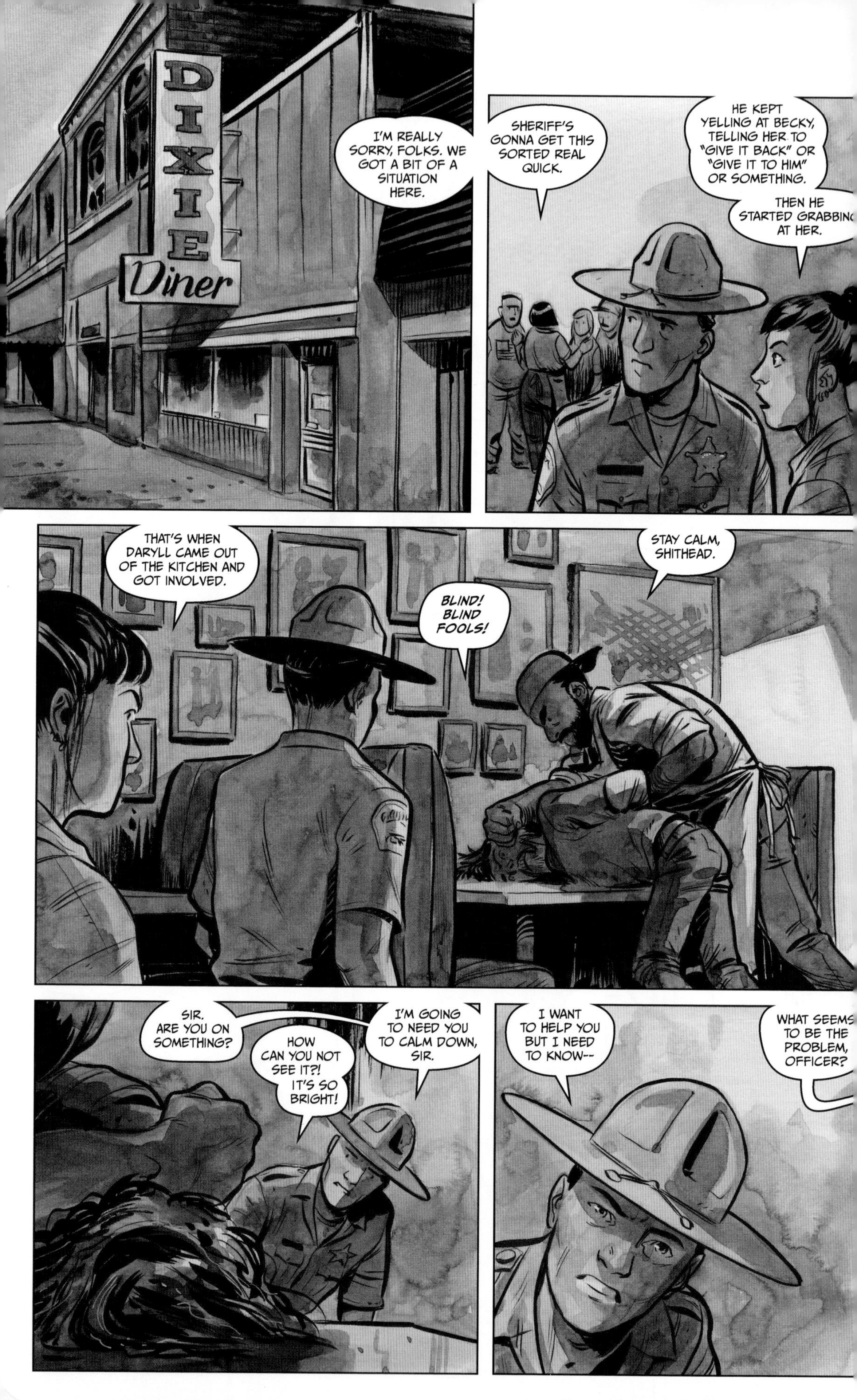
DIXIE
Diner
I'M REALLY SORRY, FOLKS. WE GOT A BIT OF A SITUATION HERE.
SHERIFF'S GONNA GET THIS SORTED REAL QUICK.
HE KEPT YELLING AT BECKY, TELLING HER TO "GIVE IT BACK" OR "GIVE IT TO HIM" OR SOMETHING.
THEN HE STARTED GRABBING AT HER.
THAT'S WHEN DARYLL CAME OUT OF THE KITCHEN AND GOT INVOLVED.
BLIND! BLIND FOOLS!
STAY CALM, SHITHEAD.
SIR. ARE YOU ON SOMETHING?
HOW CAN YOU NOT SEE IT?! IT'S SO BRIGHT!
I'M GOING TO NEED YOU TO CALM DOWN, SIR.
I WANT TO HELP YOU BUT I NEED TO KNOW--
WHAT SEEMS TO BE THE PROBLEM, OFFICER?

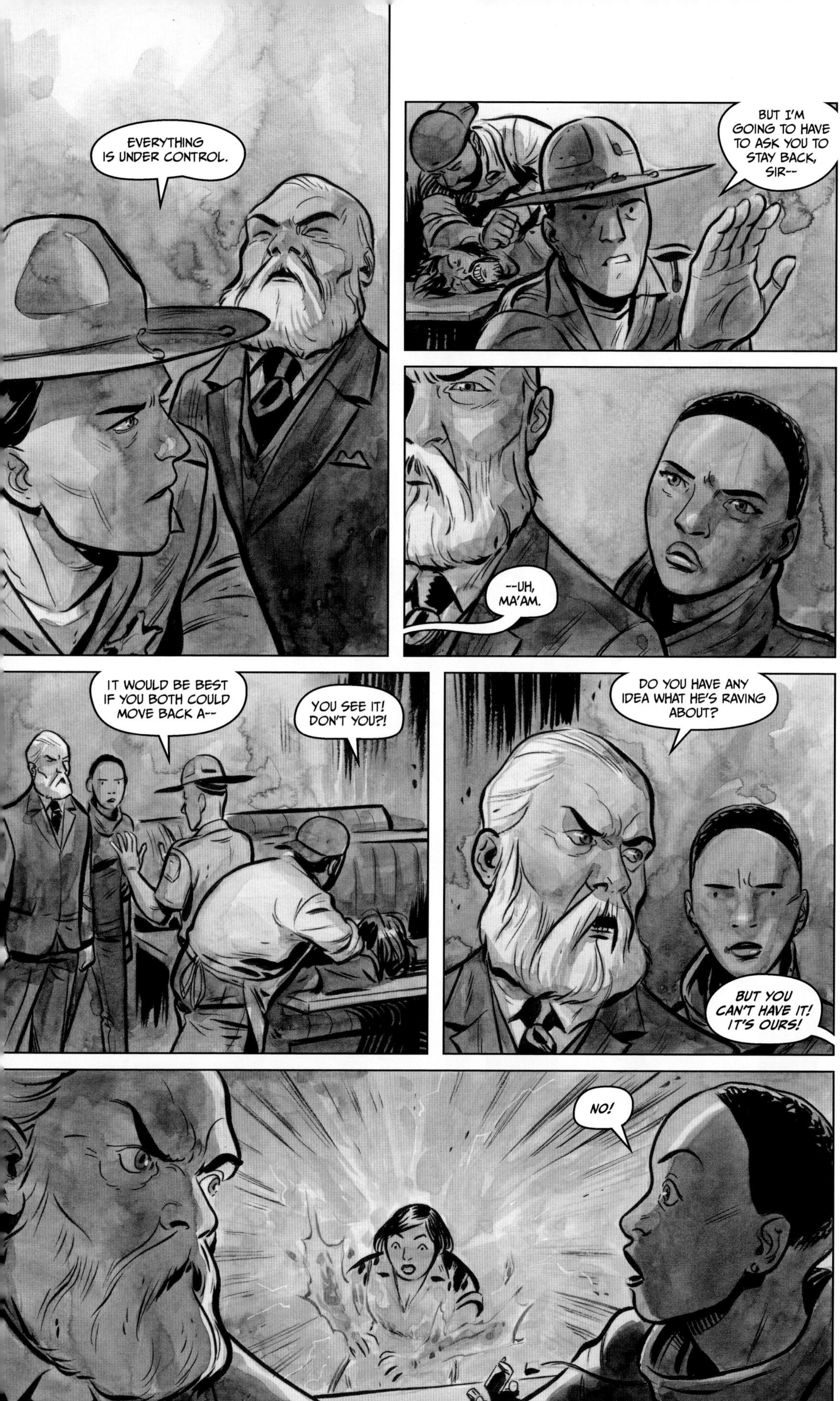
EVERYTHING IS UNDER CONTROL.
BUT I'M GOING TO HAVE TO ASK YOU TO STAY BACK, SIR--
--UH, MA'AM.
IT WOULD BE BEST IF YOU BOTH COULD MOVE BACK A--
YOU SEE IT! DON'T YOU?!
DO YOU HAVE ANY IDEA WHAT HE'S RAVING ABOUT?
BUT YOU CAN'T HAVE IT! IT'S OURS!
NO!

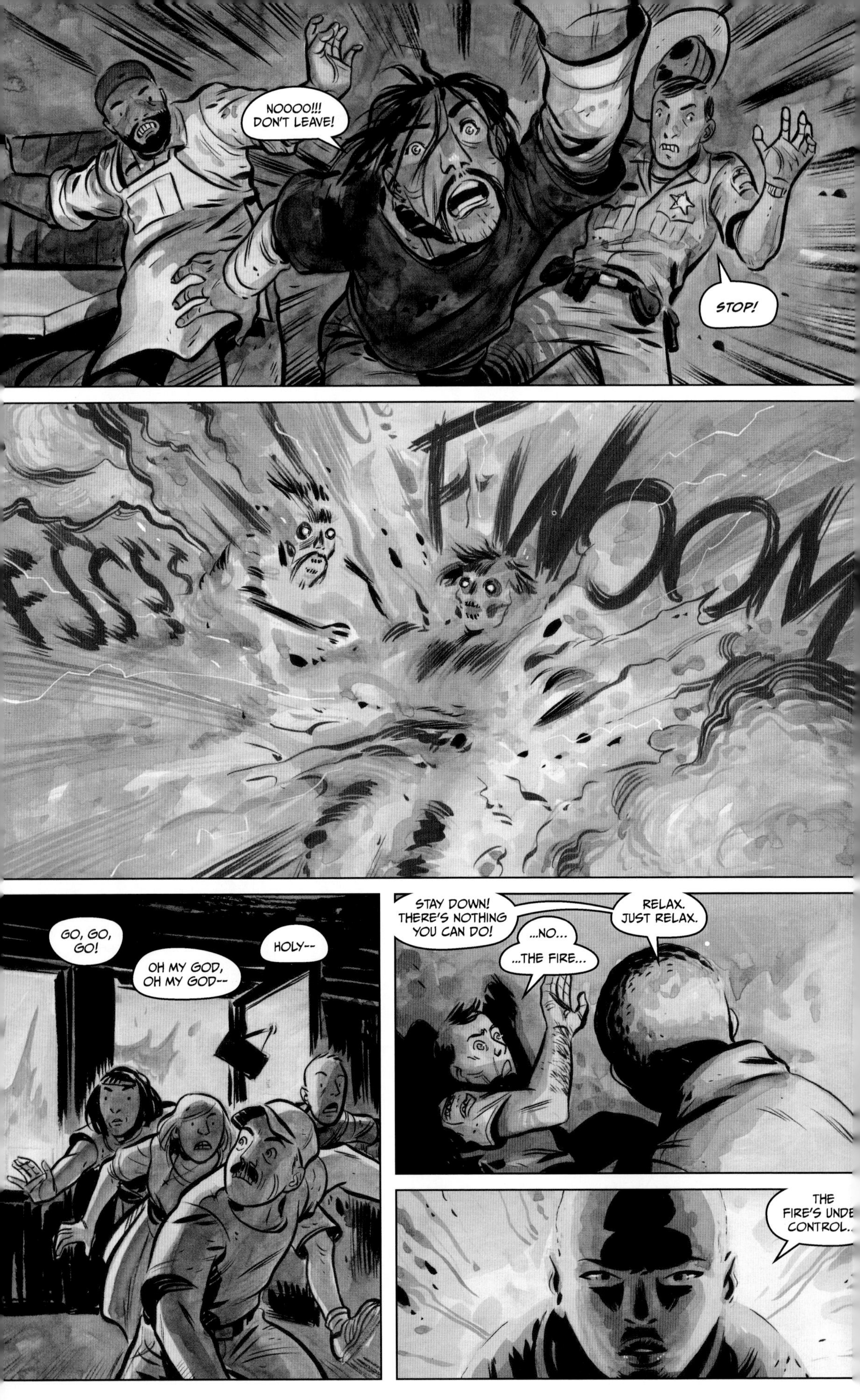
NOOOO!!! DON'T LEAVE!
STOP!
FWOOM
FSSS
GO, GO, GO!
OH MY GOD, OH MY GOD--
HOLY--
STAY DOWN! THERE'S NOTHING YOU CAN DO!
RELAX. JUST RELAX.
...NO...
...THE FIRE...
THE FIRE'S UNDE CONTROL..

"...HELP IS ON THE WAY."

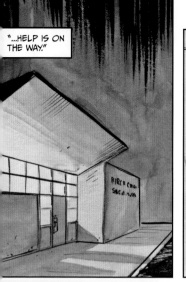

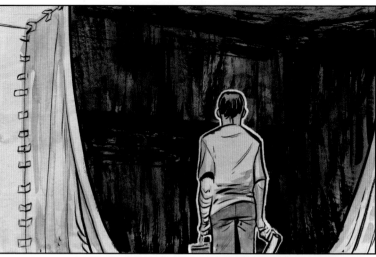

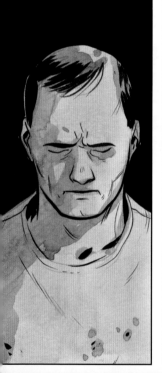

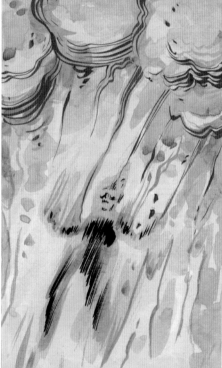

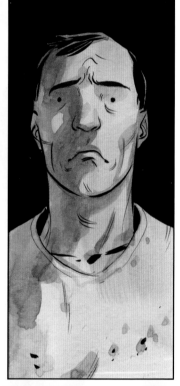

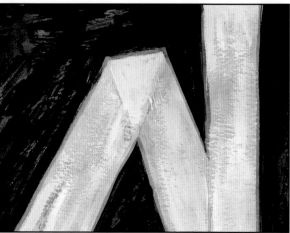

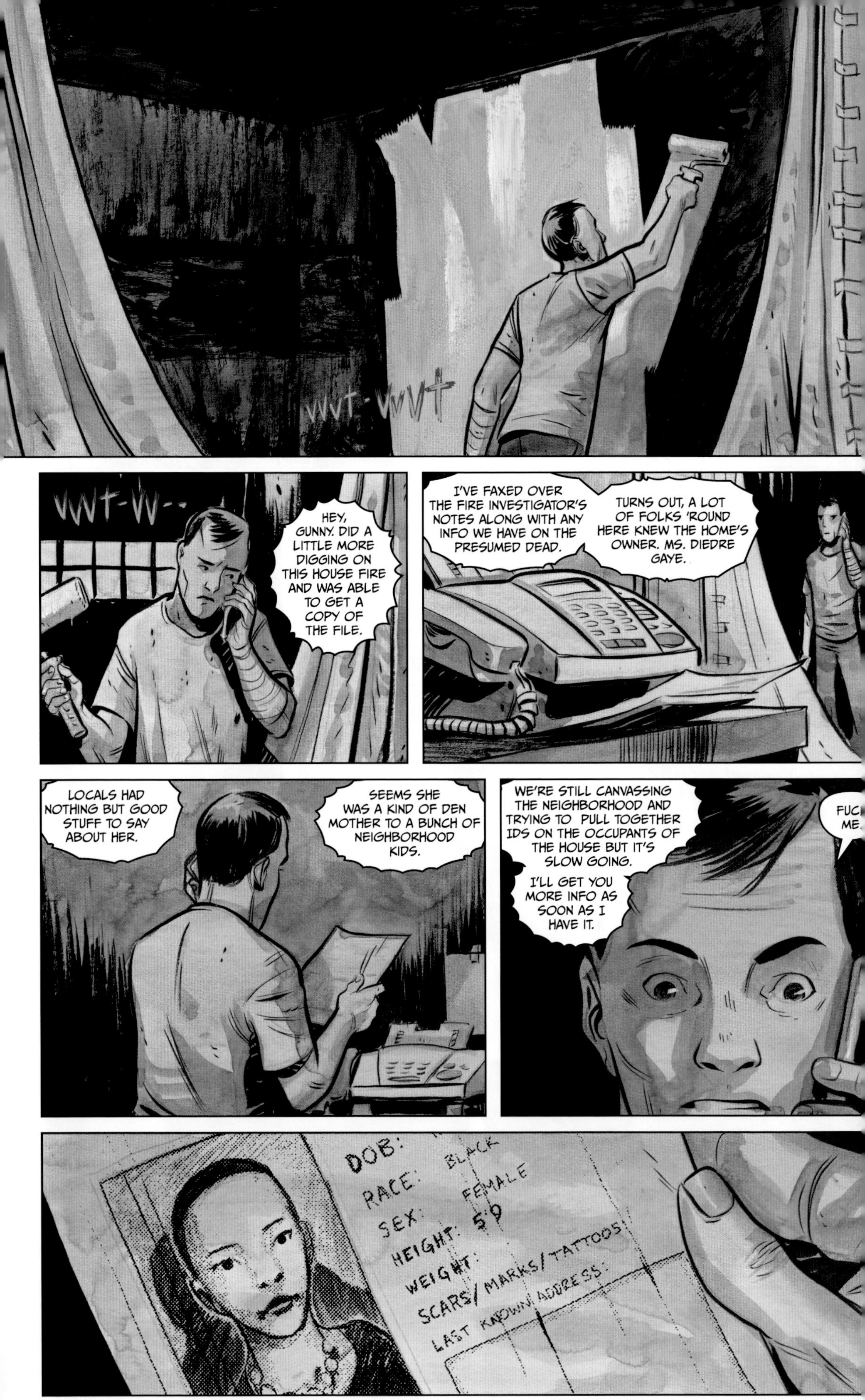
VVVT-VVVT
VVVT-VV--
HEY, GUNNY. DID A LITTLE MORE DIGGING ON THIS HOUSE FIRE AND WAS ABLE TO GET A COPY OF THE FILE.
I'VE FAXED OVER THE FIRE INVESTIGATOR'S NOTES ALONG WITH ANY INFO WE HAVE ON THE PRESUMED DEAD.
TURNS OUT, A LOT OF FOLKS 'ROUND HERE KNEW THE HOME'S OWNER. MS. DIEDRE GAYE.
LOCALS HAD NOTHING BUT GOOD STUFF TO SAY ABOUT HER.
SEEMS SHE WAS A KIND OF DEN MOTHER TO A BUNCH OF NEIGHBORHOOD KIDS.
WE'RE STILL CANVASSING THE NEIGHBORHOOD AND TRYING TO PULL TOGETHER IDS ON THE OCCUPANTS OF THE HOUSE BUT IT'S SLOW GOING.
I'LL GET YOU MORE INFO AS SOON AS I HAVE IT.
FUC ME.
DOB:
RACE: BLACK
SEX: FEMALE
HEIGHT: 5'9
WEIGHT:
SCARS/ MARKS/ TATTOOS:
LAST KNOWN ADDRESS:

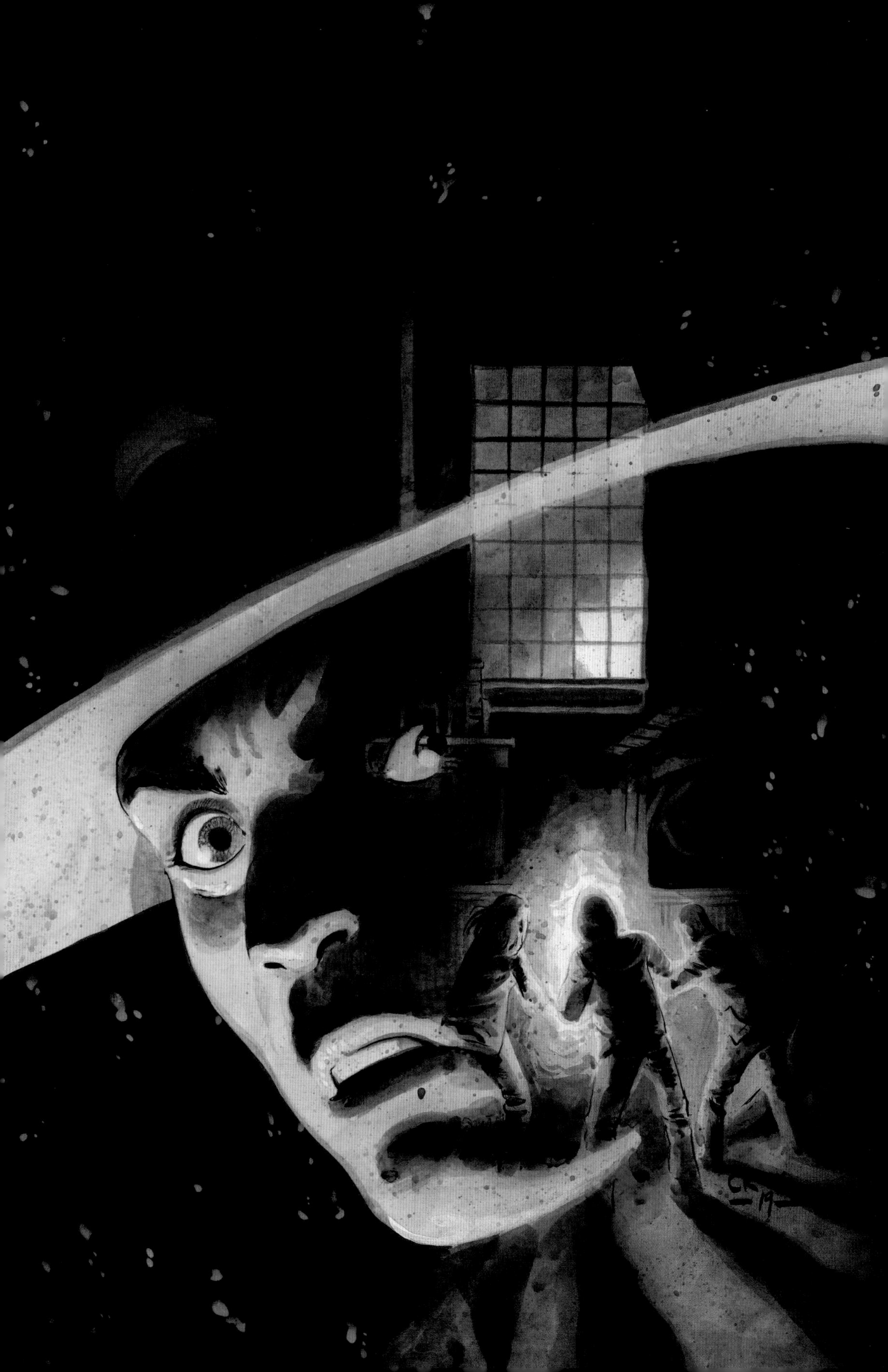

POSTED
NO TRESPASSING

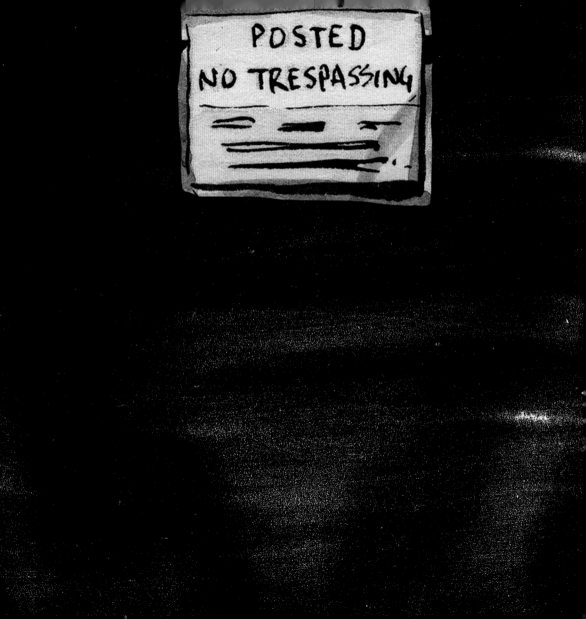

"A TOTEM HAS BEEN RELEASED INTO THE WORLD."

UNTETHERED. WILD. DANGEROUS.

YOUR TOTEM.

IT'S MY HOUSE'S TOTEM. NOT... NOT JUST MINE.

AS NEARLY AS I CAN TELL, YOU ARE THE LAST OF YOUR HOUSE.

THERE'S NOTHING I CAN DO. WHEN WE WERE ATTACKED...

...I COULDN'T STOP IT...

...ANY OF IT.

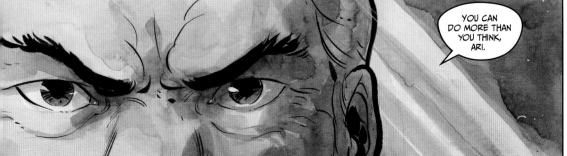

YOU CAN DO MORE THAN YOU THINK, ARI.

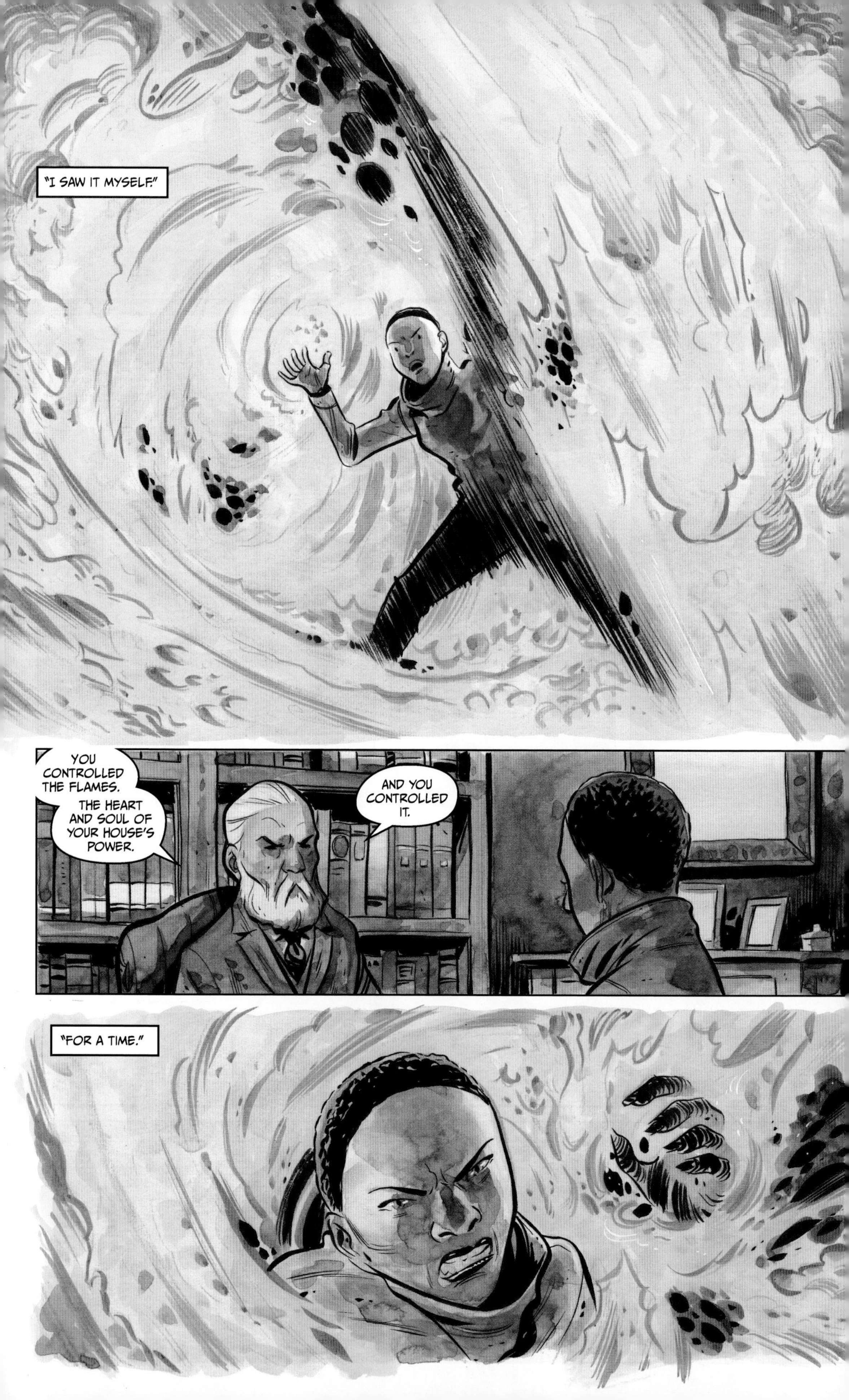
"I SAW IT MYSELF."
YOU CONTROLLED THE FLAMES.
THE HEART AND SOUL OF YOUR HOUSE'S POWER.
AND YOU CONTROLLED IT.
"FOR A TIME."

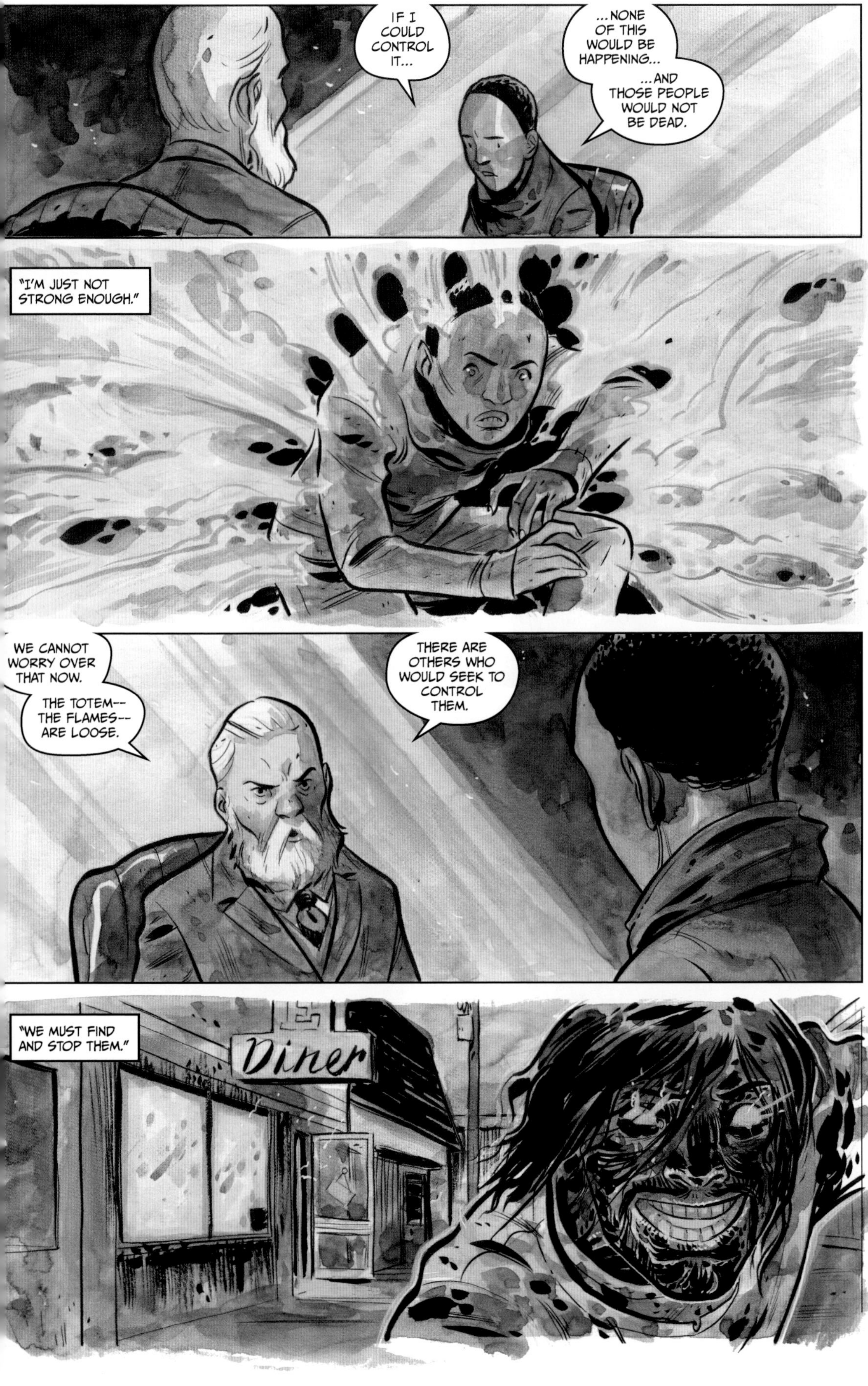
IF I COULD CONTROL IT...
...NONE OF THIS WOULD BE HAPPENING...
...AND THOSE PEOPLE WOULD NOT BE DEAD.
"I'M JUST NOT STRONG ENOUGH."
WE CANNOT WORRY OVER THAT NOW.
THE TOTEM-- THE FLAMES-- ARE LOOSE.
THERE ARE OTHERS WHO WOULD SEEK TO CONTROL THEM.
"WE MUST FIND AND STOP THEM."
Diner

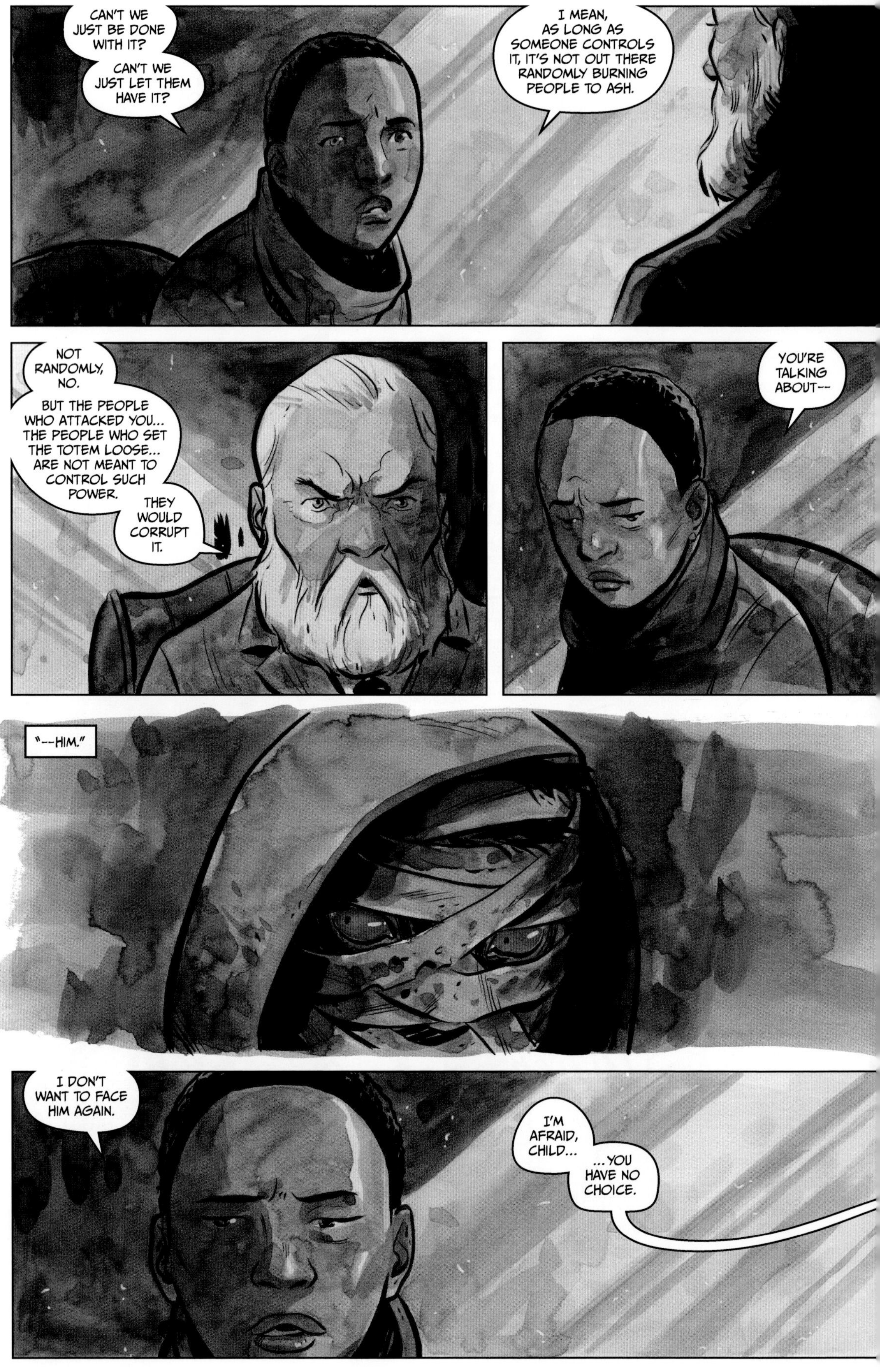
CAN'T WE JUST BE DONE WITH IT?
CAN'T WE JUST LET THEM HAVE IT?
I MEAN, AS LONG AS SOMEONE CONTROLS IT, IT'S NOT OUT THERE RANDOMLY BURNING PEOPLE TO ASH.
NOT RANDOMLY, NO.
BUT THE PEOPLE WHO ATTACKED YOU... THE PEOPLE WHO SET THE TOTEM LOOSE... ARE NOT MEANT TO CONTROL SUCH POWER.
THEY WOULD CORRUPT IT.
YOU'RE TALKING ABOUT--
"--HIM."
I DON'T WANT TO FACE HIM AGAIN.
I'M AFRAID, CHILD...
...YOU HAVE NO CHOICE.

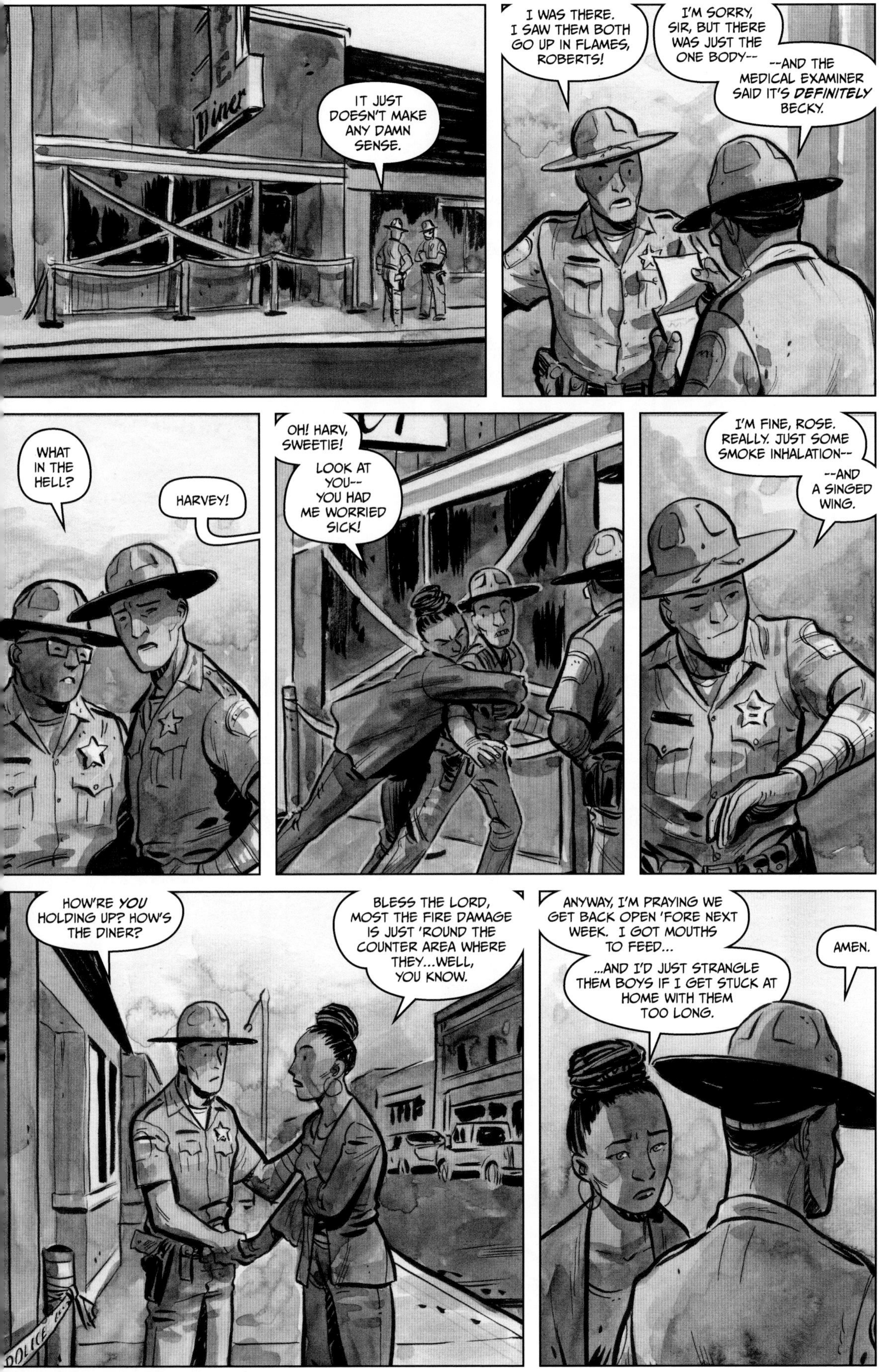

Diner
IT JUST DOESN'T MAKE ANY DAMN SENSE.
I WAS THERE. I SAW THEM BOTH GO UP IN FLAMES, ROBERTS!
I'M SORRY, SIR, BUT THERE WAS JUST THE ONE BODY--
--AND THE MEDICAL EXAMINER SAID IT'S DEFINITELY BECKY.
WHAT IN THE HELL?
HARVEY!
OH! HARV, SWEETIE!
LOOK AT YOU-- YOU HAD ME WORRIED SICK!
I'M FINE, ROSE. REALLY. JUST SOME SMOKE INHALATION--
--AND A SINGED WING.
HOW'RE YOU HOLDING UP? HOW'S THE DINER?
BLESS THE LORD, MOST THE FIRE DAMAGE IS JUST 'ROUND THE COUNTER AREA WHERE THEY...WELL, YOU KNOW.
ANYWAY, I'M PRAYING WE GET BACK OPEN 'FORE NEXT WEEK. I GOT MOUTHS TO FEED...
...AND I'D JUST STRANGLE THEM BOYS IF I GET STUCK AT HOME WITH THEM TOO LONG.
AMEN.

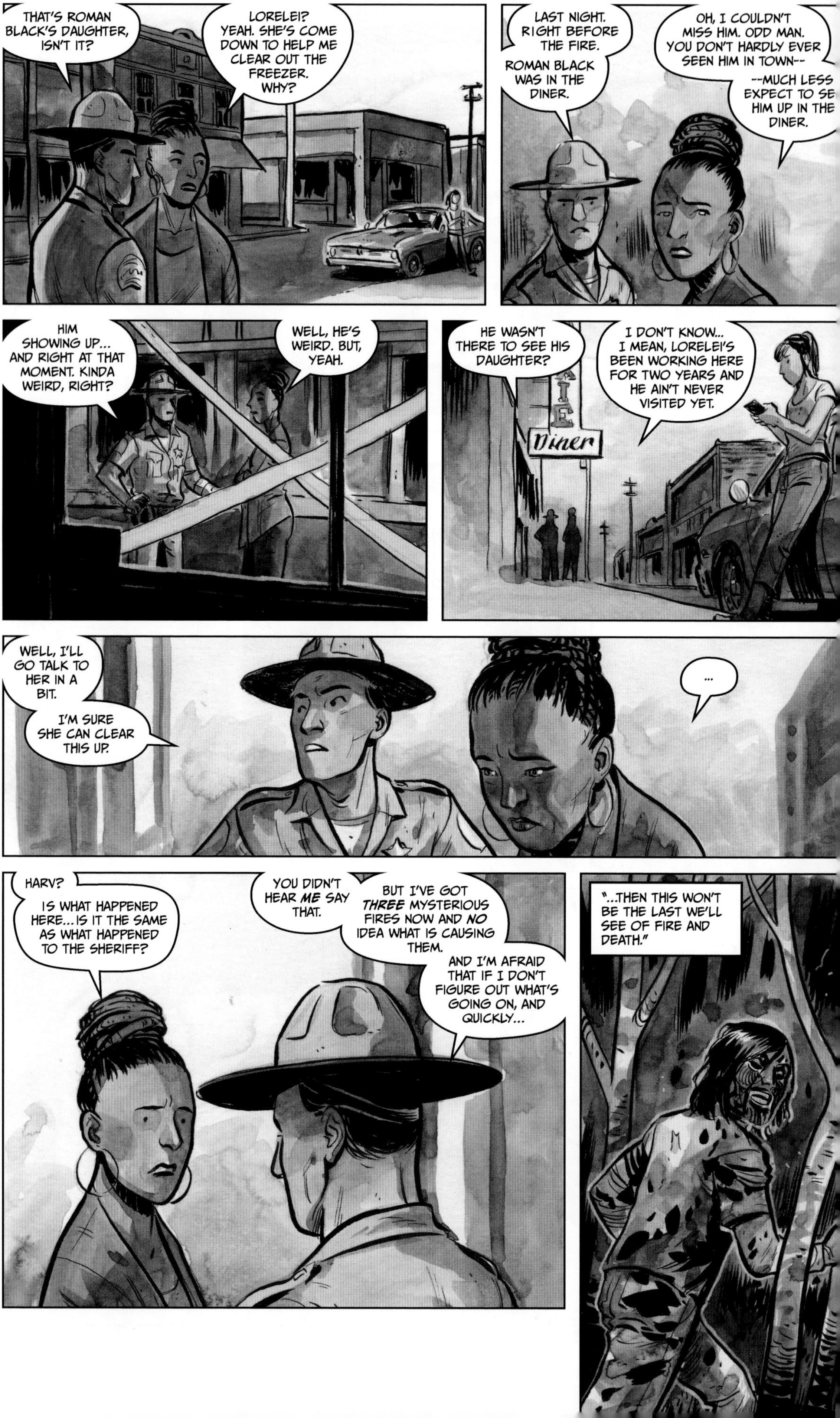
THAT'S ROMAN BLACK'S DAUGHTER, ISN'T IT?
LORELEI? YEAH. SHE'S COME DOWN TO HELP ME CLEAR OUT THE FREEZER. WHY?
LAST NIGHT. RIGHT BEFORE THE FIRE.
ROMAN BLACK WAS IN THE DINER.
OH, I COULDN'T MISS HIM. ODD MAN. YOU DON'T HARDLY EVER SEEN HIM IN TOWN--
--MUCH LESS EXPECT TO SEE HIM UP IN THE DINER.
HIM SHOWING UP... AND RIGHT AT THAT MOMENT. KINDA WEIRD, RIGHT?
WELL, HE'S WEIRD. BUT, YEAH.
HE WASN'T THERE TO SEE HIS DAUGHTER?
I DON'T KNOW... I MEAN, LORELEI'S BEEN WORKING HERE FOR TWO YEARS AND HE AIN'T NEVER VISITED YET.
Diner
WELL, I'LL GO TALK TO HER IN A BIT.
I'M SURE SHE CAN CLEAR THIS UP.
...
HARV?
IS WHAT HAPPENED HERE... IS IT THE SAME AS WHAT HAPPENED TO THE SHERIFF?
YOU DIDN'T HEAR ME SAY THAT.
BUT I'VE GOT THREE MYSTERIOUS FIRES NOW AND NO IDEA WHAT IS CAUSING THEM.
AND I'M AFRAID THAT IF I DON'T FIGURE OUT WHAT'S GOING ON, AND QUICKLY...
"...THEN THIS WON'T BE THE LAST WE'LL SEE OF FIRE AND DEATH."

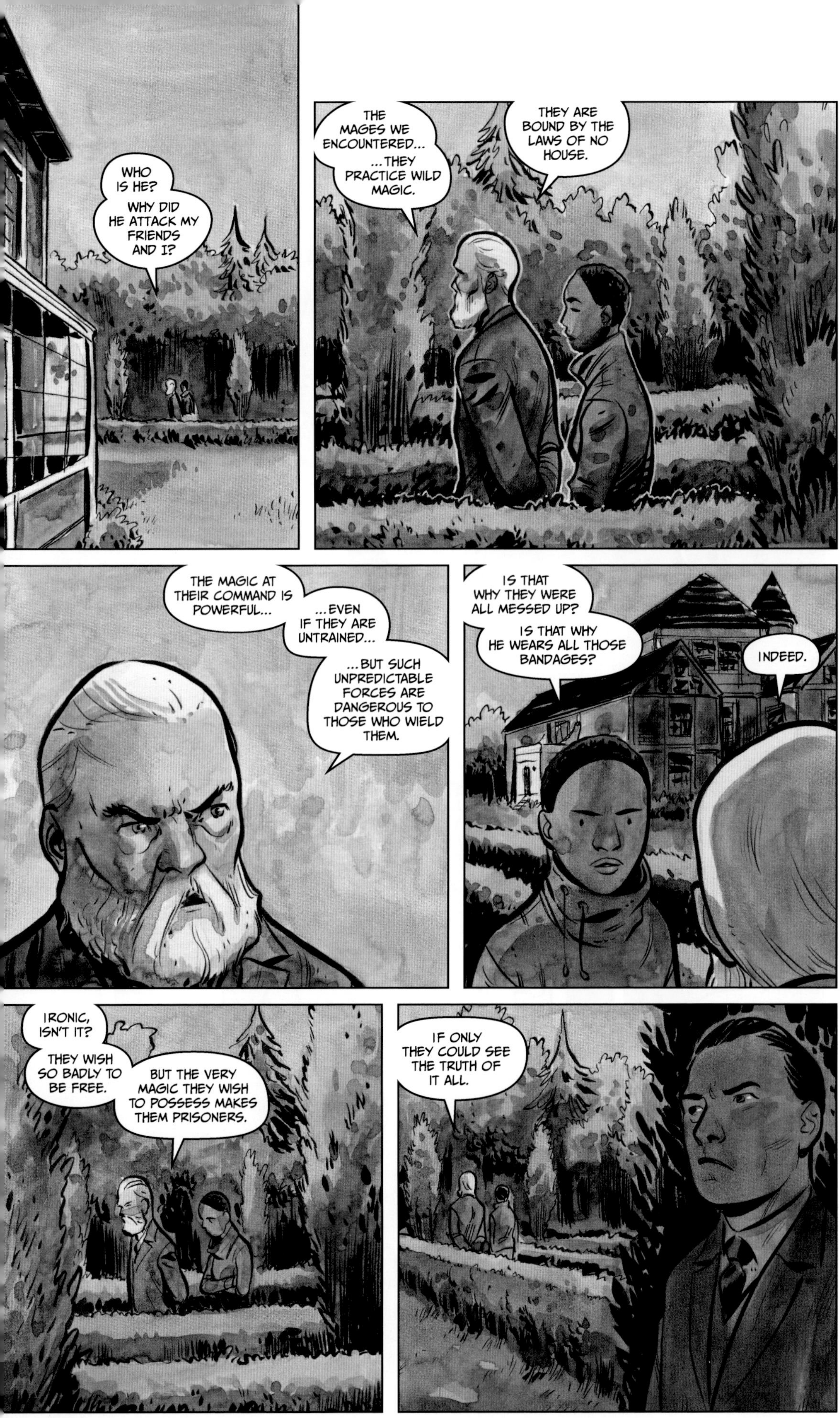

WHO IS HE?
WHY DID HE ATTACK MY FRIENDS AND I?
THE MAGES WE ENCOUNTERED...
...THEY PRACTICE WILD MAGIC.
THEY ARE BOUND BY THE LAWS OF NO HOUSE.
THE MAGIC AT THEIR COMMAND IS POWERFUL...
...EVEN IF THEY ARE UNTRAINED...
...BUT SUCH UNPREDICTABLE FORCES ARE DANGEROUS TO THOSE WHO WIELD THEM.
IS THAT WHY THEY WERE ALL MESSED UP?
IS THAT WHY HE WEARS ALL THOSE BANDAGES?
INDEED.
IRONIC, ISN'T IT?
THEY WISH SO BADLY TO BE FREE.
BUT THE VERY MAGIC THEY WISH TO POSSESS MAKES THEM PRISONERS.
IF ONLY THEY COULD SEE THE TRUTH OF IT ALL.

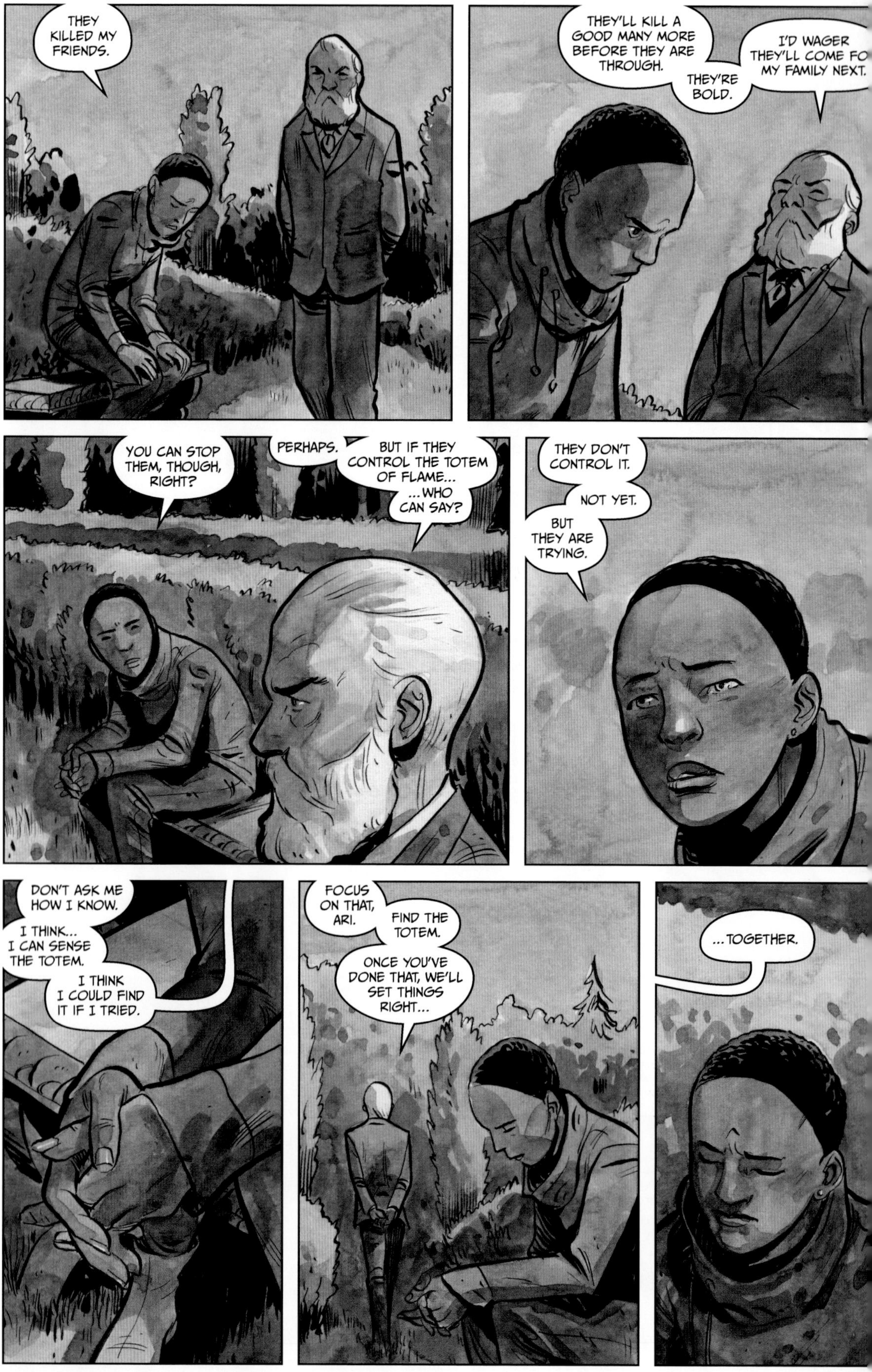
THEY KILLED MY FRIENDS.
THEY'LL KILL A GOOD MANY MORE BEFORE THEY ARE THROUGH.
THEY'RE BOLD.
I'D WAGER THEY'LL COME FO MY FAMILY NEXT.
YOU CAN STOP THEM, THOUGH, RIGHT?
PERHAPS.
BUT IF THEY CONTROL THE TOTEM OF FLAME...
...WHO CAN SAY?
THEY DON'T CONTROL IT.
NOT YET.
BUT THEY ARE TRYING.
DON'T ASK ME HOW I KNOW.
I THINK... I CAN SENSE THE TOTEM.
I THINK I COULD FIND IT IF I TRIED.
FOCUS ON THAT, ARI.
FIND THE TOTEM.
ONCE YOU'VE DONE THAT, WE'LL SET THINGS RIGHT...
...TOGETHER.

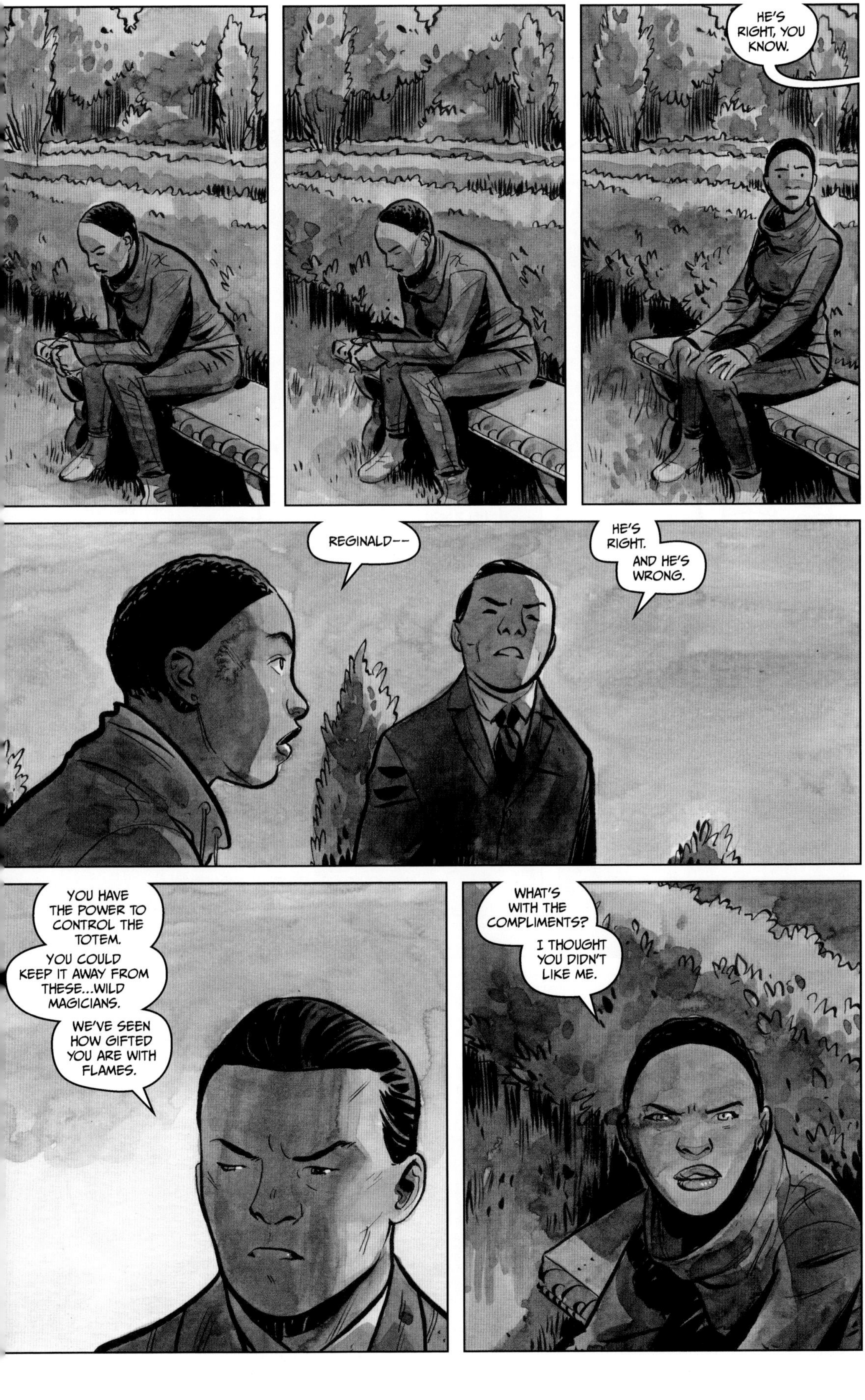
HE'S RIGHT, YOU KNOW.
REGINALD--
HE'S RIGHT.
AND HE'S WRONG.
YOU HAVE THE POWER TO CONTROL THE TOTEM.
YOU COULD KEEP IT AWAY FROM THESE...WILD MAGICIANS.
WE'VE SEEN HOW GIFTED YOU ARE WITH FLAMES.
WHAT'S WITH THE COMPLIMENTS?
I THOUGHT YOU DIDN'T LIKE ME.

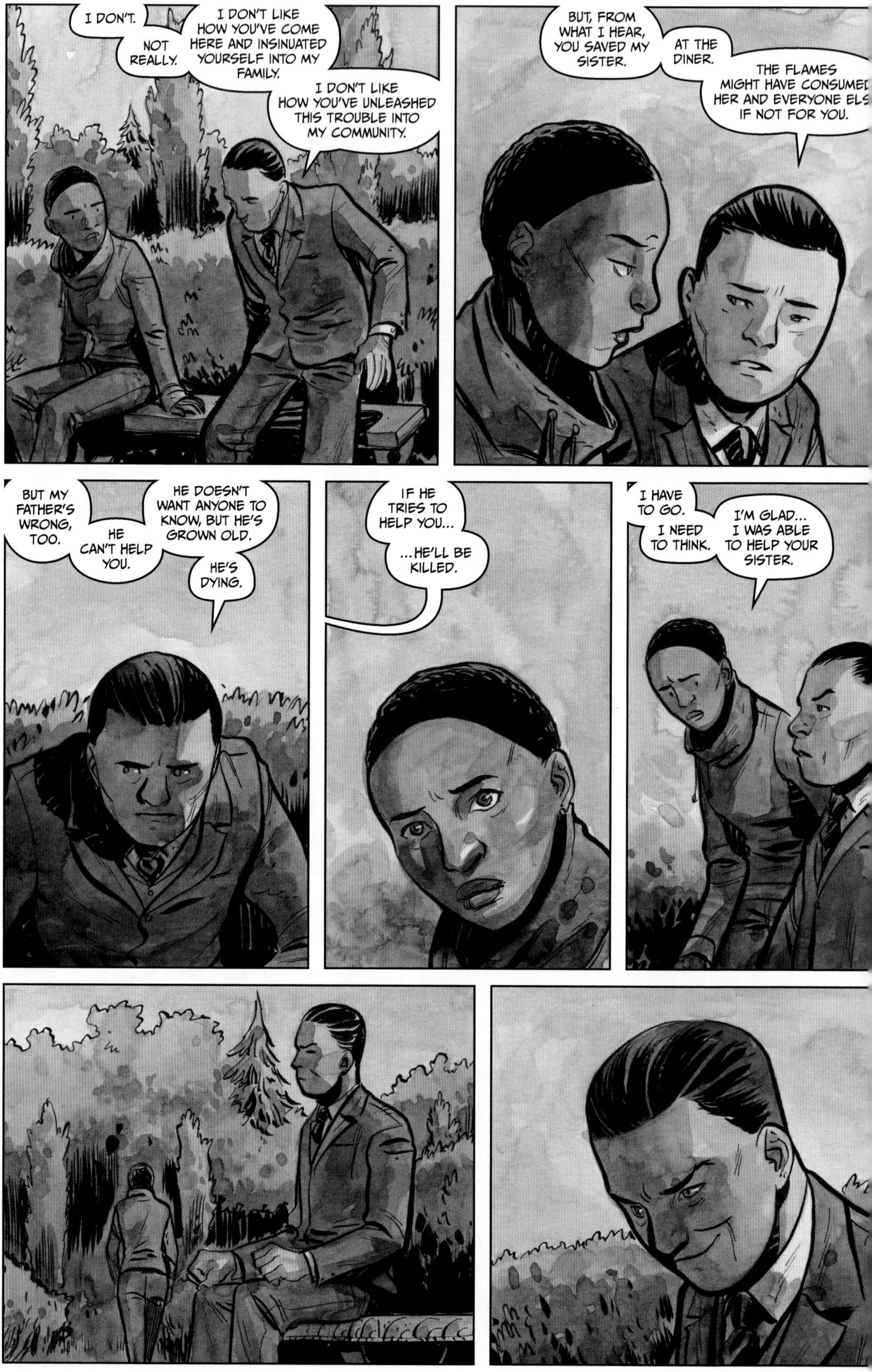
I DON'T.
NOT REALLY.
I DON'T LIKE HOW YOU'VE COME HERE AND INSINUATED YOURSELF INTO MY FAMILY.
I DON'T LIKE HOW YOU'VE UNLEASHED THIS TROUBLE INTO MY COMMUNITY.
BUT, FROM WHAT I HEAR, YOU SAVED MY SISTER.
AT THE DINER.
THE FLAMES MIGHT HAVE CONSUMED HER AND EVERYONE ELSE IF NOT FOR YOU.
BUT MY FATHER'S WRONG, TOO.
HE CAN'T HELP YOU.
HE DOESN'T WANT ANYONE TO KNOW, BUT HE'S GROWN OLD.
HE'S DYING.
IF HE TRIES TO HELP YOU...
...HE'LL BE KILLED.
I HAVE TO GO.
I NEED TO THINK.
I'M GLAD... I WAS ABLE TO HELP YOUR SISTER.

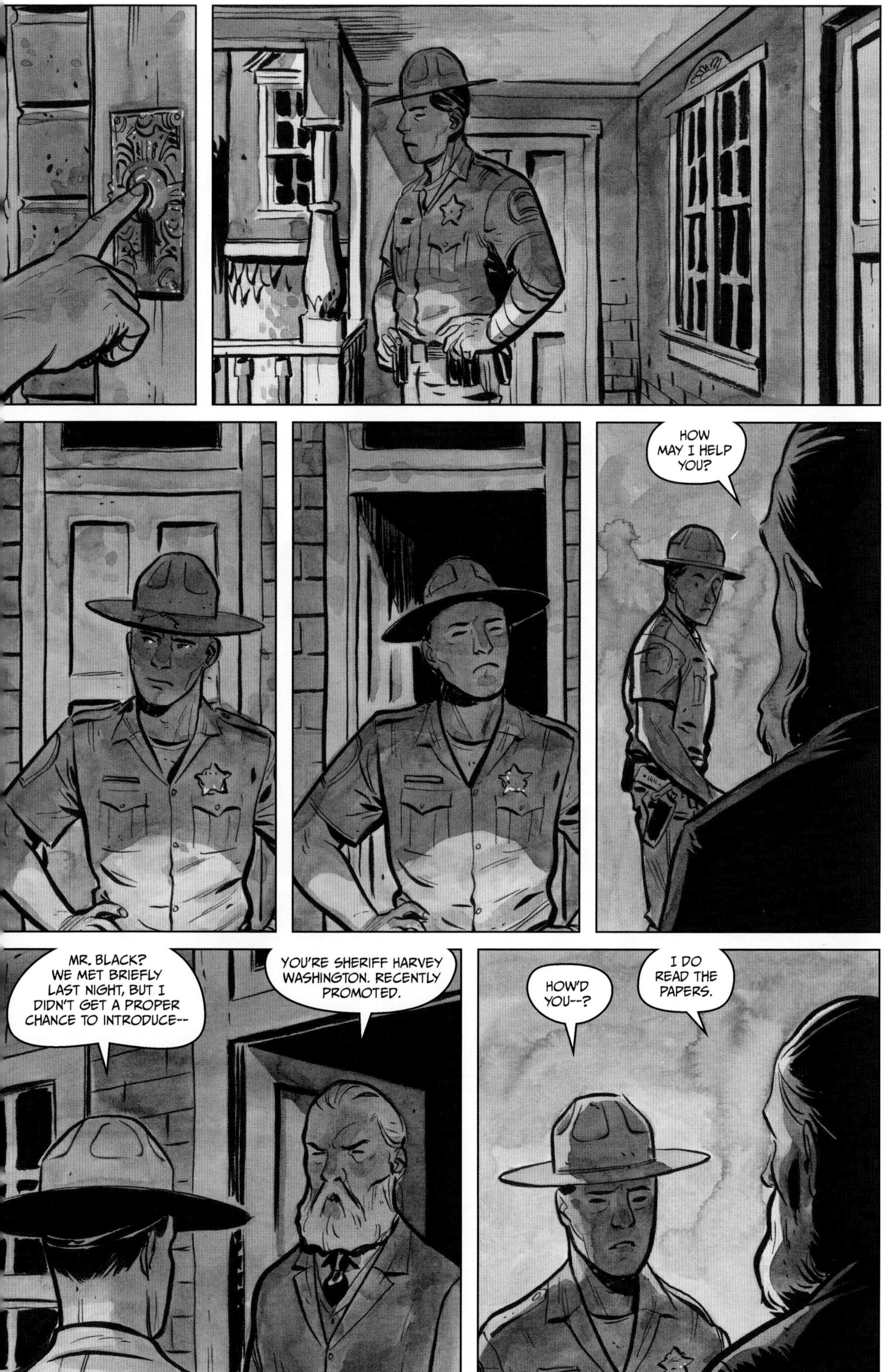
HOW MAY I HELP YOU?
MR. BLACK? WE MET BRIEFLY LAST NIGHT, BUT I DIDN'T GET A PROPER CHANCE TO INTRODUCE--
YOU'RE SHERIFF HARVEY WASHINGTON. RECENTLY PROMOTED.
HOW'D YOU--?
I DO READ THE PAPERS.

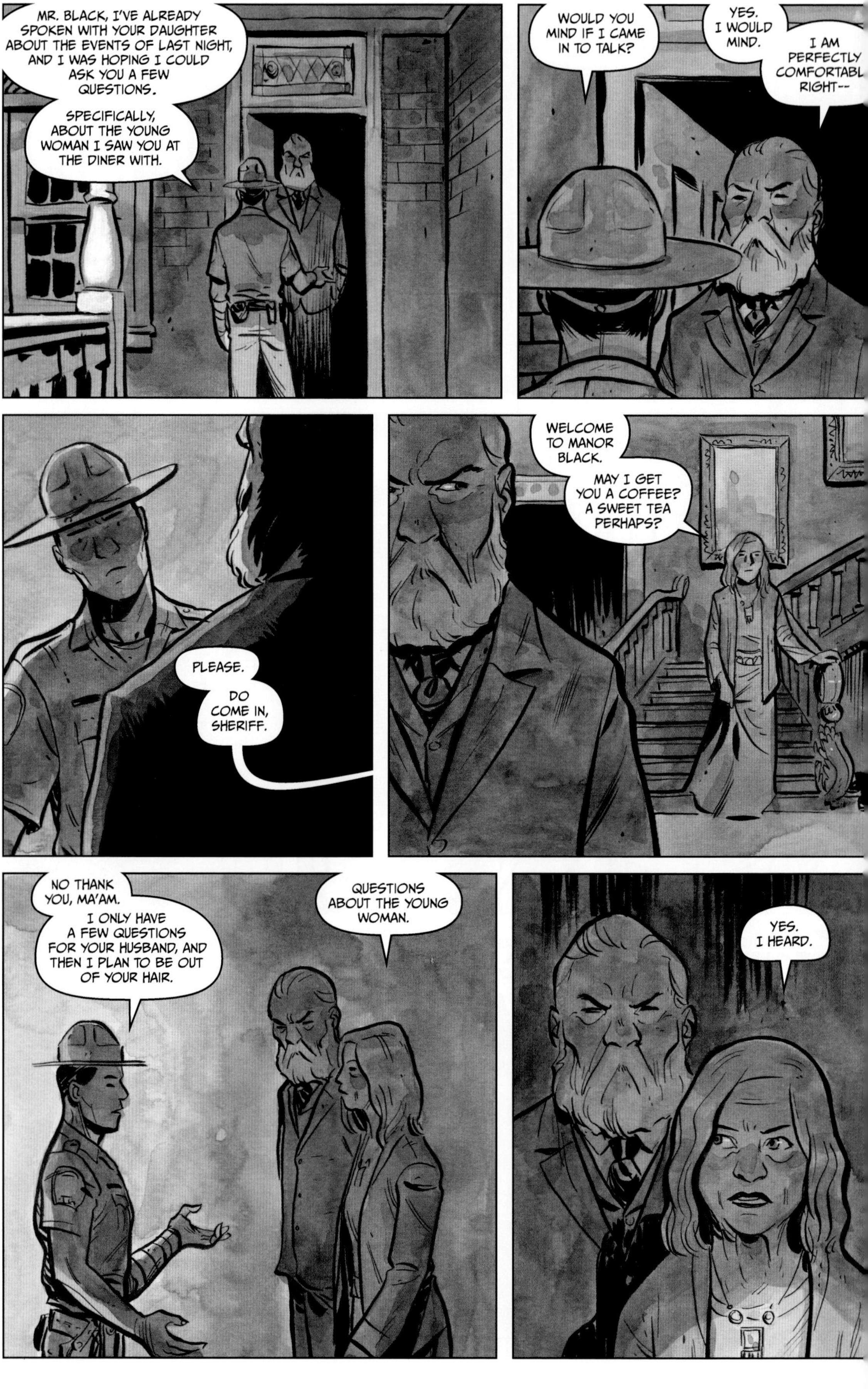
MR. BLACK, I'VE ALREADY SPOKEN WITH YOUR DAUGHTER ABOUT THE EVENTS OF LAST NIGHT, AND I WAS HOPING I COULD ASK YOU A FEW QUESTIONS.
SPECIFICALLY, ABOUT THE YOUNG WOMAN I SAW YOU AT THE DINER WITH.
WOULD YOU MIND IF I CAME IN TO TALK?
YES. I WOULD MIND.
I AM PERFECTLY COMFORTABL RIGHT--
PLEASE.
DO COME IN, SHERIFF.
WELCOME TO MANOR BLACK.
MAY I GET YOU A COFFEE? A SWEET TEA PERHAPS?
NO THANK YOU, MA'AM.
I ONLY HAVE A FEW QUESTIONS FOR YOUR HUSBAND, AND THEN I PLAN TO BE OUT OF YOUR HAIR.
QUESTIONS ABOUT THE YOUNG WOMAN.
YES. I HEARD.

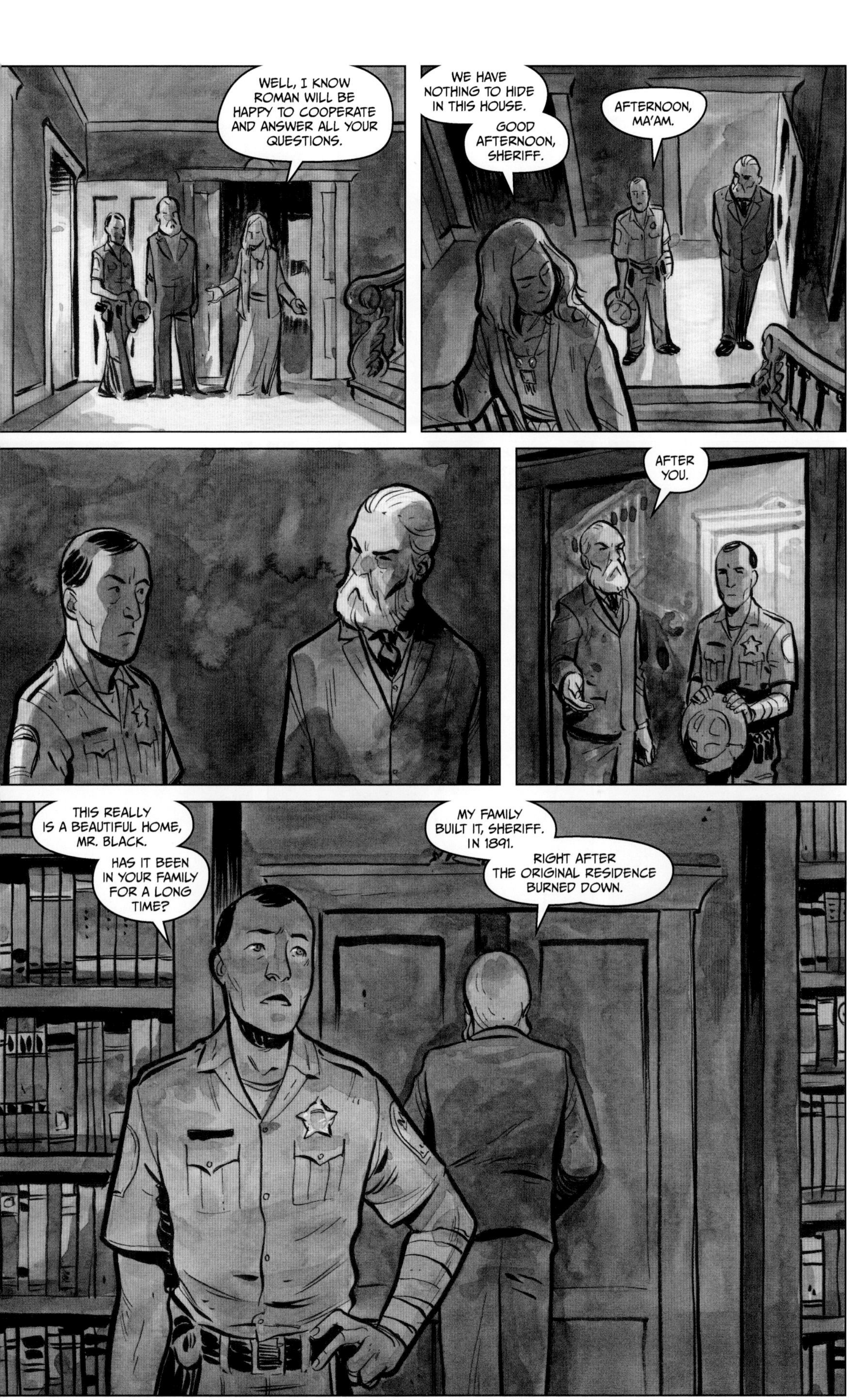
WELL, I KNOW ROMAN WILL BE HAPPY TO COOPERATE AND ANSWER ALL YOUR QUESTIONS.
WE HAVE NOTHING TO HIDE IN THIS HOUSE.
GOOD AFTERNOON, SHERIFF.
AFTERNOON, MA'AM.
AFTER YOU.
THIS REALLY IS A BEAUTIFUL HOME, MR. BLACK.
HAS IT BEEN IN YOUR FAMILY FOR A LONG TIME?
MY FAMILY BUILT IT, SHERIFF. IN 1891.
RIGHT AFTER THE ORIGINAL RESIDENCE BURNED DOWN.

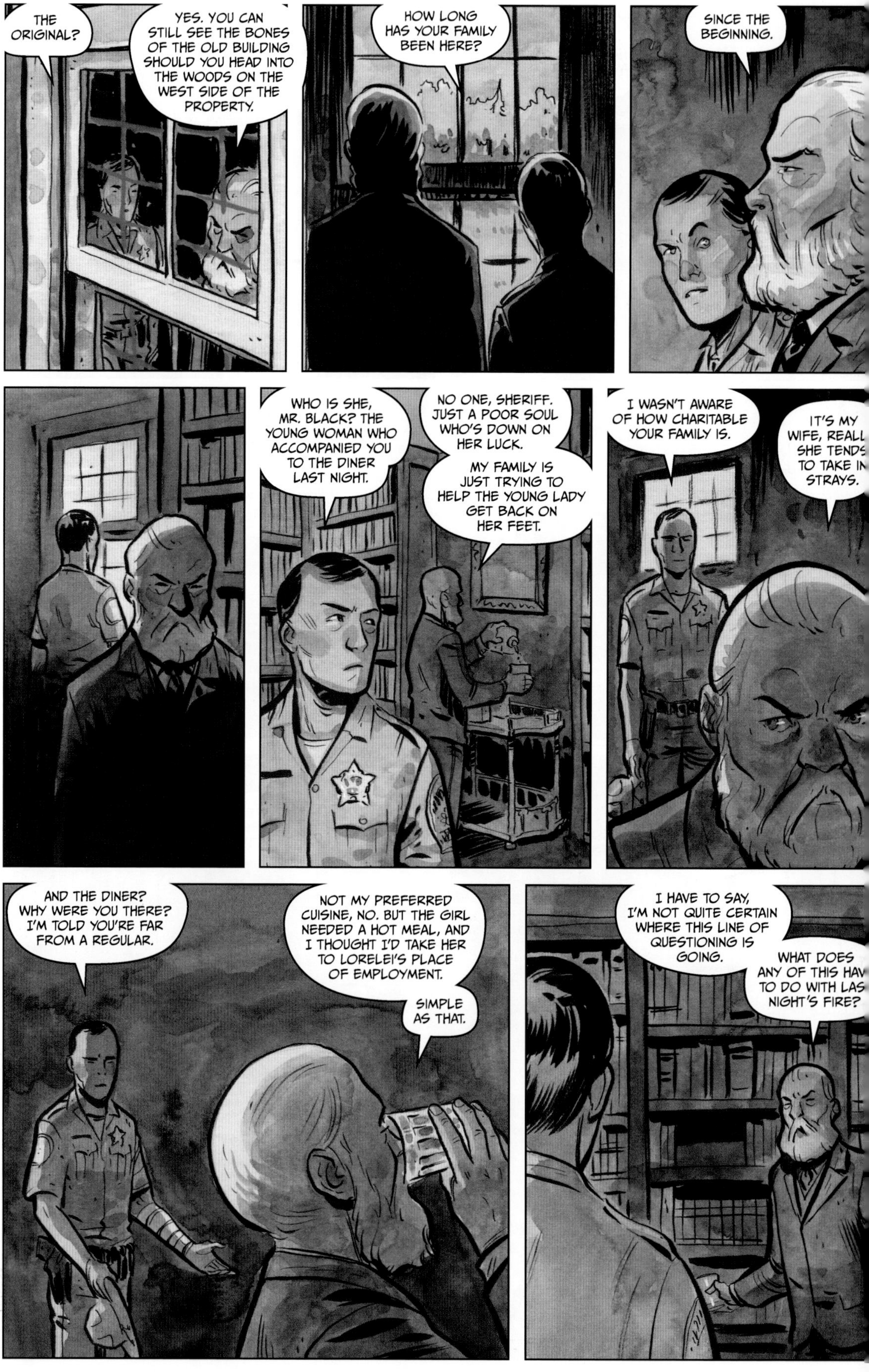
THE ORIGINAL?
YES. YOU CAN STILL SEE THE BONES OF THE OLD BUILDING SHOULD YOU HEAD INTO THE WOODS ON THE WEST SIDE OF THE PROPERTY.
HOW LONG HAS YOUR FAMILY BEEN HERE?
SINCE THE BEGINNING.
WHO IS SHE, MR. BLACK? THE YOUNG WOMAN WHO ACCOMPANIED YOU TO THE DINER LAST NIGHT.
NO ONE, SHERIFF. JUST A POOR SOUL WHO'S DOWN ON HER LUCK.
MY FAMILY IS JUST TRYING TO HELP THE YOUNG LADY GET BACK ON HER FEET.
I WASN'T AWARE OF HOW CHARITABLE YOUR FAMILY IS.
IT'S MY WIFE, REALL SHE TENDS TO TAKE IN STRAYS.
AND THE DINER? WHY WERE YOU THERE? I'M TOLD YOU'RE FAR FROM A REGULAR.
NOT MY PREFERRED CUISINE, NO. BUT THE GIRL NEEDED A HOT MEAL, AND I THOUGHT I'D TAKE HER TO LORELEI'S PLACE OF EMPLOYMENT.
SIMPLE AS THAT.
I HAVE TO SAY, I'M NOT QUITE CERTAIN WHERE THIS LINE OF QUESTIONING IS GOING.
WHAT DOES ANY OF THIS HAV TO DO WITH LAS NIGHT'S FIRE?

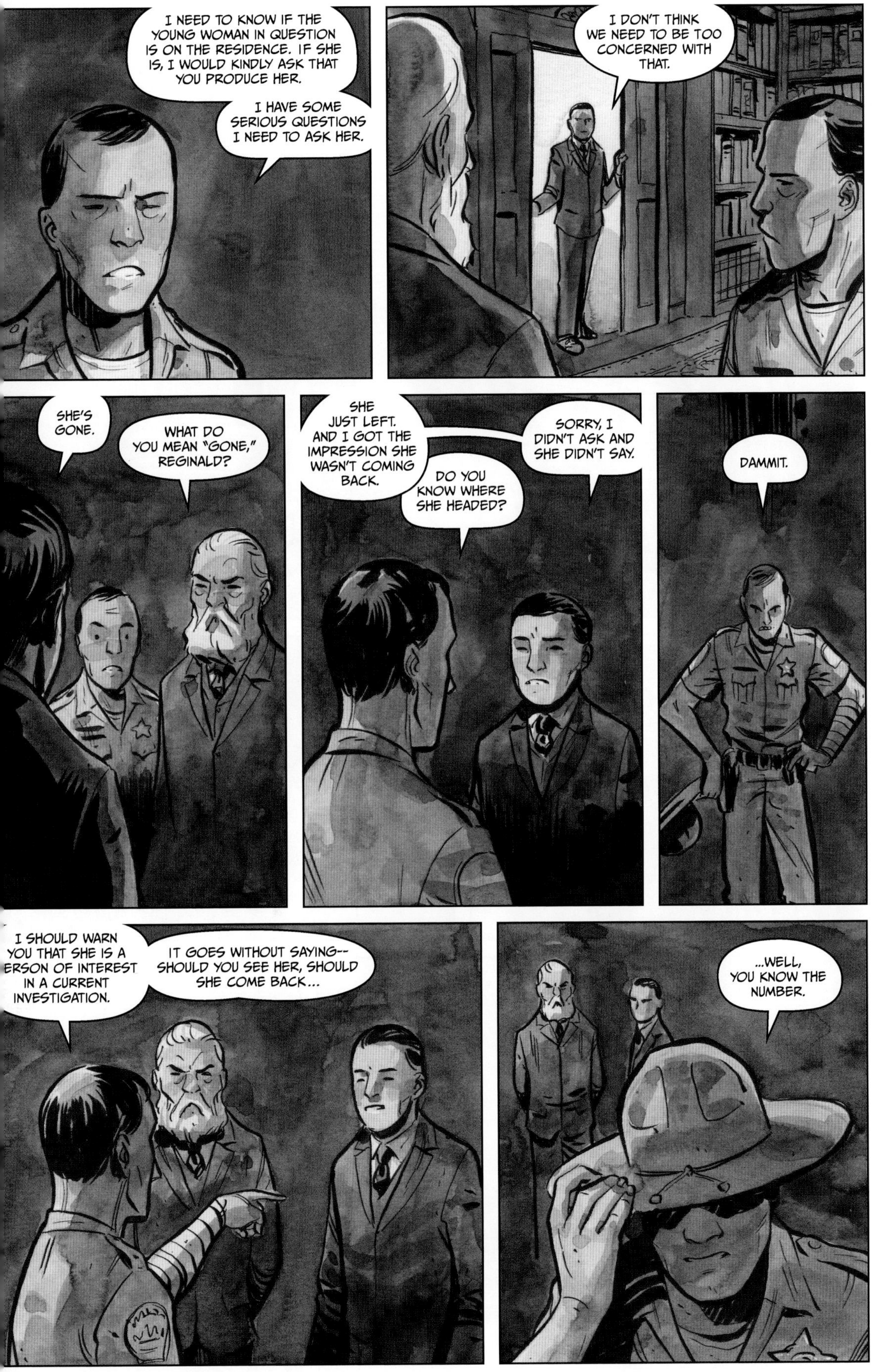
I NEED TO KNOW IF THE YOUNG WOMAN IN QUESTION IS ON THE RESIDENCE. IF SHE IS, I WOULD KINDLY ASK THAT YOU PRODUCE HER.
I HAVE SOME SERIOUS QUESTIONS I NEED TO ASK HER.
I DON'T THINK WE NEED TO BE TOO CONCERNED WITH THAT.
SHE'S GONE.
WHAT DO YOU MEAN "GONE," REGINALD?
SHE JUST LEFT. AND I GOT THE IMPRESSION SHE WASN'T COMING BACK.
DO YOU KNOW WHERE SHE HEADED?
SORRY, I DIDN'T ASK AND SHE DIDN'T SAY.
DAMMIT.
I SHOULD WARN YOU THAT SHE IS A ERSON OF INTEREST IN A CURRENT INVESTIGATION.
IT GOES WITHOUT SAYING-- SHOULD YOU SEE HER, SHOULD SHE COME BACK...
...WELL, YOU KNOW THE NUMBER.

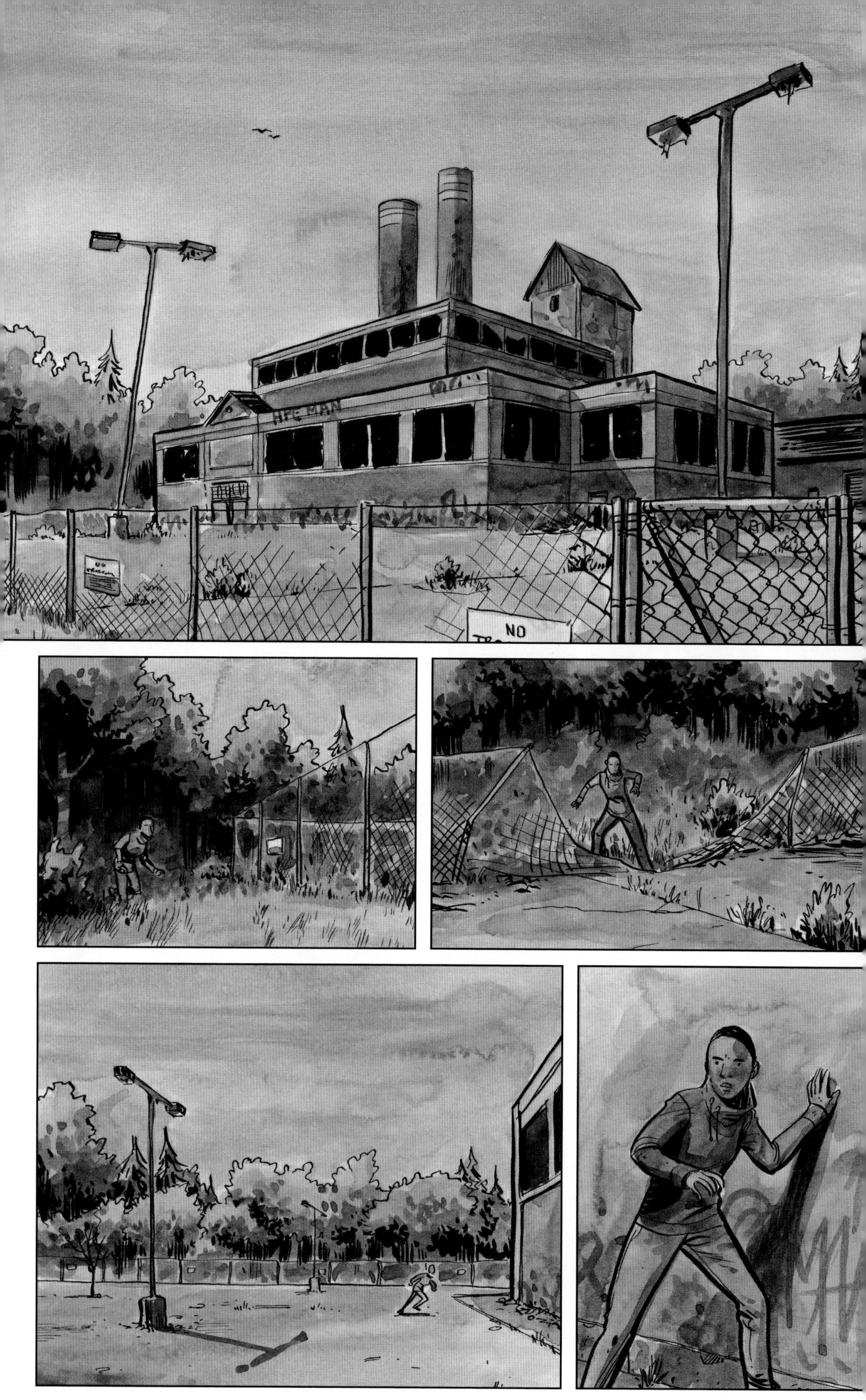
NO

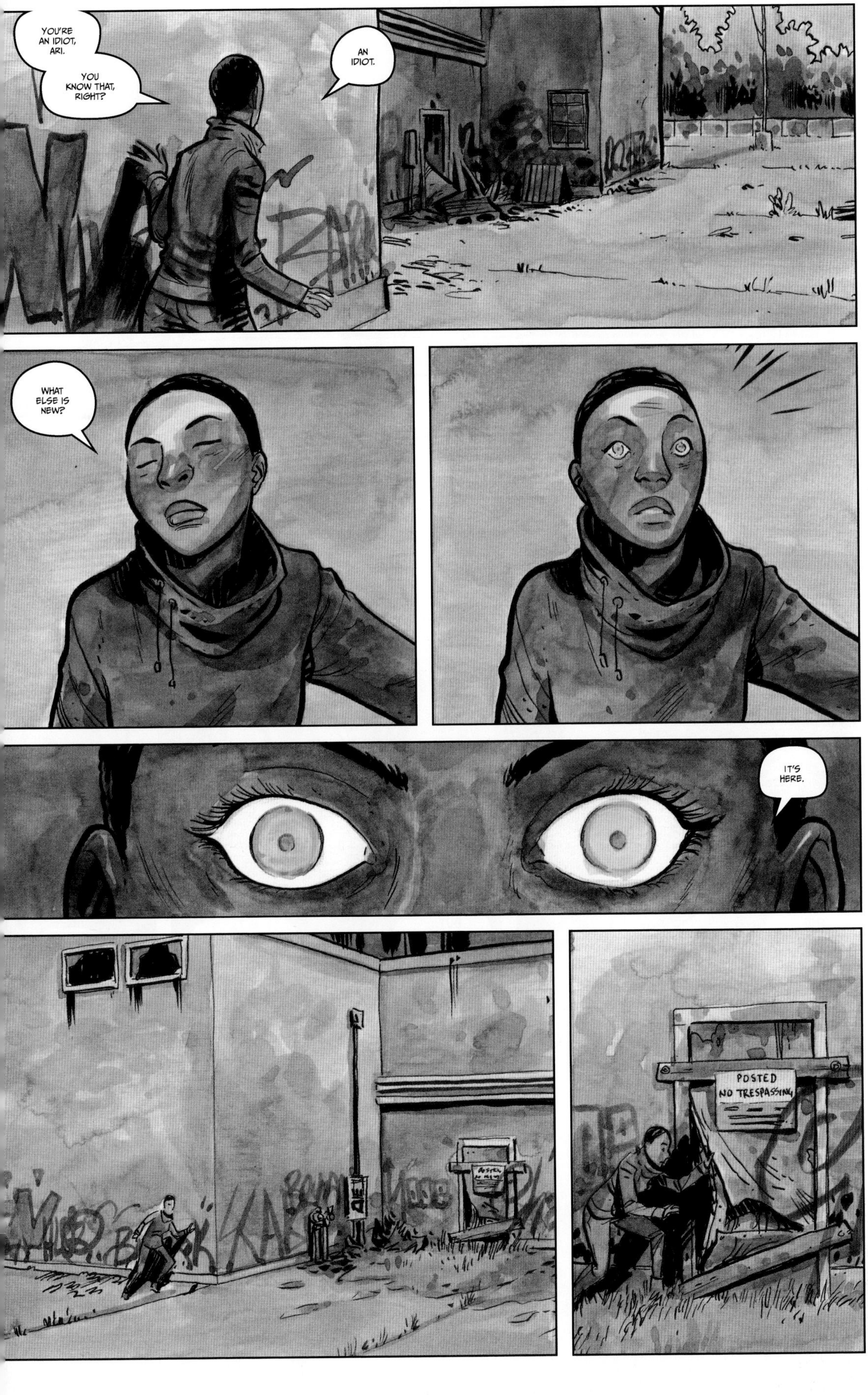
YOU'RE AN IDIOT, ARI.
YOU KNOW THAT, RIGHT?
AN IDIOT.
WHAT ELSE IS NEW?
IT'S HERE.
POSTED NO TRESPASSING

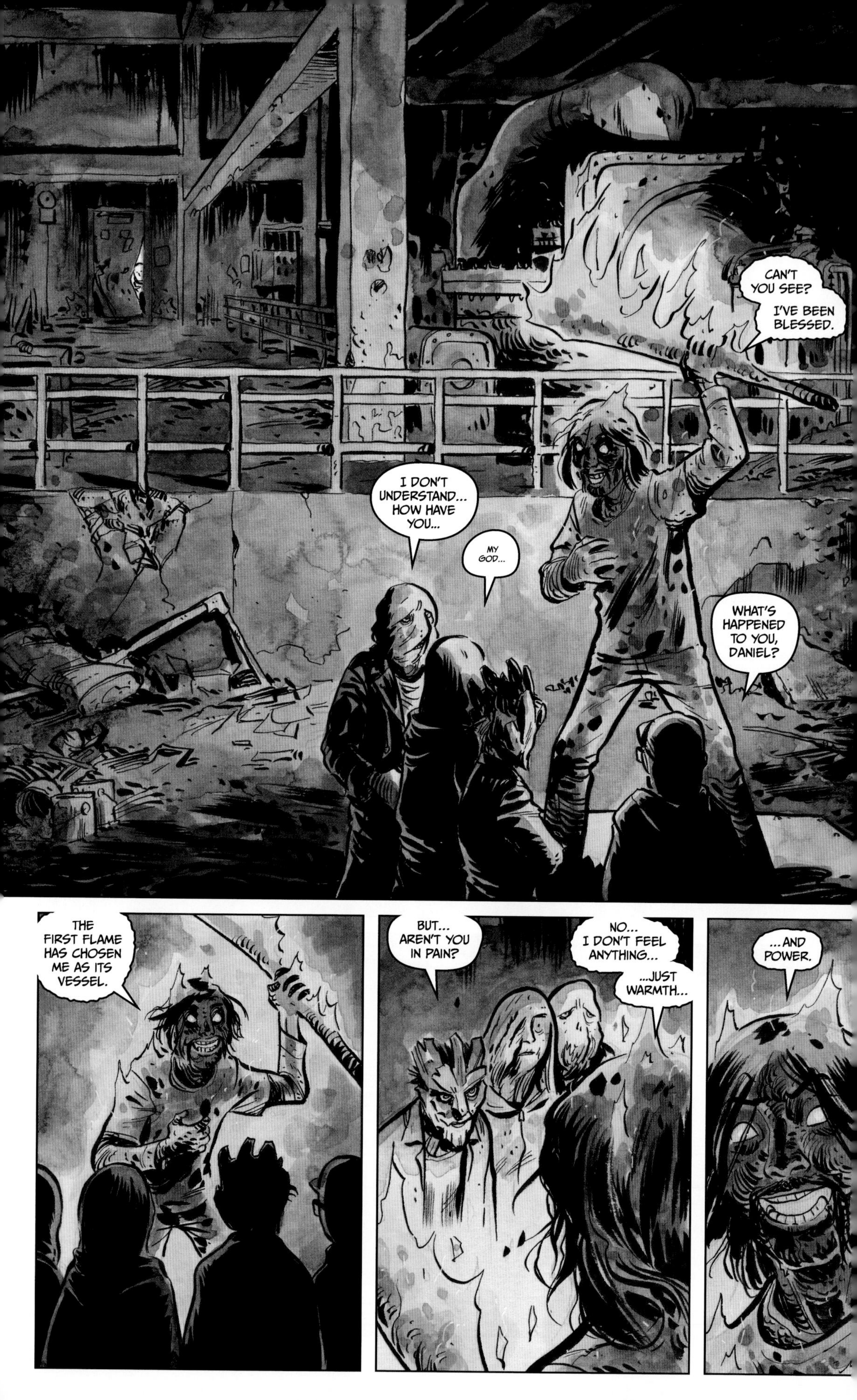
CAN'T YOU SEE?
I'VE BEEN BLESSED.
I DON'T UNDERSTAND... HOW HAVE YOU...
MY GOD...
WHAT'S HAPPENED TO YOU, DANIEL?
THE FIRST FLAME HAS CHOSEN ME AS ITS VESSEL.
BUT... AREN'T YOU IN PAIN?
NO... I DON'T FEEL ANYTHING...
...JUST WARMTH...
...AND POWER.

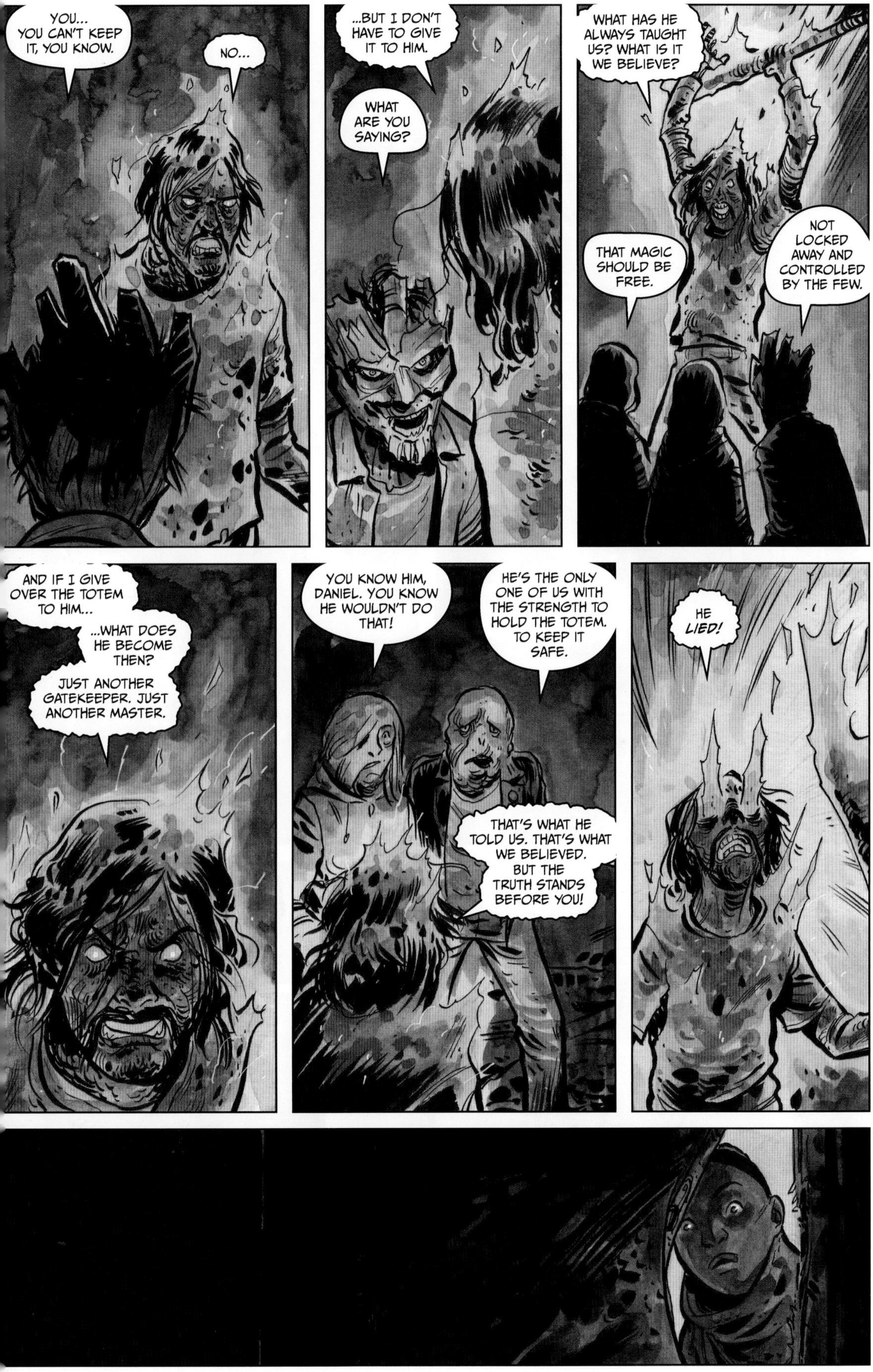
YOU... YOU CAN'T KEEP IT, YOU KNOW.
NO...
...BUT I DON'T HAVE TO GIVE IT TO HIM.
WHAT ARE YOU SAYING?
WHAT HAS HE ALWAYS TAUGHT US? WHAT IS IT WE BELIEVE?
THAT MAGIC SHOULD BE FREE.
NOT LOCKED AWAY AND CONTROLLED BY THE FEW.
AND IF I GIVE OVER THE TOTEM TO HIM...
...WHAT DOES HE BECOME THEN?
JUST ANOTHER GATEKEEPER. JUST ANOTHER MASTER.
YOU KNOW HIM, DANIEL. YOU KNOW HE WOULDN'T DO THAT!
HE'S THE ONLY ONE OF US WITH THE STRENGTH TO HOLD THE TOTEM. TO KEEP IT SAFE.
THAT'S WHAT HE TOLD US. THAT'S WHAT WE BELIEVED. BUT THE TRUTH STANDS BEFORE YOU!
HE *LIED!*

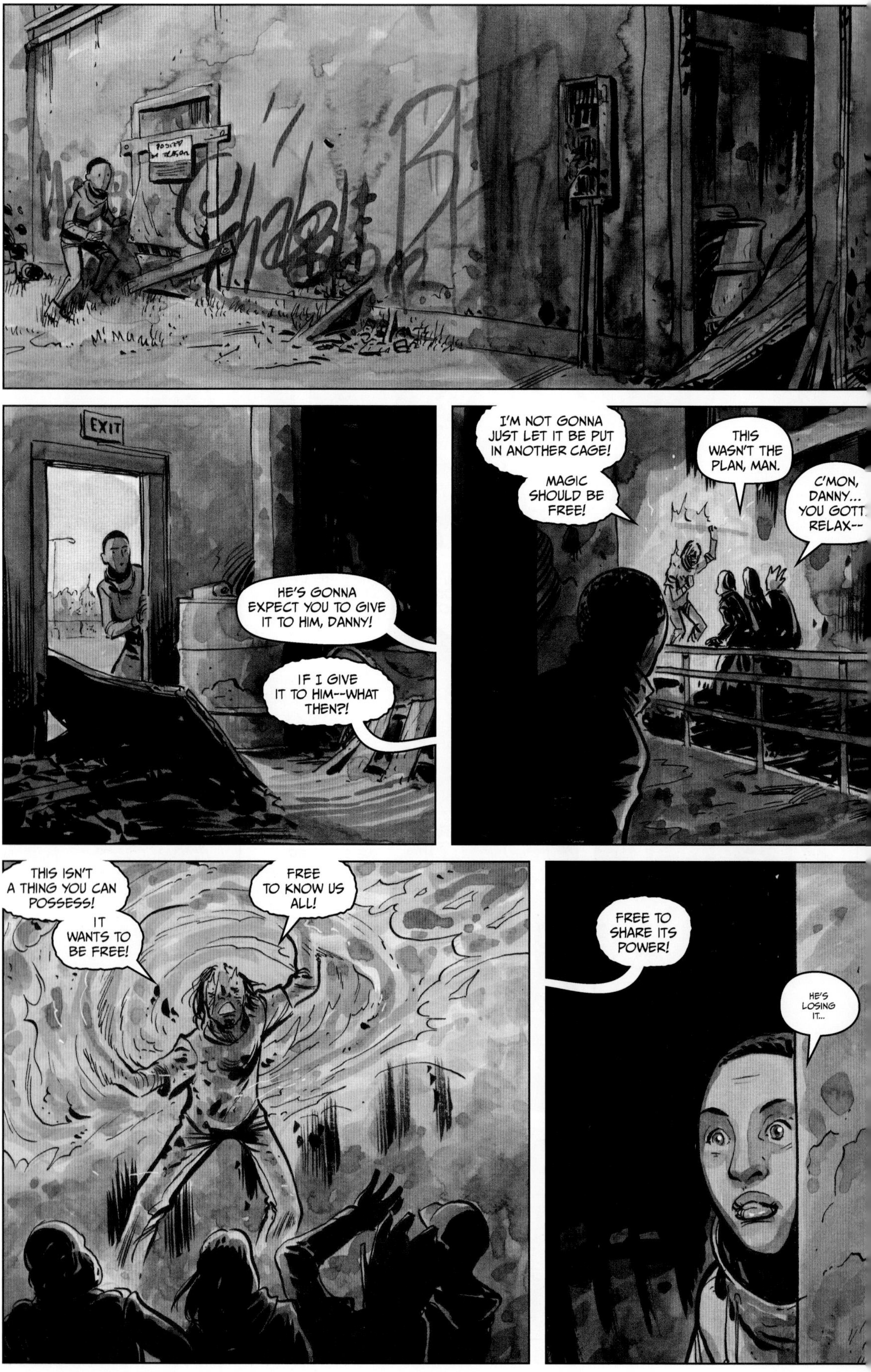
EXIT
HE'S GONNA EXPECT YOU TO GIVE IT TO HIM, DANNY!
IF I GIVE IT TO HIM--WHAT THEN?!
I'M NOT GONNA JUST LET IT BE PUT IN ANOTHER CAGE!
MAGIC SHOULD BE FREE!
THIS WASN'T THE PLAN, MAN.
C'MON, DANNY... YOU GOTT RELAX--
THIS ISN'T A THING YOU CAN POSSESS!
IT WANTS TO BE FREE!
FREE TO KNOW US ALL!
FREE TO SHARE ITS POWER!
HE'S LOSING IT...

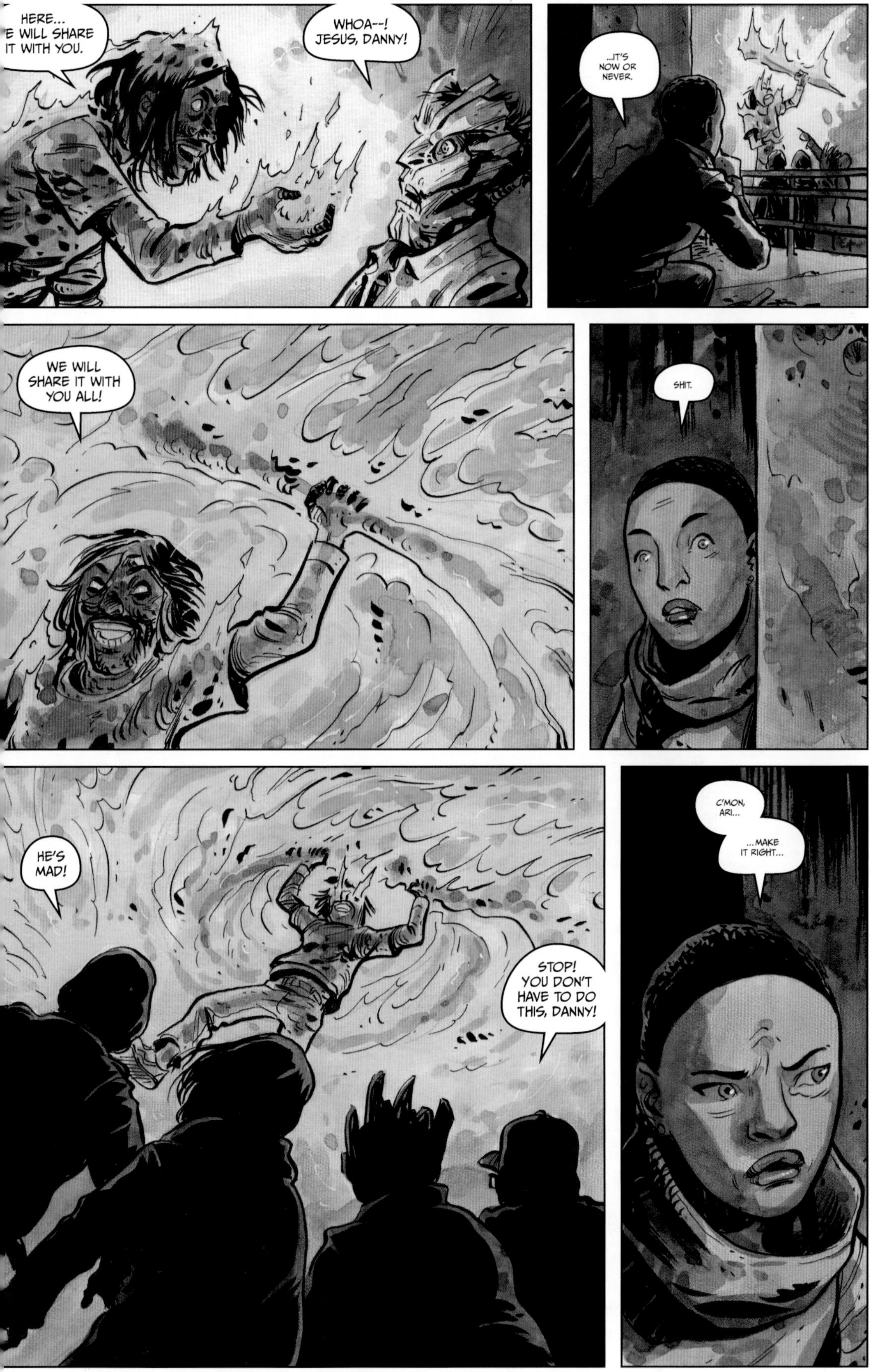
HERE... E WILL SHARE IT WITH YOU.
WHOA--! JESUS, DANNY!
...IT'S NOW OR NEVER.
WE WILL SHARE IT WITH YOU ALL!
SHIT.
HE'S MAD!
STOP! YOU DON'T HAVE TO DO THIS, DANNY!
C'MON, ARI...
...MAKE IT RIGHT...

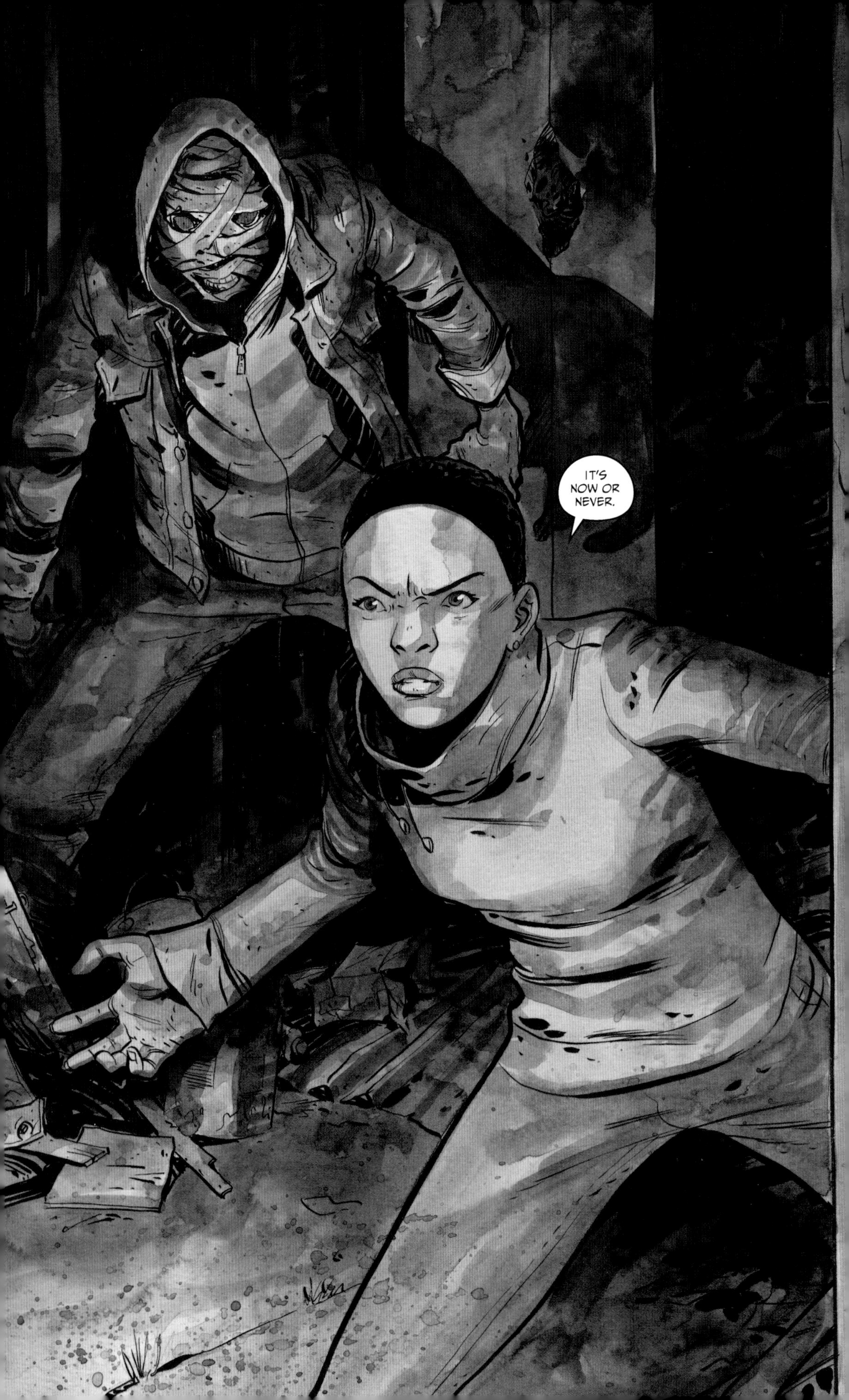
IT'S NOW OR NEVER.

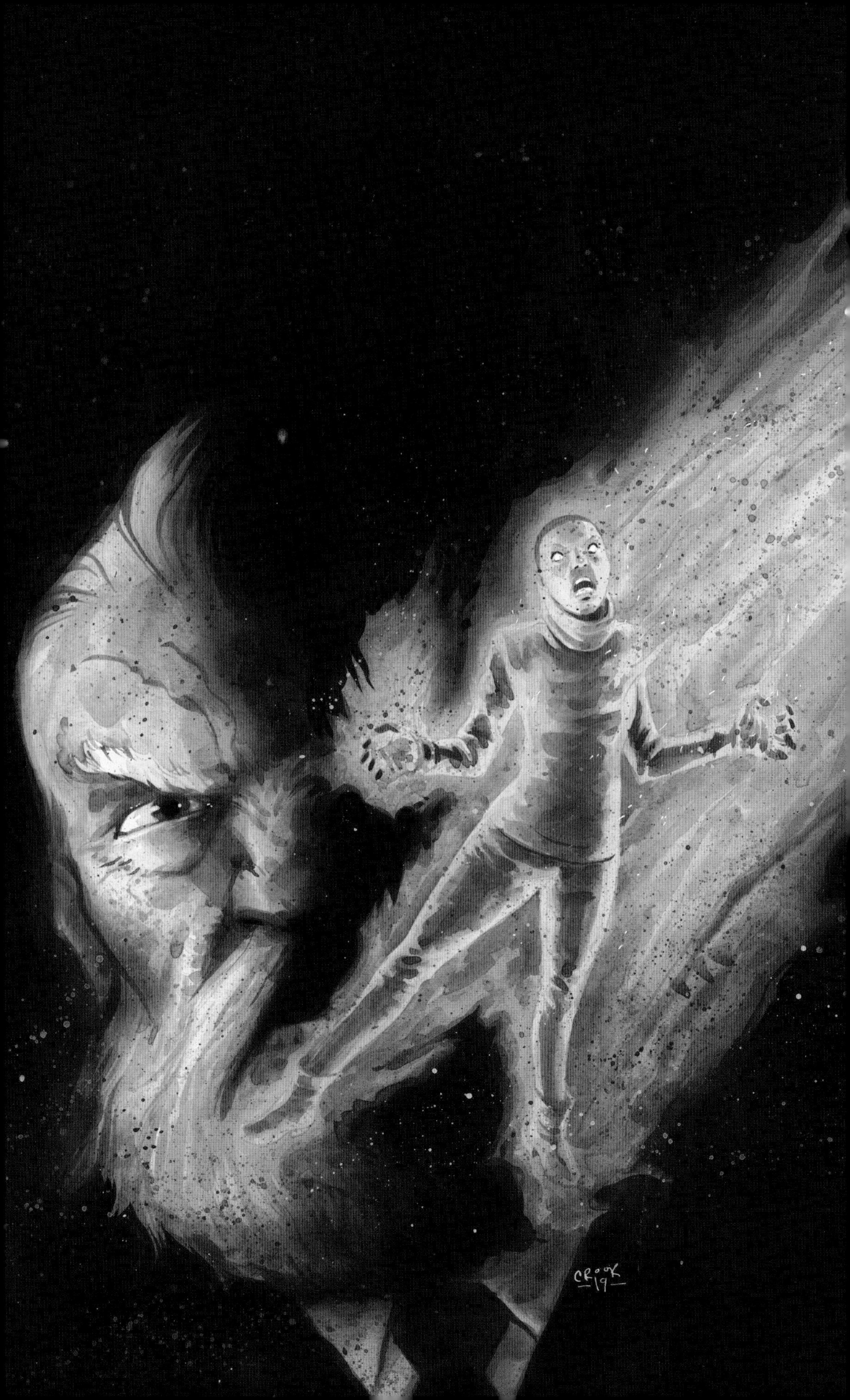
CROOK
19

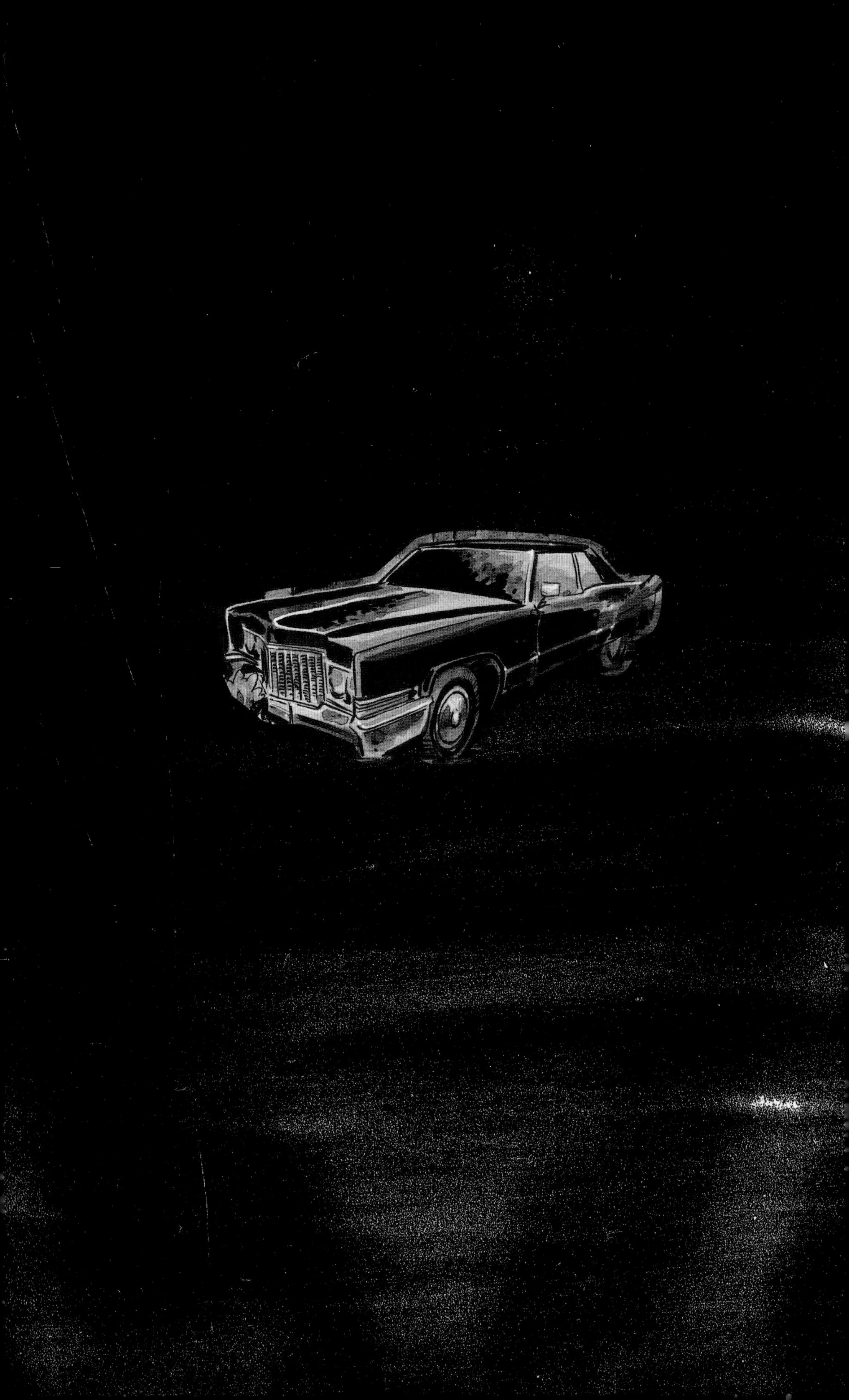

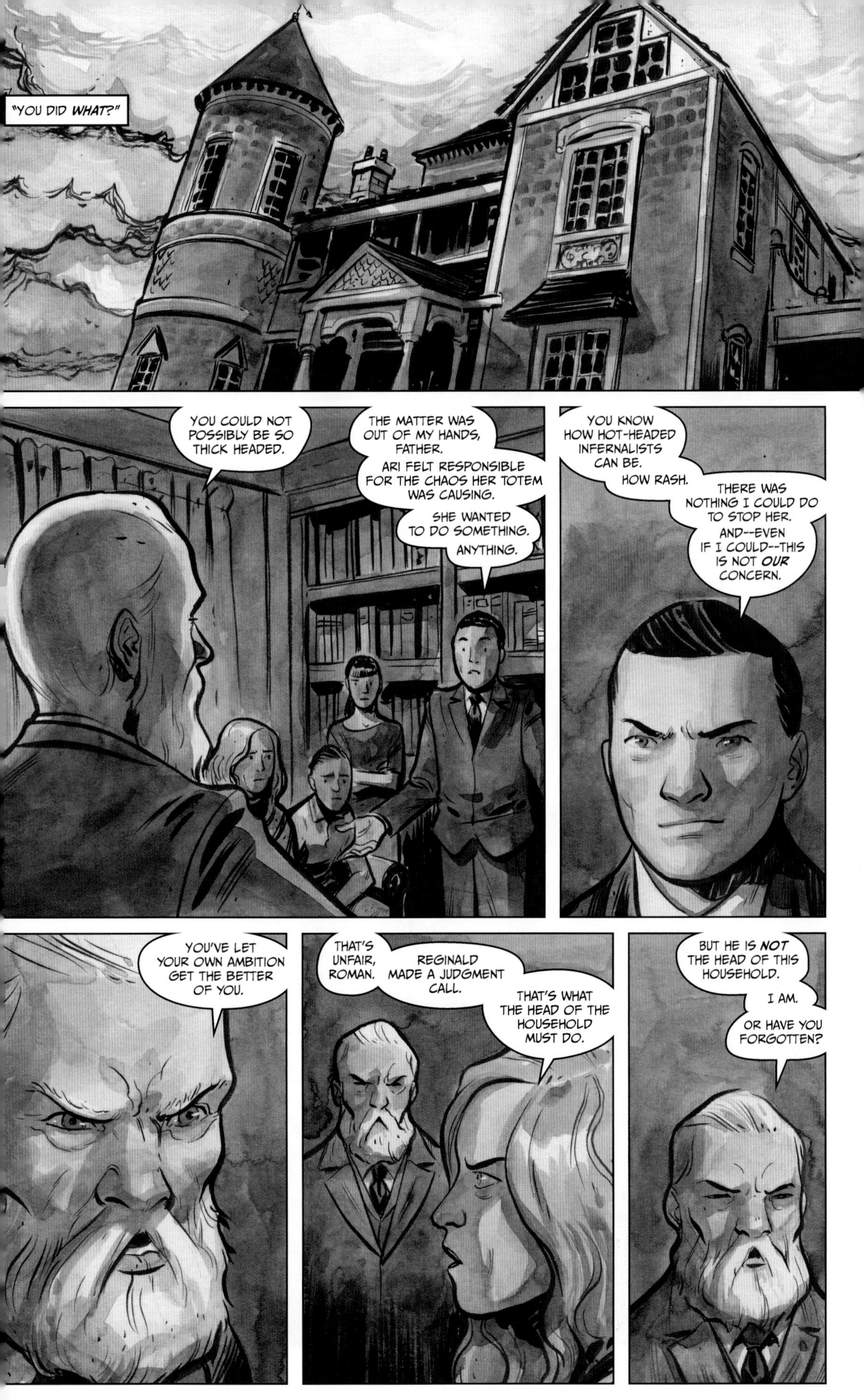
"YOU DID *WHAT?*"
YOU COULD NOT POSSIBLY BE SO THICK HEADED.
THE MATTER WAS OUT OF MY HANDS, FATHER.
ARI FELT RESPONSIBLE FOR THE CHAOS HER TOTEM WAS CAUSING.
SHE WANTED TO DO SOMETHING.
ANYTHING.
YOU KNOW HOW HOT-HEADED INFERNALISTS CAN BE.
HOW RASH.
THERE WAS NOTHING I COULD DO TO STOP HER.
AND--EVEN IF I COULD--THIS IS NOT *OUR* CONCERN.
YOU'VE LET YOUR OWN AMBITION GET THE BETTER OF YOU.
THAT'S UNFAIR, ROMAN.
REGINALD MADE A JUDGMENT CALL.
THAT'S WHAT THE HEAD OF THE HOUSEHOLD MUST DO.
BUT HE IS *NOT* THE HEAD OF THIS HOUSEHOLD.
I AM.
OR HAVE YOU FORGOTTEN?

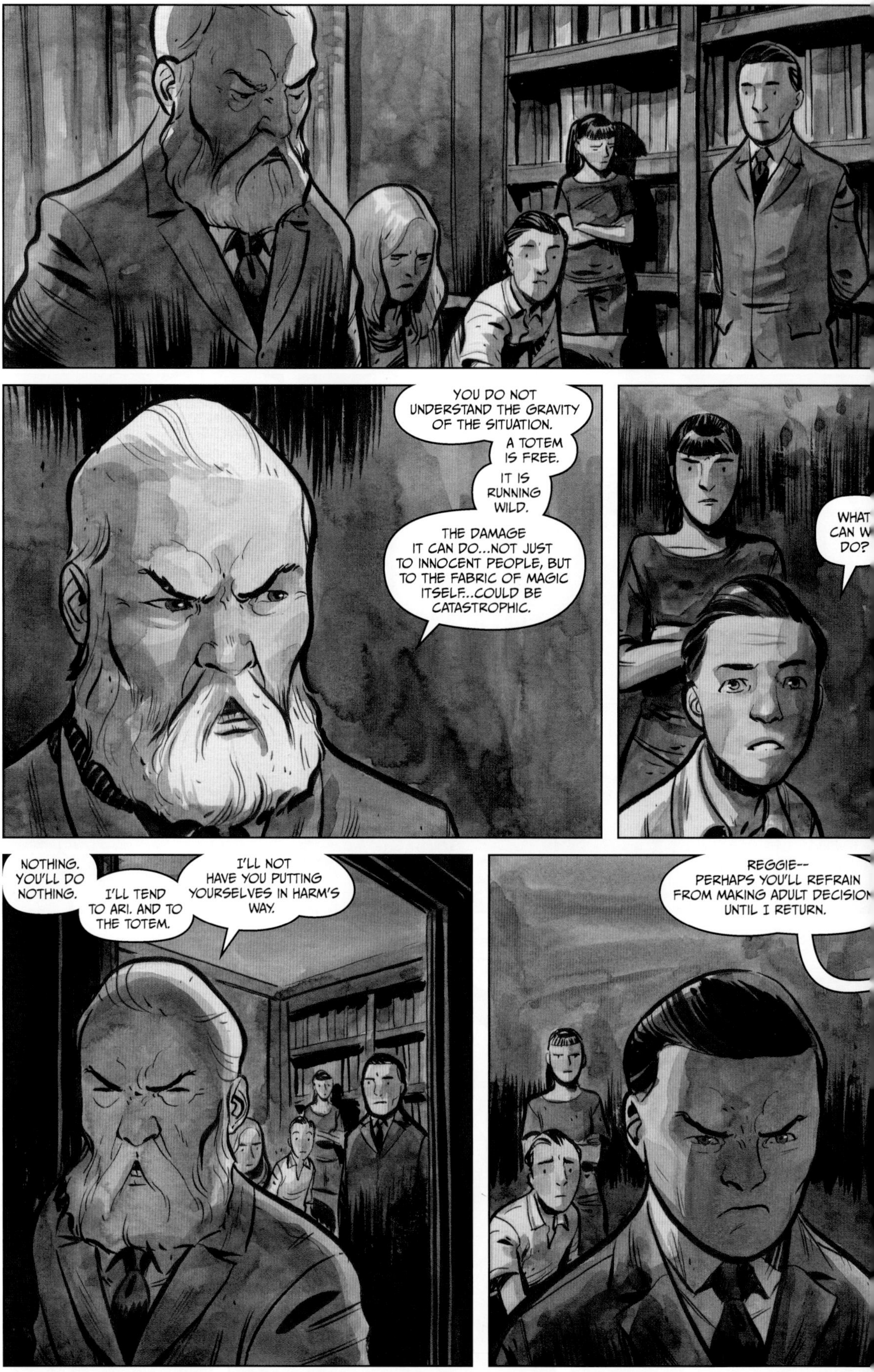
YOU DO NOT UNDERSTAND THE GRAVITY OF THE SITUATION.
A TOTEM IS FREE.
IT IS RUNNING WILD.
THE DAMAGE IT CAN DO...NOT JUST TO INNOCENT PEOPLE, BUT TO THE FABRIC OF MAGIC ITSELF...COULD BE CATASTROPHIC.
WHAT CAN W DO?
NOTHING. YOU'LL DO NOTHING.
I'LL TEND TO ARI. AND TO THE TOTEM.
I'LL NOT HAVE YOU PUTTING YOURSELVES IN HARM'S WAY.
REGGIE-- PERHAPS YOU'LL REFRAIN FROM MAKING ADULT DECISION UNTIL I RETURN.

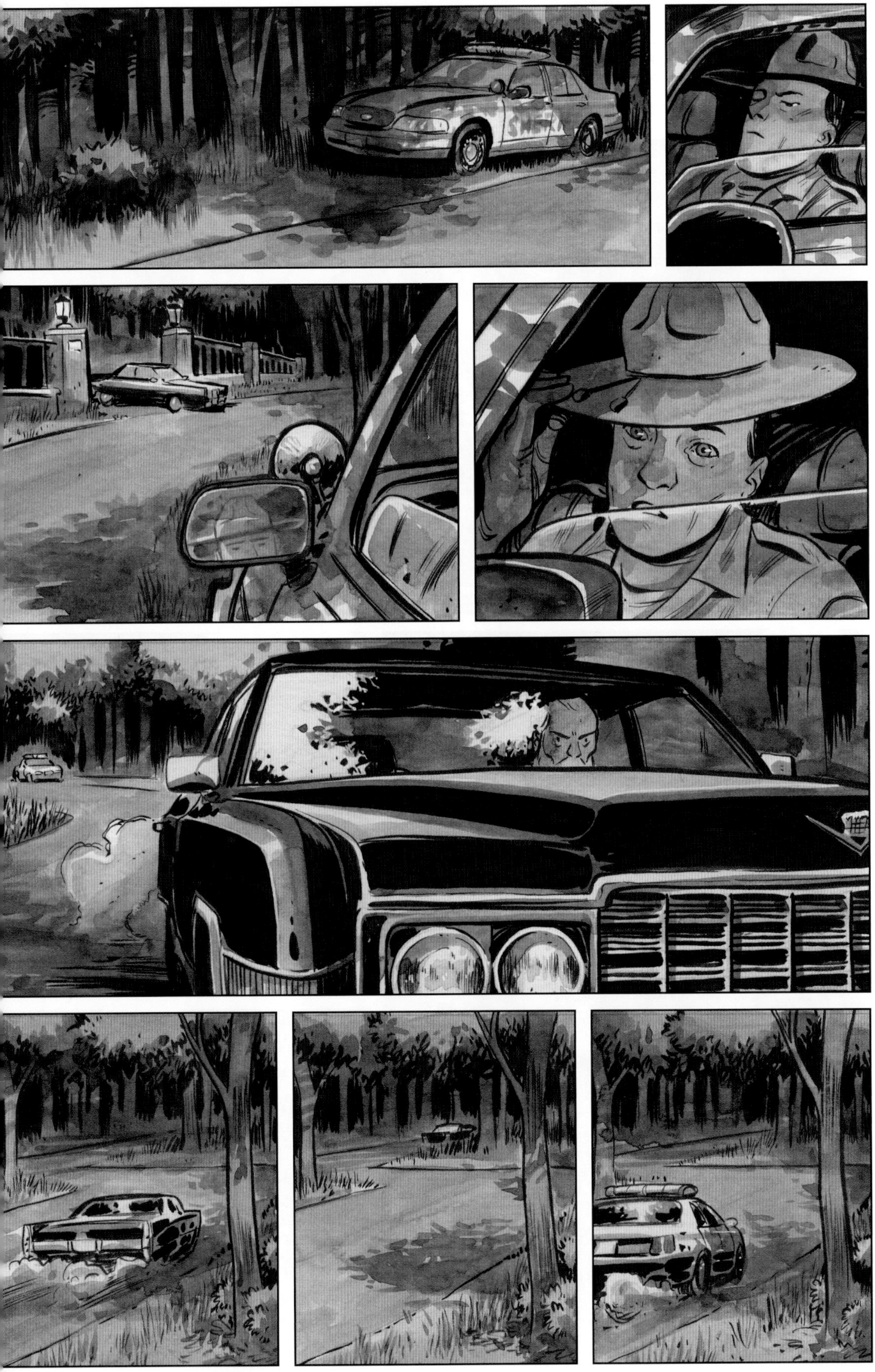

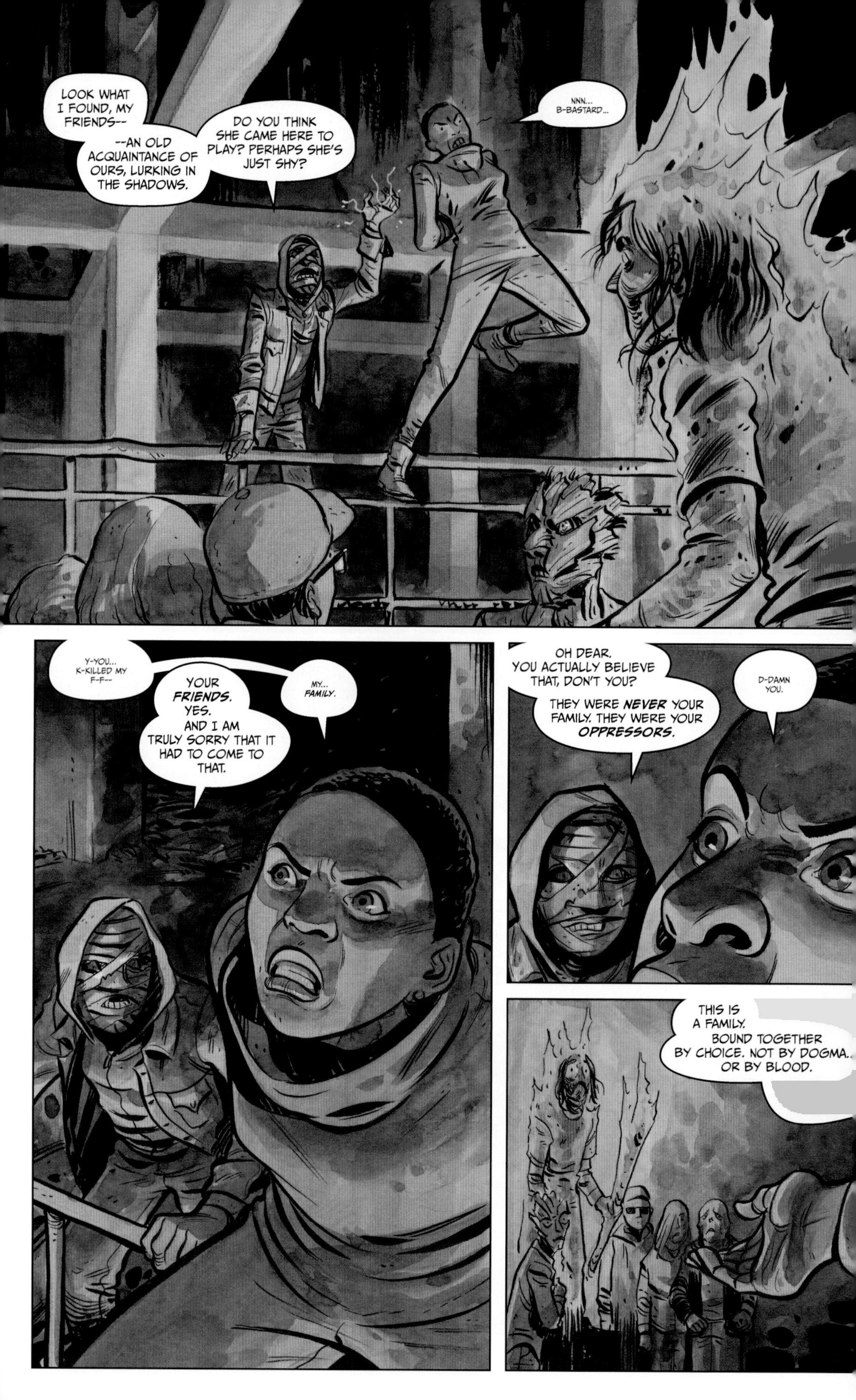
LOOK WHAT I FOUND, MY FRIENDS--
--AN OLD ACQUAINTANCE OF OURS, LURKING IN THE SHADOWS.
DO YOU THINK SHE CAME HERE TO PLAY? PERHAPS SHE'S JUST SHY?
NNN... B-BASTARD...
Y-YOU... K-KILLED MY F-F--
YOUR FRIENDS. YES.
AND I AM TRULY SORRY THAT IT HAD TO COME TO THAT.
MY... FAMILY.
OH DEAR. YOU ACTUALLY BELIEVE THAT, DON'T YOU?
THEY WERE NEVER YOUR FAMILY. THEY WERE YOUR OPPRESSORS.
D-DAMN YOU.
THIS IS A FAMILY.
BOUND TOGETHER BY CHOICE. NOT BY DOGMA... OR BY BLOOD.

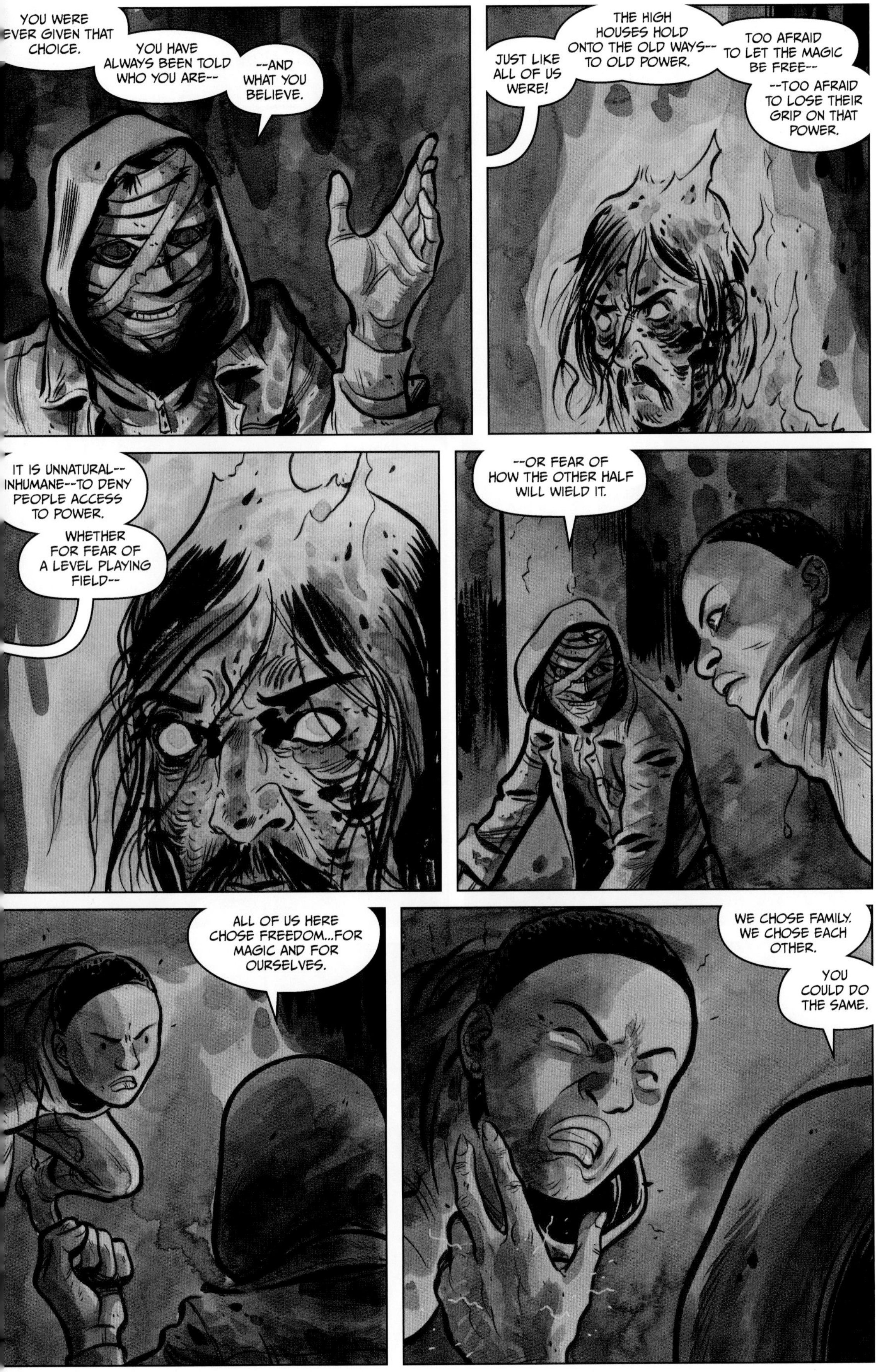
YOU WERE
EVER GIVEN THAT CHOICE.
YOU HAVE ALWAYS BEEN TOLD WHO YOU ARE--
--AND WHAT YOU BELIEVE.
JUST LIKE ALL OF US WERE!
THE HIGH HOUSES HOLD ONTO THE OLD WAYS-- TO OLD POWER.
TOO AFRAID TO LET THE MAGIC BE FREE--
--TOO AFRAID TO LOSE THEIR GRIP ON THAT POWER.
IT IS UNNATURAL-- INHUMANE--TO DENY PEOPLE ACCESS TO POWER.
WHETHER FOR FEAR OF A LEVEL PLAYING FIELD--
--OR FEAR OF HOW THE OTHER HALF WILL WIELD IT.
ALL OF US HERE CHOSE FREEDOM...FOR MAGIC AND FOR OURSELVES.
WE CHOSE FAMILY. WE CHOSE EACH OTHER.
YOU COULD DO THE SAME.

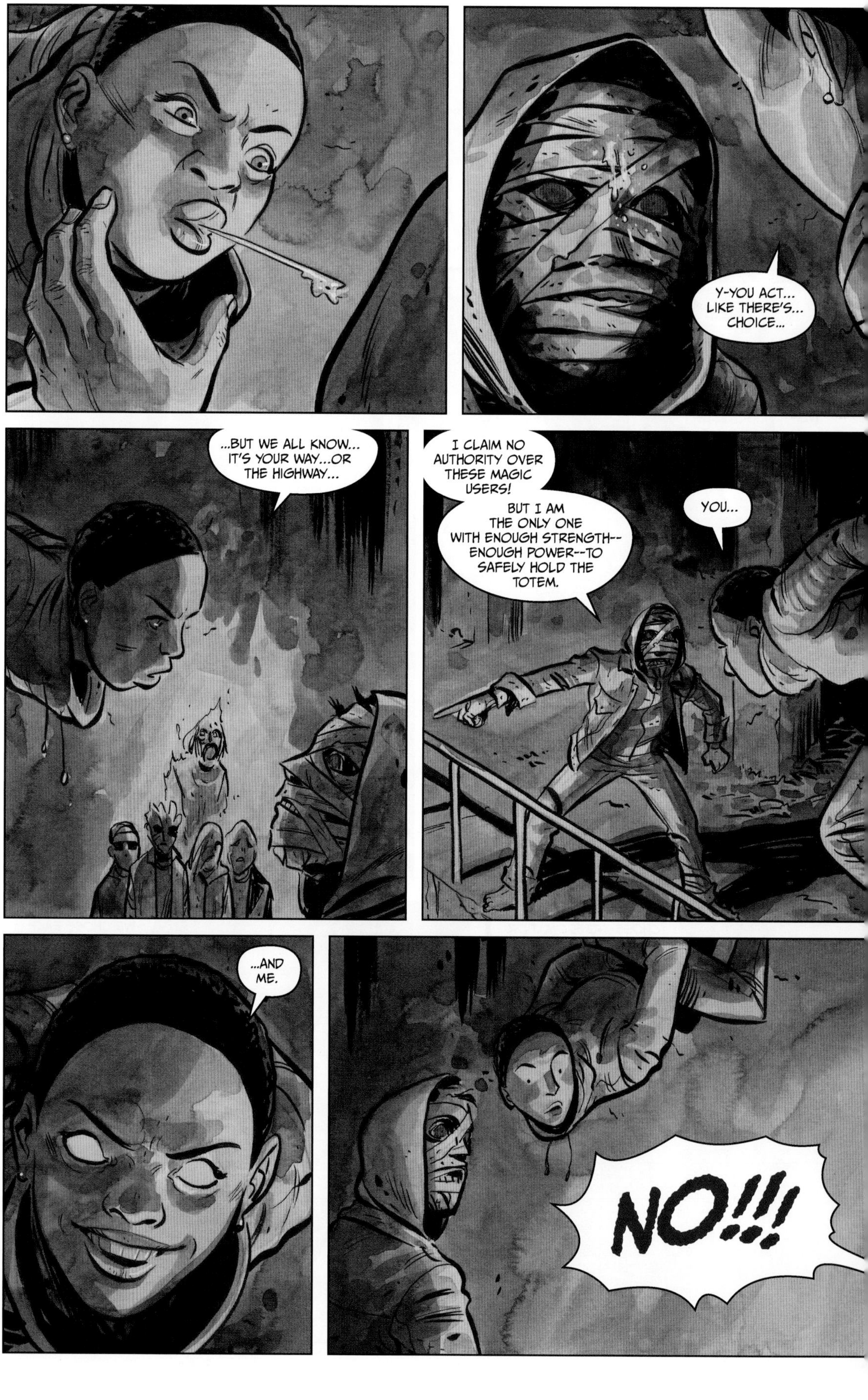
Y-YOU ACT... LIKE THERE'S... CHOICE...
...BUT WE ALL KNOW... IT'S YOUR WAY...OR THE HIGHWAY...
I CLAIM NO AUTHORITY OVER THESE MAGIC USERS!
BUT I AM THE ONLY ONE WITH ENOUGH STRENGTH-- ENOUGH POWER--TO SAFELY HOLD THE TOTEM.
YOU...
...AND ME.
NO!!!

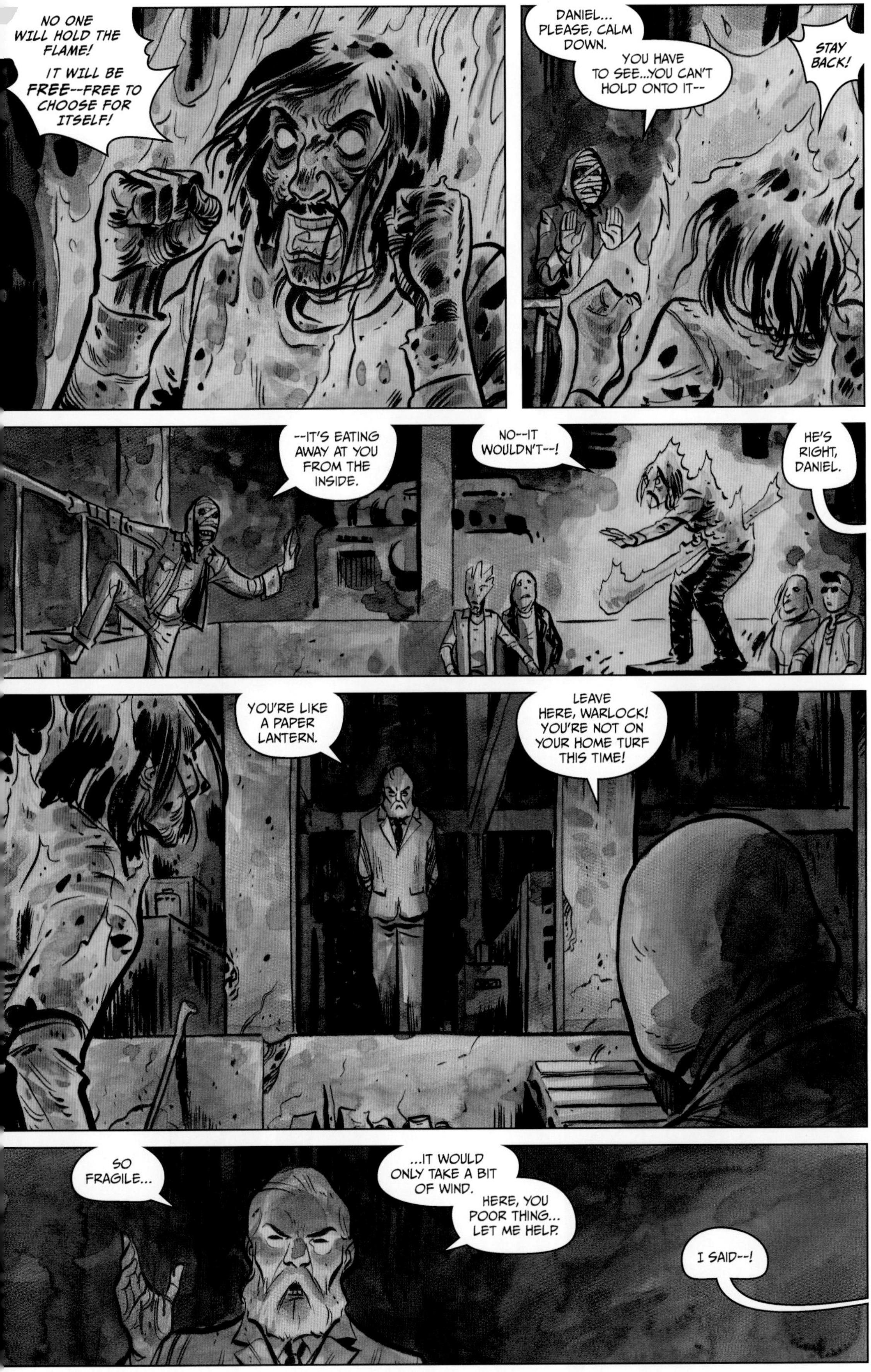
NO ONE WILL HOLD THE FLAME!
IT WILL BE FREE--FREE TO CHOOSE FOR ITSELF!
DANIEL... PLEASE, CALM DOWN.
YOU HAVE TO SEE...YOU CAN'T HOLD ONTO IT--
STAY BACK!
--IT'S EATING AWAY AT YOU FROM THE INSIDE.
NO--IT WOULDN'T--!
HE'S RIGHT, DANIEL.
YOU'RE LIKE A PAPER LANTERN.
LEAVE HERE, WARLOCK! YOU'RE NOT ON YOUR HOME TURF THIS TIME!
SO FRAGILE...
...IT WOULD ONLY TAKE A BIT OF WIND.
HERE, YOU POOR THING... LET ME HELP.
I SAID--!

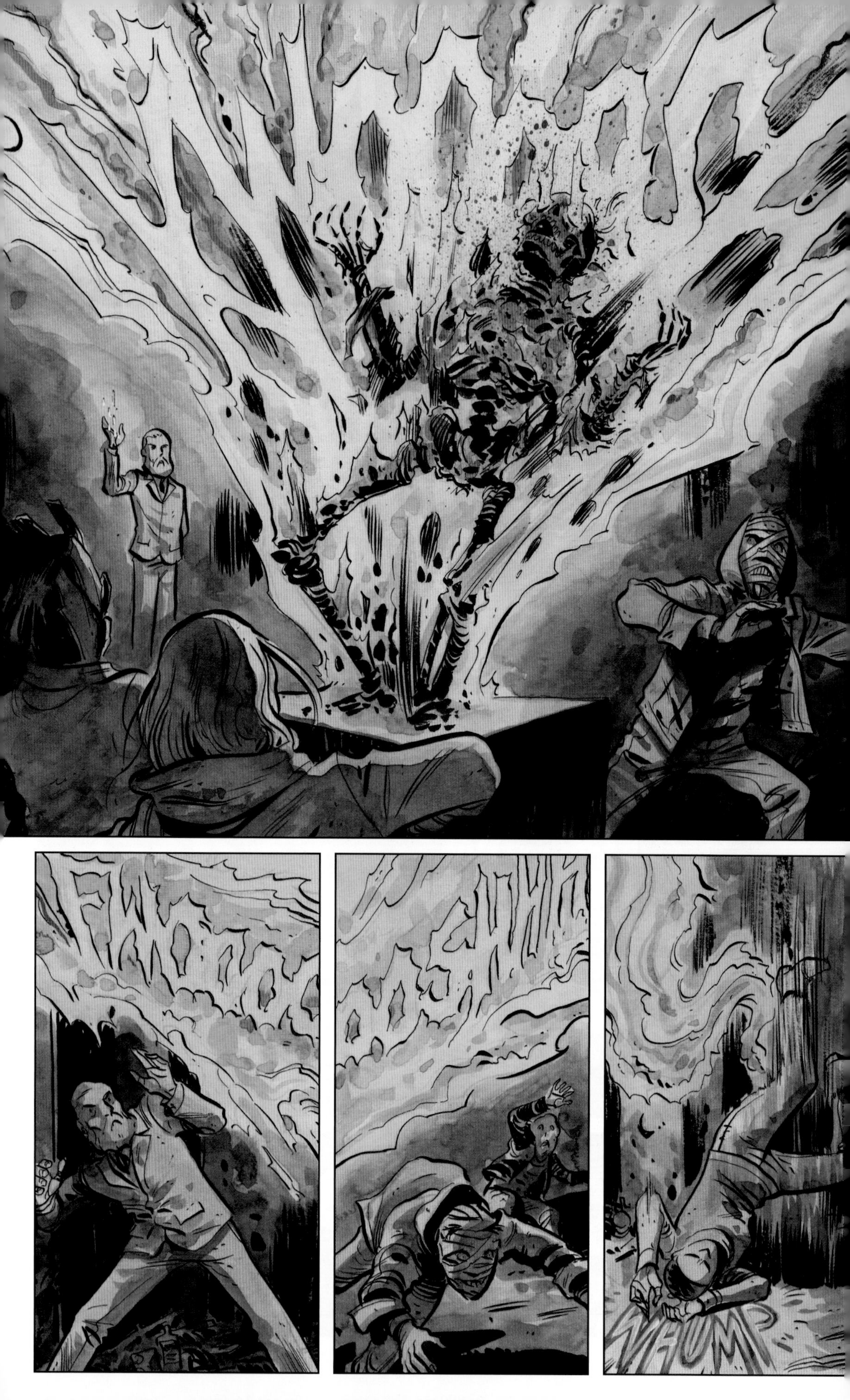
WHUMP

ARI--
ARE YOU ALL
RIGHT?

THE TOTEM--
IT'S WILD!
UNSTABLE!

IT'S BEEN
TOO LONG
WITHOUT A
HOST...

IT'S NO
LONGER YOURS
TO SUBJUGATE!

ARI...
WHERE HAS IT
GONE?! CAN YOU
FEEL IT?

YES...

...THERE.

CHNK

KKWRK

KLAN

KRANK

TINK

TINK

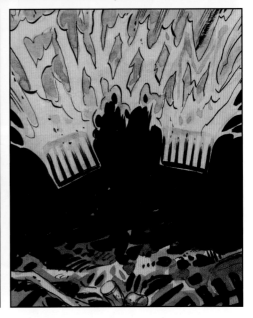

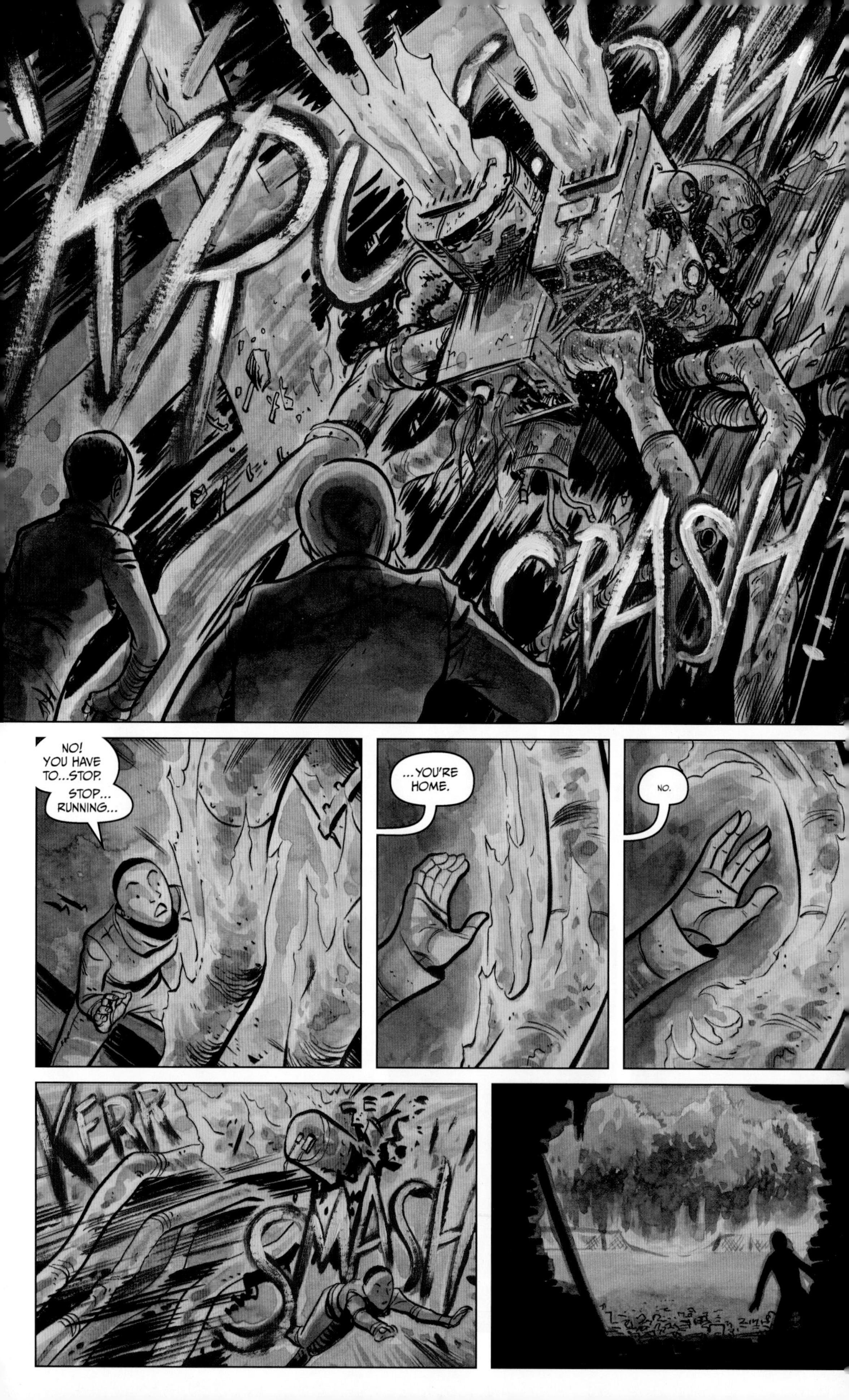
CRASH
NO! YOU HAVE TO...STOP. STOP... RUNNING...
...YOU'RE HOME.
NO.
SMASH

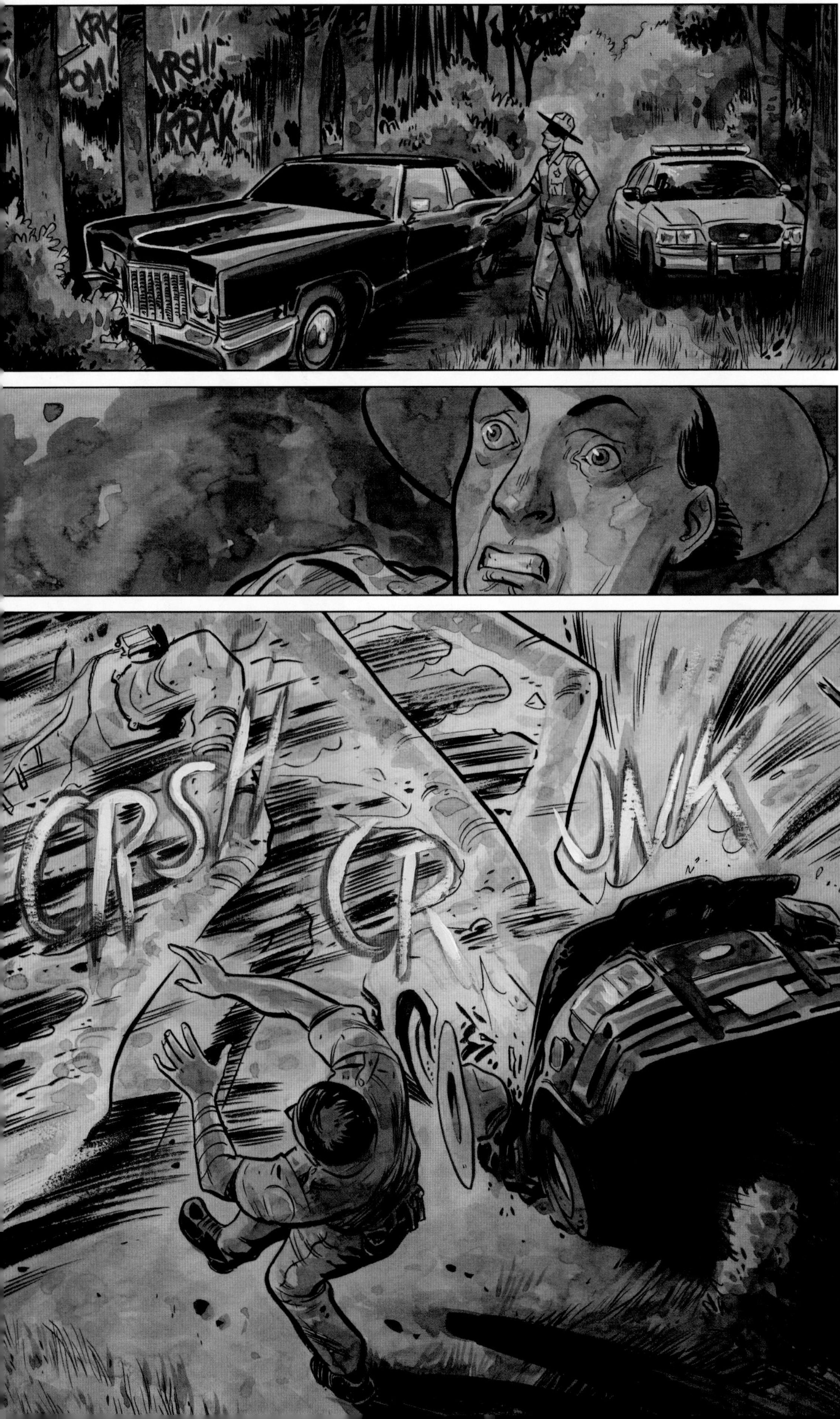
KRK
OOM!
KRSH!!
KRAK
CRSH
CRUNK

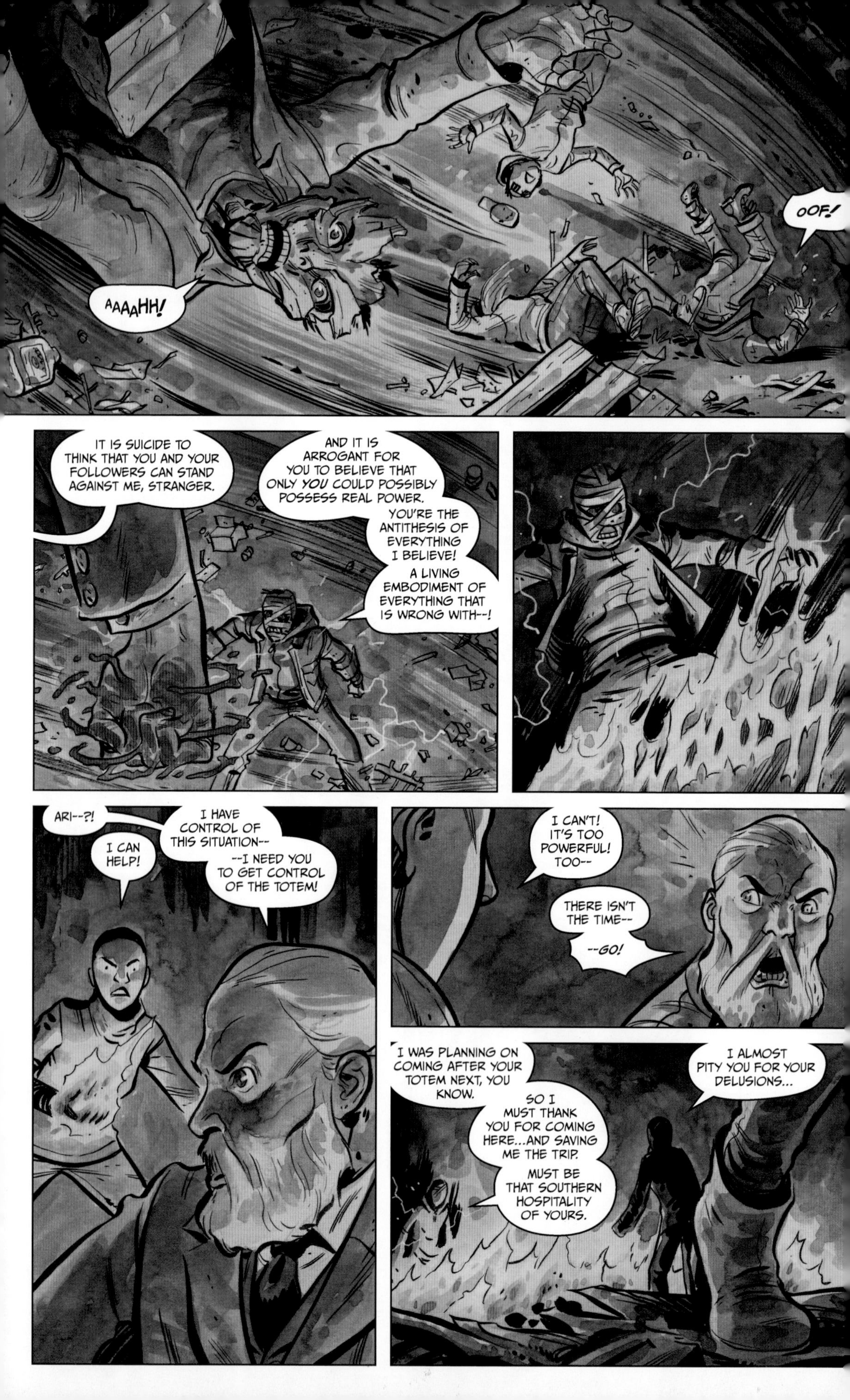
AAAAHH!
OOF!
IT IS SUICIDE TO THINK THAT YOU AND YOUR FOLLOWERS CAN STAND AGAINST ME, STRANGER.
AND IT IS ARROGANT FOR YOU TO BELIEVE THAT ONLY *YOU* COULD POSSIBLY POSSESS REAL POWER.
YOU'RE THE ANTITHESIS OF EVERYTHING I BELIEVE!
A LIVING EMBODIMENT OF EVERYTHING THAT IS WRONG WITH--!
ARI--?!
I HAVE CONTROL OF THIS SITUATION--
I CAN HELP!
--I NEED YOU TO GET CONTROL OF THE TOTEM!
I CAN'T! IT'S TOO POWERFUL! TOO--
THERE ISN'T THE TIME--
--GO!
I WAS PLANNING ON COMING AFTER YOUR TOTEM NEXT, YOU KNOW.
SO I MUST THANK YOU FOR COMING HERE...AND SAVING ME THE TRIP.
MUST BE THAT SOUTHERN HOSPITALITY OF YOURS.
I ALMOST PITY YOU FOR YOUR DELUSIONS...

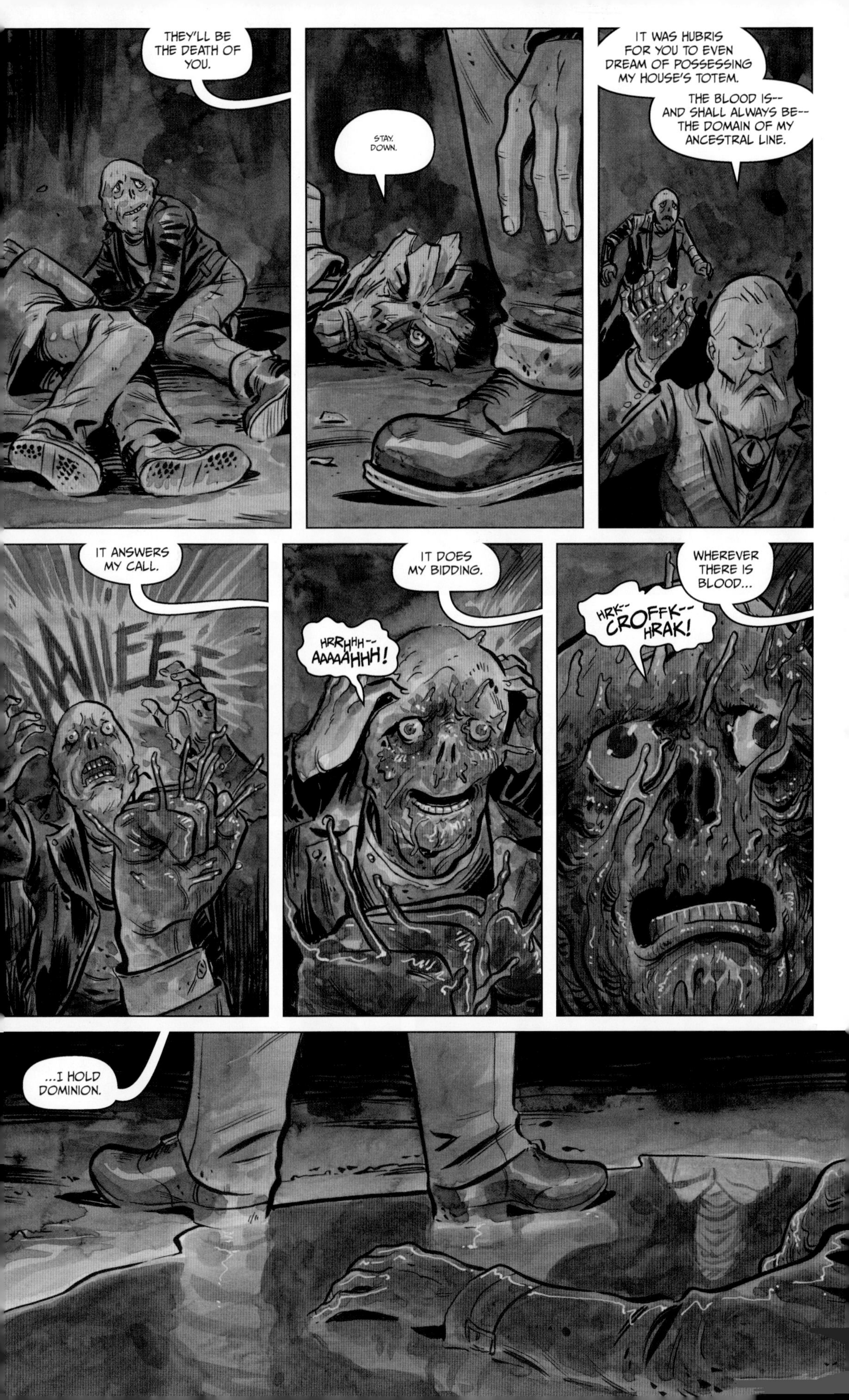
THEY'LL BE THE DEATH OF YOU.
STAY. DOWN.
IT WAS HUBRIS FOR YOU TO EVEN DREAM OF POSSESSING MY HOUSE'S TOTEM.
THE BLOOD IS-- AND SHALL ALWAYS BE-- THE DOMAIN OF MY ANCESTRAL LINE.
IT ANSWERS MY CALL.
IT DOES MY BIDDING.
HRRHHH-- AAAAAHHH!
WHEREVER THERE IS BLOOD...
HRK-- CROFFK-- HRAK!
...I HOLD DOMINION.

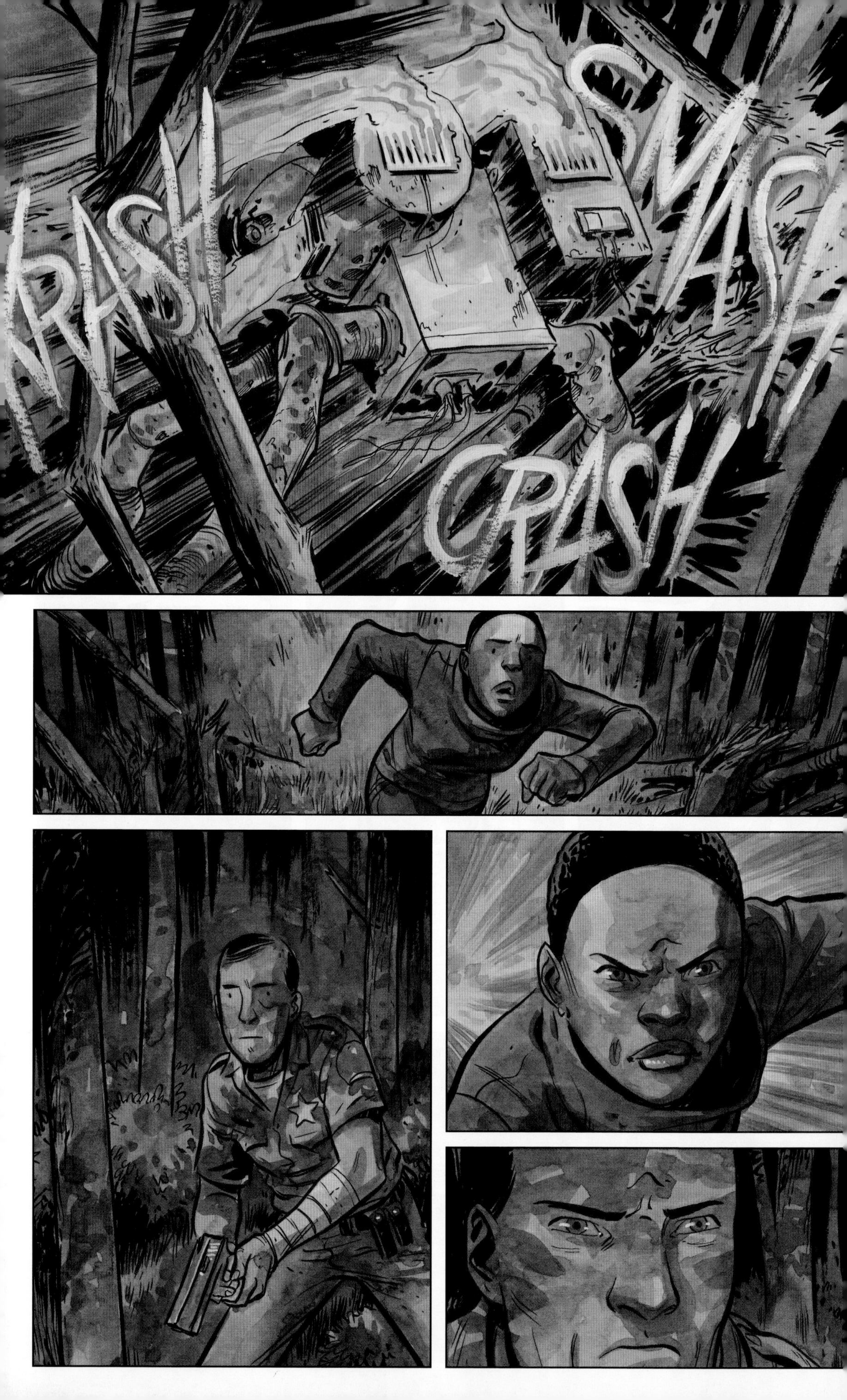

CRASH
SMASH
CRASH

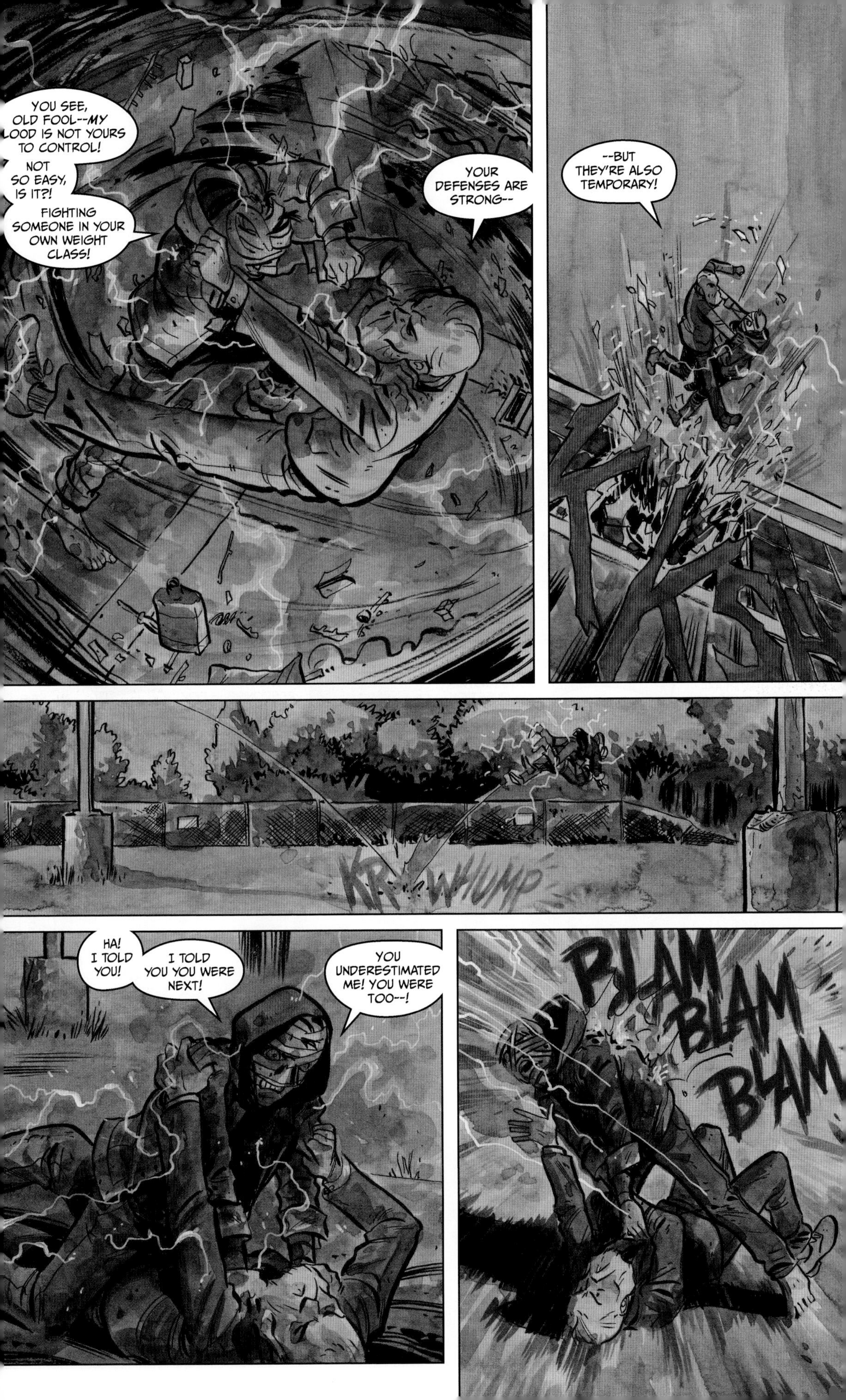
YOU SEE, OLD FOOL--MY LOOD IS NOT YOURS TO CONTROL!
NOT SO EASY, IS IT?!
FIGHTING SOMEONE IN YOUR OWN WEIGHT CLASS!
YOUR DEFENSES ARE STRONG--
--BUT THEY'RE ALSO TEMPORARY!
KRSH
KRWHUMP
HA! I TOLD YOU!
I TOLD YOU YOU WERE NEXT!
YOU UNDERESTIMATED ME! YOU WERE TOO--!
BLAM
BLAM
BLAM

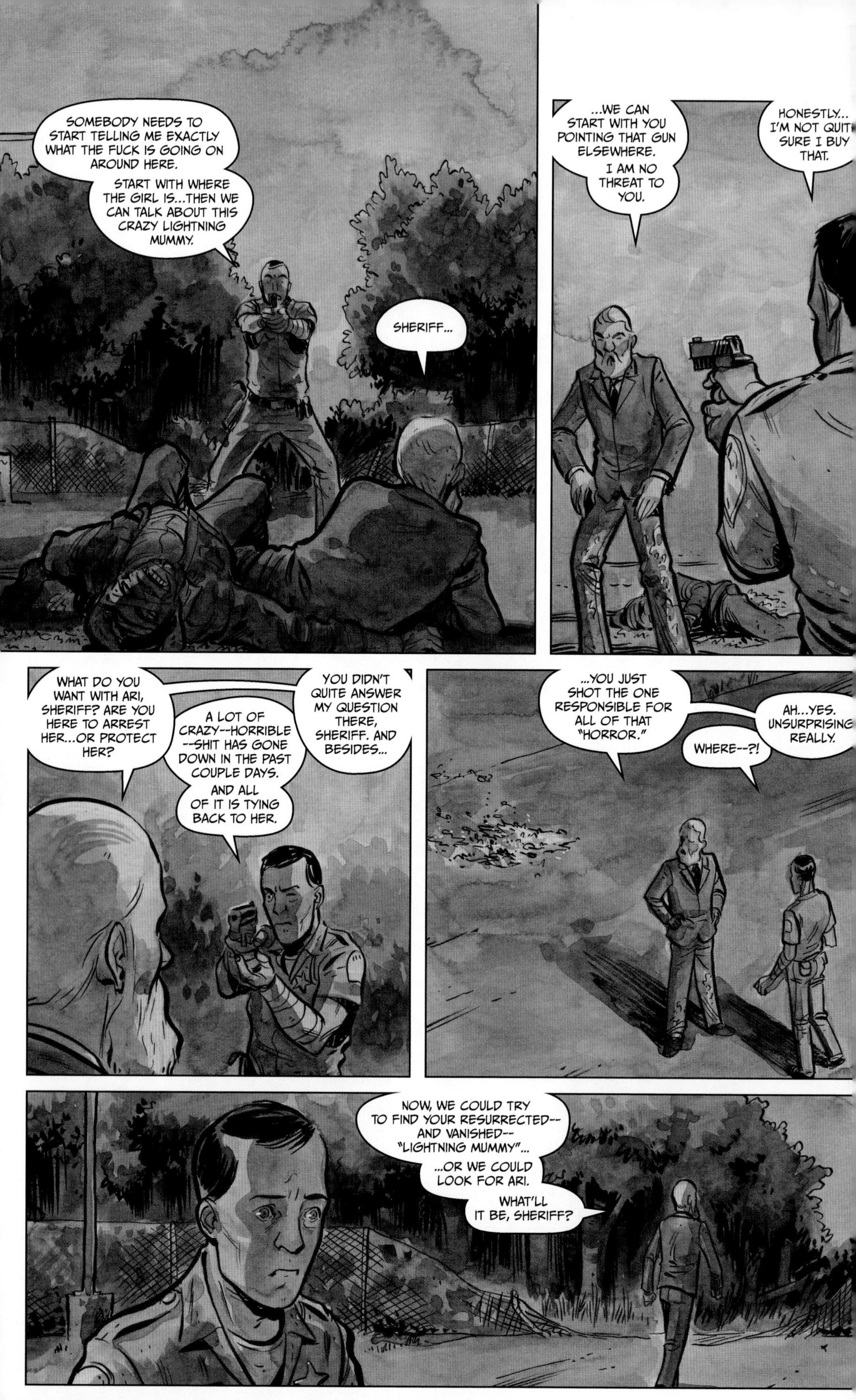
SOMEBODY NEEDS TO START TELLING ME EXACTLY WHAT THE FUCK IS GOING ON AROUND HERE.
START WITH WHERE THE GIRL IS...THEN WE CAN TALK ABOUT THIS CRAZY LIGHTNING MUMMY.
SHERIFF...
...WE CAN START WITH YOU POINTING THAT GUN ELSEWHERE.
I AM NO THREAT TO YOU.
HONESTLY... I'M NOT QUITE SURE I BUY THAT.
WHAT DO YOU WANT WITH ARI, SHERIFF? ARE YOU HERE TO ARREST HER...OR PROTECT HER?
A LOT OF CRAZY--HORRIBLE --SHIT HAS GONE DOWN IN THE PAST COUPLE DAYS.
AND ALL OF IT IS TYING BACK TO HER.
YOU DIDN'T QUITE ANSWER MY QUESTION THERE, SHERIFF. AND BESIDES...
...YOU JUST SHOT THE ONE RESPONSIBLE FOR ALL OF THAT "HORROR."
WHERE--?!
AH...YES. UNSURPRISING REALLY.
NOW, WE COULD TRY TO FIND YOUR RESURRECTED-- AND VANISHED-- "LIGHTNING MUMMY"...
...OR WE COULD LOOK FOR ARI.
WHAT'LL IT BE, SHERIFF?

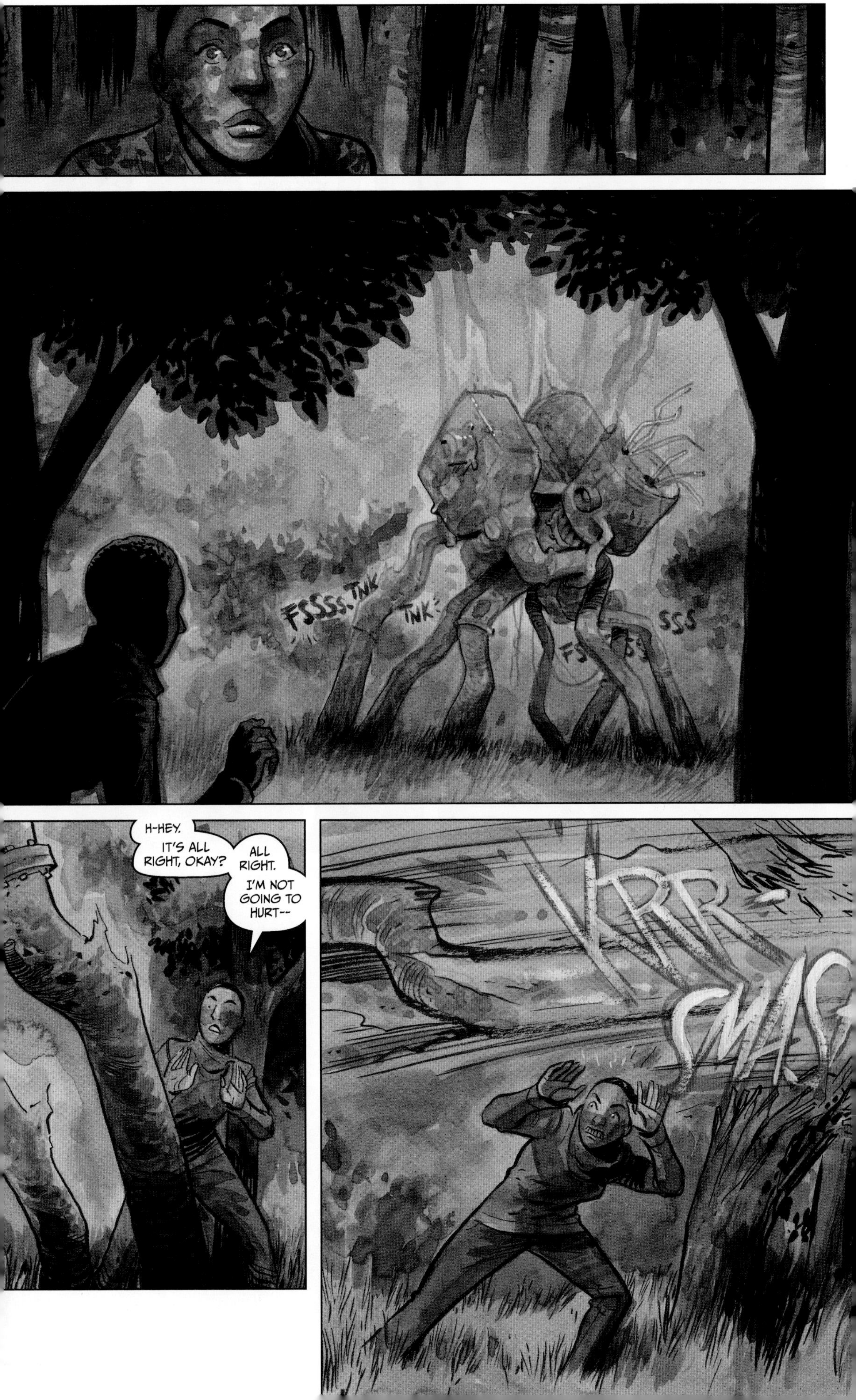
FSSSS TNK
TNK
SSS
FS
H-HEY.
IT'S ALL RIGHT, OKAY?
ALL RIGHT.
I'M NOT GOING TO HURT--
VRR-
SMAS

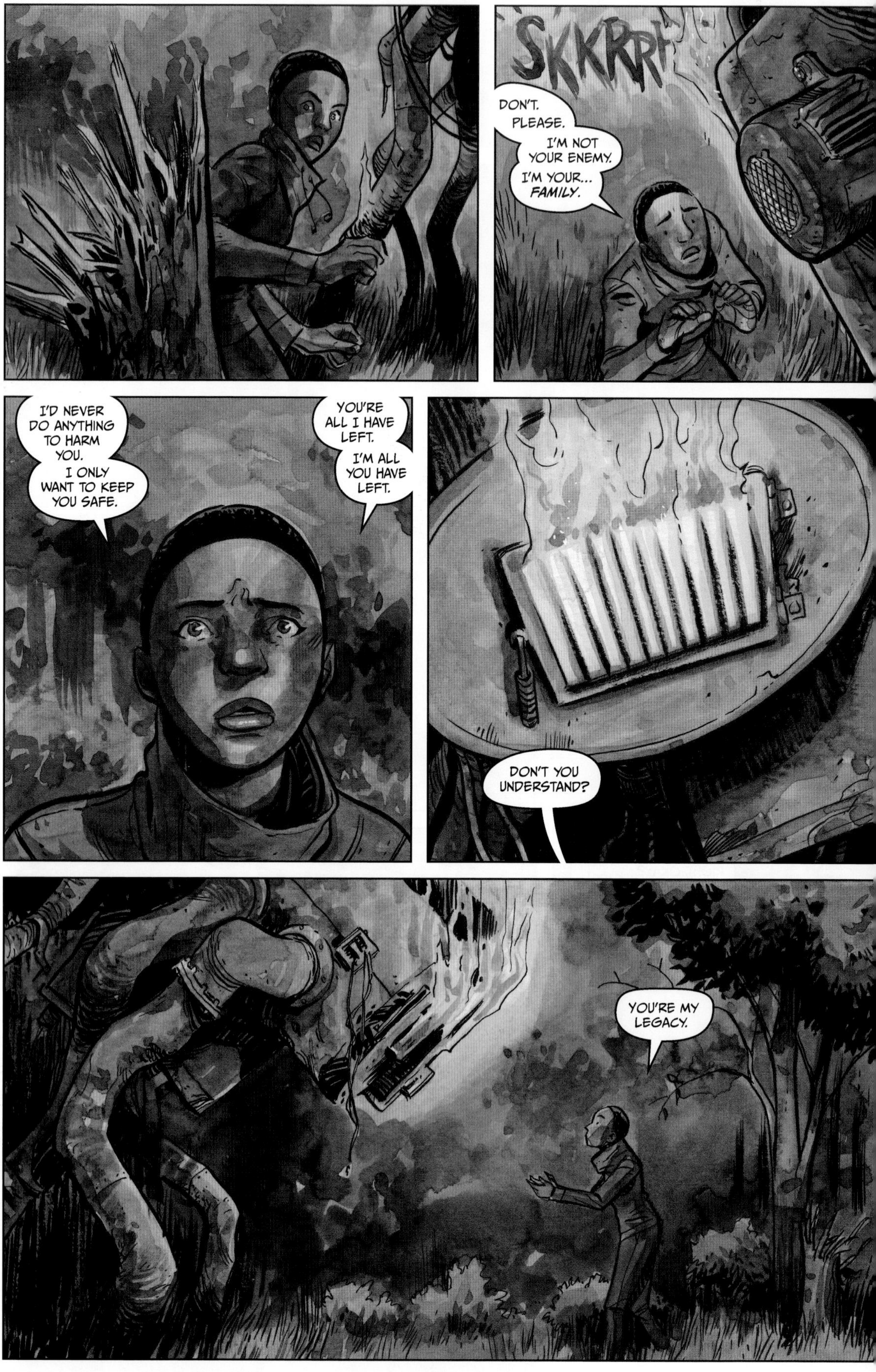
SKKRRF
DON'T.
PLEASE.
I'M NOT YOUR ENEMY.
I'M YOUR... *FAMILY*.
I'D NEVER DO ANYTHING TO HARM YOU.
I ONLY WANT TO KEEP YOU SAFE.
YOU'RE ALL I HAVE LEFT.
I'M ALL YOU HAVE LEFT.
DON'T YOU UNDERSTAND?
YOU'RE MY LEGACY.

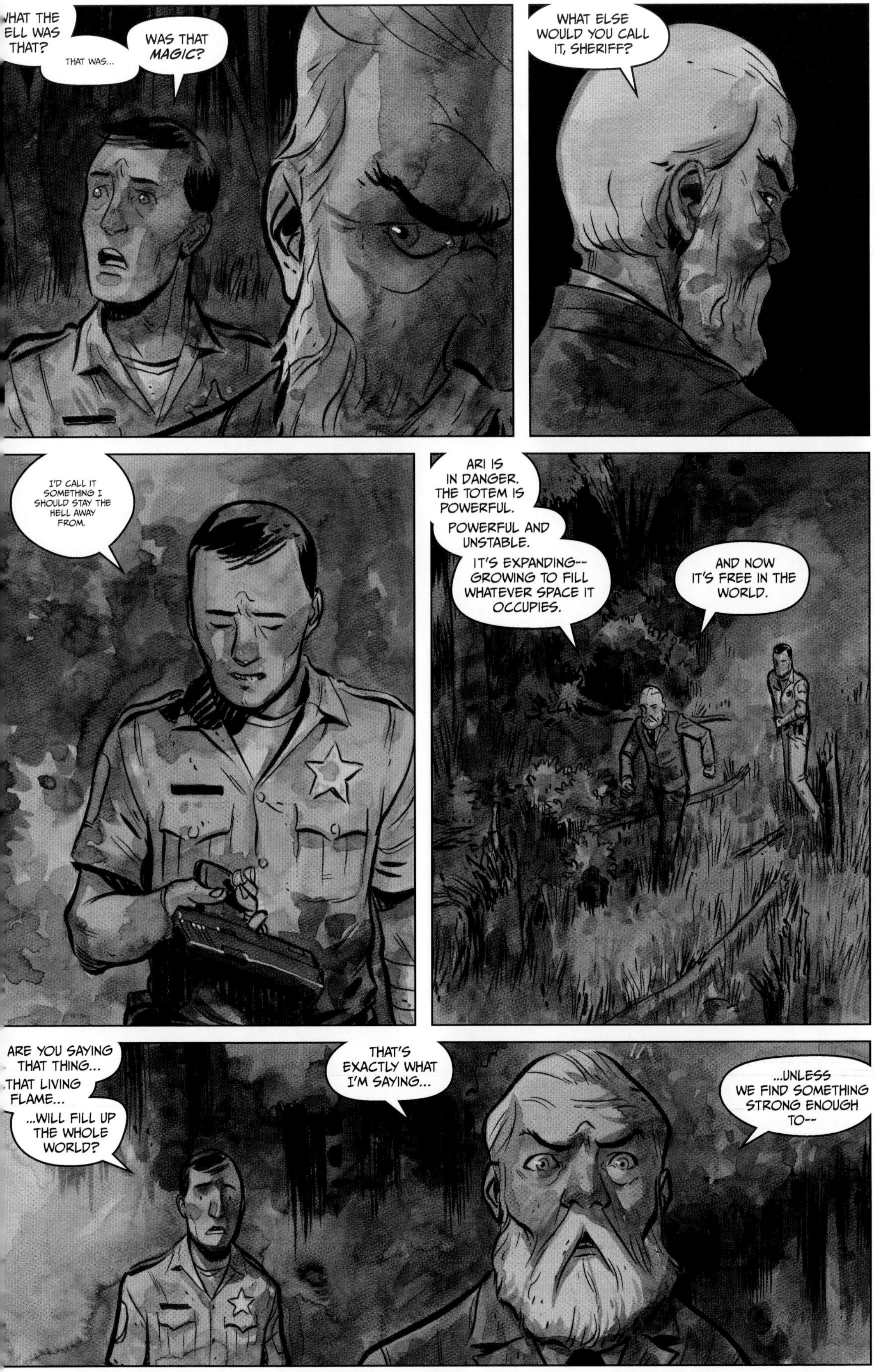
WHAT THE
HELL WAS
THAT?
THAT WAS...
WAS THAT *MAGIC?*
WHAT ELSE
WOULD YOU CALL
IT, SHERIFF?
I'D CALL IT SOMETHING I SHOULD STAY THE HELL AWAY FROM.
ARI IS IN DANGER. THE TOTEM IS POWERFUL.
POWERFUL AND UNSTABLE.
IT'S EXPANDING-- GROWING TO FILL WHATEVER SPACE IT OCCUPIES.
AND NOW IT'S FREE IN THE WORLD.
ARE YOU SAYING THAT THING...
...THAT LIVING FLAME...
...WILL FILL UP THE WHOLE WORLD?
THAT'S EXACTLY WHAT I'M SAYING...
...UNLESS WE FIND SOMETHING STRONG ENOUGH TO--

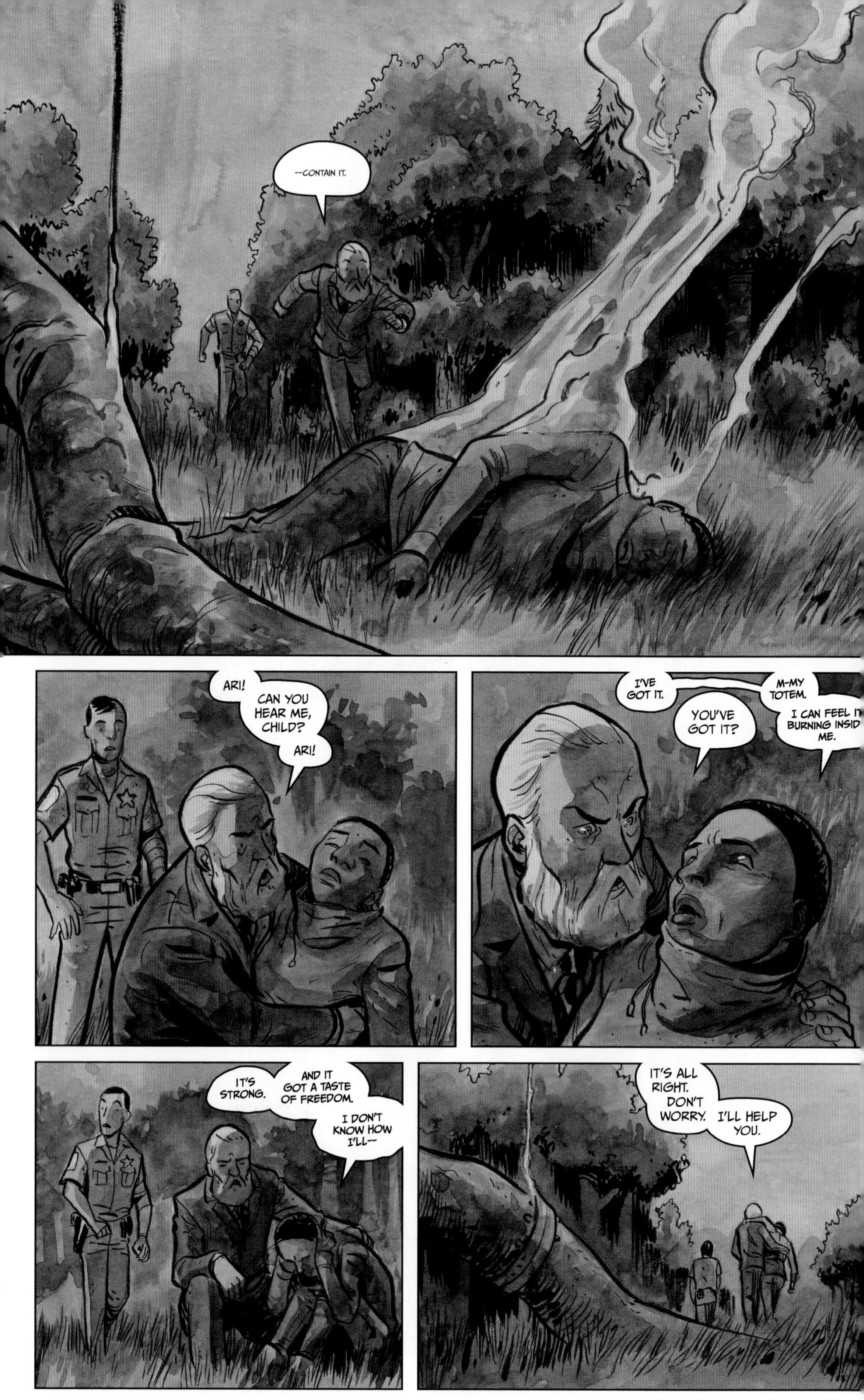
--CONTAIN IT.
ARI!
CAN YOU HEAR ME, CHILD?
ARI!
I'VE GOT IT.
M-MY TOTEM.
YOU'VE GOT IT?
I CAN FEEL I
BURNING INSID
ME.
IT'S STRONG.
AND IT GOT A TASTE OF FREEDOM.
I DON'T KNOW HOW I'LL--
IT'S ALL RIGHT.
DON'T WORRY.
I'LL HELP YOU.

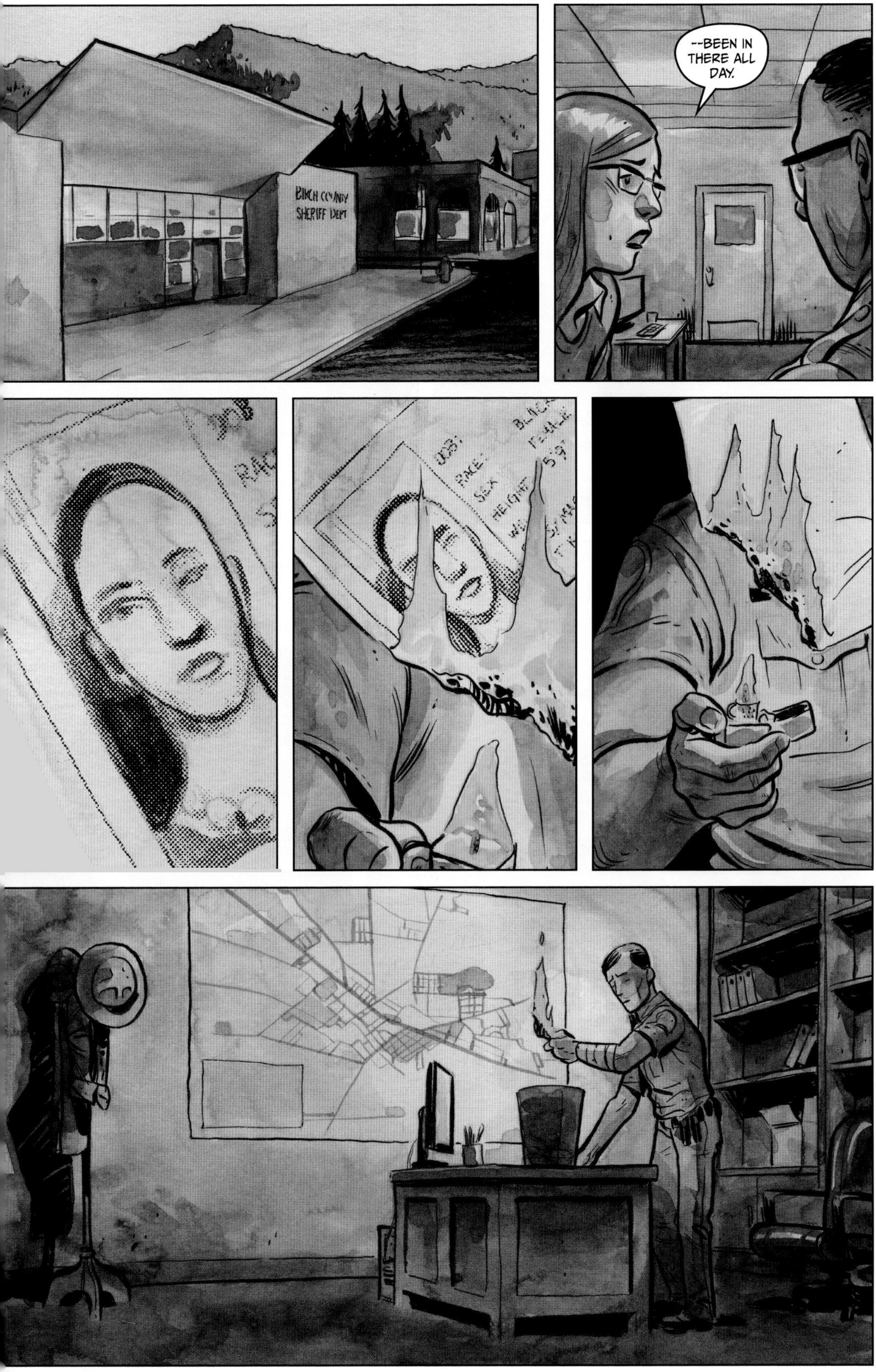
BIRCH COUNTY SHERIFF DEPT
--BEEN IN THERE ALL DAY.
DOB:
RACE
SEX
HEIGHT

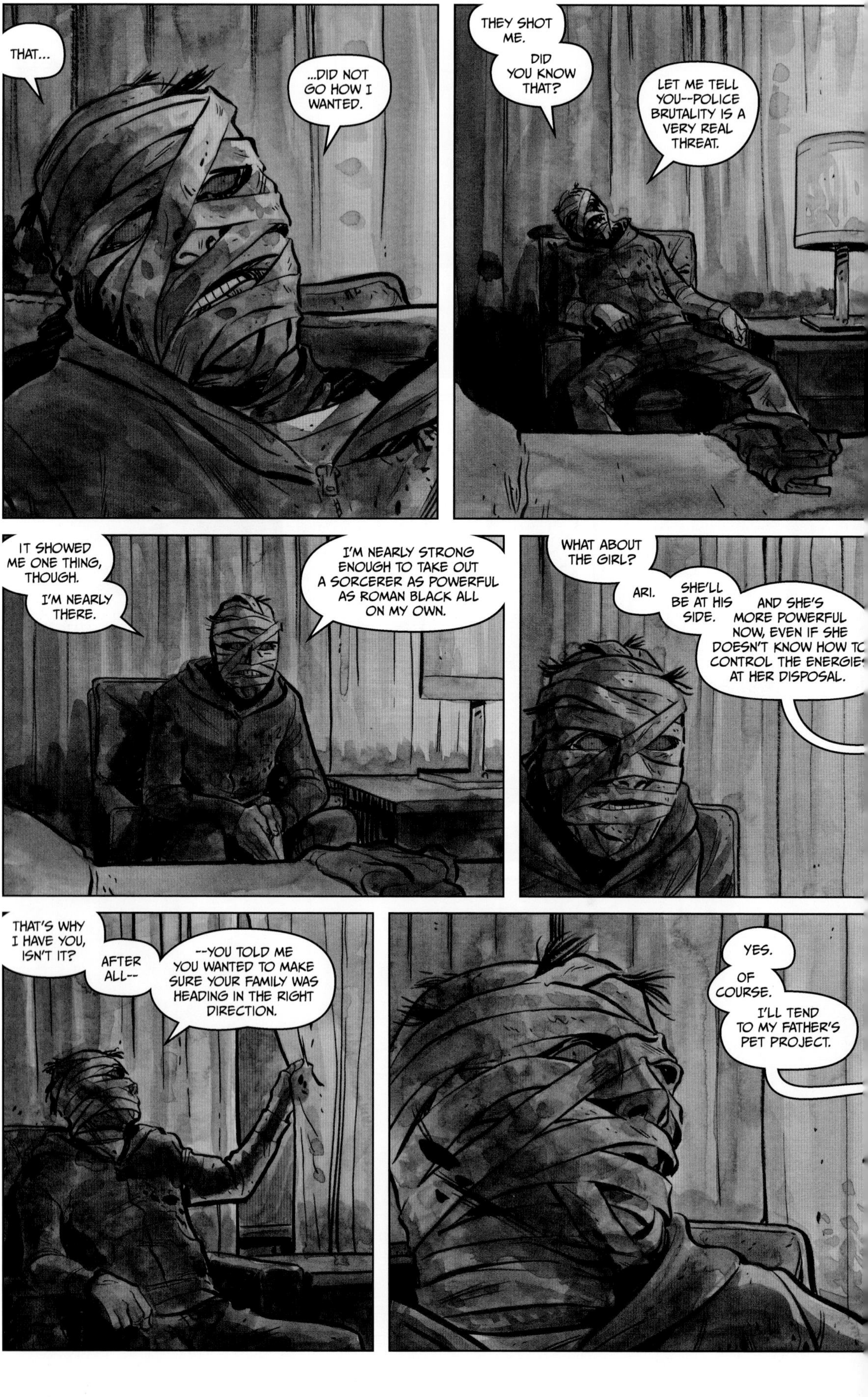
THAT...
...DID NOT GO HOW I WANTED.
THEY SHOT ME.
DID YOU KNOW THAT?
LET ME TELL YOU--POLICE BRUTALITY IS A VERY REAL THREAT.
IT SHOWED ME ONE THING, THOUGH.
I'M NEARLY THERE.
I'M NEARLY STRONG ENOUGH TO TAKE OUT A SORCERER AS POWERFUL AS ROMAN BLACK ALL ON MY OWN.
WHAT ABOUT THE GIRL?
ARI.
SHE'LL BE AT HIS SIDE.
AND SHE'S MORE POWERFUL NOW, EVEN IF SHE DOESN'T KNOW HOW TO CONTROL THE ENERGIES AT HER DISPOSAL.
THAT'S WHY I HAVE YOU, ISN'T IT?
AFTER ALL--
--YOU TOLD ME YOU WANTED TO MAKE SURE YOUR FAMILY WAS HEADING IN THE RIGHT DIRECTION.
YES.
OF COURSE.
I'LL TEND TO MY FATHER'S PET PROJECT.

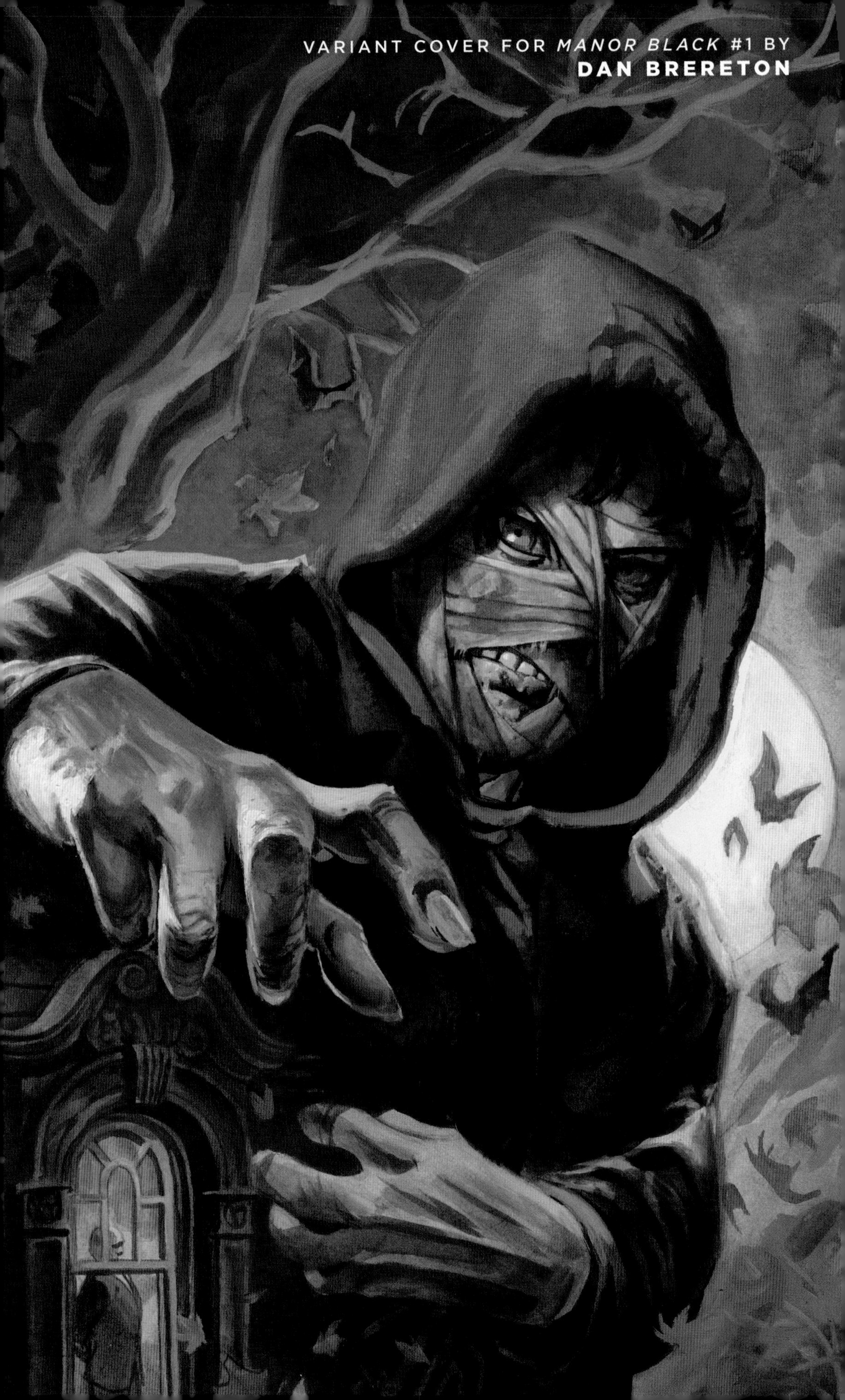

VARIANT COVER FOR *MANOR BLACK* #1 BY
DAN BRERETON

VARIANT COVER FOR *MANOR BLACK* #2 BY
JILL THOMPSON

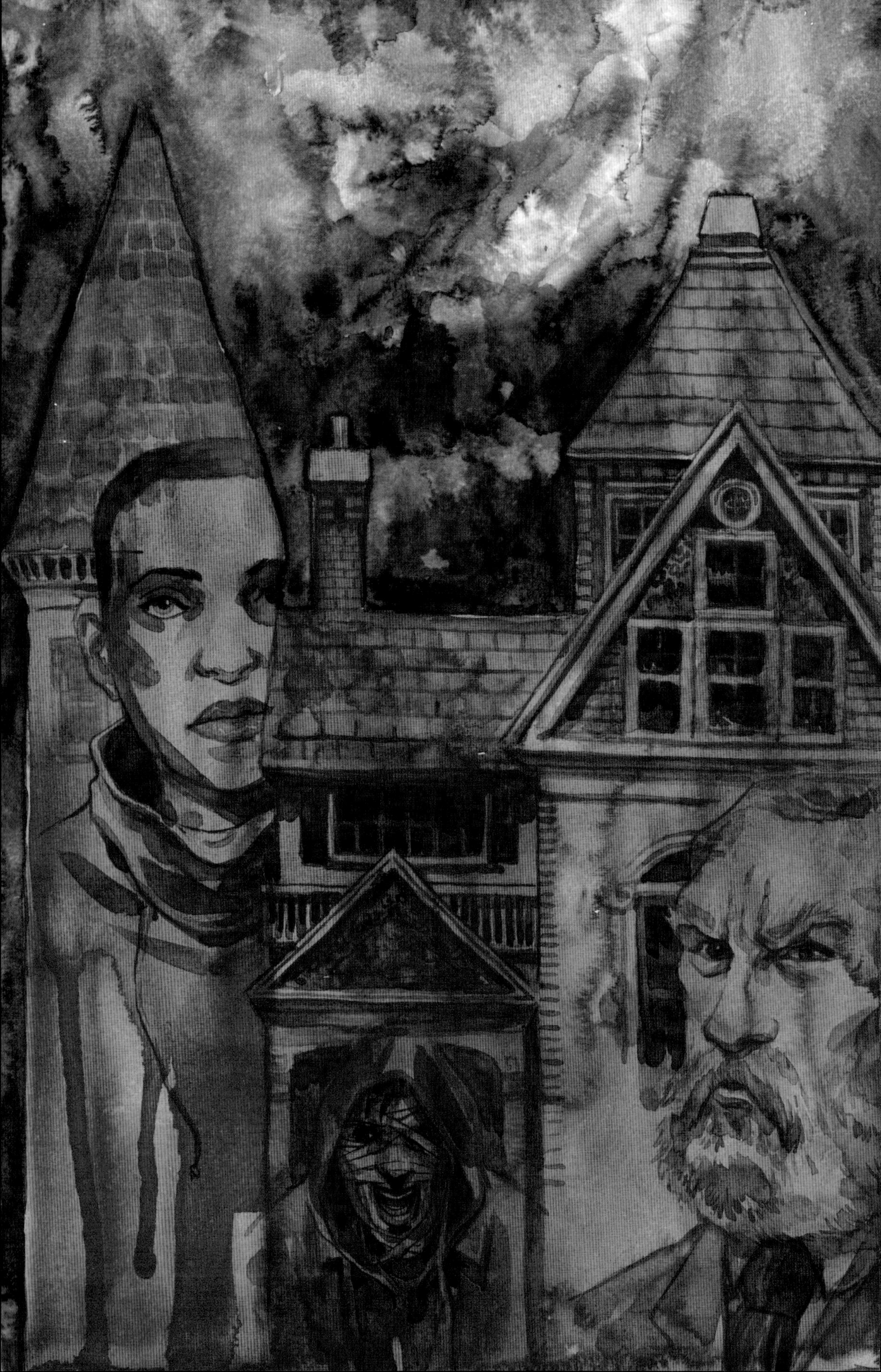

VARIANT COVER FOR *MANOR BLACK* #3 BY
GREG SMALLWOOD

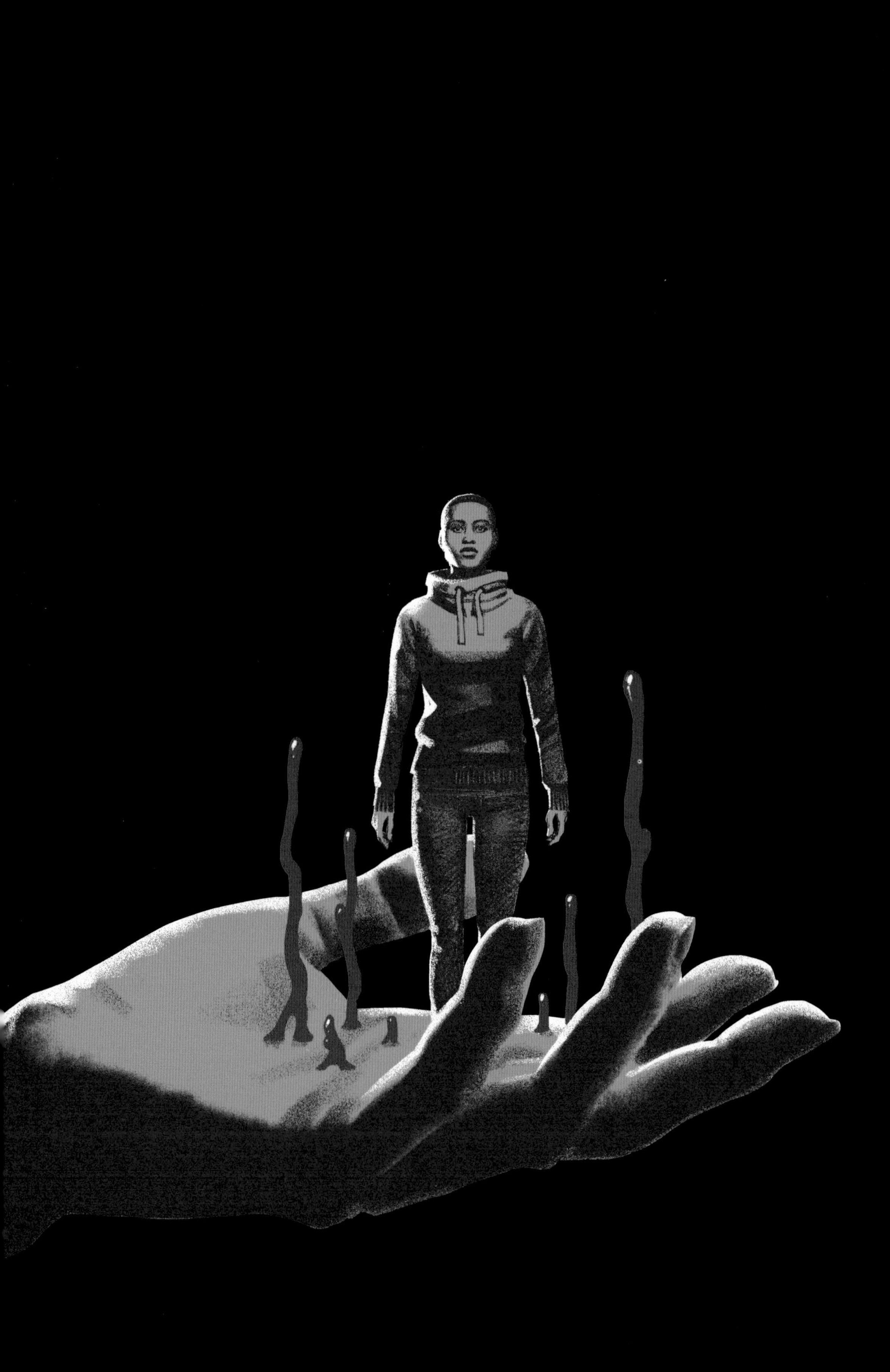

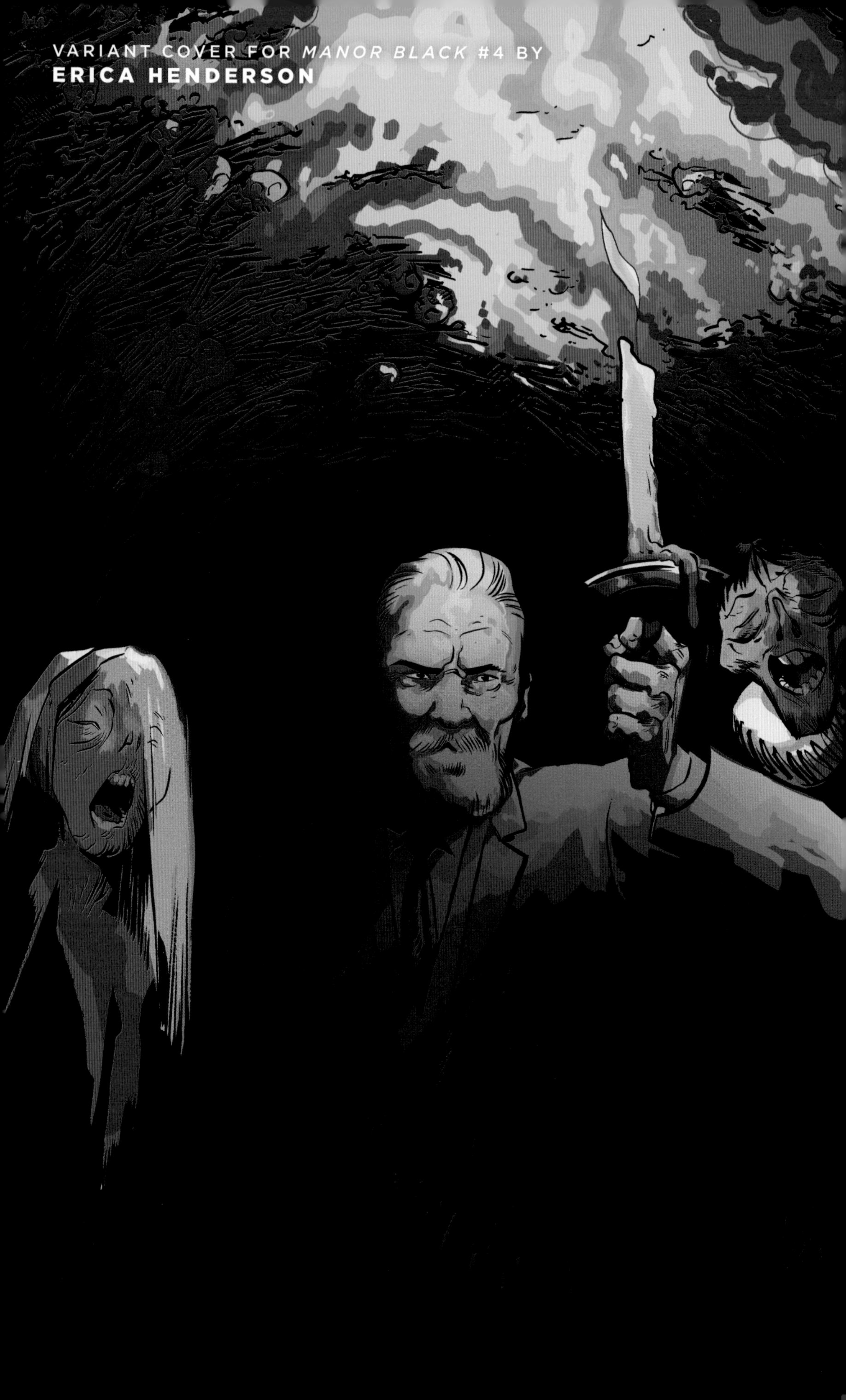

VARIANT COVER FOR *MANOR BLACK* #4 BY
ERICA HENDERSON

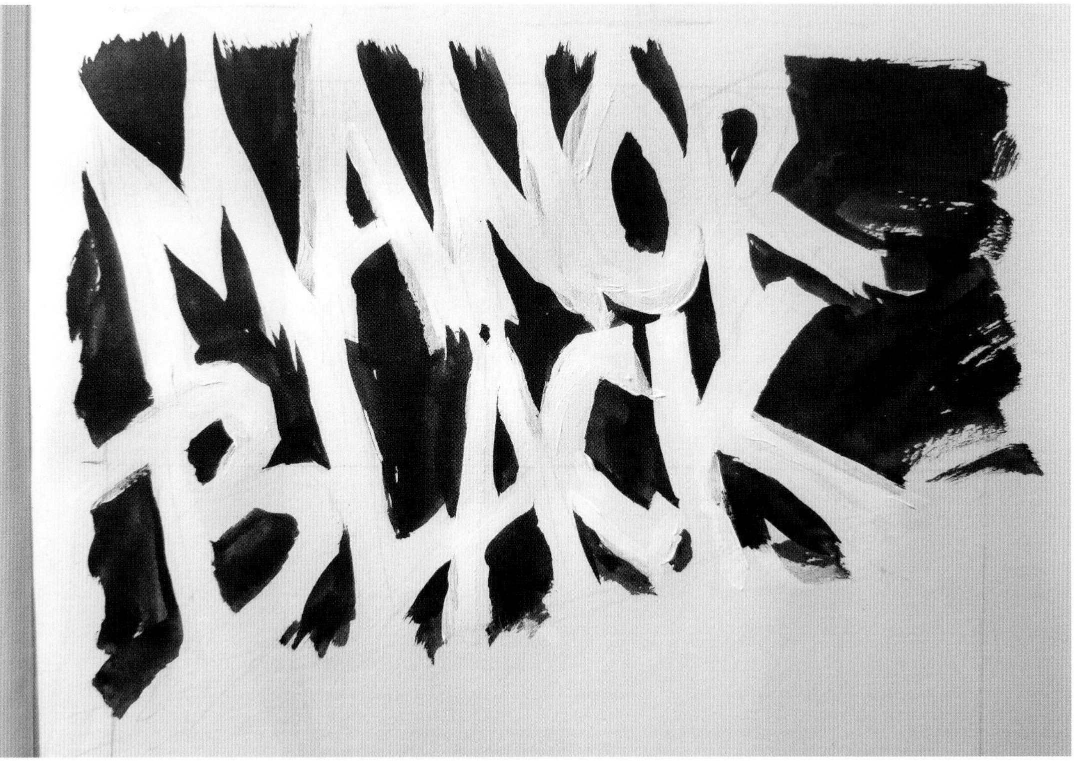
MANOR
BLACK

SKETCHBOOK

NOTES BY
TYLER CROOK

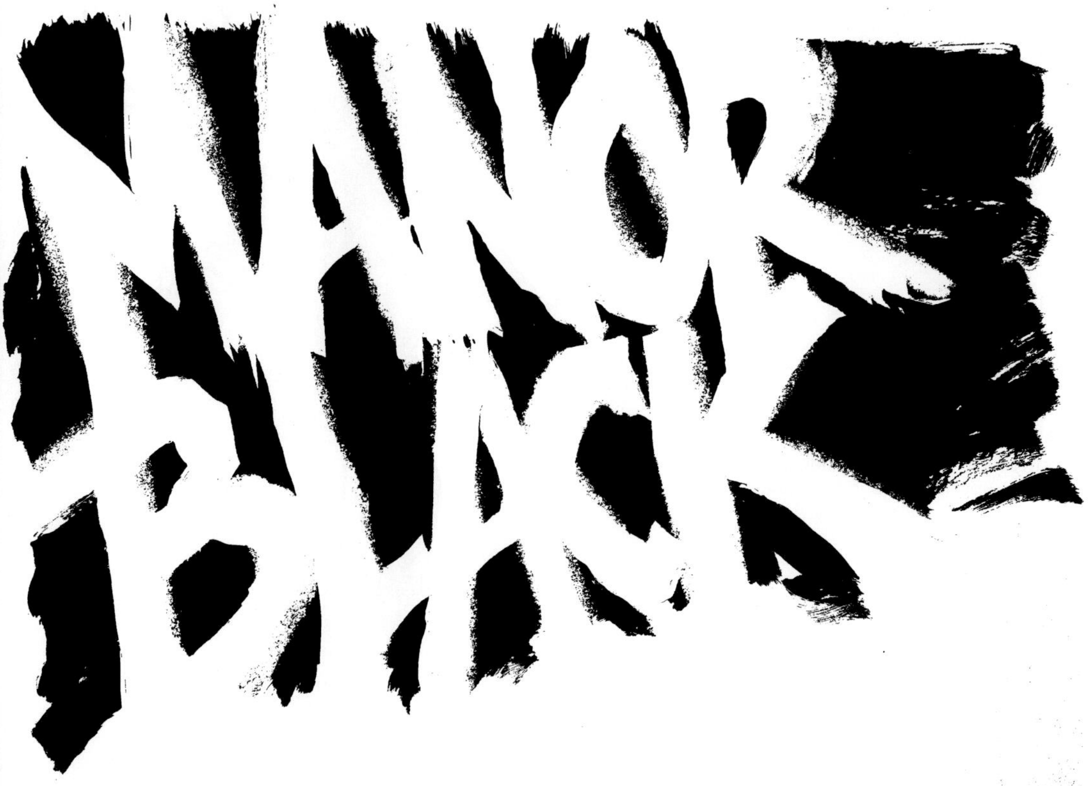
MANOR
BLACK

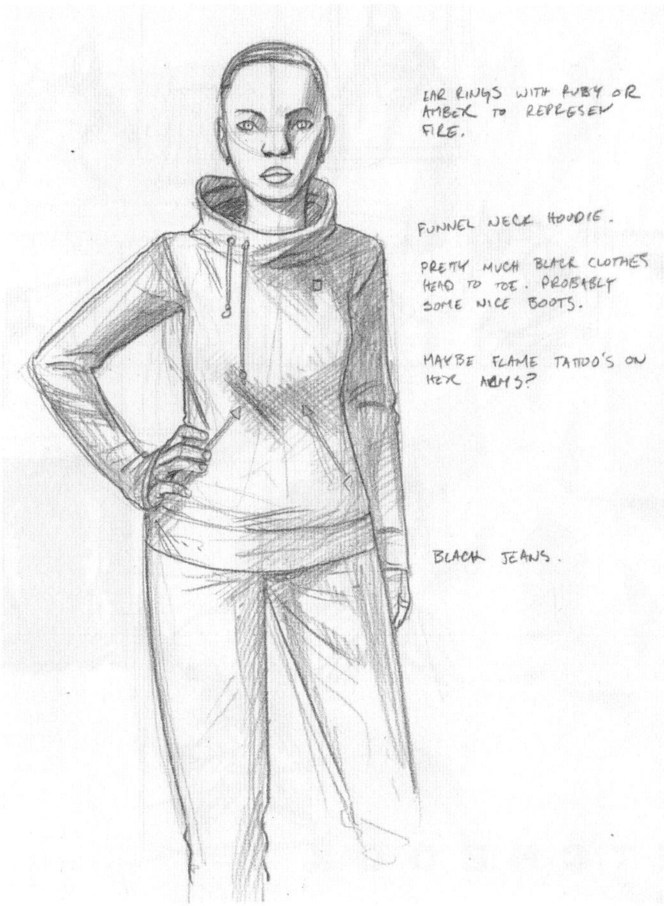
EAR RINGS WITH RUBY OR AMBER TO REPRESEN FIRE.
FUNNEL NECK HOODIE.
PRETTY MUCH BLACK CLOTHES HEAD TO TOE. PROBABLY SOME NICE BOOTS.
MAYBE FLAME TATTOO'S ON HER ARMS?
BLACK JEANS.

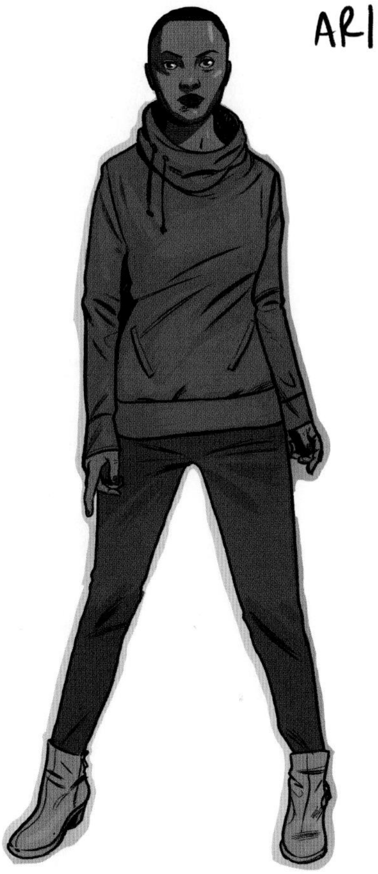
ARI

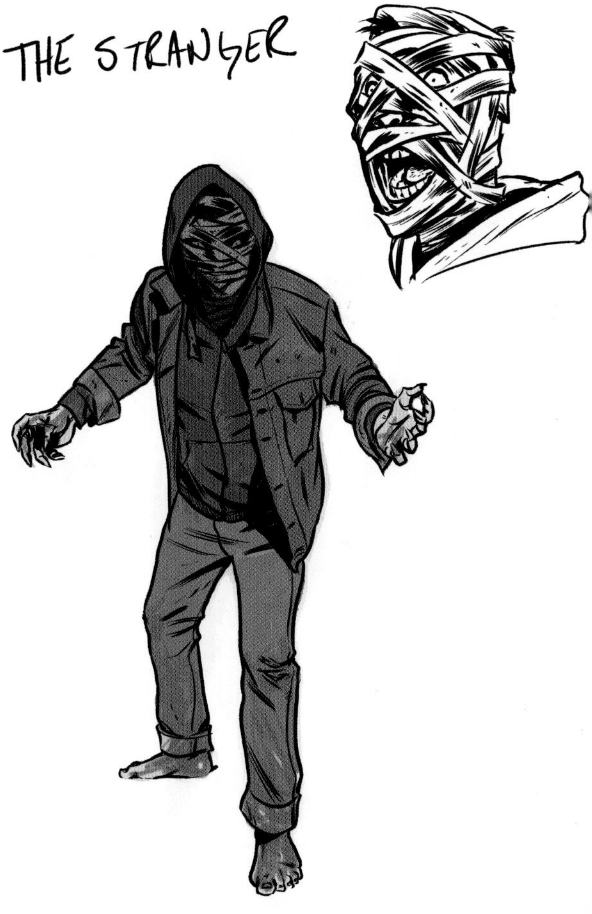
THE STRANGER

ARI

This is pretty much the first and final design for Ari. Brian explained that she was a black woman in her twenties and that she had really short hair. And that was all I really needed. I'd seen that kind of hoodie on a lady who has a woodworking YouTube channel and I though it looked super comfy, but also looked a little bit like the kind of hood a wizard would wear.

THE STRANGER

Originally, Brian wanted the Stranger to dress a little more formal—similar to Roman. But to me, he needed to look a lot more chaotic and wild. So I pitched this "dirty jean jacket" look as a contrast to Roman's nice suits.

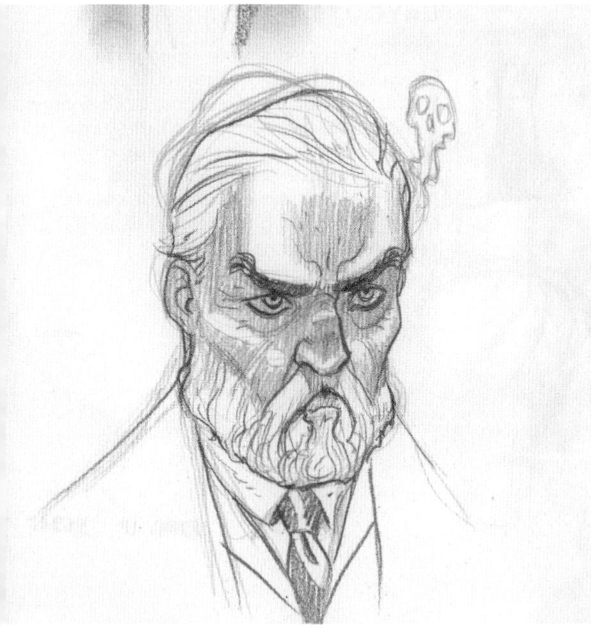

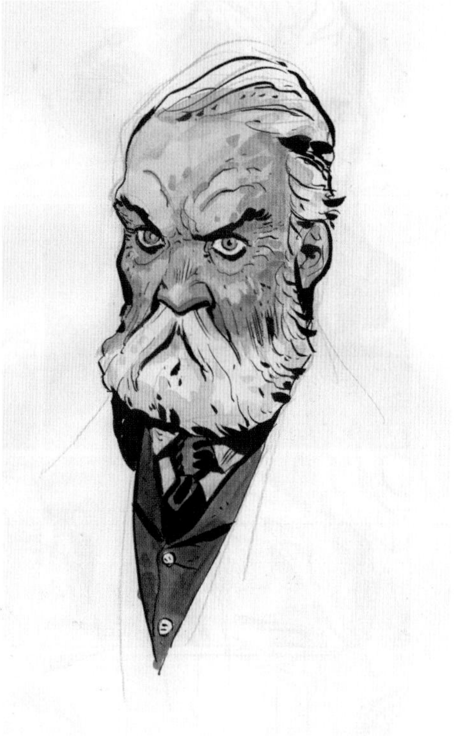

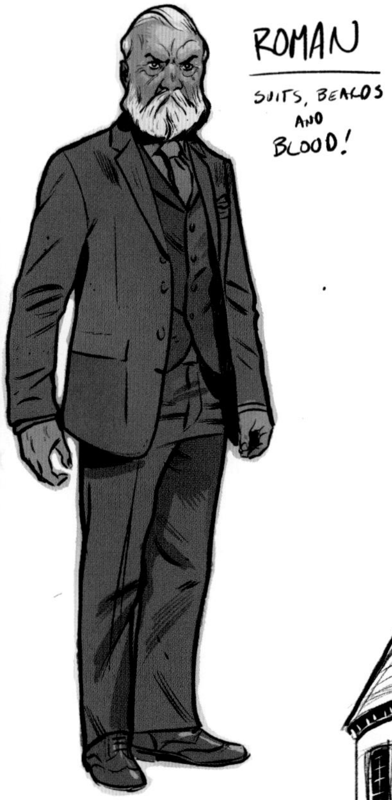
ROMAN
SUITS, BEARDS AND BLOOD!

ROMAN

I wanted Roman to look nice, but a little bit outdated. His brown suits feel like they would have been the bomb in 1983. I had initially wanted to make him very blue or gray skinned, but on deeper thought, it seemed a bit over the top. It would be weird if he was a blue dude walking around people who weren't noticing it.

THE MANOR HOUSE

I had the idea of putting the manor house in a crater at first. I thought it would have been weird and interesting, but Cullen and Brian both felt like the house needed to be able to be seen in silhouette and that would have been hard if it was inside of a hole. The house itself is a composite of a bunch of different fancy brick houses from the 18th and 19th century.

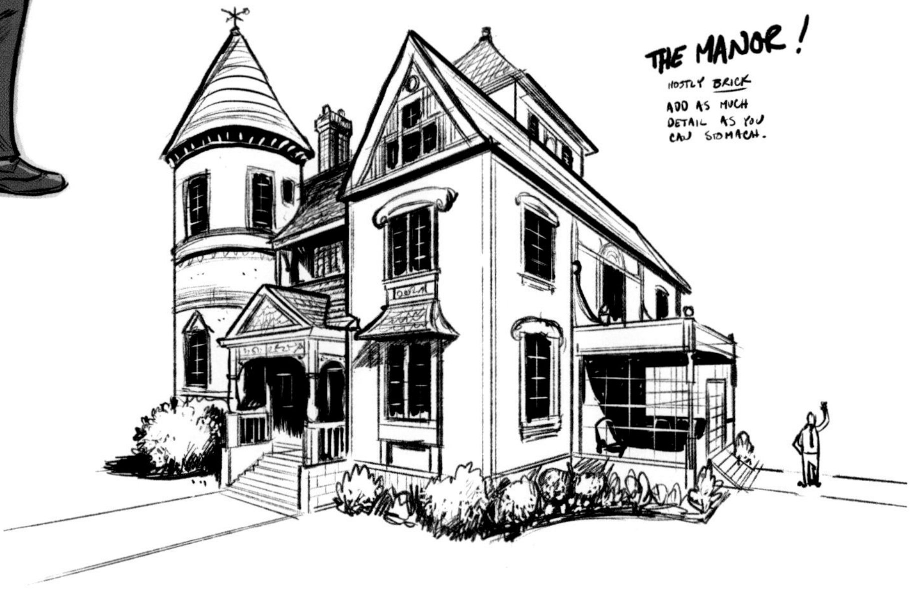
THE MANOR!
MOSTLY BRICK
ADD AS MUCH DETAIL AS YOU CAN STOMACH.

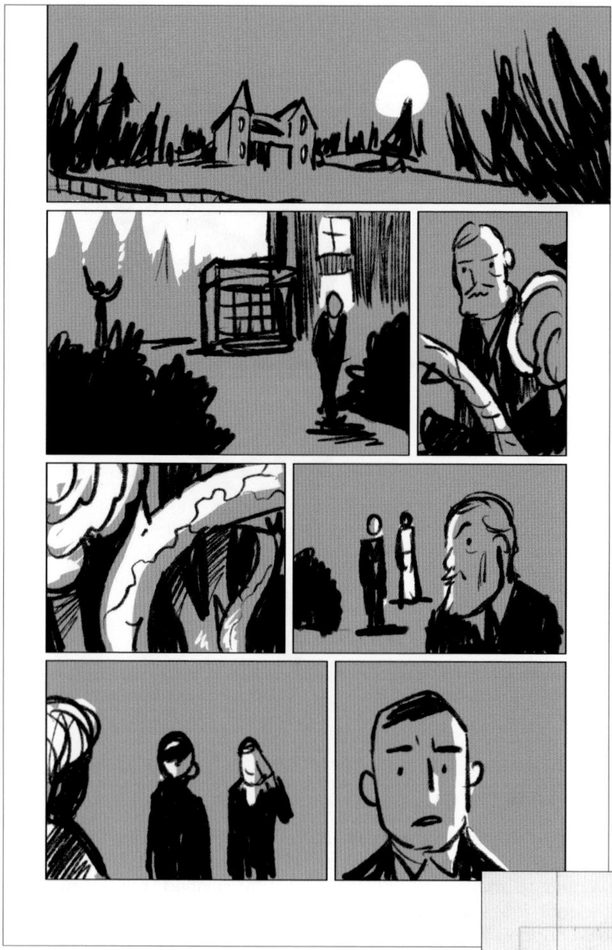

LAYOUTS

I start each page by doing rough layouts on my computer or iPad. Doing layouts is for me the hardest part of making a comic. It's a process of problem solving were I am trying to figure out the best way to compose each panel so that they make sense, look good, and have the emotional impact I want. It can take me anywhere from two to five days to lay out out a twenty-two-page issue.

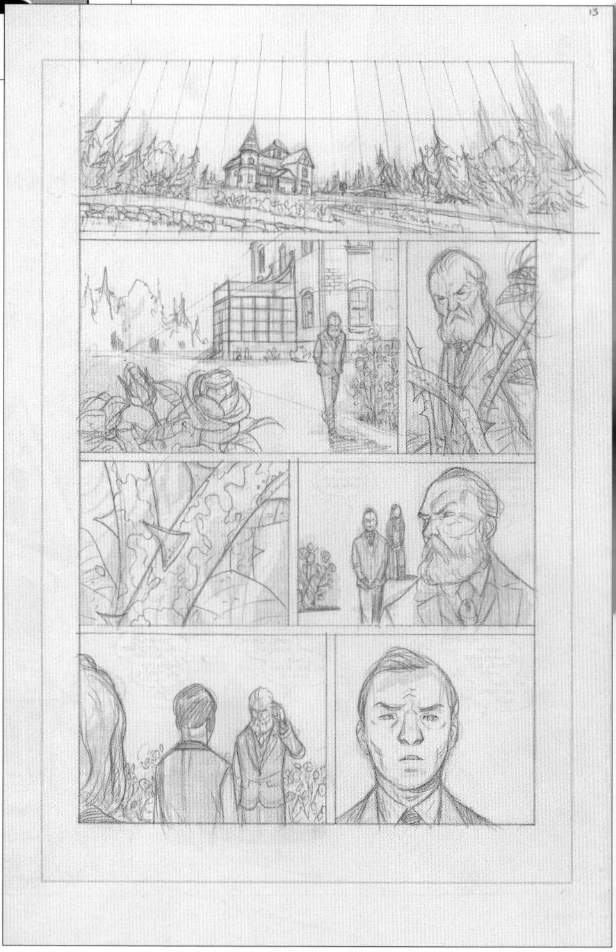

PENCILS

From there, I print the layouts on 11 x 17 paper as a light pink. I rough in all the drawings with a red pencil and then tighten up them up with a regular pencil. When I scan the pencils into the computer, I can remove all the reds and pinks, leaving just the final pencil lines.

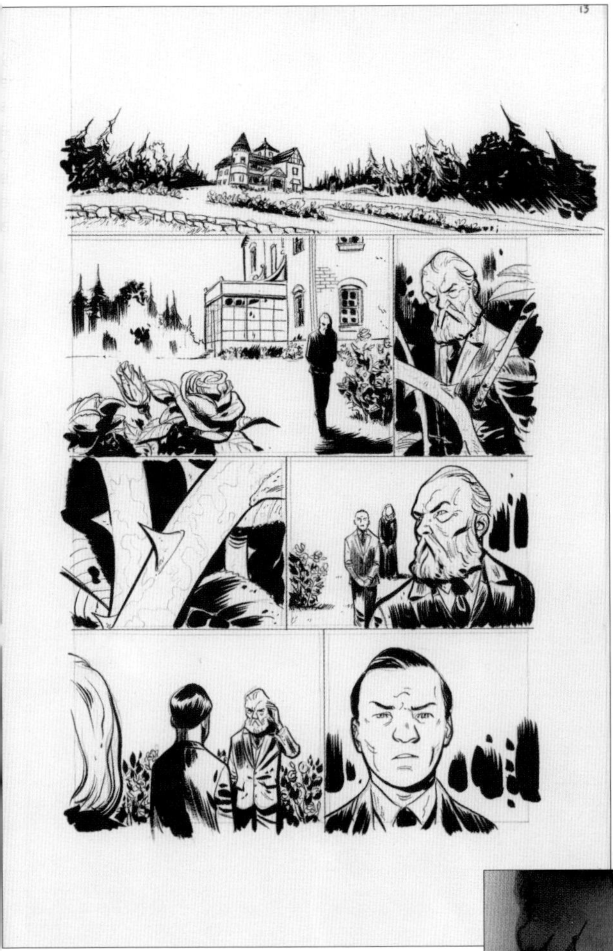

INKS

Once I get the pencils cleaned up, I print them out as a brown line onto my nice paper. I've been using Strathmore 400 Series mixed-media paper for a few years now, and it's proved to be a real work horse. I ink with FW ink because it is an acrylic ink and dries waterproof, so I can paint right over the top of it.

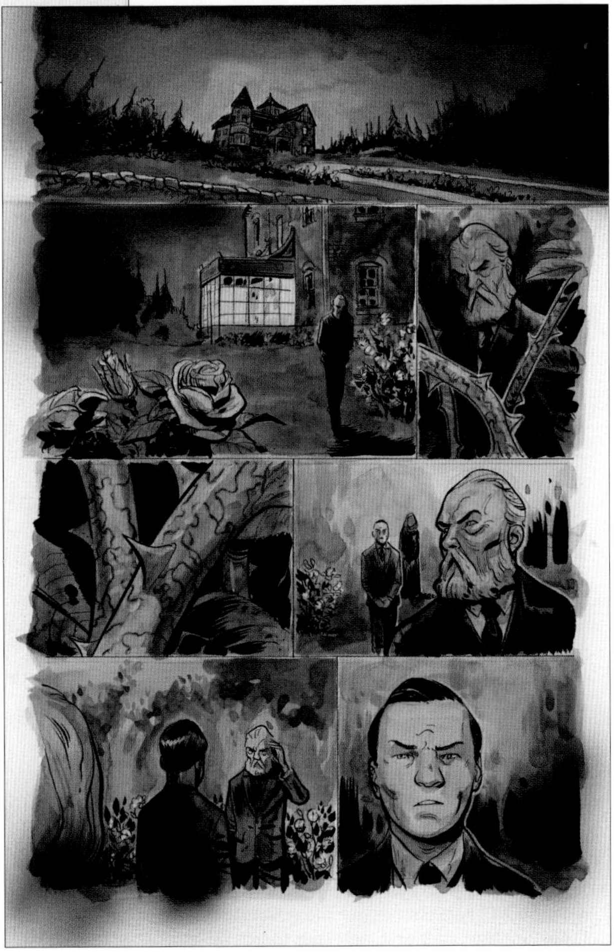

COLOR

I color my pages with a mix of watercolor, colored inks, and color pencils. For *Manor Black* I wanted to try doing the panel borders digitally in order to save time. It ended up saving me between twenty minutes to an hour on each page. In spite of the time savings, I don't think I'll do it again. It's better to see the panel borders while I'm working so I can better judge how the page is reading while I'm working on it. It was a worthwhile experiment though.

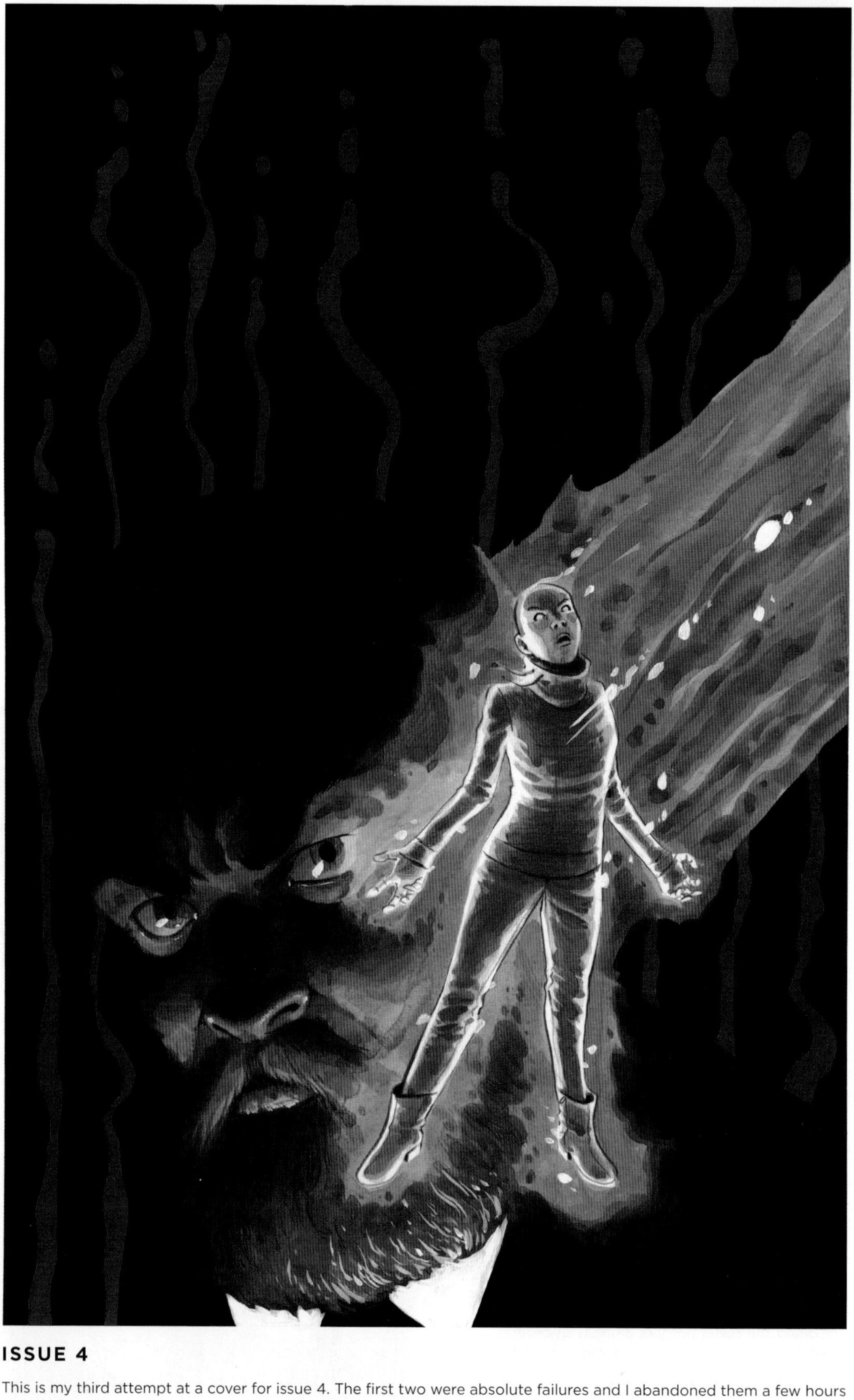

ISSUE 4

This is my third attempt at a cover for issue 4. The first two were absolute failures and I abandoned them a few hours after starting them. This one I actually finished even though I hated it the whole time I was painting it. But the deadline was calling, and so I wrapped it up and turned it in. A few months later, as I was wrapping up the interior art for issue 4, I asked if I had time to get the cover right. Luckily we had a few days before the files had to go out to the printer, so I took another stab at it, and that fourth attempt is what we finally used.

MORE TITLES FROM

TYLER CROOK, CULLEN BUNN,
AND DARK HORSE

HARROW COUNTY LIBRARY EDITION
Tyler Crook, Cullen Bunn, Carla Speed McNeil, and Jenn Manley Lee

VOLUME 1
ISBN 978-1-50671-064-8 | $39.99

VOLUME 2
ISBN 978-1-50671-065-5 | $39.99

VOLUME 3
ISBN 978-1-50671-066-2 | $39.99

VOLUME 4
ISBN 978-1-50671-067-9 | $39.99

HARROW COUNTY VOLUME 1: COUNTLESS HAINTS
Tyler Crook and Cullen Bunn
ISBN 978-1-61655-780-5 | $14.99

HARROW COUNTY VOLUME 2: TWICE TOLD
Tyler Crook and Cullen Bunn
ISBN 978-1-61655-900-7 | $17.99

HARROW COUNTY VOLUME 3: SNAKE DOCTOR
Tyler Crook and Cullen Bunn with
Carla Speed McNeil and Hannah Christenson
ISBN 978-1-50670-071-7 | $17.99

HARROW COUNTY VOLUME 4: FAMILY TREE
Tyler Crook and Cullen Bunn
ISBN 978-1-50670-141-7 | $17.99

HARROW COUNTY VOLUME 5: ABANDONED
Tyler Crook and Cullen Bunn with Carla Speed McNeil
ISBN 978-1-50670-190-5 | $17.99

HARROW COUNTY VOLUME 6: HEDGE MAGIC
Tyler Crook and Cullen Bunn
ISBN 978-1-50670-208-7 | $17.99

HARROW COUNTY VOLUME 7: DARK TIMES A'COMING
Tyler Crook and Cullen Bunn
ISBN 978-1-50670-397-8 | $17.99

HARROW COUNTY VOLUME 8: DONE COME BACK
Tyler Crook and Cullen Bunn
ISBN 978-1-50670-663-4 | $17.99

B.P.R.D. HELL ON EARTH: THE RETURN OF THE MASTER
Tyler Crook with Mignola and Arcudi
ISBN 978-1-61655-193-3 | $19.99

B.P.R.D. HELL ON EARTH: THE DEVIL'S ENGINE AND THE LONG DEATH
Tyler Crook with James Harren, Mignola, and Arcudi
ISBN 978-1-59582-981-8 | $19.99

B.P.R.D. HELL ON EARTH: RUSSIA
Tyler Crook with Duncan Fegredo, Mignola, and Arcudi
ISBN 978-1-59582-946-7 | $19.99

B.P.R.D. HELL ON EARTH: GODS AND MONSTERS
Tyler Crook with Guy Davis, Mignola, and Arcudi
ISBN 978-1-59582-822-4 | $19.99

B.P.R.D. HELL ON EARTH: THE DEVIL'S WINGS
Tyler Crook with Laurence Campbell, Joe Querio,
Mignola, and Arcudi
ISBN 978-1-61655-617-4 | $19.99

B.P.R.D. HELL ON EARTH: LAKE OF FIRE
Tyler Crook with Mignola and Arcudi
ISBN 978-1-61655-402-6 | $19.99

DEATH FOLLOWS
Cullen Bunn with A. C. Zamudio and Carlos Nicolas Zamudio
ISBN 978-1-61655-951-9 | $17.99

BAD BLOOD
Tyler Crook with Jonathan Maberry
ISBN 978-1-61655-496-5 | $17.99

WITCHFINDER: THE MYSTERIES OF UNLAND
Tyler Crook with Kim Newman, Maura McHugh, and Mike Mignola
ISBN 978-1-61655-630-3 | $19.99